"This fast-paced novel of murder and psychological intrigue will take your breath away at every turn. Like a strong rip tide it continually draws the reader in. A compelling page-turner from the very outset. I just could not put it down. What a movie this would make! Hollywood should be clamoring for screen rights!"

Anna Fenerty, a reader from Maine

"Powerful first novel takes readers on an emotional roller coaster ride. It grabs you and does not let you go. Outstanding reading!"

Carlene Christiansen, now a devoted Stevenson fan from Ogden, UT

"A 'must-read' for anybody interested in the mystique surrounding the stolen hidden treasures of the Third Reich. Wade Stevenson's characters will bring adventure, romance and humor into your life."

Barbara Schmidt, a reader from Colorado

"*The Salzdorf Wellspring* is excellent reading and action packed. Brought back lots of fun and exciting military memories."

Bob Baril, Former Third Air Postal Squadron member

"*The Salzdorf Wellspring* is a novel that grabs your attention on the first page and will not release until you finish the last. Though this thriller is gritty, sometimes grisly, Mr. Stevenson finds a pleasing balance by using a velvet glove when dealing with the romantic interest in young Steve Scott's life. Mr. Stevenson exhibits a rare and highly effective sense of humor showcasing the camaraderie and shenanigans that take place with Scott and his military buddies that will have the reader laughing out loud—as I did!"

E. Ross, Chesterfield, MO

"*The Salzdorf Wellspring* brings back a flood of memories! Mr. Stevenson has written a superb and highly entertaining novel."

R. Adams, Former ARFCOS Courier, Huntington Beach, CA

"Begun late one night, I found the combination of subject, intrigue, skill and knowledge in Wade's book a perfect recipe for an 'all nighter.' I could not put it down!"

D. Rohret, Loveland, CO

"If ever you've been in the military you will LOVE this book! It's a terrific read for civilian or military alike."

A new Wade Stevenson fan who can't wait for the sequel

The Salzdorf Wellspring

WADE STEVENSON

Rodgers & Nelsen
Publishing Co.
Loveland, Colorado

ISBN 0-9662696-3-2

First Edition 2000

Printed in the United States of America

The Salzdorf Wellspring is published by:

Rodgers & Nelsen Publishing Co.
P.O. Box 7001
Loveland, CO 80537-0001
970/593-9557
www.RNPub.com

Production Credits:

Edited by: Barbara Teel
Cover Design, Layout, and Production by: VW Design
Front Cover: Photograph used by permission of Henry Beville
                The C.G. Sweeting Collection
                WORLD WAR II:The Nazis © 1980 Time-Life Books, Inc.
Back Cover: Electronic retouching of jewelry by Dan Looper
Author Photo: Garland Photography

<u>About the Front Cover Photograph</u>
        The citation case of the Grand Cross of the Iron Cross pictured on the cover is a priceless, one of a kind work of art that was personally designed by Adolf Hitler. The Grand Cross, itself, was awarded by Hitler only once during WWII. The recipient was Commander in Chief of the German airforce, the Luftwaffe, Hermann Göring, who was given the award at the Reichstag in July of 1940 when he was promoted to Reich Marshall of the Third Reich. The Grand Cross was given in recognition of the Luftwaffe successes in the blitzkrieg campaigns in France and in the Low Countries.
        Following the end of the war and the collapse of the Third Reich, Göring was sentenced to death by the Nuremberg Tribunal for his crimes against humanity. Two hours before he was to be hanged, he took his own life with a poison capsule he kept under a false filling in one of his teeth, it is speculated. The actual Grand Cross that was presented to Göring was destroyed during an air raid at his Berlin home. He had several copies of the piece made, one of which he was wearing at the time of his surrender in 1945.
        The whereabouts of the citation case remains unknown.

Dedication

This book is dedicated to those unsung military personnel, past and present, who are responsible for moving the mountains of U.S. mail to loved ones overseas and to the military couriers who faithfully carry our country's most vital secrets. It is also dedicated to the memory of the real LaRae, Dunc and Arkee, whose days with us were far too few.

Best Wishes

Cast of Main Characters

(see page 228 for a glossary of terms used throughout this book)

Captain Karl Miller
>Sociopath, serial killer and Commander Detachment 23, ARFCOS

Master Sergeant Phillip (Pappy) Hargrave
>English born undercover CIA GS-14 who wanted one more overseas cavalier-type assignment before settling down. Steve Scott's mentor.

Master Sergeant Calvin Gage
>First Sergeant, Third Air Postal Squadron, dyed in the wool, strictly by the book-old military type. WWII hero and close personal friend of General R.P. Berg, Inspector General of the USAF.

Staff Sergeant Steve Scott
>A veteran of hard knocks as a youngster who discovers adventure, love, déjà vu and hate.

LaRae Prentiss
>Scott's hometown first love/fiancée who would join him in England.

Sergeant Duel (Arkee) Watson
>Member of Third Air Postal Squadron and Scott's friend.

Sergeant Warren Boyd
>Nervous Morning Report Clerk and nemesis/friend of MSgt Alexander.

Master Sergeant Alexander
>NCOIC of Base Motor Pool, friend and drinking buddy of Third Air Postal Squadron members. Nicknamed Axle because of job, but prefers Alex.

OTHER MILITARY PERSONNEL

Lieutenant General R. P. Berg
>The Inspector General (TIG), USAF, The Pentagon

Lieutenant General Leslie Putnam
>Commander, Third Air Force, So. Ruislip, England

Colonel Chester L. Howard
>Commander, Denham Air Force Station, England

Major David Ekridge
>Commander, Third Air Postal Squadron, Denham, England

Captain Earl Keene
>Adjutant, Third Air Postal Squadron, Denham, England

Master Sergeant Danbury
>NCOIC of Aerial Mail Terminal, Third Air Postal Squadron

Sergeant Johnson
>Disreputable member of Third Air Postal Squadron

Airman Second Class Heather MacVickar
>Clerk heartthrob of Aerial Mail Terminal

Prologue

Operation Hitlerzentrum

Like a monstrous avalanche engulfing everything in its path, Adolf Hitler and his Third Reich roared to power in 1933. In his fiery, paranoidal speeches to immediate responses of thunderous cheers from adoring crowds, he screamed, "Wir wollen ein tousand jähriges Reichs haben!" (The Reich will reign for a thousand years!) It lasted twelve.

During most of those twelve years Hitler was the Chancellor of Germany. He later became the Supreme Commander of the Wehrmacht—all of the German Armed Forces—but the title he prized most was Führer of the Nazi Party.

Twenty years earlier, the Führer-to-be spent several years in Vienna, the capital of Austria, not too great a distance from his boyhood home of Linz, Austria. In Vienna he worked sporadically at odd jobs living a largely hand-to-mouth existence. The one bright aspect of his poverty-affected lifestyle was painting in watercolors and making copies of pictures in pencil. Indeed Hitler envisioned himself another Rembrandt, Leonardo da Vinci, or Titian. For a period of time, he was totally consumed by his aspirations to become a world-renowned artist of the Old Master genre. He could not and would not accept the fact he lacked the talent of a great artist—or that his artistic skills were extremely slight. When those hard, sobering words were eventually passed to him by the rector of Vienna's Fine Arts Center they were softened somewhat with the suggestion that Hitler's interest in architecture might, instead, be the path he should pursue.

Hitler then immediately seized the megalomaniac notion that as a great architect he could draw grand buildings, museums, and a beautiful bridge across the Danube. He saw himself as a master builder and yet he always clung to his visions of personal artistic greatness.

His dreams, both day and night, were filled with visions of masterpiece paintings and other beautiful works of art.

He would have them! He must have them!

In 1910 at age twenty-one, Hitler's home in Linz was among the illiterate workers and common tramps in a flophouse, but the radical political views he developed and the heated arguments he instigated meant he was never welcome at any location for very long.

He frequented soup kitchens. He was dirty; he stank and was unkempt. His attire did not include a shirt or underwear. He wore ragged, filthy clothing often covered with mud and other stains and slept under bridges or wherever he could find shelter.

Ultimately he was reduced to begging for food. To escape conscription in Austria's military service, dirty, impoverished, and in poor health, Hitler made his way to Munich, the birthplace of the Nazi movement.

Hitler's dark journey from a failed and starving youthful artist to that of the madman who, at a whim, decided life or death for millions, was long and circuitous. But with every step of the way he clung passionately to his earlier artistic dreams.

Later, even in his role as a brave and dedicated soldier in World War I, and his subsequent, radical ascent into politics, rebellion, and imprisonment, he was still fanatically obsessed, as would be his wont throughout his lifetime, with the fascination of art and architecture. As the Führer in 1938, he assigned a group of architects to draw plans which would convert Linz into the world class art capital he envisioned for his new Europe.

His narcissistic plan for all of this he, only after a great deal of consideration, graciously acquiesced and allowed to be named *Hitlerzentrum*. The designs called for the construction of magnificent buildings and museums, which Hitler himself would help to draw. These glorious structures would house the world's greatest works of art, antiques, rare and exquisite furniture, coins, gems and books, any and all objets d'art. All of these and more in their most magnificent forms would belong to him!

Hitler's dream of *Hitlerzentrum* was never realized. But the collecting of priceless treasures and, unfortunately, more—much more—was begun immediately, at terrible, gruesome and the most horrific of costs. With the *Wehrmacht's blitzkrieg* attacks on neighboring countries and the rape of those nations' tremendous works of art, it became quickly apparent that a multitude of super secret storage areas within Germany would be required to safely store and maintain these spoils of war.

Painfully recalling his days as a tramp in Vienna—filthy, stinking, and having to beg for food—the Führer decided after Germany's first conquest that he would have his very own highly secluded concealment area. There, at that location, which ultimately only he personally would know existed, would be stored the most marvelous and glorious works of art for which he had so long dreamed of and passionately hungered.

The construction of *Hitlerzentrum* and the attendant collection of the world's priceless artworks and treasures remained a driving force within the Führer. However, the Army and its generals, many of whom Hitler did not trust and thus watched closely, constantly harped that the ever-growing need for more soldiers to make up their army, their required weapons, clothing, and food had to take priority.

With many other pressing demands upon his time, the Führer handpicked, from among Germany's elite, a small cadre of Nazi experts and professors who were most knowledgeable in their particular fields to oversee the collecting, cataloguing, and storing of these growing mountains of treasures.

In most cases these individuals reported to Hitler's second-in-command, Martin Bormann—with one exception. A Nazi SchutzStaffel Doctor Helmut Krueger, reported on the mine near Salzdorf directly and only to Hitler. It stupefied Bormann and all the others of the inner circle that only Krueger, seemingly, had access to Hitler any time he chose. And no one, save Hitler and Krueger, knew the matter of their discussions.

Although the Führer tremendously enjoyed his periodic visits to view, touch, and glory over the magnificent items, the sheer numbers involved, and his other, more urgent, war demands rarely permitted such visits. To compensate for this and to aid him in personally selecting the more exquisite prizes he wanted for *Hitlerzentrum*, photographs and detailed inventories were sent to the Führer regularly.

In addition to works of art by Rembrandt, Monet, Romney, Renoir, Titian, Brueghel, and Dürer, a more grisly accumulation of vast sums of wealth grew daily in the form of personal items formerly belonging to the millions of Jews whom the Nazis were systematically exterminating.

The Jews' money, watches, rings, silver, and even the gold from their teeth were taken. The silver and gold were melted and made into bars. Other items were placed in the suitcases the Jews had carried with them or into bags and boxes and shipped throughout Germany for storage.

Hitler, now the world's greatest plunderer of art treasures, severely restricted knowledge of each of the storage sites, but one more so than all the others. This was his own ultra secret, a long-abandoned and forgotten salt mine six kilometers from the village of Salzdorf.

The Salzdorf Wellspring was the name the Führer had given this personal and most prized cache—the single richest collection of art and wealth ever collected and stored during any known period of war. It was, perhaps, the richest cultural collection of any civilization since time began.

Berlin—bunker beneath the Reich chancellery

By April, 1945, Berlin was encircled. In rapid pincer movements the German forces were being squeezed from the east by the Red Army and from the west by the United States and British forces. With this, everyone—even the die-hard Nazis—knew that time was quickly running out.

That grey stormy Monday, a dinner of spaghetti, tossed salad and a loaf of hard bread was prepared for Mr. and Mrs. Adolf Hitler. He drank several cups of tea, which was by then extremely difficult to come by, even for him. She drank water. Amazingly, amid all the ruin and rubble, a small bouquet of early spring daffodil flowers had been collected to serve as their table centerpiece. The conversation among the small remaining group had been convivial; lots of smiles and pleasantries were exchanged despite the impending doom they knew awaited them. After the meal, and mostly without comment, there were final handshakes and hugs, pats on backs, an occasional grip and squeeze of an elbow or forearm. And, once again, the smiles. But this time they were accompanied by deep, penetrating, last looks into knowing, sad eyes.

Dressed in the impeccable military uniform his valet of ten years had laid out for him that morning, the Führer turned from the small gathering and walked away. His brilliantly shined black boots made final, hollow, thudding sounds as he walked down the concrete hallway of the bunker.

At precisely ten minutes to four on that afternoon of April 30th, 1945, in the inner sanctum of the Map Room, Hitler stepped calmly, reverently, to the blue and white velvet sofa and sat down. From the table on his left he picked up the framed 5"x7" picture he had sketched of a church in 1913, thirty-two years earlier, when he was a starving art student. He thought of his many collections of the world's most magnificent art, sculptures and other works that were still perhaps hidden and might remain so forever. Thus, they would forever be his.

All personnel with knowledge of the ultra secret storage sites had, many months earlier, been eradicated. They were killed by assassins who had no idea why they were murdering these people. Even the military troops who had ridden in the backs of the covered trucks, unloaded and stored the truck's contents without knowing their locations, were eliminated. Silenced forever also were the chosen few art professionals Hitler personally had selected to work with him on the covert aspects of his Operation Hitlerzentrum—including the proud, conscientious, Doctor Krueger. Hitler would risk no chance that they might later attempt to go back to the storage sites on their own.

Even at death's doorstep the Führer was, as always, especially concerned with his coveted and prized Salzdorf collection—his *Salzdorf Wellspring*.

Such beautiful, magnificent plans and dreams he'd had. The most wonderful art collection in the universe! Diamonds, emeralds and jewels— the beauty and abundance of which had never or could ever again be matched. A collection fit for the gods, and at this, even they would marvel.

With a heavy heart and tear-filled eyes he glanced sadly to his right. He covered her still warm hand with his own, picked it up, held it tightly for a moment, touched the platinum, diamond-studded wristwatch he had given her years before and then replaced her hand in her lap. He looked at her caringly, lovingly, one last time.

Seated beside him, wearing a dark-blue polka dot dress and still sitting upright, with her shoes off and her feet curled up beneath her, was the body of Eva Braun Hitler, his bride of one day. There was no expression on her face, no grimace of pain. It was as though she had simply fallen asleep. Eva had taken her own life by swallowing a potassium cyanide poison capsule just moments ago.

Now was the time. He took a deep breath, held it a moment and exhaled slowly. Then, looking straight ahead, he nodded his head once as if in confirmation of something.

He closed his eyes and placed the 7.65mm Walther pistol to his right temple and squeezed the trigger. A hole appeared instantly and only a small amount of blood signaled the end of his life.

The world's greatest tyrant and most evil dictator, the mass murderer of millions, men, women, children and babies included, the military leader who demanded total obedience and unparalleled bravery from his soldiers, ended his life as a coward as his supposed "thousand year reign" crumbled and fell about him and over him in ruins.

*"As the fishes that are taken in an evil net,
and as the birds that are caught in the snare;
so are too sons of men snared in an evil time,
when it falleth suddenly upon them."*

—*Old Testament*

Chapter 1

Beware the Ides of March

Salzdorf, Germany, March 15, 1928

"Ja, Helga, help is on the way," Hans Mueller shouted as he backed the door shut against a blustering cold wind while holding his arms full of several logs for the fire.

"Not to worry Helga, Mrs. Feldstein will be here shortly." He hurried to place the wood near the stove, quickly brushed his clothing and rushed again to the side of their bed where his wife lay heavily pregnant with their first child. She moaned as the waves of pain washed over her prone figure.

"This is the most wretched weather we have had all winter," said Hans trying to distract her as she lay with her hands clutching her swollen belly. "Ja, first it is like a tunnel of long and foggy, misty days; then the snow and now this freezing rain and ice with strong north winds that take your breath away." Unaccustomed to the intricacies of childbirth and himself filled with fear, Hans gingerly raised the covers and once again looked between his wife's legs, hoping to God he would not see the head of the baby appearing. So far so good.

"That's all right then. Not to worry Helga."

"Where is Doctor Erdle? The baby is coming!" Helga cried out in pain then whimpered as another strong contraction racked her body.

"Erdle is out of town—he's over at the Nenninger's farm *mein liebling*. He has been there since early morning to pull a calf, he left before dawn. Long before you started having pains. Mrs. Erdle says she has no idea when he'll return and what with the roads now solid ice he may not be back until morning. But not to worry Helga, Mrs. Feldstein has helped deliver many babies. She's had five of her own. She will be here to help any minute now. Not to worry *mein schatz*."

"*Mein Gott im himmel*, this pain! Please Hans, get me some help—now!" Glaring at Hans with a furrowed brow she screamed, "Never again!"

1

Beads of perspiration dotted her stern expression. "We will never again have sex. Forever from now you will sleep in another room!"

A frantic Hans sprang away from the bed and hurried to the kitchen. As he was picking up his coat Mrs. Feldstein knocked on the back door and Hans hastily ushered her inside.

The Jewish lady, their closest neighbor, reached to untie her head scarf and remove her coat, both of which were covered in snow and a hard crusting of ice. "Herr Mueller, please boil some water and fetch us a few fresh towels," she instructed a grateful Hans as she limped, due to her impaired right hip, composed and sedately into the Mueller's bedroom and took Helga's hand.

"It will be all right little mother. Calm down dear. Take some deep breaths and squeeze my hand." Wiping Helga's sweaty brow with a cool cloth, she continued speaking softly and reassuringly, "It's all right now, you will be fine. Deep breaths, yes, that's the way Frau Mueller. Just relax and breathe deeply and we shall soon have with us a beautiful, precious bundle from heaven."

Despite Mrs. Feldstein's expert ministrations, the labor was long and painful.

Finally, nearing midnight a strong, sturdy baby boy named Karl was born to the Muellers. A happy Helga was totally exhausted, but both she and the baby were in good health and resting comfortably when a tired, and oddly unnerved Mrs. Feldstein finally departed for home. Her walk on the frozen pathway was made all the more arduous due to her aching hip—and her alarmed state of mind.

"I have seen and helped with many birthings," Mrs. Feldstein told her husband, Arnold. "But this was the strangest. It was as if . . . well, it just gave me an eerie feeling."

"How do you mean? For what an eerie feeling? I do not understand," replied Arnold.

She struggled with words to describe what she had witnessed. "I don't understand myself; it is difficult to explain. Her labor was long, but that is nothing unusual for a first child. When it was time and he came, he came easily. It was after I cut the umbilical cord and picked up the boy to clean him. Suddenly, that moment, I was possessed by this strange feeling of fright." The midwife grimaced at the memory.

"What do you mean a feeling of fright? From what a feeling of fright?"

"I know this will sound bizarre Arnold, and I find it impossible to believe myself, but as I held the baby in the blanket it was in the fetal position. Its knees and legs were drawn up and his tiny hands covered his eyes. The baby made no sound and seemed so precious, as they all do. However, when I laid him on the table he lowered his hands and slowly turned his head my direction. As God is my witness, I believe he looked directly at me with narrowing, hate-filled eyes. This sent a shiver of chills through my body. It was as though his eyes had suddenly become brilliant and shining. They locked onto mine. His expression was no longer that of a beautiful and innocent baby, but had become one of an evil scowl. And, for the first time he made a noise. Not a cry as all babies make. It was more like a screech. An abnormal shriek of disgust or hate. Yes, I know you'll say I've imagined all of this, and that is possible. But I do not think so Arnold. I do not believe I imagined it at all. He frightened me. A tiny, newborn baby. God of my soul, please help him and us. I fear this child is born evil."

Mrs. Feldstein had little chance to repeat her views on the Mueller birth. Her ice-encrusted coat was hung, as it had been countless times before, on a wall peg not far from the hearth. Within an hour or so the extra logs Arnold carefully placed to bank the fire had completely thawed out and dried her coat. But the weight of the drying side nearest the fireplace had caused the coat to slip, lopsided, and it fell to the floor, near the open flame. A spark landed on the coat; it blinked, smoldered and eventually burst into flame. Soon the entire room was ablaze and the house filled with smoke. Mrs. Feldstein awoke and shook her unconscious husband.

"Arnold, Arnold, there's smoke!" Coughing, she tried to get out of bed, but like her husband was soon overcome by the toxic fumes of the fire. The flames weakened the overhead beams and the heavy weight of accumulated snow and ice on the roof soon came crashing down on the Feldsteins. It took a dozen strong men to dig out their frozen, charred bodies the following day.

Four years later another baby boy was born to the Muellers. His name was Otto. He was pleasant, cheerful and cuddly, and he was so different from his older brother. While Karl was tall and blond with piercing blue eyes, Otto, with his darker features, resembled his father.

Despite their aesthetic differences, the young lads grew strong and healthy and in that regard made their father proud. Physically, Karl was a perfect specimen, but the boy had a coldness and indifference to the feelings of others that puzzled his parents. He was just not a loving child. Sometimes Hans and Helga discussed these traits in Karl but ultimately, they shrugged their shoulders at the mystery. Otto was normal and kind. Karl was not. And there seemed nothing they could do about it.

The years passed and this strangeness of character with Karl intensified and ensured that schoolyard trouble was never far from him. He seemed to be prone to mean and mischievous acts. He stole and hid other children's belongings. He pinched girl students, yanked their hair forcing them to cry, and he was frequently pulled, fighting and screaming from boys younger than himself, from any that were slight or disabled. And to his parents' appalling shame, Karl seemed to have an almost hysterical dislike for every Jewish youngster he laid eyes on.

With Hans' military background and fondness for discipline, he thought the local Hitler Youth Movement would be good conditioning for Karl and thus enthusiastically presented Karl for enrollment in the training. And it seemed to work. Initially both Hans and Helga believed they had made the right move. In no time at all, Karl was a changed youngster. At last he had found something in which to channel his considerable energies. He did indeed become disciplined. He took immense pride in his uniforms, personal hygiene and appearance. He vigorously performed his assigned chores. He respected his superiors and spoke with a near adoration of Adolf Hitler, the growing Third Reich and the Fatherland. Relieved, the Muellers were convinced they had most certainly taken the correct action for their firstborn, and were delighted at the outward changes in their son.

What they couldn't see were the inward changes. A dark side of Karl, one far more sinister than his performing mean, childish pranks and his constant negative attitude, was quietly developing. In the Youth Movement under the tutelage of his Nazi stewards, Karl's capacity for hatred was both encouraged and applauded. His evil thoughts were cultivated, nurtured and even at his young age of thirteen they came to fruition. Karl Mueller harbored all the demonic and evil traits of one truly possessed just barely beneath a thin layer of constraint.

Inside the abandoned farmhouse located well on the outskirts of town, the ten-year-old Jewish girl child lay cold and whimpering on the stone floor from another era. She was naked from the waist down. Blood and urine combined in a watery puddle underneath her still form. The young girl's hands were bound behind her and a gag cut cruelly into the corners of her mouth. Her eyes were opened wide in terror as this boy she knew from the village knelt down beside her and viciously tightened the ropes that bound her.

Myra was an astute child for her age; she could easily read the look of hatred in the brilliant, icy blue eyes of this boy Karl. He had always looked at her with disdain when they were within sight of one another in town.

She had seen him in school a couple of grades ahead of her back before the Nazis, in their campaign of hate, forbade Jewish children to attend schools. But then, she reasoned, all the Jews were now accustomed to that behavior since Hitler had begun blaming them for the country's economic woes. Hitler had lit the flames of hatred and now the fires were spreading, out of control, throughout the land. Myra couldn't understand why Karl had hurt her. She was coming home from the market with the yarn her mother wanted when he had set upon her and forced her through the thick fog to the farmhouse. He was so strong! Then he had done things to her, horrible, nasty things she had never imagined would happen. He called her a Jew bitch. What had she done wrong? But he didn't give her time to think when he knelt closer to the child. The little girl's muffled screams were immediately silenced by the savage blow Karl administered.

Her family search party and several of the Jewish members of the village discovered her hideously mutilated body several hours later. Little was done to investigate the murder. But town residents still talked about the recent horror and wondered how any sane person could have performed such a shocking and grisly act.

Chapter 2

The Elite Guard

In der nahe der Grube (Near the mine) Salzdorf, Germany 1939

The night was cold and wet and the two hunters had spent most of it hidden beneath the forest's thick canopy of foliage. Now, toward dawn would be their best opportunity to get the *hasse* they sought. They personally would have taken any game, but Wilhelm's frau had given him strict instructions to bring home a couple of plump rabbits for the *hassenpfeffer* pot. His mouth watered at the thought of the meal.

"Wilhelm, why did you choose this area to hunt? You said you had us a good place to go," said his friend Oscar, sounding concerned.

"This is a good area. No others dare come so it should be a good hunting ground. Why are you worried?"

"This is a dangerous place. A hunter was killed near that strange looking building a few years ago. People have reported seeing eerie things—hooded lights in the middle of the night and rumors of big trucks on occasion. No one knows what goes on around here. That sign over there says *EINTRITT VERBOTEN* and warns of severe punishment to anyone found in this area. I would like to go somewhere else," Oscar whispered in a frightened voice.

"Don't be a *narr!* (fool) We are here and nothing has happened. Believe me, this is the best area to find *hasse*. If I come home without something for the *hassenpfeffer* pot, my frau may not let me back in the house!" Wilhelm's tone showed contempt for the stories Oscar told.

"Shhh, *dumkopf!* Don't talk so loud—someone may hear! I tell you I have a bad feeling about this place. We must go." Oscar's voice sounded an unmistakable note of panic. "I am going even if you are not."

"Oh, all right, all right. *Mein Gott* you are a *weibisch* (pansy). Let us go. But you, my friend, will have to explain to my frau," Wilhelm muttered as he gathered his hunting gear to leave.

"Ja, Ja, I will. Just move!" Oscar pleaded.

At that moment, the crack of a rifle then an explosion of bark from a nearby tree made the two hunters flatten themselves against the sodden ground. They waited for what seemed like hours, barely breathing. Not a sound, no voices, no footsteps, nothing.

"Now do you believe me?" Oscar whispered.

"Shhh *dumkopf!* I'm thinking."

"What's to think about?"

"Which way to run, of course!" Wilhelm said, his voice now edged with fear.

"Back that way is Salzdorf and home. Let's go!"

As Oscar rose and began to run from the forest, Wilhelm collected his shotgun and followed suit. Another shot exploded the back of Oscar's head, showering Wilhelm's face with brain matter, bone fragments and gore. In the next instant Wilhelm felt a tremendous thud in his back that propelled him forward face-first into a large white oak tree. After impacting the tree and even as he was falling backwards, strangely, his last conscious thought was *"Auf Wiedersehen Hassenpfeffer."*

Village of Salzdorf, Germany, 1941

Hans Mueller's spirits lifted immediately when he entered the Salzdorf Gastube. He was greeted by the muffled conversations of the bar's patrons and the warmth and agreeable odors emanating from the tavern's large fireplace. Colorful orange and yellow flames danced on top of a piece of apple tree wood, and its sweet smell mingled with that of the two hickory logs that lay cracking and popping on the grate.

Hans smiled when he saw his friend Cedric at the far end of the bar. In this atmosphere, he could forget for a moment the nagging feeling of uneasiness that had plagued him all day. It was nothing he could put his finger on, wasn't as though he'd forgotten something. It was more like a feeling of foreboding. Something just didn't seem right. The feeling reminded him of how he had felt when he stole that damn bag with the white star on it, but Dr. Krueger hadn't noticed it missing—there were so many other bags just like it.

"*Ach* then, one last stein and I must go for certain; this one must be the last!" Mueller said while shaking an index finger at his friend. He arose from the barstool, stretching his six-foot, two-inch sturdy frame and waved to the bartender for the final round. He had cut a striking figure in his German soldier's uniform during the Great War.

His dark features weren't exactly Aryan but he did have the obligatory intense blue eyes. His thick, dun-colored hair had turned prematurely grey after the war in which he had sacrificed an arm for his country. Tonight he was dressed entirely in black as was his custom for the night missions he had been called upon to complete for the glory of his Führer.

"Jawohl, jawohl, no doubt the Führer himself has an assignment for you," Cedric joked. Cedric had been blinded by mustard gas during the Great War. He and Mueller were prevented by their respective injuries from joining their countrymen to form the invincible might of the *Wehrmacht*. Mueller, after losing his left arm in battle, had later been fitted with a prosthesis just below his elbow. Aside from the lack of movement of his constantly gloved hand, the casual observer wouldn't notice his disability.

The regular references to Hitler being his friend came courtesy of the fact that both Hans Mueller and Adolf Hitler had been assigned to the 16th Bavarian Reserve Infantry Regiment and had fought on the western front. Both Mueller and the future dictator each had been wounded and awarded the Iron Cross First Class—a rare and prestigious award for military personnel of lower grade. Both Mueller and Hitler were corporals at the time, but despite these commonalties, the two men had never met. Later, like so many of his countrymen, he had been mesmerized by the Führer, his actions and fiery speeches. To him, Hitler had turned Germany around since the nation's disgrace at the end of the First World War.

Mueller had been a good soldier during his time with the 16th Bavarian Regiment. He often regaled Cedric with his heroics.

"One weekend," Mueller said, resting his good elbow on the bar at the Gastube, "several of my fellow soldiers, after a hard bout of drinking, decided to break into the Quartermaster's building. One of the drunks had convinced the others that several cases of cognac were stored in there. Too bad I had to be the Quartermaster guard because I knew and liked a couple of the soldiers. Anyway, the next morning when they woke up, they found themselves far the worse for wear. The soldiers who had tried to overpower me had broken hands and busted noses, or large lumps on their heads. And they were all in handcuffs. I received my first citation for that performance." Hans always finished the story with a chuckle and Cedric, despite his useless eyes, always looked suitably impressed and laughed loudly.

After the war Mueller had remained on the inactive register of his regiment as an Army Elite Guard Specialist. Being a recipient of the Iron Cross, he was noted as a dedicated, trustworthy and competent soldier. A good guard who could work alone.

It had been through this connection, back in 1937, that Hans Mueller had been singled out by Dr. Krueger, a Hitler appointed art and jewel connoisseur and expert. It was Krueger's duty to procure and store a tremendous horde of the art, gold and silver which would ultimately be used to construct *Hitlerzentrum* and build the dictator's new Europe.

On his way home from the Gastube late one evening—now almost five years ago—a large Mercedes sedan pulled up alongside Mueller and stopped him in his tracks. Hans tried to look inside as a dark window rolled down silently and the sole occupant of the back seat called to him.

"Herr Mueller?"

"Jawohl, I am Hans Mueller."

"Please join me for a ride. I have an employment offer for you which I am certain you shall find most attractive," said a sharp precise voice from the auto. The back door swung open and Mueller climbed inside.

The *SchutzStaffel*, SS civilian dress insignia on the stranger's collar, was momentarily illuminated as he lit a cigarette. Exhaling the smoke slowly, the SS official said, "I am Dr. Krueger." He did not offer his hand with the introduction.

"We have been watching you. We have studied your impressive war record. Your country once more, and now the Third Reich, has need of your services, Herr Mueller."

Chills raced through Hans. He was excited by this strange person sitting beside him. The doctor made Mueller extremely nervous yet at the same time, there was an aura of suspense, danger and excitement about the entire scenario. It was almost palpable.

Hans, who was long retired from anything he considered even remotely exciting, was now in this luxurious Mercedes about to be offered a remarkable assignment. His chest puffed with self-importance as he listened to what the mysterious doctor could possibly want with a one-armed retired soldier-turned-farmer-and-part-time upholsterer.

The chauffeur eased the large car through the deserted cobblestone streets of Salzdorf and out into the dark, wooded hills of the countryside.

"You will be paid handsomely," Dr. Krueger continued as he began outlining his offer to Mueller. "The work will not be physically demanding. However," and the tone of the doctor's voice turned icy, "the mission you will be involved in is classified *hochegeheim*. As you are aware, *hochegeheim* is the highest level of secrecy possible. This operation is considered absolutely vital to the *Wehrmacht* war effort, the Führer and the entire Fatherland. With this you are sworn to absolute secrecy, Herr

Mueller. Any violation or compromise of your obligation to the strictest of secrecy standards will result in not only your immediate death, but also that of Frau Mueller and your two sons, Karl and Otto. Nothing about this can be taken lightly. Is this perfectly understood?"

"Jawohl, Herr Doctor. I understand," Mueller said solemnly—more than a little unsettled with the obvious gravity of the undertaking—and that Dr. Krueger knew the names of his children.

"And do you agree, Herr Mueller? You must remain absolutely silent about this."

"Herr Doctor. *Hochegeheim*, Top Secret. I understand and I agree."

Unseen, the chauffeur silently placed the Luger pistol he had held in his hand back inside its holster.

As the Mercedes continued toward its destination, Mueller took the opportunity to surreptitiously study the doctor in the flare of the flame each time he lit a fresh cigarette. He was a chain smoker—lighting one cigarette after the other. Hans took in the doctor's stylish suit of clothing, which reeked of stale tobacco and a man's cologne, the latter of which Hans found offensive. The whole unreal quality of Hans Mueller sitting in a Mercedes and being offered a top-secret assignment, gave the doctor an air of intrigue and danger he may otherwise not have had. Dr. Krueger wore glasses with extremely thick lenses perched on the bridge of a distinctly rat-like nose. He spoke with the affected air of one born to German privilege.

When the car halted on an overgrown trail hidden to the casual observer, its passengers got out and Mueller followed the doctor toward an odd, formidable looking concrete structure. They walked silently past a large sign that read, '*EINTRITT VERBOTEN; MIT TOTE BESTRAFUNG*' (No trespassing; under penalty of death.) It was then Dr. Krueger first showed Mueller the mine.

"You will shortly receive a monthly newsletter," Krueger explained. "Give particular notice to any that has a date in parentheses on the last line. On that date precisely at 9 a.m., go to the Salzdorf Post Amt. There you will be met by your contact. Walk with him wherever he goes. Say nothing other than to repeat the time and date he tells you. He will give you a newspaper. Folded inside will be an envelope for you. The date furnished by your contact will be that of a scheduled shipment drop at the mine. The envelope will contain your pay—more than you have earned from the most bountiful harvests you have reaped and your modest part-time upholstery business—far more, Herr Mueller, than you could ever hope to acquire prior to the war or after.

"It will be your duty to be at the storage site at the appointed time to open the outer structure. You will turn on the generator, ensure that the elevator is ready, place the wheelbarrows and carts near the door, and make all other preliminary arrangements to receive the shipment and facilitate storage as quickly as possible. Our time here will be limited. It is imperative that all must be ready upon our arrival. That is your responsibility, Herr Mueller!"

"Jawohl, Herr Doctor. I understand," Mueller said. He would do as he was asked for Führer and country; Dr Krueger would not be sorry he chose Hans Mueller for the job.

Mueller told no one, not even his wife, of his involvement with the Nazi doctor or his duty as caretaker of the storage area.

Whenever Mueller received money for his clandestine work, he unearthed the metal box he had buried in the floor of his barn and put the money inside. He always covered it up with dirt and placed a wooden barrel on top of the hole. He told no one about the money and over the years his savings had grown substantially.

At 8:30 p.m. having earlier said a reluctant goodbye and leaving his friend Cedric at the tavern, Mueller stood inside a grove of trees six kilometers from Salzdorf. A slight mist and fog encircled him. He leaned against a tree for shelter, smoked a cigarette and watched for the arrival of the trucks. This evening, as always, there was some apprehension on Mueller's part, although it had grown less as time went on. But still today, all day, Mueller had had this strange feeling. Surely if Dr. Krueger suspected anything...Mueller tried to reassure himself. He had already saved a small fortune and the bag with the white star on it obviously hadn't been missed.

The structure safeguarded and concealed the entrance to a shaft that dropped over two hundred feet to a huge football field-sized former salt mine. The mine was one of many which had been built in the area, later worked to exhaustion and then deserted countless years ago. Its very existence had been all but forgotten until, after a long search, Nazi officials had seized Salzdorf's musty files regarding the site and confiscated the only recorded documentation of its existence.

Word of the hunters' disappearance spread fast and fuelled fear and superstition in the nervous villagers. That entire forest area was avoided by all but the most foolhardy. However, tonight the road would once more be traveled, not by a hunter, but by a convoy of large trucks, as it had been nine or ten times a year over the past several years.

The trucks arrived on time, and two armed guards climbed down from the first truck and took up concealed positions on either side of the road.

Mueller and Dr. Krueger would use separate keys to release the individual locks to gain access to the shaft. Mueller would then engage controls that would bring the large elevator to the bunker level. The contents of the trucks, unknown to all but Krueger, would be placed into the elevator and lowered to the bottom of the mine. There, three open railway carts traveled track that ran the entire center length of the large cavern.

All the participants, except the doctor who vigorously supervised, and Mueller, who was not permitted to handle any of the shipment, worked feverishly until well after midnight to unload and place the heavy boxes, crates, suitcases and bags on either side of the railway.

On a previous delivery when the transfer and storage had gone well into the early morning, the doctor who had been very tired, and his crew on the verge of exhaustion, were struggling to complete the mission before dawn.

"*Schnell, schnell!*" Dr. Krueger shouted to his men. "We must complete our work and be gone from here. We have very little time left."

In their forced haste, the final bag that should have been stored in the mine had been placed precariously on the side of the cart going into the structure. The soldiers, pressured and running, did not notice the bag tumble off and lay partially hidden behind the door to the building. When the inner shaft was sealed and double-locked, the doctor had left Mueller to secure the outer door and hurriedly departed with his troops.

When Mueller pulled the door to close it he found the bag. It was different from most of the other bags stored in the mine. This one had an unusual star-like symbol on it. He opened his mouth to shout at the doctor and his military detail who were already out of sight, but a sudden and uncharacteristic curiosity made him hold his tongue. For many months, Mueller had watched the strange cargo being regularly loaded into the cavernous concrete bunker. Every now and then he had wasted idle minutes wondering what the bags and boxes contained, but good German soldiers followed orders without questions—until the day came when enough time had passed since Mueller had been a good soldier.

Mueller stood listening until the sound of the convoy had faded completely. Only when he was certain he was entirely alone did he stoop and pick up the bag. He was amazed at its weight. Slowly, using his prosthetic hand to support the pouch, he undid the tie with his good hand.

"*Mein Gott im Himmel!*" he whispered as he opened the bag and saw the gleam of a pile of large diamonds resting on top of gold coins. Several of the larger stones were set into magnificent pieces of jewelry. The collection was worth a fortune.

The bag with the star on it joined the store of cash in the metal box buried in his barn.

The last delivery completely filled the enormous cave. The three rail cars left standing on the tracks were filled to capacity as well. Krueger made final notations on the worn notebook he constantly consulted. What he had stored in the bunker was beyond the wildest of expectations. Dr. Krueger's report, which he planned to deliver personally to the Führer in the morning, would show an inventory of the mine's contents: twelve and one-half million dollars in gold bricks, nine and one-half million in U.S. currency, fifteen million in Norwegian crowns, thirteen million in French francs, twenty-five million in German reichsmarks, one and one half billion in gold coins, two million Dutch gulden, and two hundred and forty-five priceless artworks by Monet, Renoir and other masters. Also, in untold billions, stacks of silver bars, diamonds, emeralds and other precious stones. Krueger glowed with pride as he anticipated the favor he would gain in the eyes of the Führer for this truly magnificent collection.

When everything had been properly stored and the locks secured, Dr. Krueger instructed the drivers to back up their trucks and for them and his chauffeur to wait for him on the main road. Mueller and the Nazi doctor then secured the cover to the entrance by each using his individual key to the double-locked vault door. Mueller closed the outer structure door, barred and locked it. The two men walked without speaking through the mist and fog down the rutted trail toward the waiting vehicles. *Just another routine night and routine shipment. So why this feeling of worry and dread I've had all day?* Or so Mueller thought.

While still under the cover of the trees, Dr. Krueger removed the Luger from his tunic with his left hand, he took a hurried step forward, turned and shot Mueller at close range.

As Mueller fell heavily to the ground, he managed to gasp a single word, "Why?"

The doctor stared down at him wearing a cold, expressionless face, and said, "We no longer need your services Herr Mueller." Krueger removed the key from Mueller's bloody trousers, stood and shot him again. Although convinced Mueller, who was covered in splattered blood from his head to his waist, was indeed dead, the doctor was bending over to check him for a pulse when his sergeant ran up the rutted road and startled him.

"*Was ist*, Herr Doctor? I heard two shots." The sergeant had his weapon drawn, shining a torch in the doctor's direction.

"Hier ist nichts passiert," (There's nothing) Krueger replied, straightening up and quickly walking toward the sergeant, shielding the light from Mueller's body. "Let's go, we are running late."

Chapter 3

Rags to Riches

The echoes of the doctor's Mercedes and the engines of the convoy had long faded when Hans Mueller regained consciousness. He woke to a deep throbbing pain in his left shoulder, matching a similar pain in his side. The earlier mist had turned to heavy drops of rain, which splashed his face. His mind was thick and he turned his head painfully to take in his surroundings. After a fashion it came to him that he was lying near the mine he had guarded so faithfully these past years. Mueller remembered barring and locking the doors to the mine and walking with Dr. Krueger when the prosthesis that was his left arm shattered from the doctor's pistol shot; the force had knocked him to the ground. Krueger's poor eyesight, further hindered by the mist, his limited experience with firearms, and his anxiety to be done with this, his first assassination, had saved Hans Mueller's life.

Mueller slowly assessed the damage to his body. His left shoulder throbbed with each heartbeat, and his left side felt as if it were on fire. He rolled to his right and gradually pushed himself to a sitting position. He sat there for several minutes until the trees and all about him stopped swirling and the waves of nausea passed. Then slowly he stood and took his first few cautious steps toward Salzdorf and home.

"Karl, Karl! Quick! Bring Dr. Erdle! Tell him Papa has been hurt!" Mueller's wife Helga shouted to their eldest son. She helped her husband into bed as Karl hurried out the door. There was no medical doctor in their small town—the closest physician was several miles away. Erdle, the local veterinarian and a close friend of the Muellers, often helped out with village emergencies until the medical doctor could be summoned.

Krueger's first bullet had disintegrated Mueller's prosthesis and continued its trajectory, penetrating his left side and creating more of a deep, jagged gash than a puncture. The second shot had gone clean through Mueller's left shoulder area without striking any bones. When he arrived, the veterinarian cleaned and sutured the wounds. He applied medication to both injuries and bandaged Hans's shoulder. Because he feared infection might set in, he placed a poultice on Mueller's stomach wound.

"You are a very lucky man Hans, you will recover quickly," assured Dr. Erdle. The veterinarian, quickly and privately assessing the situation, decided to ask no questions. Hans volunteered no explanation regarding his wounds. "And do not be concerned. No one will learn of this from me," the veterinarian offered confidentially.

The doctor gave Mueller an injection to ease his pain and to aid him in sleeping. He patted his hand. "Rest well old friend. I will be by to check on you tomorrow morning."

Mueller slept all through the day until just past midnight. For the second time in twenty-four hours, he woke confused. The pain had eased and his senses soon returned. The rain had continued and, lying in the warm, comfortable bed, Hans listened to the rain's gentle drumbeat on the roof. There were many things to think about. He knew he, Helga, and the boys were now in extreme danger. Mueller realized the Nazis had used him for their own benefit and then shot him as they would a dog. His family too had suffered. The Hitler Youth Movement had affected Karl more than Hans and Helga could bring themselves to admit. He had grown into a cold, insensitive teenager. Now, Hans could see with a clarity which had previously escaped him. If he and his family stayed, they would not survive. The picture he immediately conjured up terrified him.

Several hours before the cold light of dawn, Mueller planned his family's departure, their escape from all they had ever known. They had to leave Germany and everything they held dear with all the haste they could muster. Plans quickly formed and Mueller knew what he must do.

Helga was in a deep sleep signaled by her heavy breathing and occasional gentle snore. Mueller reached over and patted her. She awoke in a panic that suggested the last twenty-four hours had been about as much as she could bear. "What is it Hans? What has happened?"

"We must leave, Helga; we can't stay here any longer!"

"Why? Where will we go? Why must we leave?" Helga was scared and she saw a shining fever in her husband's eyes that she didn't recognize.

"Don't ask me these questions now. We must leave immediately. I'll explain it later, but we must leave now! Wake the boys then meet me in the barn. We have work to do. Go quickly woman!"

As his wife rushed to wake their two sons, Hans had little time to question how his life had changed so abruptly and dangerously. He slowly

and painfully climbed out of bed, dressed, and hurried out to their barn.
There was so little time.

Three days later, under cover of darkness, the Muellers, dirty, cold,
hungry and worn crossed over into neutral Switzerland, traveling an
unguarded backwoods gravel road that was hardly more than a worn path
through thick forest. Their crossing was at a point between Schaffhausen
and the left fork of Lake Constance, a remote farming community known as
the "Green" border Swiss plateau area.

When the wintry dawn broke, a cold but light rain turned to snow. Hans
had located an overhang in a deep, dry ravine where Helga and the boys
huddled together for warmth. In the distance Hans could just barely make
out the figure of a farmer emerging from a barn with a pail in hand. Hans
hurried toward him.

Once within earshot, the bedraggled Hans shouted, *"Guten Morgen,"*
praying that the farmer spoke German.

Startled by Hans' sudden appearance, the man replied, *"Guten Morgen"*
and being careful not to spill any, he gently set his bucketful of milk down
on level ground. As Hans came nearer the farmer asked in German, "What
are you doing up, out and about on such a foul weather morning as this?"
He noted that the stranger approaching him was thoroughly soaked from the
rain; he thought the poor fellow looked as if he was wounded and most
certainly he appeared to be near exhaustion.

"We are traveling, my wife and two sons, by foot enroute to Zürich.
Will this road carry us there?"

"Ja, it will take you to other roads that lead to Zürich, but it is a long and
tiring journey by foot, particularly in weather such as this. You have some
forty or fifty kilometers more to travel," the farmer responded. "Where is
the rest of your family?"

"They have taken shelter in that gully down by the road."

The farmer, a man of compassion, who in better times had assisted many
refugees like this stranger and his family, shook his head and smiled.
"Well, we bid you welcome here. Please invite your family to come to our
home. We can provide you some warmth and food. No one should be
afoot in these conditions and," he said looking up at the heavy, rolling
clouds, "I think we have far worse weather yet to come this day."

Thankful for the hospitable and gracious offer, Hans hurried back to
collect his family, noticing too the cluster of low dark clouds from the
northland that had suddenly begun to descend upon them.

Once inside, the Muellers, at their host's invitation, shed their sodden
coats, scarves and hats. Their damp clothing, now beginning to steam from

the inside warmth, was hung on wooden pegs by the door. Hans, standing close to the door, noted that sudden strong winds were now probing the cracks and crevices of the farmhouse making howling, whistling noises and carrying fluffy snowflakes which peppered the window and side of the house and already had begun to blanket the land. The Muellers were made comfortable at the large kitchen table. Hans and Helga each gratefully accepted a cup of hot steaming coffee and Karl and Otto eagerly drank the proffered mugs of warm milk.

Helga was delighted to learn that the farmer's wife was German from Sindelfingen, near Stuttgart. Within minutes the two ladies hugged one another and were talking non-stop as if they were long lost relations. As the farmer's wife busied herself at the big chrome and nickel-trimmed woodburning stove, the farmer and Hans walked into the closed off, frigid living room and began preparations to build a fire in the fireplace.

Perhaps it was due to his wounds, his exhausted state of mind and body, the heartbreak of being forced to leave his homeland, so many worries, concerns and unknowns, that Hans, totally out of character, took this kindly farmer and total stranger completely into his confidence. Mueller explained that he and his family were fleeing Germany and persecution by the Nazis. He told of the SS attempt to assassinate him; he told of his wounds and his family's hasty departure in the middle of the night. Hans went on to explain that because they had to flee for their lives, they were able to bring only the one suitcase they'd carried with them. He did not, however, mention that the suitcase, apart from a small amount of clothing, was completely filled with reichsmarks and a fortune in diamonds and rare gold coins.

The farmer, in addition to his natural friendly and sincere character, was caught up in the mood of the moment. He patted Hans on the back; his empathy was great and very apparent. "I understand how you might feel Herr Mueller. We have had many like you cross our threshold here near the 'Green Border.' We, unfortunately, are forced to live in strange and troubled times just now," his voice cracked with emotion.

"While maybe not so severe as yours, we, too, have heavy burdens. My wife, though she doesn't show it, is seriously ill and requires specialized surgery and a long treatment in Bern. Without this she will die. We have two children in expensive schooling, and the harvest on our small farm has been extremely poor these past two years. We are on the verge of losing everything. Bad part is even if we sold everything tomorrow, it still would not be enough. And like the farm you left in Salzdorf, ours has been in the family for generations. It breaks our hearts that we will soon have to tell our children we can no longer support their studies. Selfishly, I guess, my constant thoughts and biggest worries are for my wife and her suffering."

"I do not think that selfish on your part," Hans interrupted. "Any caring husband and father of children I know would feel the same as you."

"Ja? Perhaps," the farmer continued, "but I fear too and have nightmares about the other people crossing here from Germany. We used to be able to help them and did with many. But these bad times have curtailed most of that. Nowadays, I'm sad to say, most of them are caught and turned over to the Nazis. We don't have to wonder hard what their short futures hold. Undoubtedly they face firing squads or other horrible deaths. However, from our personal standpoint for the moment and until spring when our next payments are due, we have a roof over our heads and food in the pantry. Others, such as yourself, are far worse off—we at least have not been forced to flee our country. Still and all, enough talk of these miseries, let's have something to eat. I'm certain you must all be as hungry as you are tired."

When the two men returned to the kitchen area, the farmer took his wife aside and relayed the story Hans had told him. He suggested to her that they invite the Muellers to stay for a few days until they recuperated and the weather was more accommodating for their continued journey. The German farm wife warmly and enthusiastically agreed to the proposal.

Over a huge breakfast of *rösti*, home smoked ham and wurst sausages, *Gruyère* and *Emmentaler*, (Swiss cheese) large slabs of butter on piping hot loaves of homemade bread and *brombeere* (blackberry) jelly, the Muellers ate and drank cups of hot coffee and warm milk as though they were starved. They counted it a blessing and Helga wept tears of gratitude when the farmer and his frau invited them to stay until they were recovered and better able to resume their travels. After breakfast, the farmer's wife bustled around the house, collecting warm clothes for her guests. She boiled large pots of water for them to bathe in and gathered their dirty clothes to wash. When the Muellers were clean, dry and warm, the kind hostess, assisted by her husband, washed and dressed Hans's wounds. With most of the morning behind them, the Muellers sat by the fire and rested their exhausted bodies. All but Karl seemed happy.

Several days later at a crisp and brittle dawn, the early morning sun's rays made sparkling jewel-like reflections on the deep snow which covered the rolling plains near the Swiss farm. Completely rested and recovered, the Mueller family, all but one in high spirits, rode in the horse-drawn wagon along with the farmer and his wife. They were on their way to Zürich. The farmer had suggested that the Muellers, once arrived in Zürich, contact his son and daughter who shared a flat in the city where she was a student of architecture and he an intern at a large hospital.

The Muellers were successful in talking the farmer and his wife into also making the trip once arrangements had been made for a neighbor to tend the farmer's stock until their return. They were eager to help the Muellers of whom they had grown quite fond in the short period of time, and they were even more eager to visit with their children. After a great deal of persuasion, Hans was able to convince the farmer he had sufficient funds to pay all costs incumbent with the trip and their stay in Zürich.

"Ja, we will stay with our children and look forward to that. Also, Herr Mueller, I'm certain our son and daughter will have contacts who shall be more than willing to help with some of your needs. A bank, as you have mentioned and someone to make you a new left arm. Ja, maybe they also know a person who can give you information for your continued travels."

The farmer's son, apart from providing helpful information, expertly removed the sutures from Hans's wounds and pronounced him nearly recovered.

Later that day the teller at the World Nations Bank in Zürich looked up to see what he believed to be a person, perhaps one slightly graduated step above a tramp, approaching his window. He was quick to note the rumpled and dirty common clothes the person wore. The teller also observed the battered and dingy suitcase the apparent vagabond carried. In a haughty and demeaning tone the teller addressed the one-armed, haggard looking individual.

"And what may I do for you?"

"I am Hans Mueller and I have some valuables I need to make safe. I was told I should bring them here."

"Would you care to show me these valuables?"

Hans awkwardly lifted his suitcase to the teller's counter with his right hand. It took him several minutes to shift and position the piece of luggage so he could open it. The teller watched with a smirk, which bordered on ridicule and offered not one iota of assistance. Finally after prying both latches open, Hans raised the top of the case barely a few inches. The teller peered inside to see row upon tight row of reichsmarks amounting to thousands of dollars. The diamonds and rare gold coins were hidden beneath the currency. Hans quickly shut the top of the suitcase from the view of the amazed clerk.

Recovering from his obvious shock, the teller cleared his throat and wiped his brow with his handkerchief. Now wearing a sycophantic smile and finding his voice, which suddenly was dripping with newfound esteem and respect for Hans, the teller spoke.

"Sir, I beg your indulgence, but with a deposit of this magnitude, our bank Senior Vice President, Herr Klaus Brunner, is the person who must handle the account." Fumbling with his words he hurried around from his cage, "Would you mind following me please?"

He ushered Hans to just outside the bank official's plush office and rushed inside where he spoke in hushed conversation with Brunner. Momentarily the teller returned to Hans and with an almost comical but serious gesture of obeisance, he led Hans into the lavish, mahogany-paneled and plushly carpeted office of the Senior Vice President. Introductions were made.

"I have never used a bank before so I am not familiar with the workings," Hans said apologetically. "But I have been told I need to deposit what I am carrying with me, and that it will be secure in your safekeeping."

"We shall be happy to explain the many services we can offer you, Herr Mueller," the Vice President said with a warm and respectful smile after offering a firm, reassuring handshake and a comfortable chair to Hans. Hans had never before seen such elegance in a room. They sat facing one another over a highly polished cherry conference table.

In respectful tones reserved for the seriously rich, the Vice President spoke softly. "Please, sir, may I inquire as to how much you wish to deposit, Herr Mueller?"

"I have this suitcase of valuables which I am most anxious to secure. As to its exact value, I am not sure. But I want not to have to worry about losing any of it during our travels to Canada and the United States."

"Well, let's have a look and try to determine what we are talking about," the banker said with a smile. A wealthy new customer would help with his forthcoming annual review.

Hans set his suitcase on the table, opened it and with the help of the banker gently turned it upside down. The stacks of currency slid silently onto the table and then the gold coins, diamonds and other jewels spilled out. The Vice President sat staring, speechless, his mouth open wide in amazement.

It took several minutes for the banker to recover. He ran his hands very briefly over the diamonds, coins and currency before him. Speaking in a whisper of awe he told Hans that he would have jewel and rare coin experts come immediately to his office to appraise and give quotes on the diamonds, precious stones and gold coins Hans had presented.

"However," he cautioned, "even working as quickly as possible, it will take some time, perhaps several days, before an accurate and true value may be established. In the meantime, Herr Mueller, we will have photographs taken of all but the currency for your records." Herr Brunner summoned a clerk to count and deposit the paper money. At Hans's request a grouping of certain sized stones was set aside for his further instructions.

"As this is your first transaction with banking, all of this may be confusing to you, Herr Mueller. However, please be assured that every penny of your holdings will be perfectly safe in this bank pending a proper accounting and certification. Furthermore, you are guaranteed that all of these transactions shall be held in the most strictest of confidence." Pausing for a moment, the banker lowered his voice to confidential tones, then continued, "Herr Mueller, you will need immediate funds to er . . . perhaps purchase new clothing and find somewhere to stay, a place befitting a man of such obvious means. We shall be happy to make those reservations for you. In fact, if I may be so bold, our bank will be delighted to act as your representative with any and all such needs." The truth be told, the Vice President would have invited Mueller to stay in his own guest bedroom, such was the wealth of the battered suitcase. "Have you any idea as to the amount you might like?"

"Herr Brunner, I am a man of simple means and holdings. We do not want much, but we do have a long journey in front of us. How much can I have?"

"Herr Mueller, with what you have laid before us, your numbered account, which shall be known only to you, me and possibly one or two other officials here at the bank, is, at this very moment by no way 'simple means.' The worth of your holdings, even by the most cursory of examinations, most likely places the value in the millions of dollars. You may have any amount you desire sir."

Hans gasped in shock. He knew the stones and coins would have been worth a lot of money, that much was obvious, but more than a million dollars! It was beyond his wildest dreams.

Soon afterwards the Muellers were escorted to the opulent and magnificent Hotel Savoy Bauer en Ville, Zürich's oldest and one of its finest. Hans and Helga marveled at the beautiful pearwood cabinetry, brass and chintz. Later in the day in their own fog of amazement, each member of the family was outfitted with a complete new wardrobe. They shopped for hours in Zürich, buying new shoes, boots, coats, hats, and suitcases in which to carry their stylish and comfortable, but not ostentatious clothing. For the first time in their frugal married life they could purchase other than absolutely necessary items. Hans bought his frau a beautiful piece of jewelry—a cameo brooch that made her cry. Helga proudly presented Hans with a Swiss pocket watch bearing an impressive stag's head engraved on the cover. Otto purchased a small wood carving of an owl and Karl bought a switchblade pocketknife.

Two days later through Herr Brunner's solid and respected connections, Hans was measured and wax moldings made for his left arm and hand prosthesis. Similarly, clandestine contact had been made and work begun for Swiss passports for each member of the family along with all required entry/exit visas needed to see them through France, Spain, Portugal, Cuba, Canada and on to their final destination—the United States. The passports, although false, were being prepared by a highly reputable professional who had helped countless others, many of royal and noble standing who were fleeing wartorn Europe.

The evening prior to their departure for Spain and Portugal, the Muellers arranged to have dinner with the Swiss farmer and his wife who had so warmly and graciously helped them. This would be their first meeting since shortly after their arrival in Zürich. The Muellers had been preoccupied with all their preparations for travel, and the farmer and his frau spent every moment they had with their children. Pending the arrival of the farmer's children at the Mueller's hotel restaurant, their father and Hans repaired to the bar for a few drinks before dinner.

"So, if everything works out as planned, we have rail transportation arranged right through to Portugal and from there we will board an ocean liner to Cuba. Ja, Helga is already thinking she might be seasick, but I don't believe so. She is from stout stock. Only with our firstborn son did I ever hear that woman moan or complain. Never before and never since," Hans said with a quiet laugh. "But before we have to join the rest for dinner I wanted to have time to visit with you. I . . . all of us are very grateful to you and your frau for the help you've given us. Since arriving in Zürich I discovered that I have wealth I never imagined possible. So, for all that you have so generously and unselfishly yielded for our aid and comfort, ja, even sacrificing things you and your family will need, I would like for you to accept this." Hans handed the farmer an envelope.

The farmer, after two cognacs, and not used to drinking anything stronger than buttermilk, opened the envelope and withdrew the bank note. He nearly fell off the barstool when he saw the draft made out in his name for four hundred thousand Swiss francs. Nearly speechless and with eyes both teary and having trouble focusing on Hans, he stammered, choked, quiet words.

"Herr Mueller, I cannot accept this. Truly, I am grateful beyond anything I could say, if only I could think of something to say. But this is a fortune." He was whispering.

"Will it see your frau through surgery and her recovery, your children through their training and allow you to keep your farm? Also, I would like for you to have extra for whatever you may want to do with it."

"Most certainly. All that and more. But I could never repay this amount, Herr Mueller. Not even in two lifetimes."

"Then no more need be said my friend. You owe me nothing. You have helped me and many like me escape the Nazis and the horrors that now grip our homeland. It most certainly is we who owe you! However, and this need may never arise, but once we are settled in the United States, there might be an occasion when it would be helpful for someone to represent me here in Zürich for banking or other matters. If I could call upon you to speak for me and look after my best interests, I would be beholden to you for those favors. And I will see that you are properly compensated for that as well."

"Herr Mueller, you are a godsend and more." Unashamed, silent tears streamed down his cheeks. Neither he nor Hans acknowledged them. The farmer continued, "If ever I or my family can do anything for you we shall count it the most extreme of all pleasures. *Danke schön* my friend. *Danke schön.*"

Chapter 4

A Journey of Jeopardy

Later, resting comfortably in their first class railway compartment, the Muellers viewed the swiftly passing and magnificently beautiful Swiss countryside. The passports with which they traveled showed their recently changed last name from Mueller to Miller. Hopefully the new anglicized name would help with the riskier parts of their journey.

They were, with some apprehension, on their way through Switzerland, France and Spain bound for Portugal and boat passage from there on to Cuba and Canada. The only real anxiety they felt was with their travel through France and Vichy, in particular. Vichy was pro-Nazi and supported a large population of German troops, Gestapo and SS personnel. Trying not to worry excessively about the unknown, Hans decided there was nothing much to do about the risks except to hope for the best. He leaned back in his comfortable couch seat and rubbed his new left arm and hand.

"This arm feels and looks as if it is real," he said with a smile and immense pride to Helga. "I'm very happy to have it although it will take some time getting used to." After all he had been through, his new arm was a pleasant distraction which he had received with the delight of a child at Christmas.

"Herr Brunner told me the craftsman who made it is the very best in all of Switzerland, possibly in all of Europe."

The prosthesis Hans wore as well as the identical spare duplicate arm, which was packed carefully in their luggage, were both filled to capacity with nothing less than individually wrapped twenty-five carat, D-color, flawless diamonds. There was no seam or other indication to give the slightest hint that the arms were hollowed or capable of storing anything. The exquisitely and intricately fashioned prostheses were phenomenally light even with the fortunes in diamonds stored within. So excellent was the craftsmanship that there was nothing to give away the secret.

Helga, who with her sons was not aware of the smuggled diamonds, reached over and with a loving smile patted Hans' hand. "You'll soon adjust to it dear. I'm glad it fits you so comfortably. And it looks *wunderbar!* Herr Brunner made a good recommendation when he sent you to that prosthetist."

"Ja, Herr Brunner was of great help in many ways. And I'm truly amazed that he says we can transact financial matters long distance like that. All the way from Canada! Ja, we can bank, draw money out, put money into our account and do all these things by wire using the transatlantic cable he told me about. Remarkable! That far away. Yet he says these things are done every day with customers in Canada and the United States. Ja, this will help tremendously! It seems—" Hans was interrupted by a Jewish gentleman who abruptly opened the door to their compartment and stepped in.

Taking the Millers in, the gentleman's face registered immediate surprise. "I beg your pardon," he said bowing to Hans and Helga. "My compartment must be next door, I've entered by mistake. Please forgive the intrusion," he said, very obviously embarrassed while backing out and gently closing the curtained glass door.

While Hans and Helga barely gave the man a second thought, Karl sat like a ramrod in his seat and glared at the departing Jew. Through clenched teeth, he spewed the words as if they were venom, "*Schwein hund* Jew!"

"Karl!" Hans said sharply, "keep a civil tongue in your mouth! Sometimes I don't know what comes over you. That man has done nothing to you. He simply mistook our compartment for his. You have no cause to say such things." Once more Hans, as so many times in the recent past, was troubled and perplexed by Karl's behavior. Frequently, in private, he had discussed his concerns with his wife. "I tell you Helga, it is those *Gott*-damned Nazis and their earlier teachings! They got to our boy. They have influenced and poisoned his young mind to hate others, and not just the Jews and homosexuals, but many others. Freemasons, Jehovah Witnesses, so many who they feel are inferior. '*Untermenschen,*' subhumans, they call these people. Like the Nazis, Karl has become heartless and brutal. I see these things already. Ja, maybe in small ways only sometimes, but they are there, I tell you they are there, they are unmistakable, and they are unnatural!"

On occasions such as this, in close proximity to a Jew, Karl let his true hateful nature shine through. But it wasn't the Hitler Youth Corps or the Nazis who instilled this hate in Karl—he was born like that. The Hitler Youth training had merely given him somewhere tangible to direct his hate.

Over time, Karl had learned to mirror the behavior of those around him when he felt he should, or when it was expected. He had learned to *look* like he felt emotions, even though his soul was made of ice.

Later, as the Millers were walking to the dining car, Karl made a point of looking into the adjoining compartment. He saw the gentleman who had mistakenly entered their cubicle. As the Jew waved a friendly greeting to Hans and Helga, Karl scowled at him. He noted a young male member of the family who appeared to be close to his own age, albeit somewhat larger than himself. The two boys' eyes locked and Karl's hatred was immediately evident to the other. "I will do it!" Karl said to himself, "I must do it!"

Hans, leading the family into the dining car, was looking back over his right shoulder talking to Helga while moving slowly through the car toward an empty table. With an unexpected swaying motion of the train, Hans reached for the nearest table to steady himself. His heart leapt into his throat and he abruptly broke into a cold sweat when he saw the uniform of the Nazi SS-*Sturmbannführer* (Major) seated at the table where he had most unfortunately paused. Hans, by chance, had noticed the Gestapo identification badge half hidden on the vest of the icy-visaged person in civilian clothing sitting opposite the SS officer. The badge showed a German eagle perched on a wreath encircling a swastika and bore the agent's number above the name "*Geheime Staatspolizei*" (Secret State Police). The dreaded *Gestapo* were the fountainhead of all German terror. They tortured, grotesquely, then slowly killed any suspected foe of Hitler or the *Deutschland*.

"*Guten Tag,*" (Good Day) the SS officer said to Hans who was filled with abject fear and hatred and found himself staring transfixed into the cold eyes of the Major. "For supposedly being a straight rail this road has sudden twists and turns does it not?" the *Sturmbannführer* stated with an artificial smile to Hans.

"Jawohl, sometimes it makes a simple walk very awkward," Hans replied, his heart still, seemingly stuck and throbbing madly in his throat. He thought, *I must make a conscious effort to hide my fear. Calm yourself Hans! These people have no reason to suspect you of anything. Be calm man—for God's sake—be calm!*

"You seem to me to have a *Bayerische Dialekt* (Munich area dialect). Are you German?" asked the other person at the table whom Hans had identified as a *Gestapo*. He looked at Hans with coal black penetrating eyes, deadly as a king cobra, that betrayed more than a casual interest in the conversation.

27

"*Nein mein* Herr, we are Swiss from near Basel, which, as you may know, is mostly all German. However, we have relatives in Munich and have spent a great deal of time there, perhaps that is why I speak with such an accent. Please forgive this imposition, it is difficult to walk without holding on to something."

To Hans' terror Karl chose that moment to shove his way forward and stand before the two Nazis.

"*Heil Hitler!*" he shouted as he raised his arm in salute and clicked his heels together, standing at a rigid attention.

"*Heil Hitler,*" the two officers said as they raised their right arms in a return salute accompanied by appreciative smiles.

Hans' heart flip-flopped again as Karl boldly said, "*Meine Herren,* (Gentlemen, Sirs) I have something of great importance I need to discuss with you."

The train crossed over rough track again and caused Karl to lose his balance. He lurched forward grabbing for the table to steady himself, but instead upset a cup of tea, spilling its lukewarm contents and saucer into the lap of the SS officer. The officer quickly scooted backwards and dabbed at his lap with a napkin.

Profuse in his apology, Hans seized the opportunity to drag his son away. "I'm terribly sorry," Hans said putting both hands on Karl's shoulders. "I hope you have not been burnt with the spilled tea." Hans stooped and picked up the cup and saucer from the floor and placed them on the table. "We had best find a seat." He started to move forward.

"What is it that is of such importance? What do you want to tell me boy?" the Major said, halting the Millers' progress. There was now a note of annoyance evident in his voice.

"Please forgive my son, Herr *Sturmbannführer*, he sometimes lives in a fantasy world. He only wanted to waste your time with silly stories. Again, we beg your forgiveness for this inconvenience."

The officer seemingly dismissed the Millers by ignoring them as he continued to dab at his damp uniform. Hans took the occasion to hurriedly push and guide Karl to the empty table at the far end of the car.

"But I need to talk to—" Karl began to say wearing a sullen and determined expression. He was quieted by a hard slap to the back of his head.

"Silence!" Hans shouted in Karl's ear using the most forceful tone that Karl could ever remember hearing his father use before. "You will say nothing to no one. Do not speak another word until we return to our compartment!" Hans' right hand unconsciously squeezed Karl's shoulder so hard it brought tears to Karl's eyes and made him wince. "Do you understand me perfectly? You will keep your mouth shut Karl!"

"Yes Papa." Karl was momentarily subdued even though he knew his duty to his Führer and the Fatherland was infinitely more important to any duty he may have to his parents. *But not for long,* he thought to himself, *I have things these men need to know!*

Midway through their meal Hans saw the two Nazis rise from their table. The Major looked their way, placed his napkin on his plate and walked toward the Millers. Hans felt his pulse quicken again. "Say nothing!" he hissed to his family.

"If your travels take you to France perhaps we shall yet have another opportunity to visit again. That is a long journey." Clicking his heels together and bowing at the waist he said, "*Guten Abend,* (Good Evening) *Mein* Herr and madam, I hope you and your charming children will have a most pleasant trip."

As he turned to leave he made a point of reaching over to Karl and patting him affectionately on the shoulder and smiled. Karl returned the smile with an eye signal that begged for the opportunity to speak. *I have things I need to tell you, Herr Sturmbannführer. Important things!* Karl wanted to scream, but held silent in his thoughts. *There are some Jews on this train, probably illegally. And my parents are not Swiss, as my father said, but German. We are from Salzdorf. My father is no longer loyal to our beloved Führer and he is forcing me to leave with them. We are deserting our Fatherland and he suddenly has a great deal of money, which appeared mysteriously. You must hear me!*

Low hanging clouds, mist and still later, snow, obscured the beautiful southern Swiss and northern French countryside as their train sped on its way. Karl, after having been chastised by both his parents for his behavior in the dining car, sat quietly, his ice blue eyes watching the blur of the passing landscape. He also noted the Jewish lad from the next compartment passing their cubicle making periodic trips down the aisle to the rear. While looking a picture of remorse, Karl's mind raced with curiosity. He was curious if the Jew was passing between cars from one to another, and he wondered why he made so many trips. After repeated requests he received his parent's permission to leave the compartment for one occasion, but only with his brother Otto, and to walk and remain exclusively within their single car length, and he was to speak to no one! Once outside, Karl immediately went to the darkened vestibule, which connected the train's cars one to the other. After a hurried reconnoiter, *Yes,* he said to himself, *this is the perfect place!*

Karl made a nuisance of himself wanting to step outside the compartment and walk for exercise and to escape boredom in the car's hallway. Eventually he wore the patience of his parents and they acquiesced, but insisted he remain within their car and reiterated he should speak to no one. Karl sat patiently waiting and noticed that his brother Otto was fast asleep. Then, several minutes after Karl saw the Jewish boy once more pass their cubicle he stood and said, "I'm going for a stretch, I'll be right back." He followed in the direction the boy had gone. As he entered the dark confines of the vestibule connection area, he nearly collided with the Jewish boy and a Jewish girl who were locked in a tight embrace, kissing and fumbling with one another's clothing. They disengaged and each gave Karl an expression of intense aggravation and annoyance for his interruption as they opened the door and walked into the now dimly lit coach car.

Watching them from his dark location, Karl saw the couple halt midway into the next car where the girl took a seat. Obviously she was with her family of five or six others for all the seats were occupied by a clan of Jews. Karl was outraged; Jews everywhere! With his new knife open in his left hand, Karl removed his right shoe. He strained in the darkness to see the Jewish boy as the boy remained standing and chatting with the girl for a few moments and then he turned, preparing to return to his family's car. Karl stood behind the door and waited. Momentarily the boy opened the door and entered. As the door closed behind him Karl stepped out and swung his shoe, striking the boy solidly on the back of the head. The boy went down on his right knee and turned to see Karl, his eyes blazing and his mouth frozen in an evil grin, raising the shoe to strike again.

This was not the first time the Jewish lad had been a victim of German race-related violence. He had been chased by young thugs and adults many times. On more than one occasion the law of averages ruled against him, and he had been caught before he reached the safety of his home and was beaten. Growing persecution and harassment were the impetus for the family leaving Germany to relocate and begin a new life in Spain. Despite his father's advice the young man had learned to fight back and that is what he did on this occasion. From his kneeling position he balled his fist and struck Karl a solid blow in the stomach. The wind went out of Karl with a whoosh and he doubled over, violently striking and splitting his forehead open on the steel door handle as he fell unconsciously to the metal buffer plates which covered the cars coupling.

Minutes later in a blur, the vestibule connecting car door opened again. The Jewish boy shook his head in an attempt to clear the fuzziness.

Leaning over Karl's inert form, with everything spinning, he stared at a pair of highly polished black dress boots. His gaze continued upward to the impressive uniform trousers tucked inside the boots and finally into the piercing stare of the SS *Sturmbannführer*. He saw but could not dodge the butt of the Luger pistol the officer swung down striking the young man squarely between his eyes. The SS officer, with some difficulty due to the close confines of the compartment and the two bodies crowding the already restricted space, lifted the Jewish boy. He opened the side door and threw the youth out of the fast moving train. The body was immediately swallowed by the dark night in a snow covered ravine. He then collected Karl in his arms and made his way forward in search of the Millers' compartment. Midway of the car he saw Hans and Helga frantically searching for their son.

A French doctor from two car lengths down was attending Karl, who was stretched out in the Millers' cubicle, his head cradled in his mother's lap. This was one of the few times in his life she had been able to hold her son as if he needed her. From the very beginning, he was a stand-offish solitary child who didn't need the maternal ministrations of his mother. Now, she gently, lovingly, pulled the runaway wisps of blond hair away from the gash on his forehead.

The train's conductor was frustrated trying to translate the doctor's comments into German. "He says, 'Maybe so there is a fracture but he cannot make for certain that decision now. He will have to perform the stitches onto the boy's head and there should be absolutely no movement or jarring. Ja, very hard knock to the head and now a deep cut he has. Maybe looks like a cut down into the skull. Better he makes no movement. Most important not to jar.' *Herr Doktor* says he will be back to check on the boy periodically until the first town is reached where there is a hospital. He should be in hospital care as soon as possible. Something too about dancing, which makes no sense. Jawohl. That is what he says. I think. Nothing else I understand. The French talk funny."

"How much farther to the nearest hospital town Herr Conductor?" Hans asked.

"We are maybe two hours from Vichy. I suggest we go on to there. There may be other hospitals in between here and there, Herr Miller, but Vichy has a first-rate hospital with the finest of doctors. Your son will receive the best care there. Any other towns we might stop at would be a guess as to hospital availability and care and could result in valuable time lost. Now, if you will excuse me, we are conducting a search for the young

Jewish boy who all of a sudden is missing from the next compartment. Where on this train would that boy go? Such a trip this has become!"

The doctor and SS Officer were with the Millers when the Vichy Hospital medical staff placed Karl on a litter for transport to the hospital.

"I hope your son will be all right, Herr Miller. He impresses me as being a fine young man. Time permitting, I may be able to stop by the hospital and visit in a day or so. If his condition is improved perhaps we may still have that conversation he wanted."

"Danke schön, Herr Sturmbannführer. We are grateful for your kindness and help."

"Bitte schön," said the SS officer, once more clicking his heels together and bowing from the waist.

"I thank him, but he is driving me insane always showing up and always wanting to talk to Karl!" Hans exclaimed to Helga as soon as they entered the taxi following the hospital ambulance. "We must have Karl well and leave here as quickly as possible. We will not be safe until we are beyond France's borders and into Spain. I am becoming a nervous wreck!"

Joining his Gestapo traveling companion in the waiting staff car, the SS major said, "I want to know the hospital the boy will be in. I have a feeling about that family."

"If it is a concern let's take them in now," replied the Gestapo agent. "I'm removing that group of Jews from the train for questioning. We'll simply add these people to that collection."

"By all means, we will have them questioned. But in due course. They are stopping here so a day or more will not matter."

"Do you suspect they are lying about their status? Do you think they are German?" queried the Gestapo agent, not pausing to allow the Major time to respond. "If so, do not afford them the opportunity to escape. I'll have them arrested now!" he said, leaning forward and reaching to open the car door.

"No! They are concerned parents. They will not endanger their wounded son. I'm convinced they will remain here in hospital with him. They'll not be going anywhere. I'll stop back after I've reported in to Headquarters, and have had time to check on a couple of matters." The *Sturmbannführer* did not elaborate further on his thoughts and suspicions: *How would a Swiss farmer from a remote and isolated area out from Basel know immediately my SS insignia and rating of Major? The young lad who was obviously assaulted and wounded by the Jew boy, he so reminds me of my own youngest brother, Aryan, blond-haired and intense blue eyes. And where in neutral Switzerland would the boy have been taught to render such*

*a faultless salute to the Führer? He had stood at rigid attention, feet
and heels in perfect position, left arm at side, hand and fist properly
cupped with his right arm and palm of hand in the exact and most
precise salute form. Most definitely the lad had been taught and taught
well. In all likelihood in Germany by our Hitler Youth Corps. The
family is obviously well off financially; all wear expensive styles of new
clothing, they travel first class yet they do not act as though they are
accustomed to wealth and claim to be a small farming family. And the
youth wanted to talk to me with an intense and burning desire.
Interesting . . .*

"All we know," Hans said in response to Karl's question the next
morning, "was the SS Major said he was coming into our car and found
you lying unconscious on the metal floor of the connecting
compartment on the train. Your right shoe was off your foot. Do you
not remember what happened yourself?"

Karl lay in his hospital bed surrounded by his family. His forehead
was wrapped in layers of fresh white bandage. He had regained
consciousness later the previous night, and the doctors determined that
he had received only a mild concussion. They recommended he remain
in the hospital for a few days until his condition improved. *"Nein*
Papa, I must have slipped and hit my head. I remember nothing," Karl
lied. "But now I feel fine and I'm ready to leave this bed."

"We must wait a few days Karl, until the doctors say it is all right
for you to travel. In the meantime your Mama will stay here with you.
And I remind you, speak to no one of our travels or our family matters.
Ist das klar?"

"Jawohl Papa, *verstehen."* But Karl was hoping with every fiber of
his being that he could again talk to the SS *Sturmbannführer.*

Hans soon learned that a passenger train left Vichy each evening at
seven-thirty for several points south into Spain. They could get an
express that would take them to Saragossa with connections from there
on to Madrid. From Madrid they could easily board yet another
express straight through to the port city of Lisbon, Portugal, the point
from which they would book passage on an ocean liner for Cuba.

"But the doctors said Karl should not travel for several days yet!"
Helga exclaimed to Hans when he told her about the train schedules the
next afternoon.

"Ja, Ja, I know that Helga, but I also know that it is vitally important
that we leave here the very first instant that it is possible. We live on
borrowed time in this city what with all of the SS and Gestapo elbow to

elbow. You see them everywhere you turn. We must get out of here. I was stopped and had to show my papers twice already." The husband and wife were talking in the hospital corridor several doors down from Karl's room. Hans had no sooner passed on his concerns when he looked down the hallway to see the SS *Sturmbannführer* making his way toward Karl's room. The Nazi's hard heeled boots echoed ominously on the marble hospital floor.

"*Ach Mein Gott*, it's him again! We dare not leave them alone to speak!" Hans all but shouted as he hurried back to Karl's room. The SS Major was standing beside Karl's bed when Hans rushed into the room.

"*Heil Hitler!*" the officer shouted as he stomped his heels and raised his arm in salute before Karl.

"*Heil Hitler!*" Karl responded excitedly and threw his arm up in a return salute, which caused him immediate obvious pain. He quickly placed both hands on either side of his head and moaned.

Hans and Helga rushed into the room. Helga went quickly to Karl's side and put her arms around him. "He should not have excitement just now," Helga fussed. The bandage on Karl's head had reddened with blood and Karl's face was a grimace of pain.

"The doctor's caution that he should not talk or have sudden movement for awhile yet Herr Major. Surely you understand."

"Most certainly, Herr Miller. I just wanted to stop by and see how he is progressing. I did not want to disturb him or his recovery. I had hoped to chat briefly with your son, but I suppose that can wait until another time." In a stare filled with menace and a threatening tone in his voice, he continued, "You are not planning on leaving anytime soon, are you Herr Miller?"

"*Nein, Herr Sturmbannführer*, we must wait for the full recovery of our son. We are in no hurry except for his return to good health."

"*Das ist güte*. I, too, hope for a prompt recovery. And," he said patting Karl's foot resting beneath the sheet, "I shall be back at another time when this fine young man is feeling better and more able to talk." The Major then supposedly, accidentally dropped his hat from beneath his arm. While Hans, drawing everyone's attention, bent to pick up the hat, the Major placed Karl's switchblade knife beneath the bedcovers resting it against Karl's foot.

Karl felt the cool metal against his skin and wondered what it was. He looked at the Nazi officer who, wearing an evil smile, returned the stare and nodded his head at Karl. Receiving his hat from Hans, the Major clicked his heels, bowed at the waist and said, "Good day. My apologies for having disturbed you. *Auf wiedersehen.*"

When Karl finally slept after the doctor had redressed his wound and given him a sleeping powder, Hans whispered urgently to Helga. "The SS officer is concerned. He's up to something and he's paying too much attention to Karl and us. I'm certain he suspects us."

"Of what can he suspect? I think you are just being nervous. He likes Karl and that's all. He's just being nice."

"No Helga, I have this feeling. I'm certain he is on to us. We must leave and leave right away."

"But what about Karl's condition? We can't move him like this."

"We leave now Helga. Tonight. We must leave."

"Hans, I don't think—"

"Shush woman, do not argue with me! Do you want to go to a prison camp and be separated from your entire family to await a certain death with the Jews and others they consider enemies of Germany? We have fled our homeland. We have turned our backs on Germany. The SS have already tried to kill me. If caught with these false passports we will most certainly be looked upon by the Nazis and Gestapo as the lowest species on earth. "We must leave, we have no choice!"

Around the corner of the hospital wing, the Major lit a cigarette and watched the hospital entrance for any movement of the Millers. After an hour he returned to his office, knowing word would come from the Swiss Consulate by the next morning on this Miller family from rural Basel, Switzerland, which they'd claimed was home. He would return then, accompanied, he was certain, by Gestapo agents.

The wind on this dark winter's night seemed raw and cutting. It brought with it bitter, numbing cold and snow, which swirled in balletic patterns. Come morning the snow and wind would have sculpted deep drifts. Huddled against the elements, Helga, dressed in a nurse's uniform, made her way forward at the Hauptbahnhof, main railway station, awkwardly carrying a suitcase while assisting the bandaged Karl. The train had just pulled into the station. They walked gingerly through the light crust of snow to the boarding platform and, with the aid of the conductor, stepped into the train. He directed them to their compartment and returned to assisting other passengers to depart and others to board. Hans and Otto entered the train from the rear, wanting to avoid the main confluence of passengers, family well-wishers seeing relatives off, and the SS who had just began to congregate at the middle of the train.

The Nazis milled around through the crowd; small clouds of steam formed from everyone's breath, it circled around their heads for a moment then disappeared with the wind. The Germans tried to make eye contact with others in the gathering, looking for anyone who appeared anxious and nervous with such a confrontation. Occasionally they would stop people at random and rudely demand to see their papers. Hans thought it best that the family separate to board the train and later rejoin once the train was underway. He and Otto settled midway of the last car and tucked their suitcases under their seats. They scattered sections of paper on the floor and other nearby seats then buried their faces in newspapers, attempting to look casual, as though they had arrived with the train and were continuing passengers.

Minutes seemed like hours to Hans as they sat waiting for the boarding process. He tucked his elbows to his sides to stop his hands holding the paper from shaking. The palm of his right hand was moist with sweat. Finally, through the open rear door he heard the faint call for all to board over the alternating cadence sounds of the train's thunk, clank and hissing jets of escaping steam. He smiled and thought, *maybe, now, thank God— maybe now we go!* Just as the engine whistle gave two short blasts signaling the train was preparing to depart, the newspaper Hans held in front of him was stoutly smacked. Hans lowered the paper to see an SS uniformed *Scharführer,* (Staff Sergeant,) standing before him, wearing an angry expression.

"Papers!" he shouted. *"Schnell!"*

Hans promptly presented both his and Otto's passports. The *Scharführer* opened and looked at Hans' passport closely then glared at Hans. He appeared as if he was going to say something then staggered as the train gave a short jerk.

The Sergeant flung the passports onto the newspaper in Hans' lap. He then hurried to leave the train as it gave another jerk and began to roll forward, pulling away from the station.

Shortly after leaving Vichy and the remaining French soil occupied and considered protectorates and preserves by Germany, Hans and Otto joined Helga and Karl in their first class cuchette compartment. They closed all the curtains and a lower bed was prepared for Karl who appeared none the worse for his impromptu departure from the hospital. His headache had subsided, but he was still in a disagreeable mood due to his forced exit from Germany, the Nazis, and not being permitted to speak with the SS officer, as he had wanted. The remainder of the family, however, breathed a collective sigh of relief as their journey pressed on toward Spain, Portugal and freedom.

In Cuba the Millers had two weeks to rest and loll about on the island before continuing their journey. Helga was just getting over her violent bout of seasickness when it was time to board another ocean liner destined for Vancouver, Canada, their final port. Helga turned a ghostly pale and became ill with motion sickness on the occasion of her first step aboard each ship.

Finally, and happy to be done with the ocean going vessels, the Millers moved to the inland city of North Vancouver, Canada. There they would wait, patiently, the processing of papers that would eventually allow them to immigrate to their ultimate destination of Tacoma, Washington.

A few years before, while still in Salzdorf, the Millers had known of three German families who had immigrated to Tacoma. From members of those families remaining in Germany, Hans and Helga learned that the former Salzdorf residents had been well received and were very content in Tacoma.

During the autumn of 1942, twelve months after their departure from Salzdorf, the Millers also became residents of Tacoma, Washington, U.S.A., and began a new life. They settled quickly and comfortably into their adopted community which did indeed have a strong German influence from the many immigrants from the Fatherland who had come seeking and received asylum in the U.S. in advance of the war. With the Millers' arrival, they noted some, albeit very limited, anti-refugee prejudice. By then the Nazi brutality, barbaric and inhuman atrocities that were being committed on those fleeing Germany were well known. On the whole, they were greeted and received warmly in their community.

Although his Tacoma bank account was substantially more than adequate, and his holdings in Zürich placed him easily and quite solidly in the millionaire category, they lived modestly in their new surroundings. Hans began again to practice his small upholstery business, which grew rapidly. His ability and skill as an upholsterer, even with the lack of a moving hand and fingers on his left hand, surpassed others of that trade not likewise handicapped. The pleats, tucks and bindings he made with leather and cloth were pure artistry. After the first war, when he lost his arm and until his sons were old enough to help, Helga would assist him with the more difficult folds. But Hans made Helga nervous each time he would put a handful of tacks or brads in his mouth. He would touch the magnetized end of his tack hammer to the head of the tack or brad from between his lips, placing them exactly where needed on the material, then expertly hammer them in place. Helga always feared Hans would cough, hiccup, or maybe sneeze and swallow the pointed nails.

The entire family improved their mastery of the English language and did well in their new country. All seemed happy—all but Karl. There remained with him a coldness, an indifference and an ever-increasing cruelty in his dealings with others. All of this Hans feared was a dark and foreboding harbinger of evil things to come.

Chapter 5

The Dark Period

Thule, Greenland, February 1956

The storm that U.S. Air Force Captain Karl Miller had been waiting for was coming. Here, the daylight and nighttime hours were now solid darkness on this most northern and remote frozen island, the largest in the world. Tonight he would once again ensure that the mine his father had guarded long ago in World War II Nazi Germany would remain secure and unrevealed.

Captain Miller stepped outside the weather station and lit a cigarette. His watch showed 2130 hours. A low pressure area east of Thule over Baffin Bay was building, causing surface winds to blow off the icecap from the southeast creating a deadly storm condition of wind, snow, and sub-zero temperatures. The storm would not reach Thule for another hour, maybe an hour and a half. Miller walked the short distance to the All Ranks Club named The Top of the World Club or TOW Club. He stopped by an Air Force pickup truck and ground his cigarette into the snow. Karl leaned against the truck and listened to the wind blowing across the icecap.

It's strange here—the wind, Karl thought. It has been nearly a year now and still I am not used to it. It's a constant thing and creates this eerie sound like a cry. At first, when I arrived, the moan of the wind and the total absence of all other familiar noises bothered me. No honking of vehicle horns, squealing of tires or other traffic sounds, no birds singing, dogs barking, trains, or airplanes. Nothing! No other noises. Just the sound of the wind. Always just the moaning, wailing sound of the wind. I like it. I shall miss it when I leave shortly.

An Arctic fox darted from one snowbank to another, then quickly to the back of the TOW Club. The front door of the club opened. First Lieutenant Ronald Ramos appeared. He was Miller's replacement and had arrived at Thule several days prior. He was obviously very drunk, weaving as he walked to the truck where Karl waited. There was no one else around.

Approaching the truck, Ramos staggered, slipped, and nearly fell. He grabbed the side of the truck just as Miller reached out a hand to help steady him.

"Oops," the Lieutenant said. "Didn't see you there. Why didn't you come in and have a drink?"

With just a bit more than a trace of an accent apparent, Karl said, "Naw, I don't feel like a drink. Besides I just got here. Why don't you get in on the other side and I'll drive. Don't want you wrecking the only unit pickup we have."

"Hell of an idea," Ramos muttered. Steadying himself by holding onto the truck, he maneuvered his way around to the passenger side and got in. "Hey, you're not pissed off at me for what I said earlier, are you?"

With a sweeping right-hand motion, Karl removed his parka hood revealing his tousled shock of Aryan blond hair. He looked at Ramos with penetrating, steely eyes. "You mean what you told me the other night? About your Jewish ancestors, the Holocaust and that?"

"Yeah. I got the impression that maybe you were kinda sorta, ticked off 'cause I'm having some second thoughts about our Salzdorf venture. And you seemed surprised that I am Jewish. Nah, surprised ain't the word, you were blown away. You looked like I'd just poured a bucket of freezing water over you!"

"Naw, that's all right," Karl lied. "Hell, who knows, I might feel the same way if I were in your shoes. Like you said, we can think about it. There's nothing we should do or can do just now anyhow."

Miller was more than upset; he was hostile. His calm exterior in no way revealed the inner rage, hatred and disgust boiling within him. He was angry, shocked that he, himself, could have been so stupid. And now he seethed with a fury bordering on madness with this Jew sitting beside him who had a Spanish name and had fooled him so completely. *I shoulda known,* he chastised himself, *whenever I was around him I always had this odd sort of feeling. Goddammit, I shoulda known!* The voice screamed at him inside his head.

"I still find it difficult if not impossible to believe that you are a Jew. Ramos is not Jewish and you don't have any of the Jewish features I'm familiar with. You've never talked or acted Jewish to me."

"Yeah, well, I was only about three or four when my real father died. My mom later married my stepfather, Manuel Ramos, who adopted me and they changed my last name. But I remained a member of my biological father's Jewish faith. Had to. It was obligatory. Can't explain why I don't look Jewish, and being in the military I don't wear the Kippah, my little cap but rarely. And, Karl, to tell you the truth, over time I've gathered you didn't cotton to us Jews, so I kinda, sorta made a point of not overtly broadcasting that issue. Didn't want it to interfere with our friendship. Figured there was no reason it should. So," he continued with a chuckle, "there's no really outward revealing signs that I am a Jew, other than my Jewish insignia, which doesn't 'stick out', so to speak."

"And what's that?" Karl said with a scowl.

"My dick was cut. The Brit Milah circumcision ritual got me. Guess the opportunity to show you that just never presented itself," Ramos said looking at Miller with a drunken smile.

Miller did not return the smile.

"But with this Salzdorf thing, it's just that some of that stuff could possibly have belonged to some family members long ago. Guess it's a built-in guilt trip thing, know what I mean?"

"Yeah. I know what you mean. Forget about it."

Captain Miller started the truck, backed it up, and drove to the edge of the base away from anyone who might pass by. He then stopped to let the vehicle warm up.

"Hey, Karl, they were in there again tonight," Ramos said. "That's gonna be a hell of a thing to get used to. Just seems so . . . whatever . . . unnatural I guess."

"You mean the two Dane contractors?"

"Yup, those two. They sat at the same table. Had a candle lit and were holding hands for Crissake! Sipping wine and toasting one another. You just don't see shit like that at most Air Force bases, huh? In fact, I've never seen anything like that, 'cept the time I spent a couple of days in San Francisco. Boy, that is some kinda weird."

"You'll get used to seeing it," Karl said. "Maybe after awhile, like me, you'll just overlook it, or try to. If it were at all possible, I'd take them outside and stomp their faces into the snow. But I can't, so I tell myself it's their mouths. They can stick whatever they want in them. Unfortunately, you will see a lot of that up here with the contractors. Sick, filthy bastards. I'd like to gut every one of them!"

"Yeah," replied the Lieutenant. "I'm sure you would." He snuggled down into his parka and went immediately into a drunken sleep.

Karl's previous assignment had been with the Headquarters Armed Forces Courier Service (ARFCOS) on the East Coast. Now, as with most follow-on assignments, upon completion of a remote tour, such as Thule, he had received his base of preference assignment to Detachment 23, ARFCOS, Denham Studios, England, a former movie studio now leased by the U.S. Air Force, about forty-five minutes from London. He and Ramos had known one another for several years and had traveled the world over on temporary duty (TDY) and flying assignments. Both had volunteered for the remote Thule assignment in order to qualify for a later base-of-preference assignment in Europe.

It was on one of these trips after Karl had consumed several cognacs more than was his custom that he became too talkative with Ramos.

"I have a source for materials that will market very well in Europe, in fact, anywhere in the world," he had confided in Ramos. "And as couriers we would have the perfect vehicle to use, travel and sell these things. You could handle the states and I would work all of Europe—it would be an ideal set-up."

"What kinds of things are you talking about?" Ramos had asked.

Karl unthinking in his drunken stupor told him of some of the artwork and jewels—in fact he told Ramos far more than he should or would have normally. He mentioned that some of the items had most likely come from the concentration camps during WWII. Ramos was very interested and the two had discussed the possibilities and potential rewards at length.

Karl explained that their diplomatic status as ARFCOS couriers would lend itself perfectly to set up a network of pick-up and drop off points for things other than official U.S. classified data. Legally, classified materials were the only articles authorized, by country-to-country security agreements, that they were to courier.

By the next morning Miller, suffering from a ferocious hangover, had forgotten the conversation, but Ramos hadn't. When Ramos mentioned it to Miller, Karl turned an icy stare at him and said, "What are you talking about?" When Ramos refreshed Karl's memory of the previous evening's discussion and plans, Karl had said coldly, "We will discuss this at another time." *Such a dumkopf I am!* Karl berated himself. *How could I let myself get so drunk to lose total control and speak of these things?* he thought. *I don't even remember what I told him—surely I couldn't have told all—even drunk I am more disciplined than that. I'm amazed I said anything! What's done is done, now I must fix it.*

Shortly, Captain Miller drove out onto the *Thule Freeway*, a fjord which is frozen nine months out of the year. During that time monstrous icebergs, which were on their way to Baffin Bay and ultimately the North Atlantic Ocean, are locked there in place. He drove past the aqua colored mountain peaks of the giant icebergs jutting out of the frozen fjord, heading toward Dundas, the Innuit Eskimo village.

Adjacent to Thule U.S. Air Force Base, which is located some 700 miles north of the Arctic Circle, the four or five hut-type dwellings that comprise the Dundas settlement date back to the 10th century. The Innuit have used Dundas as a stopping over place to repair their sleds and dog harnesses. Sometimes they stopped to trade needed items with others prior to continuing their trip to remote locations farther out on the icecap. Rarely are the huts occupied during the dark period from November until February, when there is total darkness twenty-four hours a day.

Karl knew one of the huts in the Dundas area was occupied. He had driven by there earlier in the day and saw a sled being prepared for a dawn departure the following morning. With a plan in mind, which involved Ramos' future, Karl had visited with the traveler. "Have you had luck with your hunting?" he asked the Innuit, named Nuuk.

"I have done poorly with our travel. Two days ago I was lucky enough to get a small baby seal. If you would like to eat, we have some left inside." Not waiting for a response he took Karl's elbow and walked toward the hut. "We are happy to share with you," said the Innuit.

Nuuk escorted Karl inside and, ignoring his woman and introductions, he sliced Karl a piece from the remains of the small seal which were in a large, battered pan (*katta*). The hut was surprisingly warm from the heat of a small kerosene burner. The single room dwelling reeked with foul odors from the commingled, warm stench of the seal's carcass, and the rancid body smell of the Innuits.

Karl devoured the meat and was licking his fingers. His host quickly cut him another hunk of the seal. "With hunting being so bad, what do you feed the dogs?" Karl asked.

"They eat when the hunt is good. They don't eat when it is bad. We leave tomorrow morning and farther out on the cap hunting will improve. The dogs can be hungry for another day or so." Karl smiled at this bit of good news. Everything was falling into place.

The Innuit's dogs were burrowed into the snow away from the hut but tethered. Karl knew these dogs were quite ferocious. Theirs was a brutal life. They worked hard and existed on little more than a starvation diet. Only the strongest survived, often by killing and eating the weaker members of the teams. While amazingly loyal to the master, a husky would attack any other person who came within striking distance. While it shocked and amazed outsiders that such a thing could happen, it was not uncommon to learn of an Innuit toddler who had darted from his parent's control and fallen amongst a dog team. There the savage animals immediately pounced on and killed the child. *Yes,* thought Karl, *they will do nicely.*

Karl's visit extended until most of the seal was gone.

Nuuk thought, *He is looking at my woman with a lustful eye. He no doubt wants her. If he asks, I will let him. We have done so with some of the single men out on the ice where there are not enough women for all. But I will stay inside with them because I don't know this man as I knew the others.*

Karl, indeed, had pictured Nuuk's woman nude and thought about having sex with her, but instead of pursuing it, he arose. "Come with me to my truck, I have something for you Nuuk."

"Here," handing the Innuit a full bottle of vodka, Karl said, "this will make your insides warm tonight. Thank you for your hospitality. Maybe I will see you and your woman again when you return."

Later that night inside the hut, Nuuk and his woman were burrowed deeply into their fur covers and blankets. Nuuk's woman heard, for the second time that day, the unusual noise of an approaching truck. "Nuuk, wake! Listen, the foreigner comes again to visit." She shook Nuuk hard, whispering loudly, repeatedly, "Wake! Wake! He probably wants to eat again, and there is but little left."

Nuuk, his senses dulled heavily by the hard drink he had consumed, mumbled something and began snoring again.

I noticed his stares today, she thought. *He, no doubt, wants me, but Nuuk has to approve first. Why must he be drunk now? But maybe it isn't the same foreigner.* The woman sat up and reached for the single shot rifle which was always kept close by. She pointed the rifle at the small doorway and waited.

The USAF truck stopped some distance from the hut and the engine died. Karl got out and walked around to the passenger side and opened the door. He turned the Lieutenant toward him and pulled his upper body forward outside the truck's cab. That movement and the frigid blast of cold air awoke Ramos.

Startled, he looked up and said, "Where we at? What's going—"

He died instantly when he was viciously struck with a tire iron between his eyes with all the strength Karl could muster. He pulled Ramos from the cab of the truck and immediately removed his clothing. He dragged the body to an area near the dogs, took a long, switchblade from his pocket and slit the Lieutenant's throat with such force the head was nearly decapitated. A hollow, thump sound was made as Miller plunged his knife just below the center of Ramos' chest and then ripped open the stomach down to his pubic area. With a huge shove, the killer propelled Ramos forward and amongst the dogs. The huskies tore into the body even as it fell. In a short time the corpse was ravaged. By morning there would be no sign of what had taken place.

The wind from the advancing storm was beginning to pick up by the time Miller returned to the base. He quickly and quietly burned the Lieutenant's clothing in his dormitory's furnace. There would, of course, be an investigation into the missing Lieutenant's whereabouts. However, there had been other prior new assignees who, not respecting the ferocity and suddenness of the storms there, had frozen to death within yards of a shelter. Some of those people were never seen again.

In the Dundas hut, Nuuk's woman decided that any danger had passed. *Too bad it was not the tall handsome visitor. It might have been fun to lay with him. He wanted to. I could tell. Nuuk knew it too—he said so. Maybe next time we come here. Now I am concerned about the dogs and the other noises I heard. Well, whatever the problem, Nuuk can deal with it in the morning. He is too drunk to do anything now.*

The Lieutenant's skull, too large for the dogs to chew on and consume, was the only part of the body left. It had been separated from the neck. With the arrival of the strong winds, the head had already rolled far away from the hut area. Moved by the raging Arctic storms, it was possible for the skull to easily travel thousands of miles with its dead eyes staring over the nothingness of the polar icecap.

At 2220 hours the storm hit the Thule and Dundas areas with gale force winds gusting to 103 knots. The storm raged for nearly two hours, and then a heavy snow began to fall, blanketing the entire region and covering its secret.

Chapter 6

To the Future

Luke AFB, Arizona, June 1956

ot. It was going to be hot! As a premonition, at 0530 on this
Saturday morning, the sun began to rise as a fiery ball on the horizon
of the wide desert expanse surrounding Phoenix, Arizona.

The radio announcer for station KTY, the eyes and ears for the entire
"Valley of the Sun," which included the U.S. Air Force installation at Luke
Field, said the current temperature was already nearing 80. He warned the
listening area could ". . . look forward to another scorcher." The temp
would reach the 110 plus degree mark before the day was over.

Steve Scott felt great as he quietly exited his barracks and began his
daily 0600 morning run. He noted the contrasting odors of the baked
desert, sagebrush, sand, and mesquite from the nearby mess hall's frying
bacon, sausage, SOS, and other breakfast smells being carried, alternatingly,
by the fresh early morning breezes. The desert had finally cooled down and
the temperature, at the moment, was pleasant. Shortly it would heat up
again making today's base-wide parade anything but enjoyable. Steve was
in good shape physically and made excellent time with his run. Back in the
barracks within the hour and standing under the tepid shower, he was exhil-
arated and relieved that he had finally made his decision.

By 1000 the mercury in the thermometer nearest the flight line at Luke
where hundreds of troops had been assembled in parade formations had
already passed one hundred twelve and was steadily climbing. Parade
participants were promptly filling ambulances parked at the rear of the
flights. Their summer Class A heavily-starched, long sleeved, khaki 1505
uniforms, with ties, exacerbated the oppressive heat. Some claimed the
large number of fallouts were due to heat exhaustion; others allowed they
were caused by the beer farts from some sick minded bastards in the front
ranks.

The Women's Air Force, WAF, A flight was in place as the leadoff unit to march in review past the reviewing stand. Space for B flight, Steve Scott and the rest of the troops from the 4333rd Support Squadron, had been left open. Off in the distance the image of the marching flight appeared through the shimmering waves of heat rising from the tarmac, making the figures of the first four ranks look as though they were weaving, snake-like, but upright, as they marched.

The guidon's barely audible, shallow voice carried across the runway and was immediately followed by the much louder, in unison, chant-like shouted voices of the marching troops.

"You had a good home when you left."

"YOU'RE RIGHT!"

"Jody was home when you left."

"YOU'RE RIGHT!"

"Sound off!"

"ONE, TWO!"

"Sound off!"

"THREE, FOUR!"

"Cadence count."

"ONE, TWO, THREE, FOUR, ONE-TWO THREE-FOUR!"

As the marching flight maneuvered a "Column Left" and was nearing the other flights, the guidon's voice sang out again: "I don't know, but I been told, Eskimo pussy's mighty cold, sound off."

"ONE, TWO!"

"Sound off!"

"THREE, FOUR!"

"Bring it on down."

"ONE, TWO, THREE, FOUR, ONE-TWO THREE-FOUR!"

The command "Flight halt" was given and sixty-five right heels stomped as one when the flight came to rest in perfect alignment between Flights A and C.

Outraged, the WAF First Sergeant went zipping over to the incoming flight's Field First Sergeant who was standing in front of the space left for his troops. She began giving him holy hell while all the young women of the WAF flight were grinning and giggling.

"Yeah, yeah, yeah, I know!" said the Flight B First Sergeant to the WAF. "I'm gonna go take care of it now!" he said as he went stomping over and stood nose to nose with the guidon.

"Just what the fuck do you think you're doin? Don't'cha know every limp dick out here, including the Base Commander and all that brass in the reviewing stand, could hear what you said? You guys are the best marchers on the whole damn base, but you're also the biggest bunch of dumb asses I've ever known. If you can't—"

"Give us liberty, or give us death!" a disguised voice shouted from the rear of the flight.

"Goddammit!" shouted the First Sergeant. Struggling to bring his temper and voice under control, he hurried to the area where he thought the voice came from.

"For Crissake, one hundred twelve fuckin' degrees, people dropping like flies and now a fuckin' comedian! Awright, who's the wise ass? Who said that?"

From the opposite end of the flight another disguised voice yelled out, "Patrick Henry—Sir!"

This infuriated the Field First Sergeant even more. As he was about to release another barrage, the Flight Commander walked up in back of him and whispered, "Okay, shirt, I'll take over now."

"Sir!" responded the sergeant as he took a position just in front of and to the left of the guidon. The Commander gave his troops "Parade Rest."

Steve Scott, Duel Watson, nicknamed Arkee, and Warren Boyd stood about midway of flight B and were positioned side by side due to their common six-foot height. Steve whispered to Arkee to tell Warren that they should meet at the Snack Bar Beer Garden after the parade for a cold pitcher of Lone Star beer.

All agreed.

Shortly, the order "Pass in review" was called out. The band began to play. Across the flight line the commands "Tench-hut" and "Forwarrrrd March!" were shouted from flight to flight. Thankfully, the parade celebrating the Luke Air Force Base Open House was underway.

In another forty-five minutes the parade was over, the speeches completed, and the troops were dismissed. Following the formal ceremony, the USAF Thunderbirds precision flying team thrilled and awed Steve Scott and all the spectators with their magnificent aerial display.

Gene Vincent was halfway through his recording of *Be-Bop A-Lu-La* when Steve set the tray with a pitcher of beer and three frosted schooners on the umbrella covered table at the beer garden. Arkee filled the glasses.

"Well, have you guys decided to volunteer for this overseas assignment to England, or are you just gonna let 'em ship your asses over anyways?" Warren chided the group. He had already volunteered and wanted his buddies to go too.

Steve and Arkee, who were roommates and the closer buddies of the trio, had been mulling over whether or not to volunteer for the overseas shipment that had just come down.

"Yeah, we're going" Arkee said.

The Fats Domino recording of *Blueberry Hill* was playing as the second round of glasses were filled.

"Yep, in fact, we signed the forms yesterday," said Steve. "We were hoping that maybe the three of us could get together at the Manhattan Beach Embarkation Port in New York for a night out on the town before shipping over. But it looks now like my training won't let that happen."

Steve had been accepted in the Airmen's Education and Commissioning Program, which meant he would shortly be leaving for his Officer Candidate School, OCS, training. He would transfer overseas as a Staff Sergeant. Later, when he completed the last semester of his college education, he would be commissioned a Second Lieutenant. Even with this he had been assured that he would be assigned either with or near his friends in the Third Air Postal Squadron, (Third APS) in the United Kingdom.

"Gonna take some adjustin' seeing you as a fuckin' second louie after all this time we've been Enlisted Swine together," Warren said.

"Won't be a problem Warren. Just always remember to bow, scrape, and praise each time you look at me once I'm commissioned. And remember, I'll be knowing what you're thinking each time you try to give me one of your sloppy-assed salutes," said Steve, trying to look serious.

With large smiles plastered on their faces, Warren and Arkee gave Steve a smack on the back, a mock salute, and said, "Yessir!"

"Can-do easy for you pal," Warren said and they all laughed and clinked their glasses together in a toast to one another and to Jolly Olde England.

They had become real buddies during their two-year assignment at Luke. Warren was the eldest and rascal of the trio. He'd met a lovely girl and fallen madly in love shortly after the three had arrived at the base near Phoenix. The two had planned an early wedding, but four months ago, shortly after picking her up on a date, Warren's car had been sideswiped. He had been knocked unconscious, but wound up with only a lump on his head. Tragically, his fiancée had been ejected from the car, run over, and killed. Warren was just now beginning to return to his former impish self.

Arkee was the most reserved, but had a terrific sense of humor. Prior to joining the Air Force everyone called him "Kee," which referred to his Cherokee Indian heritage, and that was the nickname he preferred. But once in uniform and being from Arkansas, his nickname had been changed to "Arkee." He didn't mind it that much. Arkee had never traveled prior to joining the USAF and was filled with excitement about the coming overseas assignment.

Steve, on the other hand, was anxious. Not only about the shipment to England where he would, just as soon as possible, have his fiancée LaRae join him to get married, but also getting the college degree he'd worked so hard for, his pending OCS, and furlough. So much to be done in such a short time.

It seemed to Steve Scott that his life had done nothing but speed up and continued to accelerate since he got on the Greyhound bus back home to leave for St. Louis and his induction into the Air Force. Exciting, adventuresome and fascinating times for him!

The trio downed several more pitchers, made all kinds of semi-drunken vows and promises, then staggered back to their WWII wooden barracks.

The future lay ahead and would affect them in ways they could never have possibly imagined.

Chapter 7

Reflections

Denham Studios, England, November 1956

M aster Sergeant Phillip Hargrave was the spit and image of the movie actor David Niven—albeit slightly heavier. These attributes included the pencil thin mustache and a slight British accent, which due to his English roots, could be exaggerated to perfection in seconds. Hargrave was nicknamed Pappy, but was called that only by a very private and select few. He was filling in as Acting First Sergeant of the Third APS. The prior First Sergeant had been accepted for Officer Candidate School and follow-on helicopter training and left before his tour was completed.

The Squadron Adjutant, Captain Earl Keene, had for two months served additional duty as Commander of the newly generated Detachment 23, ARFCOS. The incumbent scheduled to fill the ARFCOS position, a Captain Karl Miller had been delayed at Thule AFB, in the Arctic due to a personnel replacement problem there.

Staff Sergeant Steve Scott was also new. He was the Special Actions and Passport NCO. Buck Sergeant Warren Boyd was assigned as the Squadron Personnel Actions and Morning Report Clerk.

There had been numerous personnel changes. However, now with a New Year right around the corner, and the huge organizational build-up with new troops and replacements all but complete, most were hoping things would settle down to normal and into good, routine, and smooth running operations for both the Third APS and the new ARFCOS courier detachment.

It soon became apparent that those hopes were pipe dreams. Regrettably, assigning Sergeant Warren Boyd as the unit's Morning Report Clerk would be only one of many problems that lay ahead. And even though it appeared minor, that was a problem!

Unfortunately, Warren Boyd was probably the most hyper, excitable and nervous Personnel Specialist (and typist) in the history of the U.S. military since General Custer's Morning Report Clerk at the "Battle of the Little Bighorn" on June 25th, 1876. To make matters worse, the deadline for the submission of the report to the Base Commander's Office was 1200 hours daily. No excuses accepted!

Preparation of the Morning Report was a pressure packed and highly stressful job for anybody. Boyd was certainly no exception.

"Goddam Steve," Warren lamented in a near panic stricken voice, "that fuckin' report has gotta show everything going on in the unit—and not just ours, but the ARFCOS detachment too! Makes me nervous as a whore in church. No shit, my hands get wet with sweat just thinkin' 'bout the damn thing! Gotta give a complete and total accounting of all activities for Crissake!" Warren continued ranting as he paced the floor in small circles. "Everything from what poor bastard has come down with the syph or clap to overall troop strength, people on leave, those hospitalized, and everyone on Temporary Duty. Can't skip or leave out nothin! Know what the biggest problem is Steve?" Warren asked and then suddenly sat down on a corner of a desk and began to stare at the floor while absentmindedly biting a fingernail. He was obviously very deep in thought.

"What?" Steve asked.

Warren, with a puzzled expression looked at Steve and said, "What what?"

"You asked me what the biggest problem is and then you just quit talking."

"Oh, yeah. Well, the fuckin' thing has to be totally error free. No shit! Not one strikeover. No erasures. Not even so much as a comma or period can be out of place. And, get this, all the small letter x's have to fit exactly in those tiny little assed Yes/No boxes provided on the form. They can't even touch any of the black bordered squares. Now, ain't that a crock! I tell you Steve, that report is giving me nightmares. Know what? Any more I'm dreamin about the damn thing more'n I do Brigitte Bardot!" The report had to be totally flawless. Perfection—nothing less was acceptable.

Boyd soon learned his best efforts were obtained by typing the report on the small typist table that his knees would just barely fit under. And there, hunched over the typewriter, he would type each entry one at a time. A slow, painstakingly, calculated, peck at a time. Peck by nervous peck. Block by nervous block.

Whenever he made a mistake everyone in his office would know it by his stifled yell, muffled scream or loud curse. Sometimes he bellowed all three in unison when he made the mistake in the last line of the report.

Seemed like Shit, Hell and Damn! had become Boyd's favorite morning words.

This particular Monday morning Boyd had performed in spectacular fashion and completed the nerve wracking, lengthy Morning Report in record-breaking time. To reward himself, he joined Sergeant Hargrave and Steve for coffee in the cafeteria. The three of them were going through the short order line.

Standing before the chrome-fronted grill, Boyd was reading about the filming of *Moby Dick* starring Gregory Peck in the morning issue of *The Stars and Stripes*.

"How'd they make that big assed whale?" he asked no one in particular.

Warren's regular morning fare, without exception, was ham and eggs.

Martha, the cafeteria's short order cook and main waitress, had taken a liking to Boyd. Often she'd joke around with him, hoping to arouse his hormones. This morning, trying to get Boyd's nose out of the paper, Martha, in jest, said to Boyd before he could place his order, "We've just scratched something you fancy daily and like very much from the main menu."

Boyd, without looking up from the outstretched paper in his hands mumbled, "What?"

"I said we've just gone and scratched your favorite thing."

Boyd lowered the paper where he could just barely look over the top and directly into Martha's smiling face and said, "Well, then, go wash your hands and fix me some ham and eggs!"

"Oh, wot a cheeky blighter—you're a proper rotter—you are!" Martha scowled.

At their table Hargrave said, "I've had a call from the new First Sergeant. He's here unaccompanied. Arrived last Thursday, and he'll be reporting for work tomorrow."

"Where's he gonna be staying?" Steve asked.

"He has thirty days temporary lodging in Uxbridge. Seems to me he said he'd be at the Queen's Bell Inn."

"Do you know anything about him, Sarge?" Warren asked.

"Not a lot. He's something of a mystery to me personality wise. But I know he has some terrific credentials just based on the thumbnail sketch we've received from his 201 File. He's been around for awhile.

"His name is Gage, Master Sergeant Calvin Gage. Evidently he's strictly 'Brown Shoe,' from the old school, R.A. (Regular Army) type; goes pretty much by the book. Kinda think that he'll settle in and smooth out once he gets to know everyone and how the unit works. May be interesting for awhile, but I'll be glad to turn over the First Sergeant duties and just concentrate on MY job. He'll probably be all right."

Martha placed Boyd's ham and eggs plate on the table in front of him, lightly punched him on his shoulder and with a smile said, "Blimey, what a wretched person you are!"

Boyd looked up at Martha and with his curly edged, strawberry blond crew cut and captivating smile warmed Martha's heart with a quiet "Thank you, Luv!" He waited until she left then removed the upper partial plate that served as his four front teeth. He placed the false teeth in his shirt pocket and began to eat his breakfast.

Sergeant Hargrave continued. "Got another bit of news. Sergeant Danbury's new Admin Clerk will be reporting in before long, so you guys won't have to be doing all the Aerial Mail Terminal's (AMT's) typing anymore."

Master Sergeant Danbury was the Non-Commissioned Officer-In-Charge of the AMT where all the mail destined for delivery throughout England and Scotland was received, sorted, and hurriedly further routed on to the final delivery base.

"That's some great news," Boyd said. "Where's he coming from?"

"It isn't a he; it's a she, and she's coming here from Scott Field near St. Louis where she went to Admin School. She's originally from Scotland; only been in the Air Force from Scotland about a year. Think her home is Edinburgh, or near there, so she's not too far away to visit. It'll be good to have her. I hope Danbury will be able to keep her away from all those wolves downstairs. Believe everyone of those bugger's middle name in the AMT is horny!"

"Wonder what she looks like," mused Warren.

The following morning wasn't nearly as good as the previous day for Boyd. He'd already made four mistakes and was starting on his fifth attempt at the Morning Report.

The new First Sergeant had been waiting at the Orderly Room's outside door when Warren, the first worker, arrived.

When Boyd had said, "Good Morning, Sergeant," the new Top Shirt looked at him unsmilingly, nodded his head, then looked at his watch as if asking, "Where the hell have you been to keep me waiting here?"

"Who's got the key?" MSgt Gage snapped.

Boyd, thinking to himself, *Oh shit, Oh dear! We got a good one here*, said, "Right here, sir. Sorry to keep you waiting."

When Sgt Hargrave arrived, he escorted the new First Sergeant from office to office introducing him to everyone present in the Orderly Room.

"When will the Commander, Major Ekridge, arrive?" Gage asked.

"Believe he was gonna stop by to see the Base Commander about our new barracks first thing this morning. He also had to go to the Office of Special Investigations, our local OSI shop, about some stolen mail, but he should be showing up any minute now."

"Right. I'll wait for him here by the Bulletin Board."

"Suit yourself," said Hargrave. "I'll be in my office." Hargrave thought, *He's one of the sharpest NCOs I've ever encountered.*

Recalling the ribbons on Gage's Ike jacket, Hargrave walked over to the Armed Services Awards and Decorations chart on the wall and found his suspicions to be true. The new "Shirt" was sporting the Distinguished Service Cross, a Silver Star with one cluster, and the Purple Heart with two clusters!

Wow! I'll be damned, he said to himself. *We have us a real hero here. He must have a hell of a lot more decorations than those he's wearing by the looks of all the hash marks and hershey bars on his left sleeve. If I remember right, he was even wearing aerial gunner's wings above the ribbons.*

All of this, combined with his commanding presence, the sharp crease of his pants, and the way he wore his garrison hat squarely on his clean shaven head, made Hargrave think of a recruiting poster he had seen once. Phil suddenly had a deep foreboding that maybe the unit was in for some sort of a shake-up. Perhaps there would also be a profound change in duty performance as well as the loose living conditions with the arrival of this new "Top Shirt," at least in the enlisted men's department.

Well, we'll just have to wait and see, he thought. *Interesting.*

He didn't have long to wait.

Hargrave had just sat down at his desk. Everyone in the Orderly Room was quietly hard at work. Boyd, knees locked together under his little table and all bent over his typewriter, was nervously pecking one letter at a time, completing the last line of his report when the Commander, Major Ekridge, opened the outer door and stepped inside by the Bulletin Board.

The entire Orderly Room reverberated with the ear shattering shout of the new First Sergeant: "Orderly Room—tench hut!"

Boyd, already wound up tighter than a four hundred day clock, and scared to death that the next key typed would mean disaster, bolted straight up out of his chair. The table and his typewriter went flying helter-skelter across the room, the typewriter one way and the table another.

Hargrave said, "What the hell . . . ?"

The entire staff, startled, looked from one to another wondering what was going on. The Commander seemed to be in total shock. His eyes were opened wide in fright; his garrison hat was setting skewed crosswise on his head. He was very obviously quite unnerved by the shout that had left his ears ringing.

Major Ekridge looked at the new First Sergeant who was standing right beside him at ramrod attention and staring straight ahead.

The Commander coughed and said, "Um, we uh, we don't do that kind of thing around here, Sergeant."

The First Sergeant still standing rigidly at attention, solid as a rock, again, at the top of his lungs, yelled, "As you were!"

The Commander, wearing a dumfounded expression, was staring at Sergeant Gage when Sergeant Danbury flew up the stairs to the Orderly Room. Danbury had heard the yelling and the thud and thunk of Boyd's typewriter and typist table hitting the floor. Danbury flung the door open and ran smack into the still startled Commander standing just inside the door.

"Sorry," Danbury said, "I heard some shouting and banging and thought something was wrong. You all okay?"

"Yeah, we're fine Sergeant Dan, thanks for checking. Sergeant Gage, let's go to my office and talk," Major Ekridge said coolly.

In his office the Commander, obviously perturbed with his new First Sergeant, motioned for Sergeant Gage to have a seat. They both sat and for moments just stared at one another. The immediate dislike between the two of them was evident.

"This is an unusual unit and operation Sergeant. And I can see right off you are gonna have to make a lot of adjustments. What we have is anything but the typical Air Force or Army unit you may have been used to in the past. We provide a vitally important service to every U.S. military person in the United Kingdom including Scotland. We deliver as fast as humanly possible what, over here, is probably the most important thing in the world to our U.S. military members—their mail from Moms or Dads, their wives or husbands, fiancées or sweethearts, friends, whomever.

"Ours is a very important mission. The work is hard, dirty, and demanding. The hours are long. And while the rest of the Air Force and this base might close down at night, weekends, and holidays, we operate three hundred and sixty-five days a year.

"You won't see spit and polish in our squadron—not with me—not with our people. I don't expect it. I don't want it. Our troops are always in fatigues, except for here in the Orderly Room, and they're routinely lifting fifty pound bags hundreds of times a day.

"We receive mail from ocean liners, from intercontinental flights, foreign mail channels and classified information up to the Top Secret level from our ARFCOS armed couriers. Oftentimes we have to work around the clock. Spit and polish don't last three minutes in our work. If you're used to that, I'm telling you to forget it—now!" The Commander's face had reddened noticeably.

Gage, the first instant he saw him, observed that the Commander's uniform looked as though he had slept in it, and his shoes seemed to be thirsting for polish. He hadn't heard much of the Commander's diatribe.

"For all these reasons, I've relaxed the typical military routines around here," the Commander continued. "I don't want any inspections, especially room or clothing inspections, no formations of any kind. We're too busy and don't have time for that stuff. Our troops don't pull K.P. or any other details. No parades, base clean-up efforts, or other host base activities. I've found if I just leave 'em alone, our guys do us a damn good job. I expect you to follow the same procedure and then we'll all get along just fine."

Gage stared at the Commander.

"I'm kinda busy just now. If you have anything you want to talk about, look me up a little bit later on. So, for the moment, welcome aboard. Get yourself settled in. If you have any problems, see Phil Hargrave. I'm sure you're gonna enjoy England.

"Oh, and, by the way, don't go 'round yelling 'tench-hut' anymore. You scared the cowboy shit outta the entire squadron, me included."

The Commander didn't offer a handshake, or smile, or even bother to look up again at Sergeant Gage. Instead, he picked up a paper from his in-basket and appeared to be totally involved with that, summarily and rudely dismissing his new First Sergeant.

Master Sergeant Calvin Gage sat looking intently at the Major for a long moment, his jaw muscles twitching and his eyes glaring. He then rose from his seat so fast you would have thought he'd just sat on a bed of red hot charcoals.

He crossed the room and slammed shut the partially opened door of the adjacent office which the Adjutant, Captain Earl Keene, used.

He walked back, stopped, and stood in front of the Commander's desk just as close as he could get without bending over. Gage locked eyes with Major Ekridge, who had suddenly disengaged himself from the paper he had been reading.

With obvious restraint, Gage spoke slowly and forcefully, emphasizing each salient point.

"Major, I am a pro-fessional soldier. I have been in this man's Army most all my life. I have engaged the enemies of my country in aerial combat in the skies and on the ground, in hand-to-hand combat, where one or the other of us would most certainly die," Gage continued.

"I have survived two wars and have been a First Sergeant longer than you've held a commission. I know the rules and regulations of the United States Air Force inside and out, backwards and forwards. And, Sir, whether you like it or not, I've been assigned the duty of First Sergeant of the Third Air Postal Squadron, and not as your personal prat boy. I intend to fulfill those duties in keeping with that office the way I was trained and the way I know those duties are to be, should be and will be satisfied.

"I learned long ago to do my homework. I knew a great deal about you personally, and your undisciplined unit, long before I got here. If what I have witnessed in the few short hours since my arrival is representative of the proper management of Air Force resources, then I must be in Laurel and Hardy's Foreign fuckin' Legion!

"And, Major, had you done your homework, you would have received me in an entirely different fashion. I know, for example, that you spend more time in the air under the guise of 'maintaining flying proficiency,' albeit authorized by regulation, than you do in your primary assignment, which is Commander and manager of this outfit.

"Major, let's you and I get things straight right off the bat. You fly the goddam airplanes to get your flying time in so you can collect your green flight pay and whore around with your Rest Over Nights in your favorite sin cities. Go do it! And I'll run this goddam outfit like it should be run—by the fucking book!

"One other thing. That poor excuse for a First Sergeant who you endorsed outta here for Officer's Candidate School should instead have been Article 15'd for dereliction of duty and sent back to basic training. Now, Commander, now that we're through talking, I'll be in my office should you like to discuss any of this further.

"Thanks for your generous, warm hearted welcome, but I strongly suspect that once I've done my job as I see it needing to be done, I won't be around here long enough to enjoy myself all that much. Been a real pleasure meeting you."

With that he snapped a smart salute, said "By your leave, Sir," and without waiting for a return salute, smartly turned on his heel and walked out of the Commander's office. He deliberately left the door open behind him.

Captain Earl Keene, the Squadron Adjutant arrived late that morning. As soon as he entered his office adjoining Ekridge's, the door between them had slammed shut. Curious, he listened intently to the conversation with his ear pinned to the door. After he heard Gage leave, he entered Ekridge's office, closed the door and sat down. Major Ekridge was just sitting there looking straight ahead with a vacant, trance-like expression on his face. His eyes looked twice as large as normal.

"Well Dave, that seems to have went over 'bout as well as a turd in the punch bowl. I've been trying to call you since 10:00 last night. I heard about this guy from the I.G's Exec at the South Ruislip O club last evening. Master Sergeant, First Sergeant Calvin Gage seems to be a legend. He's described as an enlisted Steve Canyon. Not sure how we were lucky enough to get him here or why. But he is dynamite!"

Captain Keene waited for a reply. When none was offered he continued with his scuttlebutt.

"They say his assignments are tightly controlled out of the Pentagon through Senior NCO Assignments at Randolph Field in Texas. He's known for straightening out units, then moving quickly on. That's why I can't figure why he's come here. Hell, we're not in bad shape; in fact, we're in pretty damn good shape. Anyways, let me tell you what I heard about him. You ain't gonna believe this."

Again Keene waited. No response.

"During WWII he was a young aerial waist gunner in a B-17G Flying Fortress outfit flying with the 8th Air Force. On a mission over occupied France, his aircraft was shot up pretty bad. The Aircraft Commander (AC) lost control, but managed to crash-land in enemy territory and was knocked unconscious.

"The navigator and co-pilot were also pretty well banged up and semi-conscious. The rest of the crew, 'cept Gage, were all dazed. Wounded and bleeding like a stuck pig, Gage pulled and led all the others out. They knew the Jerries would soon be on their asses, so they got clear of the aircraft and scrambled into some nearby woods.

"Gage then realized that the Norden Bombsight which was still fairly new and highly classified, and the recently developed classified electronic jamming gear, were still intact inside the aircraft. He ran back and climbed into the smoldering plane that was in danger of exploding any minute and destroyed the equipment with a fireaxe.

"He was just a second from tossing the emergency thermite grenade when, by luck, he happened to see the pilot was still belted in his seat and had been overlooked by everyone.

"Trying to get the unconscious pilot unstrapped and out of his seat, he looked out the cockpit window and saw a platoon of Jerries bearing down on the road from the port side of the aircraft.

"Although wounded and groggy, Gage hurried to the 50 caliber machine gun in the window of the side gunner's post facing the Jerries and single-handedly wiped out all but two of the platoon.

"He was wounded again by flying shrapnel from return fire and knocked unconscious temporarily. He came to minutes later to see one of the Germans with a combat dagger in his hand poised to cut the throat of the AC who was now drifting in and out of consciousness.

"Gage grabbed the outstretched arm holding the dagger and snapped it down across his knee, breaking the German's arm. He picked up the knife and slashed the soldier's jugular vein. Gage grabbed the AC's 45 pistol out of his holster and put three rounds in another German who was just coming in through the open belly turret. To make the rest of this long story short, Gage passed out next to the AC."

The CO's silence was beginning to unnerve Keene.

"As fate would have it, a unit of the Free French underground, searching for the downed aircraft, came upon the plane in the approaching darkness and took everyone to a safe house. Through the resistance pipeline, they managed eventually to get the crew back safely to England. Gage was awarded the Distinguished Service Cross for that performance.

Keene rattled on. "He also became a hero in Korea. Got his ass shot up again a couple of times over there and received two Silver Stars in the process. Those for Gallantry in Action. He was offered a direct commission but nixed it. He also refused follow-on invitations to go to OCS—said he was too old to begin playing officer with a bunch of snot-nosed college boys.

"But, here's the kicker with all this, Dave. That young pilot, back then a Captain, the one Gage saved in France—he's now no other than Lieutenant General R. Peter (Moose) Berg—the Inspector General for the whole fuckin' Air Force!"

Keene caught his breath and waited for some sign of life from the CO. When none was forthcoming, he added one more tidbit.

"We may have a problem here Dave. The Third Air Force I.G. Exec, the guy I was talking to last night, said General Berg and Gage are locked tighter'n a ruptured duck's nuts. So, whadayathink?"

Ekridge, by now staring blankly at his fingers drumming nervously on the edge of his desk, sighed heavily. "Earl, believe you're right, I think we do have a problem!"

Upon leaving the Commander's Office, Sergeant Gage walked to his desk, passed Boyd using Steve's typewriter, and said, "Hurry up with that Morning Report! I want to look it over good before it goes out. I'll go with you when you take it to the Base Commander's office."

Warren Boyd's stomach, already in knots, lurched, and he felt like he was about to shit some clinkers.

Gage dialed Phil on the intercom line and asked if he would be interested in walking to the cafeteria for a cup of coffee.

Hargrave said, "Sure, just stop by whenever you're ready." *Well,* thought Hargrave, *our rather banal and tranquil operation here might be in for a bit of a titillating turn of events. Well, again, we'll just have to wait and see.* And, again, he didn't have long to wait.

Chapter 8

Nightwatch Sends Regards

Gage and Pappy had entered the long hallway enroute to the cafeteria and hadn't gone more than twenty yards or so when a group of four Airmen walked past them going the opposite direction. One of the Airmen had his fatigue shirt half in and half out of his pants and was walking with an exaggerated limp/shuffle nearly dragging the toe of his right foot. Gage heard him say, "And then I tell this muffucker, 'Man you don't know what good muffuckin' leg is 'till you set it up here like this an'—" with his hands around his imaginary female, the airman was humping his hips like crazy while the others laughed loudly.

Angrily, Sergeant Gage grabbed him and spun him around. "Airman, just where in the hell do you think you are?"

"Say what?" The Airman looked at Gage with a frown on his face. He yanked Gage's hand off his shoulder. "What's that, let go me man, you crazy or somethin'?"

Gage shoved his face nose to nose with the Airman and hissed through clenched teeth, "I want to see you snap shit right now—hit it!"

The Airman's eyes went wide; he looked at Gage dumfounded, taking in, for the first time, all the stripes on his arms, the hash marks on Gage's sleeves, and row upon row of ribbons on his chest.

Gage, still nose to nose, yelled, "Goddammit, I told you to get to attention soldier and you damned well better do it and right now!"

The Airman's body sprang backwards like a bow as he snapped to attention. Gage glanced menacingly at the remaining three other Airmen. They, too, with the whites of their eyes now showing, bolted to rigid attention. The First Sergeant stepped back and with a scowl took them all in.

"Just where in the hell do you think you are? Your uniforms are a disgrace. Your footwear is as filthy as the language coming out of your mouth and none of you is showing the slightest regard as to who may be within earshot." Drawing nearer he said quietly for their benefit only, "I heard the word motherfucker, which should not be in any civilized language, spoken by you five times openly and loudly in this common walkway."

The Airmen said nothing. Gage continued.

"All right, I don't know any of you, but you can bet your young asses I'm going to. Gimme your I.D. cards and Class A passes, one at a time, while you step here in front of me and report your name and unit. Do it now—move it!"

When the person with the exaggerated walk reported to him, Gage asked, "Something wrong with your leg Airman?"

"No, Sir," replied the Airman.

"Then why you walking like you got a cob up your ass and a twenty-five pound weighted right toe?"

"I dunno, I was just doing that."

"If I see you doing it again, we'll first go to the Dispensary and get your leg checked out. If it's okay, and I think it will be, you'll then go to the chow hall for a month's solid K.P. You got that?"

"Yessir."

"And," Gage went on, "if I ever hear any of you using filthy language like that, see you acting like an animal having sex in public, and wearing a uniform unfit for a dumpster, you'll regret the day your daddy ever looked at your momma with a gleam in his eye. Do you understand me?"

"Yessir!" the four shouted in unison.

"Now, all of you, straighten your uniforms! Go directly from here to your unit First Sergeant and report to him. I'll be calling him. Understood?"

"Yessir!" the four responded.

Gage and Pappy continued on toward the cafeteria. By the time they got there, Gage had a handful of Class A passes and several names and units written on his little pocket note pad.

Martha saw them enter and was at Pappy's favorite table waiting for him and saying, "All right then Ducks, what'll it be for you this mornin'?"

Pappy said, "I'll have a cuppa me usual please Martha, strong as sin, black as hate, and hot as love."

Martha lightly slapped Gage on the shoulder and said, "Gawd, I love it when 'e talks like that. No one else orders coffee the way your mate 'ere does. And wot'll it be for you, luv?"

Gage said, "I'll have the same as him, thanks."

Their orders in hand, Martha left.

Gage looked discretely around the room then scooted his chair back. Pretending to tie his shoe, he looked under the table, straightened himself, and said quietly to Pappy, "Nightwatch sends regards."

Pappy's eyes narrowed. In little more than a whisper he asked, "What's going on?"

"We have a new assignment, Phil. Actually it's an additional assignment. Your Company credentials, GS-14 grade and clearance tickets have been certified through DoD to Third Air Force and other U.S., U.K., and European agencies for the purpose and duration of this assignment. You'll be briefed on this further next week. For the moment, and until we can talk more privately, I've been asked to tell you only that you need to be aware that you're back in-status, to take usual precautions, and decide which weapon or weapons you want to carry. All other duties are to be carried on in the normal manner. This comes directly from Nightwatch who sends personal best wishes and numbers three, twelve and twenty-one in confirmation, okay?"

Pappy mentally added his number thirteen to the numbers just given him. They reached the total forty-nine, which substantiated that the message was in fact from Dulles, head of the CIA himself—Sergeant Hargrave's friend and boss back in Virginia.

"Okay," said Pappy. "Are you Company?"

"No, I work directly for General Berg. I'm sort of on loan for this one. I've had a couple of short assignments more like details with the Company, but nothing ever like this though. It's gonna be interesting."

Pappy said, "I'm sure it will be. They always are."

Chapter 9

Near the Firth of Forth

Captain Karl Miller had been to the submarine base in Scotland on four prior occasions, each one on an ARFCOS classified courier run. On this occasion he had traveled via rail on the overnight trip. For runs within England he and his couriers used USAF automobiles or small pickups, and for all travel outside England and Scotland they flew on commercial airlines. As a rated officer Miller, logging mandatory flying time, would sometimes carry ARFCOS materials aboard the military aircraft he flew, but that was infrequent. This was a good trip for Miller; he liked Scotland. It reminded him of Salzdorf, home, and Germany.

On prior visits after delivering the classified materials to his U.S. Navy counterparts, he spent some additional time in Edinburgh. Those stops gave him the opportunity to further scope out the art dealer he had decided to work with in the sale and transfer of more of the stolen art treasures he had brought with him from the Salzdorf salt mine repository.

He had met with his new Edinburgh dealer once at his art shop and another time at the store owner's residence. He wanted to know where the art dealer lived in case it would ever be necessary to drop something off late at night. This was a typical procedure Miller had established with most of his drop-off points.

Karl changed to the civilian clothing he'd purchased in London to make his dress look strictly European rather than American. He had also applied his artificial mustache and the large fake mole. He was extremely conscious of his German accent. He tried hard to disguise it and spoke in only guarded and very limited conversation.

"It must be perfectly clear," Miller had told all his art dealers during their first contact, "that any of our transactions must be considered strictly on a one-on-one basis. Absolutely no fanfare or discussions between anyone but myself, you, and the individual who will make the actual purchase.

"With this understanding," Karl assured the art dealer, "you'll find the object, whether it be a painting, sculpture, rare coins or whatever, to be worth a figure nearly double the amount for which I shall sell it to you. Always, in these dealings, you will make a handsome profit." Karl continued, "The article will not appear on any kind of a current police stolen object or Hot List warrants. However, it must never be viewed by anyone but the person to whom it is being sold." While Karl asked and immediately received tremendous prices for the works, his profit was considered miniscule when compared to the actual value, and worth of the pieces, which could only be described as priceless.

With those assurances Captain Miller had, earlier in the day, shown a rare and beautiful porcelain figurine and small sculpture to the storeowner.

"The historical card accompanying the items detail their history and authenticity," Karl had explained. "Each item, by itself, is worth a small fortune. However, as agreed, I will sell you both items for only a nominal fee, in this case thirty thousand pounds sterling."

The art dealer anxiously agreed to the transaction, but Karl thought, *He acts strange. I'm sure he's a homosexual, but apart from his effeminate walk, talk and gestures, he seems, all of a sudden, to be shifty and evasive. I don't trust him—better check things out a bit more.*

For these reasons Karl made arrangements to meet with the storeowner at the dealer's residence at eight that evening to finalize their transaction and deal.

In the early evening's darkness while the art dealer was just closing his shop, Karl, wearing rubber gloves and expertly using his burglar's lock kit, entered the front door of the dealer's remote home site which was located near the Firth of Forth. He was greeted as soon as the door swung inward by the bachelor owner's pet Scotty dog "Teddy," whom he had played with during his last visit. Teddy hesitated, barked, and growled at Miller initially, but shortly came forward to have his head patted while his tail wagged in a friendly greeting.

Karl picked up the pet, quickly snapped and broke its neck, opened the back door and tossed it out into the bushes beside the house. He then made himself comfortable on a chair in the hall larder off from the parlor. He kept the door just barely ajar. He didn't have long to wait until the art dealer arrived.

The storeowner unlocked the front door and was surprised not to have Teddy there jumping all over him as usual, wanting to be loved, petted, and to go outside. He called the dog's name several times while hanging up his coat and hat on the clothes rack. With a frown, he started toward the kitchen, calling "Teddy" when the phone rang. He stopped in the hallway, picked up the receiver and said, "Yes?"

The call was from the distributor he phoned after Karl had shown him the porcelain and sculpture earlier in the day.

"Hello McCloud. Has he arrived yet? Are they authentic?" the voice on the other end queried.

"No, he's not here yet, but I expect him any minute. We can't talk long. This makes me nervous. The man I'm dealing with frightens me, and yes, the items are as I told you. They are definitely not fakes. They are positively originals, worth several fortunes. At least one hundred twenty thousand pounds."

"The sculpture is a Rodin. Can you believe that?"

"A Rodin. My God! Are you certain mon?"

"Aye, I'm convinced of that! It 'tis a Rodin and that's a fact! I could scarcely believe it meself as I held it in me hand—a Rodin and he's selling it for a pittance. I'm positive it was stolen by the Nazis when they stormed Paris, and just as certain this chap hasn't the foggiest notion of its true value. Dumb silly thing. He's giving away a bloody fortune!"

"And you'll be placing no restrictions on me as to where it goes, except that it must leave Scotland and England?"

"No, I'm not interested in to whom you sell it. Just make certain that you bring me the cash we discussed earlier when you come by later. Call first, 'round 'bout nine-ish. He should have been and gone by then. Now, I've got to go. He's due any minute, and I've yet to set up me recorder. This time I'll tape our conversation and also make certain I get something with his fingerprints on it. I know someone who can find out who we're dealing with here. Then, perhaps, we can sit in the driver's seat with this business! I anticipate the sky's the only limit. Anyway, I'm busy just now and I've got to find me dog. Ring me back later on then."

The art dealer set the phone down, turned around, and stared into the glaring eyes and demonic grin of Karl Miller.

"Ghastly!" the Chief Inspector exclaimed as he looked at the body slumped over in the dining room chair. It was manacled by odd-looking handcuffs binding his hands behind him. The inspector had been called shortly before midnight. The art dealer's house was swarming with policemen, detectives, the coroner, crime photographer, and others.

"I've seen lots of horrible crimes, but this one takes the bloody prize," the inspector said. "Are you through, doctor, and do you have any preliminary findings?"

"Yes, I'm all but done. However, this, of course, is just a guess until I perform the autopsy." Lifting the dead man's head, its eyes still open and its facial features frozen in horror, the coroner pointed to the tissue stuffed into the corpse's nostrils.

"Nasty business this one, Chief Inspector. These are pieces of wet tissue that would make it impossible for the poor bastard to breathe through his nose. His tongue was cut out and stuffed down his throat. His genitals were severed and also stuck into his mouth. I'm confident he choked to death on his own blood, but I'll have to let you know that for certain later on, after I've performed the autopsy. Should have it for you by early this afternoon."

With the coroner still holding the dead man's head back, the inspector pointed to the corpse's chest. "What in God's name is this?"

"It's difficult to say absolutely due to all the blood, but it looks as though the words *'Lügner* and *Warmebruder'* were carved into his chest, then strips of skin about two inches in diameter forming a border around the two words were cut and stripped from his body. I would hazard a guess the poor bugger was still alive at that point, and then made to suffer the agonies of hell as his penis was excised and stuffed into his mouth. I've guessed his death to have occurred between seven and eight p.m."

"The letters would appear to be German?" questioned the Inspector.

"Yes, you're quite right about that. One of your policemen chaps knows German and roughly translated the words to mean 'Lying homosexual,' but again, it's difficult to say what with all the blood. We'll know better later on. Another guess, Chief Inspector."

"Yes?"

"The killer is, of course, a fiend. I do believe that's a given. And I would guess that he very much enjoys seeing his victims suffer, actually causing the pain and relishing its effect. He is most likely driven by that, or thrives upon it. I strongly suspect sir, that this is indeed the work of an insane person. A madman, or someone very near that."

"Well, his day will come," the Chief Inspector said, feigning a certainty which he didn't feel.

Chapter 10

Hug, Mug, or Slug?

S cott, a little over a month before, had moved in with MSgt Pappy Hargrave, as a temporary room assignment. Billeting was tight. Hargrave's was the only two-man NCO room available. A new barracks for the Third APS influx of troops was being negotiated with the base commander. Also, a new policy allowing single NCO's to reside off-base and draw separate rations was, on a trial basis, just being implemented.

Even though MSgt Hargrave wasn't all that thrilled with having a roommate, Scott kept to himself. He was studious and spoke only when spoken to. Hardly knew he was there.

Noticing Steve gingerly touching the recently healed wound above his eyebrow, Hargrave asked, "So, how'd you get the knock?"

"I've told most everyone that I was in an accident, but I got this in a fight back home on leave."

"Wanna talk about it?" Hargrave asked as he lit a cigarette and stretched out on his bunk. He reached over to his large console Telefunken player and turned down his favorite Joni James' recording of *Have You Heard*.

"Yeah, guess so," Steve said reluctantly. "The Commander'll probably be getting a letter about it from the sheriff back home any day now. Kinda surprised he hasn't already received it." Steve had been worrying about the problem.

In addition to his normal job, he'd carried the heavy academic burden of nine quarter hours constantly. Worked damn hard, six and seven days a week and nights too. OCS training recently completed, his pending commission and, most importantly of all, bringing LaRae over to England to marry him—all of this was now in jeopardy.

Stubbing the cigarette out in the ashtray resting on his chest, Hargrave got up, set the ashtray on the Hi-Fi, and freshened his Cutty Sark on the rocks. He offered Steve a drink, which was politely refused. Glass in hand, Hargrave lay back down on his side and looked at Steve inquiringly.

Steve, sitting on his bed, looked across the room at Sergeant Hargrave. He was deep in thought, remembering, and began . . . . .

He'd gotten off the Greyhound Bus at the Ancell, Missouri, and Highway 61 junction. It had been a long ride from Phoenix, Arizona. With all the stops, crying and screaming children, and everyone that sat next to him wanting to talk about everything from WWII, probably because he was traveling in his Class A uniform, to Johnny Cash's latest song *I Walk the Line,* Steve had gotten little rest. When the bus stopped, he pulled his duffel bag from the luggage compartment, hoisted it up on his right shoulder, and started toward his grandmother's house about a mile distant.

It was warm for October. By the time he reached Arnold's Granary near the railroad tracks, Steve was ready for a rest. He dropped the heavy bag from his shoulder and sat on it. He heard the train whistle long before the Cotton Belt diesel engine and long line of freight cars came into view, slowly passing in back of the Granary.

When he'd been in school, Steve used to hop the freights. He'd hang onto the car's ladders and ride the two miles from Ancell to Illmo where the train always stopped to change crews or for the engine to be turned around at the roundhouse. Often Steve walked the rails, stooping frequently to pick up stones from the track bed. With a developed, unerring accuracy, he would throw and hit telephone poles, tin cans, and other various targets as he walked or jogged along the iron rails.

The only movie theater in the area was in Illmo. Steve and LaRae used to go there Saturday nights. They would hold hands and every now and then scoot down in their seats so no one could see them sneak a kiss.

Except for coming home to LaRae, he wasn't looking forward to his furlough. Ancell held very few pleasant memories for Steve. His childhood, after his mother and father's divorce when he was three, had not been a happy one. His mother was twenty-one when divorced and at that young age, after having married too early at sixteen, evidently felt that life was passing her by. Employment and romance opportunities were both scarce in Ancell. Steve's mother moved away. The day she left a stranger had pulled up in front of his grandmother's house where they lived. His mother's luggage was soon loaded in the trunk, and she took Steve in her arms to say a hurried goodbye.

"Little Rock isn't that far away, and I'll come home and be with you as often as I can," she said unconvincingly. "You'll have lots of fun with your cousins, you'll see, everything'll be just fine. I love you. 'Bye honey."

Steve watched until the car was swallowed up by dust from the gravel road. He sat down, leaning his back against the porch column and stared off into the woods in front of the house. Quiet tears ran down his cheeks.

Steve became the sometimes ward of his uncle, who was an engineer on the railroad and frequently gone. At other times he stayed with his grandmother, but she was the cook on a Mississippi riverboat and would be away for six weeks at a time. He was alone a lot.

The years passed and Steve grew. His aunt would remark from time to time that he had matured much earlier than his peers and noted too that he was remarkably "broad at the shoulder and narrow at the hip." He had blond hair and intense blue eyes. Steve's handsome features coupled with his honest and caring demeanor immediately attracted others to him. His mature directness accompanied by a compelling boyish humility set him apart from others.

His childhood was pretty much patterned after Mark Twain's Huck Finn in that his guardians had their own families and responsibilities, which took precedence.

Although very limited, Steve was guided, periodically, by his uncle and grandmother. He admired and respected both of them tremendously. Under their tutelage, Steve grew to be well mannered, quiet, and unassuming. He was courteous and respectful to his elders, and he was also a good worker. He always had at least two jobs going at the same time and his work at the local sawmill from his early teens through high school gave him a terrific lean, but muscular build. Years of working with the hard oak and hickory logs in constructing wooden pallets gave him amazing strength. Girls were not real big on his interest list even at age fifteen. That changed, however, on the day that he was at the home of his best friend, Duncan, nicknamed Dunc.

It was Dunc's birthday and he'd invited a few guys over. "You gonna be doin' anything later on?" Dunc asked Steve after his other friends had left.

"Nope," replied Steve, "I don't have anything going on."

"Then how 'bout going with me over to Billie Jo's, after while?" Billie Jo was Dunc's girlfriend. Her closest friend, LaRae Prentiss, was staying overnight with Billie, and it was on this occasion that Steve first met LaRae.

LaRae was fourteen when she and Steve became friends. She stole his heart the very first instant he saw her. She had beautiful dark brown eyes that looked right to his very soul and never wavered. Cute freckles lightly peppered a gorgeous nose and her high cheeks. She had full lips that Steve hungered to kiss the moment he saw them, and they always presented him

71

with a beautiful smile. They could sometimes be pouty, too, in a sexy kind of way. She had dark silky hair that reached to her waist. It had a wave in the front that partly covered her forehead and sometimes shadowed her left eye. At other times she wore her hair in a French braid which was also very striking.

LaRae had this way of tilting her head just a tiny bit to the left when she stared at Steve, seemingly hanging on every word he spoke, for LaRae was as taken with Steve as he was with her.

Miss Prentiss had developed early with a beautiful body and, already at fourteen, her breasts were firm and full. With her wasp waist and attractive derrière, she always turned boys' heads whenever she walked by. LaRae was in the school band and was also a cheerleader. Every Sunday she played the piano in the 10:00 a.m. service at her family's Baptist church. LaRae's beauty and talents were matched in kind by her wonderful sincerity and personality. To Steve, LaRae was everything perfect.

This afternoon she was wearing form fitting Levis and a blue oxford shirt with a button down collar. She was fantastically beautiful and radiant and Steve was hopelessly in love.

The day's late shadows became early evening and darkness. The fireflies were in abundance and the cicadas up high in the whitewashed trees had begun their nightly cacophony of song. Billie Jo and Dunc were holding hands, sitting in the front porch swing, swaying gently. Steve and La Rae were sitting on the top porch step when Dunc suggested they play the game Hug, Mug or Slug.

"Never played that. In fact, I've never even heard of it," Steve said.

"Well it's easy enough to play," Dunc responded. "You'll catch on fast, and I'll betcha you'll like it."

Billie Jo and LaRae both laughed, disappeared briefly into the house and returned with an empty Royal Crown Cola bottle.

The four of them relocated down to the lawn and the shadows of the side of the house.

Dunc said, "Okay, LaRae, you can go first." LaRae spun the bottle and it stopped, pointing at Billie Jo.

"Well, that spin needs a little help," Dunc said as he pointed the bottle at Steve.

LaRae walked up to Steve and said, "What'll it be, Hug, Mug or Slug?"

Steve said, "I don't know."

"Yeah you do," Dunc said. "Tell her, Mug."

Steve said, "Mug," and with no hesitation whatsoever, LaRae placed her gentle hands on either side of his face and kissed him full on the lips, long and hard.

Surprised, Steve awkwardly put his arms around LaRae and kissed her back. That was Steve's first real kiss. He felt like his heart was racing at least three hundred miles an hour in a ten mile per hour zone.

There were a lot of Mugs after the first spin of the bottle. Later, lying in his bed, his heart still raced when he thought of LaRae. Steve had a hard time getting to sleep that night and when he finally did, he dreamed of her.

Steve graduated at eighteen and immediately after enlisted in the U.S. Air Force. The next summer LaRae and her family drove out to Phoenix, Arizona, and picked up Steve at Luke Air Force Base where he'd been sent after basic training in Texas. They all visited the Grand Canyon, and it was at this time that Steve gave LaRae a Promise ring.

Young romances often waned, particularly when the lovers were separated by distance for a long time, but not theirs. LaRae and Steve remained true to one another. Dunc helped by being such a close friend to them. They wrote to each other almost daily.

Steve called LaRae every weekend. The only single problem they had was with Ernie Thompson. Ernie Thompson was into his second year of college and had done very well on his football scholarship. Ernie was strong as an ox, formidable in all sports, and a bully, first class. He had a couple of football pals, but for the most part, the majority of his school-mates avoided Ernie and his friends.

Ernie, along with his two constant thug companions, crashed the local high school prom. He immediately zeroed in on LaRae who stood out easily as the most beautiful girl. LaRae was, as usual, accompanied by Dunc now that Billie Jo and her family had moved to Ohio. She and Steve decided that neither she nor Dunc should miss out on their prom and Steve trusted Dunc completely.

Ernie had watched LaRae and Dunc dance. He was captivated by the way LaRae moved her body as they danced the Stroll to Fats Domino's recording of *I Want to Walk You Home*. To Ernie, her every move broadcast her sexuality.

Ernie elbowed his way to LaRae and asked for the next dance.

"Her dance card is already filled Ernie," Dunc said after LaRae had politely tried to tell Ernie she didn't care to dance. That didn't matter to Ernie. As the next song began, he reached down and grabbed LaRae by her elbow and pulled her to her feet.

73

"Hey, she told you she didn't want to dance," Dunc said, rising from his chair.

LaRae, not wanting to cause any more of a scene than the one already created, said, "It's okay Dunc, I'll dance with him," as Ernie was already pulling LaRae toward the floor.

The instant they were on the dance floor, Ernie held LaRae's body close to him and, with no regard for the tempo or beat of the music, gyrated his pelvis into hers. He immediately sprang an erection. When he placed his hand on her lower back with his outstretched fingers on her buttocks and pressed her in closer to him, LaRae jerked her body backward.

"You pig!" she shouted in his face and walked past the table, telling Dunc, "we're leaving now!"

LaRae said nothing more of the incident to Dunc on the way home or to Steve when she wrote him her nightly letter.

Ernie, however, marked the occasion later to go into minute detail on how he'd had sex with Little Miss Hot Pants LaRae Prentiss. While most doubted his boasts, many also envied the conquest.

Monday at school LaRae told Dunc, "I wish we hadn't gone to the prom. Ernie Thompson has been telling all kinds of lies about me and all I did was dance with him for just a few seconds. God, how I wish I hadn't gone! Whenever I hear the lies I try to stop them."

"LaRae, don't let that bother you," Dunc said, trying to console her. "The people who really know you know you're not that kind of girl."

"I'm afraid Steve will hear all this when he comes home."

Steve, of course, did learn about Ernie's lies and decided he would deal with that problem during his leave.

Coming out of his reverie, Steve looked up to see the train's caboose well off in the distance. The red light was rotating in the lantern on the back platform, and he could barely hear the clickity-clack of the freight's wheels turning. He stood, picked up his duffel bag, put it back on his right shoulder and crossed the tracks, walking the last half-mile or so toward his grandmother's house.

LaRae was on Cloud 9. She was so thrilled and excited to have Steve back home, and Steve wanted to spend every minute of the day with her.

"Grandma Bertha has made a list of things she wants me to do for her," Steve was telling LaRae. "It's not that much, and it'll keep me busy some of the time while I'm waiting for you to get off work. But boy, how I hate being home and not being able to be with you all the time."

"I know. I feel the same way. And it's hard for me to concentrate at work cause I'm always thinking about you, missing you, and wanting to be with you. Time goes so slow!"

Still concerned about the Ernie Thompson lies, LaRae was worried about Steve's quiet reaction. "Promise me that you'll stay away from that lout Ernie Thompson. Everyone knows he's a liar. Please don't let him ruin any part of the short time we have together on your leave. Promise me Hon, okay?"

Steve avoided a response.

With his work completed at his grandmother's, Steve worked on some chores at the Prentiss home. He spent every minute he could with LaRae. They went to the skating rink, the movies in Illmo and Cape Girardeau, and picnicked at Big Springs in Van Buren. They frequently took night drives out to Commerce and parked by the river. When passing tugs and barges rounded the bend and swung inland to avoid the sandbar, Steve would flash the car's headlights on and off. Momentarily the huge, brilliant spotlight from the boat would engulf their car. The boat's eerie foghorn would give a short blast for "Hello."

They were deeply in love, completely and totally infatuated with one another. This was in the way that only a young and all-consuming first love can be.

Sitting in the car, parked by the Mississippi's edge, LaRae said to Steve, "You know what? I really believe that God has made this special place in time just for us." The Platter's recording of *My Prayer* had become their love song and was playing on the radio. The lyrics said everything that was in their hearts. LaRae put her arms around Steve and looked lovingly into his eyes.

"I just know that no two people on earth have ever shared a love like ours. I really believe that. I say a prayer of thanksgiving every night for you and for us having found one another. You are my life and, God, how I love you!"

Steve's leave flew by when he was with LaRae. On this particular Friday night as his leave time was winding down, LaRae had to work late at the bank.

"I'll just hang around with Dunc till you get off work," Steve had told LaRae, "and after if you want, and you're not too tired, the two of us can go to the Blue Hole Bar-B-Que in Cape for a snack. Then maybe we can drive up to the Cape Rock Drive lookout point for a while."

"Sounds great to me and I can tell you right now that I won't be too tired," LaRae responded with a smile.

Passing the time waiting for LaRae, Steve and Dunc sat in Dunc's Studebaker with two other friends. They were having a Coke at the Saveway Restaurant. Steve, responding to a question from one of his friends in the back seat, said, "Yeah, I've heard about Ernie Thompson's lies. Guess he gets some kinda kick outta starting rumors and hurting people's reputations. Made me so mad I coulda bit a spike in two."

Just then, as if on cue, Ernie and his two cohorts pulled up beside them in Ernie's '49 Plymouth. Ernie got out and walked over to the passenger's side where Steve sat.

"Heard you wanted to talk to me about some supposed rumors 'bout me and your girlfriend," Ernie said to Steve.

Steve remained in the car. "Yeah, I want to talk to you about that, but not here. Let's go over in back of the skating rink."

"Sounds okay to me," replied Ernie. *I can handle this little bastard with one hand. Maybe then sweet pants LaRae'll appreciate me more. This should be fun!*

Both cars crossed Highway 61, passing between Walker's Tavern and Walker's Roller Rink.

"Steve, remember what LaRae told you. Ernie Thompson and his lies don't matter a whit. Don't get into a fight with Ernie over this," Dunc cautioned Steve. "'Sides that the big lug probably outweighs you seventy or eighty pounds. And he's got a height and reach advantage." Dunc saw he was getting nowhere with this. He sighed and resigned himself to the fact that his best friend was determined to fight and, unfortunately, was probably gonna get beat up pretty bad.

The tires crunched on the gravel as they drove to the rear of the skating hall and parked next to a small field where no lights showed from the buildings or the highway.

"Dunc, I'd just as soon not fight him, but the lies gotta stop!"

Ernie lost no time getting out of his car and followed by his two friends, walked a little way into the field. Talking didn't look promising. Steve, Dunc and their two friends followed.

Steve came face-to-face with Ernie, who stood with his hands on his hips. The others formed a ring around the two.

"Okay, Mister Air Force," Ernie said, "I guess now that you've been in the military for a while, you're a trained killer and wanna kick my ass, huh?"

"Ernie, you know as sure as we're standing here that you lied about having sex with LaRae. I'd like you to admit that."

"Well, I had my hard dick on her and that ain't no lie. So what'cha gonna do about it Flyboy?"

"Well, Ernie," Steve sighed, "I don't really want to fight you but . . ."

Ernie swung his right fist as hard as he could, hitting Steve squarely just above his left eye. Steve, with no guard up, was totally unprepared, and his eyebrow split wide open. Gushing blood, he went down on his back like a sack of rocks.

Ernie with a superior smirking grin leaned over and spat in Steve's face. He struck Steve again, this time in his stomach, and then grabbed him by both shoulders and lifted him up. "Some trained killer you are, Candy Ass!" Ernie pulled him closer until their noses were nearly touching. "You didn't have to worry about fighting me Candy Ass. You ain't even gonna get in a punch." With a taunting laugh, Ernie was preparing to hit Steve again.

Steve shook his head quickly. All he could hear was Ernie's filthy words, "Well, I had my hard dick on her" echoing louder inside his head. His rage exploded. He was blinded with a fury that channeled his entire being into a consuming hatred for this obscene piece of shit who now collared and belittled him, and had insulted and pressed his slimy, filthy body against his LaRae.

Steve's eyes narrowed to tiny slits of pure hatred and suddenly there was a loud roaring in his ears that drowned out everything. Like a snake striking from a coil, Steve's right arm shot up between the hands that clutched his shoulders. With a vice-like grip he locked onto Ernie's windpipe. Ernie immediately released Steve and began to gasp for air, his eyes bulged as if they would pop out of his head, and his fingers feebly covered Steve's hand at his throat.

Steve, while still holding Ernie's trachea in a claw-like seize, grabbed a handful of Ernie's hair and jerked Ernie's head down savagely. At the same time he thrust his forehead into Ernie's nose, which shattered. The sound of breaking bone and cartilage could be heard by everyone, and blood splattered over both the combatants.

Ernie fell backward gasping for air from both his destroyed nose and his already swelling throat. Steve, his eyes still blazing with hatred, walked over to Ernie and with his right foot spread Ernie's legs. He viciously stomped and ground his shoe into Ernie's crotch causing Ernie to scream and then make gurgling, strangling noises.

The others standing around were stunned by all of this, but finally sprang into action and tried to suppress Steve. But they weren't quick enough to prevent Steve from savagely kicking Ernie full force in the testicles. Finally it took Dunc and all the others to restrain Steve and lead him away. They sat Steve down in some grass and then went back to attend to Ernie.

Steve shook his head trying to clear the cobwebs and pressed the handkerchief Dunc had given him to his still bleeding eyebrow. The roaring in his head had finally ceased. Dunc returned and was bending over him.

"That was one helluva fight Steve. You were fast as lightning and kicked the crap out of the asshole. I reckon I've never seen anything like it. Are you okay bud?"

"Aw, this cut is numb, that doesn't bother me. Ernie asked for most everything he got and I'm not sorry I stomped the piss outta him." But he was shocked about the amount of anger Ernie had been able to trigger in him. "Dammit, Dunc, I lost control. I coulda killed him," his voice trailed off. "I really wanted to kill him."

Dunc shared none of his friend's worries. "Well, he damn sure brought all this on himself. And you didn't wanna have to fight him Steve—you told him that, but you put him away good. And there for a minute or two I thought you were gonna kill him. You kicked him in his nuts so hard I thought they'd fly right up and outta his ears! Tell you one thing Steve, I don't think you and LaRae'll ever have any more trouble from Ernie Thompson. Can't you hear him groaning? He's still crumpled over there in the weeds. They've called an ambulance from the bar and it oughta be here pretty quick now."

Dunc helped Steve to his feet and over to where Ernie was lying on his back. Ernie was struggling for ragged breaths in between bouts of vomiting, moaning "Oh God, Oh God!" and rolling from side to side with his hands between his legs.

"Let's go," Steve said as he staggered toward Duncan's Studebaker.

Dunc drove to Steve's grandmother's house and helped his friend inside.

His clothing, face, and hair were soaked with both his own and Ernie's blood, but he would not let Dunc do anything to help him clean up. Instead he dampened a washcloth, put it over his eye and stretched out on his bed.

It seemed like only moments later, but nearly an hour had passed, when he awoke to find LaRae, her beautiful eyes brimming with tears, sitting beside him on the bed. She removed the washcloth and winced as if hurt herself when she saw his cut face. Her gentle touch and the warm wet cloth she was using to wipe away the dried blood covering his face, throat, and hair felt good. He tenderly took her wrist and kissed her hand. Dunc was standing beside her, holding a pan of water and towels.

With obvious concern, LaRae said, "Steve, why did you do this? We know Ernie lied, and it doesn't matter what anyone else might think. I belong to you. I could never give myself to anyone else. You have to know this!"

"I'd never question that. But I wanted him to stop telling those lies."

"Well," said Dunc, "I think you oughta go see the Doc and get some stitches. That's a pretty bad cut, Steve, and it's wide open."

But Steve didn't hear anything—he'd fallen asleep again. LaRae sat by his side on the bed watching him and gently ran her fingers through his hair for long, silent moments. Finally she leaned over and softly kissed his bandaged brow. "Hey boy," she whispered, "somebody loves you—sleep well my heart."

"Don't worry about him, LaRae. I'll stay with him tonight. He'll call you in the morning the first minute he wakes up."

"Thanks Dunc. You're such a good friend." Giving him a quick hug, she said, "Goodnight."

"Night, LaRae." Dunc opened the door and LaRae ran lightly down the steps to her car.

Ernie, after reconstructive surgery, with bandages wrapped all around his nose and head and an ice pack on his crotch, spent a very uncomfortable night. He just knew nobody's nuts—nobody's in the whole wide world ever—could come near to hurting even half as bad as his did.

The next day the cut above Steve's eye was still open and bleeding. Finally he went to Doc Tillison who first fussed at him for not coming in when he got the cut, then stitched up the eye.

Steve had received an early morning call at his grandmother's house telling him the sheriff wanted to talk to him, so he headed for the jail. "Mornin' Sheriff. I was told you want to see me," Steve said.

"Hey, Steve. Yeah, we need to have a little talk. Grab a chair." The sheriff had known Steve for a long time and had watched him grow from childhood—he liked Steve. "How're you feelin' son? Is your eye all right? Heard you had a little scuffle."

"Yessir, I'm fine. Doc Tillison gave me a pretty good chewin' out for not coming in sooner. Am I in trouble Sheriff?"

"Ernie Thompson's dad stopped by. Said you beat the shit outta his young'un and he wanted to swear out a complaint against you. I went to see Ernie in the hospital and got his side of the story. Ernie told me he wouldn't sign a charge. Said he was the one that caused the fight. So, there'll be no formal charge made, but Mr. Thompson insisted a copy of the incident report be sent to your commanding officer. I'd just as soon not send that report, but you know how Mr. Thompson is. He'll raise hell with the mayor and city hall till the report is sent. I'll make certain the accounting places the blame for the fight where it should be, with Ernie. I'm hopin' this won't cause you any problems at your overseas unit. Thanks for coming by Steve, I thought you oughta know this."

The sheriff stood, indicating an end to their business. "Guess maybe it ain't my place to say this, but I'm proud of you, Steve. You've done well, and you've already carried a heavy load a lot further, and better than most young people I know could have, had they been given the same cargo."

The day before he was to leave for England, Steve, LaRae and Dunc went to the Southeast Missouri Hospital to see Ernie.

When they walked into his room, Ernie's eyes widened when he saw Steve and the others. He moved his head slightly and moaned. Dunc thought Ernie looked like a mummy the way his nose and face was all wrapped up in bandages. Dunc struggled not to smile. He wanted to laugh, but instead kept a straight face.

Steve walked over to Ernie's bedside and stared down at the hard eyes locked onto his own.

"Ernie, I'm sorry this went so far," Steve said.

Ernie raised his right hand in sort of a wave. In a weak voice he said, "Hey, I'm the one who started it with my dumb ass mouth. And I threw the first punch." Ernie looked at LaRae and said, "LaRae, I apologize. I'm sorry—I'm really sorry about everything—the lies and any hurt I caused you."

LaRae said nothing, but nodded her head yes a couple of times.

"How're you doing? Any word on when you might be released?" Steve asked.

"The doc said he'll take these bandages off tomorrow and we'll know then, but he's already told me that my football playing is over with, for this season anyways."

"I feel bad about all of this."

"Naw, no need. Like I said, I was the one that pushed it all. Besides, now that I can't play ball anymore, I'll hunker down and get my schoolwork straightened out."

Surprising everyone Ernie raised his right hand to Steve and said, "Heard you're leaving for overseas tomorrow. Probably won't see you again, so I'll wish you good luck now."

Steve took the proffered hand. "Thanks Ernie. Guess you're a lot bigger guy than I thought you were."

As he was turning to walk away Steve thought he saw something in Ernie's eyes. Something that negated all the nice things Ernie had just said. He thought he saw a deep, burning hatred.

MSgt Hargrave stood and walked over to his liquor cabinet to pour himself a nightcap. "Well," sounds to me like this Ernie chap was being a proper rotter. Hells bells, you were just defending yourself. Unless the sheriff's report says something totally different, I don't think you have a bloody thing to be concerned about.

"I guess so. Thanks for listening Sarge, and I hope you're right." He felt better after talking about all this, but he was still worried, and with good cause.

Chapter 11

SNAFU, et al.

Master Sergeant Gage, Pappy, Warren Boyd and Steve enroute to the snack bar entered the long and wide, main building corridor. Once inside it quickly became apparent that many enlisted personnel walking their way from the opposite direction zeroed in on Sergeant Gage. The First Sergeant's reputation had spread immediately throughout the base. If any of the troops had a doubt about the condition of their uniform, haircut, or footwear, they either took a sharp right or left exit from the main corridor when they recognized Gage walking toward them.

"Bald-headed fucker's got lines formed and backed up all the way outside the barber, laundry, and dry cleaning shops," Major Ekridge complained to Captain Keene. "Sometimes you gotta wait fifteen to twenty minutes just to drop off even a small bundle of laundry. He's pulling everyone's passes, including those people living off base, because of the condition of their uniforms. Fuckin' barracks already filled to overflowing and he's restricting off-base personnel from going home till they get a haircut, shine their shoes, or spruce up their uniforms. Guys're racking out in sleeping bags on barrack floors. I saw two airmen turn around and run over the three guys in back of them when they saw Gage coming their way. You're hearing Article 15 more than you hear people talking about Brigitte Bardot anymore, for Crissake! Hell of it is all the other First Sergeants and most of the Commanders on base are supporting him like crazy."

"Have you noticed how hallway traffic here seems to go in fits and starts," Gage smilingly said to Hargrave. "Like now, suddenly it has really thinned out in front of us. And as soon as we're at the other end of the corridor, this part will be crowded."

"I do believe the game's afoot, Sherlock," Phil Hargrave joked back.

Seeing Danbury and the Base Motor Pool NCO, MSgt Alexander, already seated in the cafeteria, the four newcomers made their way over to the two sergeants' table. Alexander was well known and liked by all the

Postal and Courier personnel. He showed favoritism to them by making certain they always had the truck or automobile they needed for duty, day or night. Those that knew him well called him Alex. His bar and pub drinking buddies called him Axel (due to his vehicle duty assignment,) but only when they wanted to get a rise out of him or to piss him off.

"There, that's the guy. Him! The one just now getting a cup of coffee at the coffee urn," Alexander said excitedly.

"What's up guys?" Pappy asked.

"Alex here swears he knows the guy up there at the counter, but can't remember from where," Sergeant Danbury explained.

"Yeah! Yeah, I know that I know him, but I can't for the life of me figure out where from! Damn, anymore my memory's 'bout as long as a chigger's dick," Alex complained.

"Well shit," Warren Boyd said, "go up and talk to him about it, for Crissake—just ask him." As an afterthought Warren asked, "By the way, how long is a chigger's dick?" Alex gave him a friendly punch on the shoulder.

"Naw, that's always embarrassin' to me. You go through all this rigmarole like, 'Well, back in '45 I was with the 82nd in Germany; stateside I was in SAC in Omaha; MATS at Scott field; AAC at Elmendorf,' and so forth. Then after goin' through all those assignments and places, you still can't make the match. It's embarrassin'. I'll just forget about it," Alex decided.

"Yeah, well, then forget about it!" Danbury said, becoming slightly agitated with Alexander's rantings. He turned to Pappy. "What's the latest Phil?"

"Gage here says it looks like we're gonna get our new barracks and boy do we need it! Your administrative clerk's arrival is still on schedule and, of course, you know we're still wrapped around the axle on these suspected mail thefts. Sure wish we could catch that bugger."

The squadron's operations section was working with the OSI on a rash of suspected stolen mail pieces. The missing items were monthly allotment checks, large numbers of *Playboy* magazines, and occasionally, expensive articles of men's clothing. *Playboy* had just recently been accepted for shipment via APO mail channels. It was expensive and hard to get as well as extremely popular in Europe. The magazine was a hot black market item in downtown London. The allotment checks were military subsidized monthly pay being sent to military dependents in the U.S. or the U.K., and amounted to thousands of dollars. The officials were hard-pressed to determine where the mail thefts were occurring.

"Yeah, this really gives us a black eye," Danbury complained. "Here we work our balls off three hundred and sixty-five days a year, conscientiously trying our best to get everyone's mail through as fast as possible, and some Yayhoo comes along and makes us all look bad. Thankfully we have a very small number of these, but when one goes bad, everyone else is dumped into the same category. Damn I hate this! It's especially bad during Christmas time when folks back home, children in particular, will have to go without needed things. I'd sure like to be the one to catch the son of a bitch responsible."

"Goddammit, this is driving me nuts," Alexander shouted, totally oblivious to the discussion taking place at their table. "I'm certain I know that guy. But where in hell do I know him from? Betcha we were together back in SAC. Mighta been at Tripoli in Libya. Geeeesch!"

Ignoring Alexander, Warren Boyd said, "Well Sergeant Dan, we'll be getting your port call pretty quick and then you can go into FIGMO status and forget all of this."

"Yeah. Maybe," Danbury replied.

"I gotta talk to this guy," Alex said. "I'm gonna go bonkers if I don't find out where I know him from."

"Axle, old chap, you're obviously in a frightful muddle over this and if you don't bloody well ask the fellow, I'm going to," Hargrave said with some desperation. "Here. He's coming our way now. Haul your ass up and ask him and then be damn well done with it. You're driving us nuts!"

Alexander stood as the Sergeant approached. "Excuse me Sarge, but I know that I know you from somewheres and I just plain can't place where."

The Sergeant looked at Alexander somewhat oddly and said, "Yep, you're right, I do know you."

"See there you smart asses, see, I told you I knew this guy from somewheres. I told ya. I may forget a name, but I'm hell on rememberin' a face. Yessir, I'll never forget a face!" Alex all but shouted to the group at the table. "Where was it Sarge? Where'd we know each other from? Bet it was Africa—over in Tripoli wasn't it?" Alex asked expectantly.

"Nope, I was in your office 'bout an hour ago and coordinated a paper on a truck transfer."

Alexander mumbled, "Oh. Yeah. Well, thanks Sarge," as he sat back down to a silent table and the grinning faces of his friends.

To interrupt the deafening, pregnant silence, Alexander cleared his throat and asked Boyd, "Well, um, what was that you was saying about FIGMO? What's a FIGMO?"

"You gotta be shittin' me. Here you are a Master Sergeant in the Air Force, probably been in since Ike was a corporal. Probably had buffalo shit on your boots during the battle at the Little Big Horn. You been in all this time and you don't know what FIGMO means? What about SNAFU and ASAP and HSORI and—"

A chagrined Alex interrupted Boyd. "All right, all right for Crissake, you don't have to make a fuggin' federal case outta it Boyd. I know what it is, but it just slipped my mind. What does FIGMO mean?"

"Stands for: Fuck-it I Got My Orders, and SNAFU is: Situation Normal-All Fucked Up and ASAP—"

Alexander cut Gage off this time with, "Yeah, yeah, I know all those, I just forgot 'em. Shit, I can't remember anything anymore. I'd swore I had been stationed with that guy somewheres and here he just stopped by my office an hour ago."

"Yeah, well, don't forget HSORI, Axle" Boyd said. "You must know what HSORI means, right?"

Alex, acting somewhat puzzled and a little miffed, said "Yeah, yeah, sure, HSORI I'd never forget—everyone knows that one! Gotta go, see you guys later."

Once outside and slowly making his way to his motor pool office, Alexander nearly collided with Staff Sergeant Johnson, one of the postal squadron NCOs who was pushing a cart. The sergeant had hurriedly departed the AMT and didn't look in Alexander's direction. Alex had seen the sergeant in his motor pool frequently when Johnson was there picking up or returning a borrowed truck for mail runs.

"Hope you don't drive my trucks like you're operating that cart!" Alex shouted to the sergeant—he was still slightly ticked off.

"Huh?" The sergeant, just then noticing Alex, was jumpy and his nervousness and ediginess showed. He looked startled at Alex and then all around him to see if any others were nearby. "What'd you say?" Johnson obviously did not want to stop or chat with Alexander.

"You just damn near ran into me with that cart. You oughta be watchin' where you're goin'."

"Yeah, you're right, I'm sorry."

"That's okay. You goin' to the Pool for a truck?"

"Yeah, I gotta make a run to the airport."

"I'll walk along with you, I'm goin' back to work."

Alex did not see the expression of anxiety and frustration flash across Johnson's face caused by his now having to walk with the senior NCO.

"Hey, Sarge, I got a question for ya," Alex tossed out casually.

"Yeah, what's that?" Johnson responded nervously.

"Have you ever heard of the accrominism HSORI?"

"I don't know what you're talking about," the sergeant responded. He didn't want to walk with or talk to Alex. He was trying his best to hurry and was annoyed with Alex tagging along beside him, slowing him down.

"HSORI—you never heard of HSORI? It's a accrominisn. You know, like FIGMO and SNAFU and stuff."

"Nah, I ain't ever heard of HSORI," Johnson said, resigning himself to Alex accompanying him. "But I know the others. What's it stand for?" he asked, not really caring or wanting to know.

"Hell, I don't know. If I knew I wouldn't be asking you!" Alex said, his anger and frustration returning. "Forget it."

The two continued on inside the motor pool gates with no further discussion. Once inside the truck yard Johnson hustled away and never looked back. He thought he was had when Alexander first yelled at him as he was coming out of the terminal.

The cart Sergeant Johnson was pushing was heavily-laden with large, empty mailbags. The mailbags would be placed in the bed of a small motor pool pickup truck and driven to Heathrow airport to be used as needed there. Beneath the empty bags were several bundles of *Playboy* magazines, and on the inside of his field jacket the NCO had three stacks of government checks held together by fat rubber bands. These would be dropped off at his apartment enroute to the airport.

Settling into his office chair Alex asked himself out loud, "Wonder what in the hell HSORI could stand for?"

Alexander's HSORI enlightenment would soon be a dramatic revelation to him.

Chapter 12

Auf Wiedersehen Schatze

Paris, France

The earlier evening mist had turned to rain and a cold north wind drove the rain in sheets, buffeting the side of Captain Karl Miller's rental car as he parked at the art dealer's storefront.

He tilted the rearview mirror and checked his reflection to ensure his false mustache and the large fake mole near his left cheekbone were in place. Karl then reached for the covered painting on the front seat beside him, making certain it was well protected from any rain or dampness. He left the car and knocked on the front door of the store.

The proprietor looked at the wall clock and noted the time. It was 8:00 p.m. and his visitor was, as always, just as punctual as he was mysterious. This strange, late hour caller had phoned the storeowner the morning before and said he would be there at that hour the following day. The dealer had closed his business three hours earlier. He unlocked the door, admitted his visitor, and then pulled the front door shade down. He led the way, without speaking, to his office in the back of the store and turned off the main storefront lights. They spoke in English.

"You've brought the painting?"

"This is it."

"You're certain of the title," the art dealer asked in hesitant disbelief.

"The title and available history is on the card inside the envelope attached to the back." Removing the card and handing it to the dealer, Karl said, "Here, read for yourself." The man took the card.

"Forgive me, but I have studied the work of that title. If this is that piece, it will be a miracle, truly an incredible miracle. It is one of the greatest works of religious art ever created." The card read, "Christ Baptized in the Jordan by John." The art dealer knew it had been painted circa 1320 by the unknown artist referred to by chronographers and biographers as the "Master of Zilina."

The store owner, reaching for the painting, whispered, "May I?"

Karl handed him the covered canvas.

With trembling hands the dealer carefully wiped the rain from the outer wrapper with a rag, then laid the painting face down on a large table and turned on a crookneck lamp, bending it over the covered article. He gently unwrapped the framed canvas, and when he turned it over his breath caught in his throat as he looked at the magnificent painting. He, unconsciously, made the Sign of the Cross and whispered something to himself.

The art dealer, squinting and peering closely through his large magnifying glass, examined the entire surface of the canvas, and murmured a hushed "Oh" several times. "Unbelievable!" he whispered in awe. "Truly, this is among the greatest of all religious paintings!"

With the damp cloth still in his hand, he wiped his brow now suddenly wet with perspiration and, still in a whisper, he said, "Do you realize, Monsieur, that this most magnificent painting is more, much, much, more indeed, than just a painting? This is a national treasure! It is a great Czech masterpiece not seen since 1938. It was believed destroyed. Monsieur, this painting is priceless beyond any figure!"

Handing him a card with numbers on it, Karl said, "I'll take one million U.S. dollars for the painting payable, as before, to this account in Switzerland. I will confirm the transaction tomorrow morning. And, as before, the painting must go to one who will display it solely for his own enjoyment. No others may see it. Understood?"

"Understood perfectly, Monsieur. I shall look forward with great enthusiasm to your next visit."

Over the short period of a year and a half, numerous fantastic works of art, long considered lost to the world, began to surface at various points throughout Europe and the western United States. These masterpieces mysteriously appeared in the private collections of only the very wealthy. For the most part, they were the unscrupulously wealthy who shared the magnificence of the treasured art pieces but rarely. There were, however, among this number, the occasional proud owners who could not keep their fabulous great fortune and tremendous art works to themselves. Very selectively, they boasted of and grandiosely showed the sculptures, paintings, rare coins, jewelry, and other exquisite objets d'art to astonished visitors who eventually passed the knowledge of the collections on to others.

In time, Interpol in Europe, the FBI in the U.S., and other international law enforcement and investigative agencies, were alerted to the fact that art collections, confiscated and collected as loot by the Nazis during World War II, still existed. Countries raped of the art by the Nazis and the surviving members of the Holocaust began to fuel interest in the hope of recovering these stolen treasures because now, quite suddenly, several masterpieces and other rare items, long thought to be lost to the world, were beginning to mysteriously appear again.

The rain continued as Karl Miller, now satisfied with the sale, locked his rental car a block away from a bar. The outside neon lights identified it as The Rendezvous. He made certain the boot containing his small leather bag was securely locked. He pulled his greatcoat collar up against the wind and rain. Thunder rumbled overhead as he walked toward the lounge on Rue St. George. Inside, without looking in their direction, he passed the bar and the seven or eight customers engaged in conversation with the bartender and waitress. A lone prostitute who appeared extremely bored was seated at the end of the counter nursing a drink.

Karl, in civilian clothing and still wearing his artificial mustache and false mole, slid into a darkened booth at the rear of the building. The only lights were from a dim, low hanging, Tiffany-style ceiling fixture several booths away and the flickering candle sconce on the wall above his table. The waitress appeared and took his order for a double cognac. As she was turning to leave, she bumped into the prostitute who had suddenly appeared at Miller's booth.

"Would you like some company, Monsieur?" she asked in halting French, her German accent very apparent.

"Do you speak English?" he asked.

Noticing, no more like hoping, she had caught a bit of a West German dialect in his speech. She said, "Not nearly so well as German. *Sprechen sie Deutsch?*"

In perfect German, he invited her to have a seat, offered her a cigarette, and asked if she would like a drink. When the waitress returned and placed his cognac before him, she looked at the prostitute with a quizzical expression.

"I'll have what he's having," the German girl said. Sitting opposite Karl, she leaned forward for him to light the cigarette he had given her. When her drink arrived, they clinked glasses and said, "*Prosit.*"

The girl's name was Gretchen Schneider but she called herself Amanda. She was twenty-four and had been living in Paris for two years. She came to Paris from Frankfurt, and after some limited success as a model in the fashion quarter, she had been introduced to drugs. Her modeling career then plummeted. Her work now as a hooker supported her drug habit and paid for a modest apartment where she discretely took her paying customers.

It was to that apartment two hours and several drinks later where she opened the door and admitted Karl who carried his small leather bag with him. After letting her out near the front door, he parked his car a block away and walked back to Amanda's flat. In the meantime she had hurriedly snorted a couple of lines of cocaine. Coupled with the alcohol she'd consumed, Amanda was enjoying a real high. When she opened the door, her condition was apparent to Karl. And so also was the bottomless, sheer pink negligee she was wearing. Soaking wet, Miller removed his coat and handed it to Amanda.

"The bathroom and towels are there," she said, pointing to a closed door.

He set the leather bag down near the bathroom door and made sure the zipper and latch were closed tight. He went into the tiny bathroom, closed the door, urinated, washed and toweled himself dry. After a few minutes he returned to the bedroom and found Amanda on the bed with her shorty nightgown pulled well up over her waist and open at the top, exposing her beautiful breasts. With a quick glance he also noted that his bag, not quite zippered shut, had been turned in the opposite direction from which he had set it down.

Karl sat on the edge of the bed, and Amanda immediately pulled him backward into her arms. As she kissed him, she placed her hand on his crotch and expertly unzipped his trousers, reached inside, and slowly began to knead him. In seconds he was erect and experienced a throbbing ache in his loins.

He knelt on the bed and pulled Amanda to him, bending her over into the doggie-style position. He cupped her sex mound with the palm of his hand and played his fingers from just below her navel across her vagina and anus several times until she moaned and became wet. Then entering her, he moved in long, slow, steady strokes. The girl made pleasant moaning sounds with each of his thrusts. He pressed his thumb against her anal area and she bolted forward, dislodging him abruptly.

Laughingly she said, "No-no, not there! That is *verboten* (forbidden) territory."

He said nothing but placed a hand on each side of her hips and pulled her back near him. He then leaned forward and put his left hand on her left shoulder near her neck. He took his penis in his right hand and rubbed it first against her vagina, then her anal area, and then savagely he thrust himself inside her anus solidly to the hilt as she began to scream in pain, which was muffled by his strong hands now clasped around her neck.

Bent over her back and deep within her, he plunged time and time again, tearing her insides while strangling her with both hands which were locked tightly around her throat. He released his choke-hold allowing Amanda to draw a few ragged gasps of air. "Where have you hidden what you stole from my bag?" Karl demanded.

"*Du hast mich sehr weh gepan*" (you have hurt me bad), Amanda wheezed between tortured breaths of air.

Ramming his penis into her again, "*Drekische-sow!* (whore-pig) Answer me! Where did you hide what you stole from my bag?"

"*Die brosche ist im der schublade*" (The brooch is in the dresser drawer.) Amanda was just barely able to whisper in between coughs. Karl smiled and immediately resumed his choke lock. He increased the pressure on Amanda's throat as he accelerated his thrusts into her body. His eyes glazed fiercely, and he smiled as he could feel her straining and gasping for a last breath within seconds of the resumption of his torture. In death, she fell forward with him still enclosed.

Her last client climaxed as her body spasmed and jerked several times. Then Amanda lay still.

Finally, he withdrew his sperm-streaked bloody cock. He washed himself and, using the same towel, wiped everything clean of fingerprints. He put his bag on the bed beside her body. Karl opened the case. He hurriedly surveyed the satchel's contents; a dazzling disarray of diamonds, rubies, sapphires, pearls, emeralds, opals and other precious stones that had graced Europe's royalty and wealthiest personages as small tiaras, pendants, bracelets, earrings, lockets, and rings. He replaced the brooch Amanda had removed. As far as he could tell, everything looked the same. Nothing more seemed missing. But, he had no way of knowing that Amanda had also removed and hidden a diamond and ruby stick pin beneath her mattress while he had busied himself in the toilet. Nor was he aware of the minute engraving on the jewelry that identified the house of royalty to whom the pin had once belonged. Of course that marking rendered the item traceable.

Again, using the towel to open the door, he said to Amanda "*Auf Wiedersehen Schatze*. Damn shame about your being so curious. I don't guess you'll be doing that again, huh? *Danke schön* for a real interesting evening!"

Karl, his carnal and blood lust appetites sated for the moment, thought, *all of this pleasure, these pure delights and for this I also receive a million dollars in the process—wunderbar!* The thrill of killing continued to grow within him. It had become an addiction. He looked forward to the occasion of his next victim and had already narrowed his sights on that Third Air Postal Squadron member.

Chapter 13

Heather Arrives

Martha was cleaning the grill in the cafeteria when she saw Hargrave, Boyd, Gage and Steve walk in and sit down at their usual table. While she always complained about having to serve them, she nevertheless quickly washed her hands, grabbed an order sheet, and hurried over to their table before the other waitress could head in their direction.

As Pappy looked up at her she said, "I know, I know, your usual cuppa—strong as sin, black as hate and hot as love. Will there be anything else, Sergeant Hargrave?"

"No thank you, me darlin'. That'll do nicely."

She turned to Warren Boyd, her favorite. "Now, don't go takin' the Mickey out of it. Just tell me what you want—in the food department—I know what else you're always wantin', you cheeky rotter!"

Boyd, remaining silent, just stared at her intently for long moments until he had everyone's attention. "I see it in you Martha! Others don't, maybe, but I see it and you can't hide it or deny it—it stands out like brilliant, flashing, neon lights!"

"Geet out of it! You're off your ruddy rocker!" said Martha.

She bent down closer to Boyd's staring eyes. "Wot is it that you see then, Luv?" she asked in a cautious, curious voice.

Boyd, with as serious an expression as he could muster, replied, "I see the intense fire that burns within you whenever you look at and lust after my body."

Martha grabbed the towel off her shoulder and whacked Boyd with it several times while everyone laughed, herself included.

Orders completed, Hargrave said, "Well, Sergeant Dan's new clerk, the Scottish lass Heather MacVickar, will be reporting in this morning. This is going to be interesting. Especially her using the powder room because, as you all know, Heather is the only female in our Squadron and we don't have a Ladies room." Hargrave added with a grin, "She'll have to come upstairs and use our restroom. We'll put a hook and sign on the door so we'll know when she's using it. Can't have her using the can in the AMT. Dan don't trust those animals, 'fraid they'd walk in on her, sign or no sign. Also, our facility is, shall we say, well, just more suitable."

"I'm anxious to see her," Boyd said.

"Me too," Steve added. "And I think her using the latrine upstairs is a great idea. Sergeant Dan is right. Our guys downstairs probably wouldn't respect her privacy, and that's putting it mildly."

All activity stopped dead when Steve escorted Airman Second Class Heather MacVickar into the AMT. In the monstrous, hangar-sized building, one could hear a pin drop as they entered the terminal.

The first thing any guy noticed about Airman MacVickar was her beautiful, bright red hair. The next thing was her knockout body that filled out the U.S. Air Force uniform like no one in the Third APS had ever seen before. Heather had a gorgeous body and great looks.

She also had a wonderful personality. She was outgoing, flashed a brilliant smile, and captured the heart of every single guy working in the AMT the first second he saw her. Steve walked her up the stairs to Sergeant Danbury's open balcony office area and made the introductions.

Johnson had been assigned from the Paris Twelfth Air Postal Squadron about a month ago, and he was mesmerized by Heather, just watching her walk up the stairwell.

"Never, never, in my entire life have I ever wanted to kiss a female's belly button as much as I want to kiss hers," he said.

Arkee, like everyone else in the Squadron, had already, several times over, heard about Johnson's fetish for French style love-making with his mouth.

"Damn Johnson, are you mellowing? You only want to kiss her belly button?" Arkee questioned.

"Yeah," said Johnson, "but from the inside."

"Damn you're gross, Johnson!" said Arkee and eight of the other troops standing around them said, "No he ain't, I want to, too! Yeah, and right now this minute I wanna dick her so bad my teeth hurt," another added. Heather's entrance had commanded everyone's attention.

After Heather's In-Processing was completed, Sergeant Danbury escorted her throughout the AMT to the Receiving Section, the Sorting and Routing Sections, the Registry Cage, the Window and Mailbox areas. With each stop he introduced her to each of her new co-workers. Heather quickly extended her hand and with a surprisingly firm handgrip gave her new fellow-Airmen co-workers a beautiful dimpled smile. Within the first hour on the job, she became AMT's Sweetheart of the Terminal.

While Heather was completing her Base In-Processing and being assigned her WAF Barracks area, Sergeant Danbury called a hasty staff meeting of all the male workers.

"All right guys, I ain't pullin no punches with this 'cause I want you to understand right up front what's gonna happen here. Everyone, that is every swinging dick here, is gonna treat MacVickar like the nice, sweet young lady she is. She's young enough that in a lot of cases she could be your little sister. Treat her like that. Respect her and be nice to her. Since we've not had any females around, our language has gotten raunchy. So two things right off: clean up your act and clean up your language. I don't wanna hear anymore filthy talk. Understood?"

There were a few "Yeahs" mumbled.

Danbury yelled, "I said, is this understood?"

A shouted chorus of "Yessir!" responded.

"Okay, when she gets back here, I want each team or section leader to show her what is done in your area. She needs to know everything we do here and how it's done. She'll be doing all your reports for you so she needs to know what's what, the terms we use, schedules, routines, all that crap. She'll be doing all your typing and filing. She'll be a great help to us. We haven't had an Admin Clerk for four months, and it's been a pain in the ass. MacVickar has good records, and I'm certain she'll do us a good job. Just look at her like she's your little sister back home. Treat her nice and help her however you can. Okay, that's it. Remember, she's your baby sister. She's sweet. She's innocent. And I'll have the nuts of the first one of you that forgets it!"

The second day on the job Sergeant Dan had Heather's desk turned sideways because the guys were all bunching up down below, looking up and through the open middle section of her desk, gawking at her beautiful legs and thighs. Heather reached across her desk for the glass jar that held her pens and eraser pencils and accidentally tipped the container over. It rolled off her desk and broke on the floor. "Oh fuck!" she yelled.

Once again, all activity, shuffling, and talking, everything stopped abruptly throughout the entire AMT as every troop in the building looked up at her in the balcony office area. Then, the entire group, as one roared in laughter.

Heather's face turned as bright a red as the beautiful hair on her head. And all the guys thought, *Hey, our little sis is gonna be okay.* At that moment Heather was immediately accepted into the AMT Postal family. One of her fellow AMT airmen, without knowing it, would sorely regret that particular family addition.

Chapter 14

Shipment from Bremerhaven

Wearing his European attire and sporting his artificial mustache and facial mole, Captain Miller drove his rental car into the gigantic shipping yards of the port of Bremerhaven, Germany. He went to the far northeast corner of the yards to a small shop he had frequented many times before. From the boot of the car he removed the old family ottoman. This aged cushioned footstool had been his grandfather Mueller's favorite piece of furniture. It was attractive with a lush red velvet floral design on a heavy buff colored fabric. It had cabriole legs with ball feet and had been in the family since 1830. It was beautifully upholstered and the artistic carpentry work was exquisite. It also had hidden inside a fortune in precious stones, jewels and magnificent Nazi military medals and awards.

Even though Karl and his brother Otto had played on the ottoman as children and it had supported and rested many tired feet over a span of several decades, it had been cared for and remained in pristine condition.

Locating his contact in the Packing and Crating shop, Karl placed the 16"x24"x16" ottoman on the workbench before him.

"Same as before?" the German worker asked.

"Jawohl," Karl responded and spoke in impeccable and crisp German, "exactly the same as before. Package, crate and ship this to my parents in Tacoma, Washington, USA. Here are the address labels and the customs declaration form. Your friend in customs will certify the form as in the past—no problem?"

"Ja, no problem and as I told you on the telephone, there is a ship bound for Seattle, USA due in port in two days. Your footrest will be properly crated, certified and on that liner. It should have a fast crossing."

"How much do I owe you?" Karl asked.

The workman quickly measured the ottoman and told Karl the amount. When Karl placed the money in the man's hand the worker looked up at

Karl in vivid surprise. Karl had given him three times the amount the workman had stated.

"But you have given me far too—"

"This piece of furniture is very old," Karl interrupted him in mid-sentence, "but it is of great sentimental value to my father. He is most anxious to have it—he looks for it daily. I appreciate your extra care in its handling and prompt shipment. *Danke schön.*"

"*Jawohl. Jawohl. Bitte schön!*"

Tacoma, Washington, nine weeks later

Thelma's truck driver husband Homer had been getting up to use the bathroom at least every forty-five minutes nightly. He complained that he'd just start to pee and everything would shut down on him. Still felt like he had to urinate, but nothing would come out. He'd go back to bed and be up again ten minutes later trying to urinate. Aggravating. Worrisome. And, after a fashion, painful.

Anymore, his over-the-road trips were out of the question, and he was having problems with local hauls. The loss of sleep and growing discomfort soon forced him to see a urologist who had prescribed some medication. It helped little. Eventually Homer had to have the surgical procedure called the Trans Urethral Resection of Prostate, or TURP.

According to Homer, they used a so-called roto-rooter gizmo to go down through his dork and unclog the passageway. After the TURP, they'd stuck one of those catheters in him for several days. Homer hated it. Humiliating. Embarrassing. Awkward as hell too! Its going in hadn't bothered him because he was out of it. However, Homer had worked up a king-sized dreaded fear of its removal. That happened five weeks ago and today, and despite the heavy fog, he insisted Thelma drive him to town to see his doctor. He was still having bladder spasms and, recently, night-mares that he would again need a repeat of that damned catheter!

Homer had been extremely short-tempered about all of this. The entire procedure had exacerbated him.

In the hospital, when they decided to remove the catheter, Homer knew damn right well that Little Miss Cutesy, the blonde nurse who titty-bounced around acting like she knew she was the cutest, smartest, and world's best nurse ever, hadn't let all the water out of the end of the damn thing. They had explained the water balloon end was what kept it anchored inside him.

When she grabbed hold of his groznik and tried to jerk the catheter out, Homer, with an ear-piercing shriek, all but flew up off the bed.

"Hmmmm—it must be stuck," the nurse had said.

Homer, who had broken out in a cold sweat pounded on his mattress like a downed wrestler smacks the canvas mat, and yelled, "Will you please get away from my dick!"

When Miss Cutesy summoned someone who knew what he was doing, the catheter was quickly and painlessly removed.

The doc insisted Homer drink lots and lots of water. He did. He drank water all day and was so bloated he could barely move and felt as if he was going to explode any second. Clearly, he didn't want anything more to do with that frigging catheter! And, still, he could not pee. Back in went the catheter! The next day Homer had cold sweats all day long, fearing the removal of the catheter. But it came out easily this time.

"Drink lots and lots of water," Nurse Cutesy advised Homer. "And if you have a hard time going tinkle, just turn the water faucet on in your lavatory. Hearing the tap water run will help you go tee-tee," she had instructed in her most caring, nurseful tone.

Yeah sure thought a somber, sore penised, Homer. *Dumbest pair of nipples I ever saw—can't piss so listen to water run—make me go tee-tee. That's what she said for Crissake—make me go tee-tee. Who the hell she think she's foolin'?*

But damned if it didn't work! And now, whenever Homer heard water running he had to pee like crazy! Even if he'd just gone, hearing water run made him have to go again. *Damndest thing* Homer thought. Just after having surgery down there, he couldn't hold it back. They'd cut the muscles or something. When Homer had to go, he had to go and right now!

Done pissed my pants three times cause I couldn't get to the can fast enough, Homer embarrassingly reminded himself. For this reason, he kept a plastic urinal in the car whenever he and his wife went anywhere.

And today, the problem continued. *Wouldn't you know it,* he thought, *and after I made a point of peeing just before we left the house.*

Driving into town the radio played hell with Homer! A commercial for "Crystal Clear Marble Springs Drinking Water" came trickling over the car speakers. The water could be delivered directly to your house by calling the following toll free number. When Homer heard the sound of the rippling water coming over the radio, he started scrambling like mad for his urinal. Bringing it from the back seat to the front, the urinal clipped Thelma's shoulder. The urinal tumbled and fell to the floor. There it lodged between the brake and the accelerator.

Trying to keep her eyes on the road and steer the car, Thelma struggled to kick the urinal out of the way with her foot. Instead, she inadvertently pushed the accelerator to the floor where the urinal kept the pedal tightly lodged. Homer's big Lincoln Town Car shot forward while Thelma screamed and Homer peed his pants again.

Otto, Hans and Helga Miller were driving north on Interstate Five from their home in Tacoma heading for the Port of Seattle. Hans had received a call the day before that a large crate had been received from Bremerhaven, Germany, and was being held for him at the port. Karl, on one of his trips to Salzdorf, had packed and shipped the container a couple of months back.

The Millers were on their way to pick up the shipment. Otto was driving the car as he always did since Hans' stroke last Christmas day. They had just passed the Interstate 5 and 18 Interchange, opposite Lake Killarney, when the huge Lincoln Town Car burst instantly out of the dense fog, its lights barely visible.

Helga looked up to see Thelma's face frozen in terror, revealing the certain knowledge that collision was imminent. Helga didn't have enough time to scream when the grillwork of the Lincoln came crashing through her side of the car, crushing her, Otto and Hans against the far side of their Volvo station wagon. The force of impact and the momentum of the Lincoln carried both cars well off the Interstate and close to Pacific Highway, which ran parallel to I-5. The three Millers were killed instantly.

Thelma and Homer's heads cracked the front windshield of their car. Thelma died that night in the Intensive Care Unit. Homer had a fractured skull and was comatose. When he died two days later he had not awakened to learn he was once more sporting another catheter.

The crate from Germany with its hidden compartment and contents sat in an isolated corner of Seattle's Pier 9 holding area—waiting.

Chapter 15

Salzdorf Revisited

C aptain Karl Miller and Buck Sergeant Warren Boyd were delivering classified ARFCOS materials to Royal Air Force Station Upper Heyford, England, when the Detachment Commander asked the Captain to please come into his office.

Captain Miller was told he had an important telephone message and was given the phone. The Detachment Commander quietly left the room and closed the door.

The message was the tragic news that his family, Hans, Helga and Otto had been killed in an automobile accident. Captain Miller and Boyd returned to Denham Studios immediately so Karl could catch the next morning's first flight out of Heathrow Airport in London for the States.

Karl was in his parent's home in Tacoma the next night. With a cold, seemingly total indifference, he made all the arrangements and buried his family. Later, after receiving another call from the Seattle Port Office, he drove to that location in a rental car and collected the crate his family had been enroute to pick up when the accident occurred. Back home he uncrated the ottoman, carefully removed the lining at the bottom, then the pressed board and some matting. Finally he lifted the volleyball sized cloth container which bore an unusual looking white star. He took the bag to the kitchen table, loosened the drawstrings, and emptied its contents. Diamonds, opals, emeralds, gold and silver heirlooms and fantastic exquisitely jeweled medals spilled from the bag.

Karl picked up a strikingly beautiful replica of the military citation case for the Grand Cross of the Iron Cross medal. The presentation case was patterned after the original Hitler had presented to Luftwaffe Chief Hermann Göring after the fall of France. The Führer had seen to it no expense was spared with Göring's unique case and medal—the only one of its kind. The original case was in black leather and dotted with thirty rubies and a dazzling array of diamonds formed in the shape of a swastika in a golden wreath beneath the Reich party eagle. The opulent citation case alone was worth a staggering sum. Karl watched the hundreds of sparkling reflections cast by the overhead light off the large cluster of diamonds and brilliant red stones. This particular piece he remembered his father had personally selected and placed in the bag at Salzdorf when they were last there together.

"Ever the consummate soldier, huh, Papa?" he said. "You always liked the military awards and decorations."

Karl sat, mesmerized, staring at the replica of Göring's presentation case. He was remembering the countless times his father had proudly shown him his classic military decoration, the prestigious Iron Cross the elder had received during World War I. He recalled the thrill and excitement of their going back to Salzdorf and rediscovering the mine and its fantastic contents. Remembering this it seemed to him as though it were yesterday....

It was in the spring of the year during the early 1950s. After having exhausted all efforts via correspondence, lengthy telephone calls, and even intercession by his Washington State U.S. Senator and Congressman, Hans and his two sons returned to Germany. Hans Miller's stated mission was to regain the Salzdorf farm home and properties they'd been forced to vacate so abruptly many years before. However, his primary concern and goal wasn't the old farm, but rather the fabulous riches that he hoped still rested undisturbed in the ancient Salzdorf mine he had guarded for the Nazis.

Hans Miller frequently wondered and worried, *What if the Nazis had gone back and removed it all? Perhaps the U.S. or its Allies had located the secret storage site. After all, they had found the Führerbau, the Schloss Thuerntal, Schloss Neuschwansein, Schloss Steiersberg, Schloss Kogl, Bad Aussee, the Hohenfurth monastery, Alt Aussee, the Merkers' Salt Mine and so many others. Could it be the bunker and underground mine had been bombed and burned, destroying—without knowing—the fantastic, unimaginable wealth that was stored there?*

For many anxious years Hans had followed closely all reports dealing with Nazi loot discoveries. *But maybe that particular one had not been reported*, he fretted.

He also followed, with great interest, the efforts of Holocaust victims and their remaining families, searching for the vast wealth and fortunes taken from their people in the Nazi death camps and throughout Europe. The untold millions stolen from them, their gold and other treasures stored in bank vaults and safes in Switzerland and elsewhere. He read of the countless demonic and horrific experiences of untold millions of Jews during that time. But he could find no mention of a Salzdorf mine as a repository for the looted treasures. His anxiety and worries, one way or another, would be put to rest with this trip back to Salzdorf.

Hans Miller parked his rented automobile off the main road and walked once again the old trail to the mine. It was now heavily overgrown with briars, bushes, small trees and weeds. Miller, accompanied by his two sons, held high hopes the millions were still beneath them as they walked up to the large mound of rubble which had been the concrete structure covering the entrance to the vault.

He looked carefully. He knew Lt. General George S. Patton's Third Army advance tank forces had passed through this area. Quite obviously they had zeroed in on the site. They had taken no chances it could be a pillbox, bunker, or other enemy held fortification back during the close of the war when the Allies rooted out all isolated pockets of German resistance.

Miller could find no evidence that the mine's entrance had been disturbed. Heavy slabs of concrete covered the top of the access entryway. Miller then took photographs of the old trail from the arterial highway and recorded as best he could the exact location of the property. He would attempt to purchase the ten wooded acres encompassing the mine. Hans, reluctantly, had to give up all efforts to regain his old farmhouse and land.

"Ja, I understand what you are telling me, Herr Miller," the stern-faced and curt sounding woman at the German Wohnungsamt, Housing Authority, said to Hans. "Lots of us suffered under the Nazis, but it is as I say, you voluntarily left your Salzdorf property. Even though it was during the war, if it was not taken from you and you were not forced out of your home, then you are considered to have deserted the property. Herr Miller, if you are able to provide documentation or witness confirmation that you were forced, through no fault of your own, to leave, then perhaps we can do something for you. Without that, unfortunately, your claim is quite impossible. The problem is even more complicated with Germany being divided as it is by the Berlin wall. There are many people still held captive in East Germany who may have return rights and privileges and legal ties to properties here that we know nothing about. Consequently, all sorts of realty transactions must be held in abeyance. It is complicated Herr Miller, surely you can see—"

"But that farm was mine!" Hans interrupted. "I owned it for years and it was my father's before me. No one else could possibly claim it. And I was shot by the Nazis—they tried to kill me—I had to leave. We would all be dead now, my entire family, if we hadn't left as we did."

"I'm sorry Herr Miller, you have nothing to support your claim and we cannot move the current owners out just on your word. Is there anything else?"

"Jawohl, there is something more . . ." Hans explained his desire to purchase the wooded acreage south of town. He was calmed and encouraged by the lady's response to his intentions to buy the property encompassing the mine.

"Ja, with regard to purchasing property previously held or owned by the Nazi political party—all that now belongs to the State," she explained. "However, documentation must be provided showing the property does not now, nor had previously belonged to others. With that it is possible for an interested party to submit a bid at fair market prices via certified and licensed Amt Real Estate Offices. Lots of red tape, Herr Miller. I suggest you contact a local realtor who is familiar with these things."

Hans did just that through his old friend the town veterinarian. The veterinarian's nephew was a licensed realtor in the area and assured Hans he could help him.

"Two things I want," Hans told Horst, the realtor, "I want to buy back our old farm and I want to purchase the ten wooded acres I've shown you."

"I'll do what I can," Horst responded.

"*Das ist güt,* but," Hans cautioned, "do not draw attention to me or this transaction. I want everything done as quietly as possible. Speak only to those absolutely necessary and do not mention my name except as a last resort. I do not want others knowing my business. *Verstehen?*"

"Completely, Herr Miller," Horst replied and quietly, but enthusiastically went about his mission.

"I am sorry," Horst reported to Hans the next day, "but it is quite impossible for you to buy back your former residence. The new owners are sympathetic to your situation, but they have no intention of selling. They have, however, invited you to visit them. Evidently many of the former furnishings, pictures and other belongings you left have been stored in the barn. Perhaps, they said, you may be interested in those. I am exploring the possibility of your purchasing the ten wooded acres. It is early with that, but all indications point toward success. I shall keep you informed of any progress."

At the new owner's invitation, Hans, Karl and Otto visited their former homesite.

"I was born here in that room," Hans said pointing to the master bedroom. Karl and Otto were both born in that room." Hans was moved by their return.

"*Ja*, I will be happy to purchase the old couch, chair, ottoman and any other furnishings you will sell me. *Frau* Miller will be very happy to have them back." Hans was delighted to learn that his upholstery table and all his upholstery tools had also been stored in the barn. He would, if things worked out as planned, most definitely have need for those.

Horst, the realtor, at Hans' insistence, reported to the old man routinely. Day after day Horst could only say, "I am continuing with the research, *Herr* Miller. It is a slow, time-consuming process. Please have patience— this cannot be rushed." Finally, after nearly a week and an exhaustive, but accelerated search, Horst knocked hard on the Miller's apartment door in the late afternoon.

"*Erfolg!*" (success!) Horst shouted startling Hans as he opened the door. "I have been able to prove to the Housing Authority that no record exists showing the property you want to purchase was ever owned by anyone other than the Nazis and now the State. *Herr* Miller you have been authorized to purchase the ten acres!"

It took quite a while for Hans to locate a contractor with equipment to remove the large pile of concrete rubble covering the mine. Finally, he found one. He also contracted to have a solid, windowless building constructed once the rubble was removed. Materials for that structure were ordered and would be standing by in readiness.

Hans made himself a nuisance with the removal of the rubble. As soon as the tractor bucket lifted up a piece of the concrete, Hans was immediately there looking beneath the raised piece to see if the entryway to the mine was being revealed. The construction worker repeatedly had to halt his work to avoid colliding with Hans, who was darting in and out, beneath and around the huge slabs being removed.

"*Herr* Miller, I cannot move this rubble with you constantly in the path!" the contractor, stopping his rig, shouted at Hans again. He was frustrated with Hans who would not stay out of the way. "If you insist on examining every piece of concrete I move, then I am leaving now. It is impossible for me to do my job with you in the way like this. You will be injured and I haven't the time to work slower. I have other jobs waiting!"

Hans knew from his initial search that he had been lucky to employ this man and his backhoe. At this time of the year construction activity was at its busiest level.

Miller pointed out that the job was nearly completed.

"Surely only a few more hours will see the entire job all done," Hans said, trying to appease the contractor. "I promise you I will stay out of your way." But that didn't last long.

Inevitably, Hans was struck on the head by a piece of re-bar jutting out from a broken piece of concrete. The wound was not severe although bad enough that his younger son, Otto would have to take him to the local doctor for stitches and a bandage.

With blood streaming down his face and shoulders from the gash on his head, Hans paused to tell the contractor, "Be absolutely certain to leave the last bit of concrete near the ground's surface alone! My sons and I will do the last of the removal. *Ist das klar? Verstehen?*"

"*Jawohl*, Herr Miller," the contractor acknowledged, even though he did not understand why that was necessary. Nevertheless, he agreed to the instructions and went about his business as Otto sped Hans to town and the doctor's office, leaving Karl to oversee the work.

With Hans out of the way, the job quickly accelerated. In no time the last piece of concrete was visible. Karl was out of sight in the woods when this point was reached. The contractor was anxious to complete the job and get his equipment the five kilometers back home before nightfall. Very efficiently, he picked up and stacked the slab of concrete against the pile of rubble a hundred yards distant from the site. Immediately the contractor noted the large, double steel doors that quite obviously covered an underground entryway. Puzzled and extremely curious, he stopped the backhoe. With its motor idling, he jumped down and hurried to the double doors. Almost in a whisper he said to himself, *Was ist vieses*? (What is this?) *Obviously, steel doors lead to something underground. I wonder, could this be an entrance to a mine? I'm told there used to be a lot of salt mines in and around this area way back before the wars.*

Noticing the reduced motor noise of the tractor, Karl returned to the site. With the idling engine drowning out his footsteps, Karl walked silently up behind the worker who was kneeling, closely examining the metal doors. Feeling rather than hearing Karl's approach and nearness, the contractor turned, startled, and stared at Karl's evil grin.

Karl's eyes appeared brilliant and sparkling as they glared down at the worker. He seemed to be enjoying the moment and the man's fear that he had created.

"You shouldn't have been so curious my friend," Karl said calmly as he swung a piece of metal pipe in an arc, crushing the forehead of the worker. The impact of the pipe caved in his frontal lobe and slammed him against the steel doors.

Although killed instantly, the worker's eyes remained open. His face was frozen in terror. His body jerked a few times and his hands and feet spasmed and twitched.

Karl nonchalantly stooped down and draped the body over his shoulder and carried the corpse out of sight into the woods.

Hans had the feeling that something was wrong when he and Otto pulled up to the site and got out of the truck. Karl was standing near the tractor, and the contractor was nowhere to be seen.

"Why has all the rubble been removed?" Hans shouted. "Goddammit, I told you I didn't want the last part removed! Where is that idiot? Can't he understand instructions? Why did you let this happen, Karl?"

"I was in the woods, Papa, when he removed the last section. When I came back, he had already uncovered the doors and was examining them. I had no choice but to take care of him. Back in town, he would tell everyone what he had found." Calmly and coolly, Karl continued, "I carried his body into the woods, and now we've got to hurry and decide whether to dig a grave and bury him, or make it look like he had an accident driving the tractor back on the road to Salzdorf."

Hans stared at Karl dumfounded. *"Ach Mein Gott!"* Hans exclaimed. "Karl, don't you realize what you have you done? You have killed a person! You have murdered a man, Karl!" Hans sat on the running board of the truck, his head in his hands.

Over the years Hans and Helga had noted flashes of cruelty in Karl's behavior. Sometimes, especially in competition, Karl became overbearing. He always wanted to dominate and seemed particularly aggressive toward others with handicaps or any non-Caucasian Gentiles. In sports or play it was never enough for him just to win; he wanted to humiliate and degrade the loser. The Millers had trouble with neighbors and others whose pets sometimes wandered into their yard. More often than not, the pet wound up with its throat slit, head bashed in, or was found grossly mutilated and hanging in a neighborhood tree. They suspected Karl of torturing and killing the animals. Hans and Helga feared Karl had a dark, evil streak. They blamed this on the Hitler Youth Group and their teachings back in Nazi Germany. They had worried about Karl over the years, but did nothing. They hoped he would outgrow his bad traits but he didn't. In fact, they intensified and became even more sinister. However, in this case, Hans greedily rationalized, *this was the only thing that could be done. Everything, would be lost otherwise. It had to be dealt with as it was.*

Finally Hans, in desperation, stood. *"Ja. Ja."* Hans said in agreement. *"Ja,* you did what you had to do Karl, I guess it had to be done. But now we must decide and act fast." Hans' heart was thundering and his head throbbing. He pondered the next action to take.

"This is what we do. Go, fetch that piece of tarpaulin and put his body in that, then load him in the back of the truck. Otto and I will drive the truck and, Karl, you drive the tractor back toward town. It's nearly dark now and suppertime. Maybe there will be no one on the road. We can't meet anyone going back to town. We'll put him back in the tractor and run it off the road there at the deep ditch down by the bridge. *Ja,* that's better than burying him, I think. Make it look like an accident. *Ja. Ja.* That's what we do. Go. We must hurry now before it's too dark!"

Later, as evening shadows were falling, Karl, with no lights on, steered the tractor to the edge of the road toward the deep ditch and paused. Hans and Otto, also without lights on the truck, had followed and removed the body from the back and struggled it up to Karl.

Karl stood on the axle, and, finally, was able to seat the contractor forward with his arms through the steering wheel spaces. The tractor's operator compartment area was tight and low, so Karl wasn't concerned the body would fall out prior to crashing at the bottom.

He got off the tractor and moved around it to the other side. He put the tractor in gear with his foot on the clutch and leaned across the body. He moved the throttle to full speed, then let off the clutch slowly, staying with the tractor for a little way. Then he leaped to the ground as it picked up speed. The tractor, with the body still seated, ran straight for a short distance. Then, as if steered by the dead contractor's arms, it went off to the side, into the ditch and overturned. It came to a rest on its side, pinning the dead man beneath.

Satisfied with their work, the three Millers rushed back to their truck and returned to the mine. They quickly burned the tarpaulin, hurriedly covered the mine's entrance by stacking planks of wood on top of it, and went over their story again several times until they each had it down pat. It was well after dark when they returned to town and the apartment they had rented for their stay. That evening and the next morning Hans was so excited he could hardly contain himself.

Even with all the excitement of the preceding day, Miller had noted before covering them with wood that the solid steel doors leading to the mine had been scarred and bent inward. The heavy concrete that had fallen against them had taken its toll. However, the seal of the door and the hinges and locks all appeared to be in relatively good condition.

Of course they could not further explore the mine until the police and whoever else connected with the accidental death of the construction worker had stopped visiting the area. Also they needed immediately to construct a good, solid building over the mine's entrance. Hans wanted this building windowless, very sturdy, and he wanted it built quickly. But he had to first convince himself that all of this effort was not in vain. He had to know that the underground cavern over which they stood still contained at least some of the fortune he had once guarded for the men of the Swastika.

"So when you hurt your head and the three of you left for the doctor in town, that was the last time you saw Mr. Burcheit. That was yesterday afternoon about 2:30?" the Inspector queried Hans at the mine site.

"*Ja*," said Hans. "*Ja*, that's the last time we saw him. And so today, later, I was going to stop by his house and pay him for the job. He was finished and gone when we came back from the doctor. I told him earlier I'd pay him at home if he was gone to the other jobs when we came back. He was in a hurry to finish here and go on to start his next job, but I don't know where that was. You say he didn't come home all night?"

The body of Mr. Burcheit, the contractor, had been found beneath the tractor by the bridge that morning. It had been noticed by a pedestrian walking across the bridge. He had paused and almost missed seeing the tractor off to the side, near the water's edge. Evidently Mr. Burcheit had lost control of his tractor. It plunged off the road, turned over, and crushed him beneath. The death was ruled an accident.

Hans Miller stopped by the Burcheit residence to deliver his payment for Mr. Burcheit's services later that day and to pay his condolences. The Millers then hurried off to Munich to find a good locksmith.

In Munich, Hans asked and was shown how to make a good wax impression so a key could be fashioned for each of the door's locks. He also purchased a quality oil for the hinges and a good lubricant to put into the locks. Back at the mine Hans and his sons made several wax impressions and returned them to Munich where new keys were promptly made. Pulleys, long ropes, a block and tackle, a large basket filled with two lanterns, and flashlights were procured and placed near the mineshaft. Finally, all was ready for the locks to be worked and the vault doors to be opened again.

Now, after all these years, coming back and standing here, Miller had a cold dread and fear, wondering if the football field sized mine would be empty or filled as he remembered it his last fateful visit so many years ago. *I have spent a great deal of money in this effort. We, Helga and I, have made so many sacrifices, and the legion of risky chances I have taken. Now, and now, mein Gott in Himmel, we have even murdered! It has all been a gamble up to this point. For years I have wondered whether the mine would still be filled with fantastic jewels and art and wealth beyond all dreams, or if this ancient salt mine will be completely empty. The countless nights I have lain awake wondering and worrying!* His hand was shaking so badly Karl had to help steady him and insert the first key into the lock. Initially, it seemed the key would not fit, but after several attempts and jiggling, the key went all the way inside the lock, fitting snugly.

Hans tried to turn the key, but the locking mechanism would not move.

"Goddammit, it has to work," shouted Miller. "Spray in some more lubricant! Spray more in both locks! There must be some grit and dirt particles clogging the tumblers. This has to work!"

Karl did as instructed and took the key from his nervous father, and inserted it again. He tried opening the lock several more times but the mechanism still resisted. Then, ever so slowly and reluctantly, it yielded and slid open. With a huge grin an even more nervous and excited Hans, with a shaking hand, inserted the second key. As with the first key, the second was sluggish sliding in, but once in, the lock's tumblers turned as quickly and silently as clockwork.

For the first time in over twelve years—the same number of years that the Third Reich had reigned, raped, slaughtered and ravaged—the vault doors to the Führer's personal cache were unlocked.

It took the three of them to open wide the rusty, heavy steel doors. Of course the generator and elevator could not be used, but in their stead the pulley and long coils of rope were employed to lower Hans, with flashlights and basket, to the bottom of the mine. It seemed to Hans to take three forevers before his feet finally touched earth beneath him. Though filled with anxiety and wonder, he had kept his eyes closed and purposely left the flashlight turned off during the long trip down. Now, standing firmly on the ground, he pushed the button on the large light in his hand, and the brilliant beam illuminated the top of the huge cavern.

Holding his breath and, with a shaking trembling hand, he lowered the light. In a voice choked with emotion he shouted, "*Ach, mein Gott!*" as the shaft of light revealed, once again, row upon row of bags he knew now to be filled with gold and other rare and precious coins. He surveyed boxes stacked six high as far as the light's beam would show, hundreds and hundreds of suitcases, large, wooden cloth-covered crates. *These crates must be the famous works of art I've read about having been discovered in other similar hiding places,* he thought to himself, nearly hysterical over his find. *But those storage areas—they were all different. They could not be compared to this. This most fantastic and vast secret holding was Adolf Hitler's personal prize! This belonged to the Führer himself! Incalculable wealth probably in the billions; magnificent art and other treasures beyond belief, imagination and description. And all of this still remaining just as I last saw it on that night I was shot and left for dead by the Nazi Doctor Krueger. And now, all of this is mine!*

Overwhelmed, and suddenly drenched in a cold sweat, Hans Miller sat down on one of the wooden crates and tried to catch his breath and to calm his palpitating heartbeat.

It took even longer to first haul up the basket with a bag of the gold coins and then Hans himself. The two boys helped considerably and, Miller sitting in the seat harness with the rope in the bend of his left arm, helped his sons hoist by pulling with his right hand.

On the way up he was determined that they would, on the morrow, remove the old generator and take it in his veterinarian friend's truck to have it made serviceable. They would also grease and service the old elevator and cable, for they would most certainly have need of their efficient operation. Busy times now lay ahead of them.

Arrangements were made and construction began immediately on their metal building. Lumber remained stacked on top of the mine's storm cellar type entrance doors, concealing them, during the work. A thick concrete foundation was poured for a twenty foot by forty-five foot steel structure. The building would have no windows and a heavy steel, roller-sliding type of door with two heavy duty locks. A four-inch thick concrete floor was poured after Hans, Karl and Otto laid forms and first poured the flooring closest to the mine's doors. The entrance to the mine was guardedly concealed. A bolt type iron bar would secure the door from the inside to keep out any unwanted visitors when the Millers were down working inside the mine. No trespassing signs had also been posted to discourage stoppersby. The building went up quickly and the outside and roof were painted a dark green to blend inconspicuously with the color of the tall pines and other surrounding trees in the forest. The generator was soon humming like a new sewing machine. The elevator worked superbly and the Millers installed new lights in the mine.

Although rather Spartan, the new building was furnished with the family's old couch, a storage cabinet for canned goods and other supplies, and a few other odd pieces. Hans' old upholstery table with skirting and four heavy-duty wheels hid from view the metal doors leading to the mine. With the wheels the table could easily be rolled away from the mine's entrance by a single individual. Several other original furnishings from the old farmhouse were stacked one on top of the other along the back wall. Hans removed large sections of the furniture's former coverings and stuffing, reinforced the framework and constructed boxed areas within the pieces where items from the mine could later be stored. Then the reupholstered pieces would ultimately be transported via ocean liner from Bremerhaven to the Miller residence in Tacoma, Washington.

The Millers went about their chores quickly and very efficiently. Their stay in Germany was rapidly drawing to a close. Hans had yet to finish up with several of the pieces of furniture he intended to use to smuggle some of the contraband back home. With that exception, and for a hurried visit to the Swiss Money Market, and to deposit in his Zürich account a respectable amount of Norwegian crowns and French francs, most of their work was done, for this trip, but there would be many more.

Chapter 16

Down by the Green Parrot Pub

It didn't take long before Phillip Hargrave and Steve became friends, despite the fact that Steve worked for Hargrave. The gap that divided lower rank from senior NCO was, by necessity, fully and completely respected. Steve always addressed the senior NCO as Sergeant Hargrave both in public and private. Master Sergeant Hargrave didn't suggest anything different.

Hargrave had the reputation of being a heavy drinker. He was capable, however, of handling his booze and maintaining himself so as not to discredit his grade and position. Alcoholic beverages were not permitted in the barracks, but that didn't seem to apply to MSgt Hargrave who had a well-stocked liquor cabinet in his room. His favorite drink was Cutty Sark Scots whiskey with the tiniest splash of water.

On a couple of occasions after Hargrave had had more than a few drinks in their billet, instead of addressing Steve as Scott which was his normal custom, he'd called him Lad or Laddie.

Use of that term seemed to demonstrate a liking for Steve by the senior NCO. After a fashion, Hargrave left a standing invitation for Steve to help himself if he cared for a drink. Steve had respectfully declined and, at the most, would only have a beer now and then when he went to the Green Parrot Pub or the Airman's Club with squadron friends.

Just outside Denham Studios, maybe a quarter mile from the Denham Village train station, was the Green Parrot Pub. A small tavern, and due to its close proximity to the USAF base, was always filled to capacity. Once a drink was served, it was almost necessary to hold your elbows in close to the body in order to have your drink without being bumped or jostled, causing the drink to spill. Friday and Saturday nights were the busiest.

The jukebox up near the bar played non-stop and to the Americans' delight had most of the latest hits from back home. Acceding to the requests of their young American customers, the English beer and lager, instead of being served warm the British way, was chilled in a walk-in cooler.

The Green Parrot was a well-known favored hangout of the Yanks and their lady friends. This did not bode well at all with a local gang of Teddy Boys who would go to various nearby towns looking for a Yank or two who were out on their own and easy targets for activity ranging from rough-housing to beatings and robbery.

These Teddy Boy gangs were made up of young male Brits wanting to show their defiance of law and order and their dislike of Americans living in their country. They dressed ostentatiously and very similar to the Zoot Suit U.S. style of the 1940s—exaggerated shoulder pads in their suit coats and jackets, and the long chain hanging from vest pocket to pants pocket.

They ordinarily avoided areas where American troops congregated in groups. They had previously taken on several of these GIs and found the Americans were not at all hesitant to fight back. The Yanks willingly gave them a proper scrap of it all and frequently resulted in the Teddy Boys coming out on the short end.

For this reason a small number of Teddy Boys had been cruising around the Green Parrot this particular late Saturday night in mid-December. There they saw Sergeant Hargrave walking, with a noticeable stagger, from the train station, past the Green Parrot, making his way back to the base.

The Sergeant had caught the 9:40 p.m. train from Marylebone after having spent the larger part of the late afternoon, early evening, and night at The Little Sweden near Soho. This was a small but popular district in Westminster, London, which was noted for its foreign restaurants, lounges, and clientele. In Little Sweden, Hargrave had been able to demonstrate his expert knowledge and usage of the German language to his favorite group of regulars in the lounge who spoke their native German, Swedish, Hungarian, and other languages.

Phillip was also using the occasion to further solidfy his relationship with Olga, the Nordic beauty, who had, in the past, appeared rather cool and standoffish to Phillip. As time progressed and his visits to the Lounge and his polite and respectful conversations with her became more frequent, Olga had begun to warm to Phillip and his courteous, but definite (even if sometimes comical) romantic efforts. Phillip just knew success was near! He had begun to ogle Olga with a libidinous eye.

The Sergeant departed the train at the Denham station and was a short distance beyond the Green Parrot when he heard running footsteps coming up behind him. He turned. . . .

It was near closing time and Glen, the manager of the Green Parrot, was trying to shout above Ferlin Huskey's recording of *Gone* on the jukebox. The loud talking and laughter in the Pub didn't help as he began to make his last call announcements.

"All right, all you Texans, Georgians, Californians, New Yorkers, Alabamians, and the rest of you Yank lot, order up now. This is your last call for the evening!"

It usually took Glen several calls to even get the GI's attention. Routinely, it would be another hour after that before he could get the Americans headed out the door. Closing the pub on weekends was always a chore.

"I'm gonna head on back to the base," Steve said to Arkee with Glen's first call. "I just stopped in for this one beer with you—gotta get back to the room and that darn course I'm taking."

"What is it?" Arkee asked.

"Philosophy and it's a booger! See ya later."

There'd been a moderate fog and slight drizzle earlier. Now, as Steve was making his way to the main gate of the base, a heavy fog began to roll in from the English Channel. Up ahead he saw a group of people, maybe four or five off the sidewalk a little ways. They appeared to be scuffling.

Steve had heard tales of the Teddy Boys in the area recently. One of the guys in the squadron had been beaten by several of them at the bus stop near the base just last weekend. Finding nothing available to use as a weapon, Steve stooped to pick up several good-sized rocks from the edge of the road. As he got nearer he yelled, "Hey, what's going on?"

The figures had been bending over. Hearing Steve, they straightened and one of them said, "Well, looks like we've gone and got us another Yank who'd like to get his head bashed proper like." Through the fog and mist Steve could see a figure lying prostrate and thought he heard a moan.

"Hey, okay, guys, I don't want any trouble. I'm just on my way back to the base," Steve shouted back.

"Well, like it or not, you've got our attention now Yank. We'll just give you a bit of what we've dealt your mate here!" the obvious leader of the gang said. They advanced toward him in a group.

Steve backed up and selected the largest stone he had. He hesitated for just a moment until they got nearer, and then he threw the rock as hard as he could into the middle of them. He heard a thunk sound and a groan. One of them dropped to the sidewalk. The remaining three paused. Steve quickly threw another stone.

"Wot the bloody hell? He's throwing stones at us!" With that they began to run at Steve. Steve quickly threw his remaining stone as hard as he could and then braced for the fight.

His last stones had had a modicum of success and the group of four was now a scattered line of just two in front. The third was on his knees and the fourth was sitting on the sidewalk. Steve ran at the leader and hit him with both a body block and a savage forearm to his head. The Teddy Boy went down immediately. Steve was off balance with the impact, but spun around as the second person was taking a boxer stance. Steve rammed into him as the gang member let fly with a swing at Steve.

The blow caught Steve on his left eye and nose. He saw stars, heard a strange roaring in his ears, and felt his nose gushing blood. Although staggered, Steve was able to grab his assailant. He enveloped the gang member in a headlock and squeezed as hard as he could. The roaring continued to grow inside Steve's head, and he felt himself becoming dizzy.

Afraid he would black out, he bent forward. Dropping to the ground he rammed the Teddy Boy's head into the hard turf alongside the concrete walk. Steve rose wobbly, stood for a minute, and caught his breath. He then kicked his assailant in the side and walked toward the third member.

That Teddy Boy raised himself from a squatting position with his right arm hanging limply. "That's enough for me mate. Me arm's gone right the way numb and I can't raise the bloody thing. Your stone hit me dead on in the shoulder."

Steve went to the fourth assailant who was still on his knees. His forehead was bloodied and he was mumbling incoherently. Deciding to check the injured man, Steve was surprised to find the person lying off in the grass was Sergeant Hargrave! He knelt and rested the Sergeant's head on his knee. Hargrave's face had been pounded, and he was bleeding from his eyes, nose, right ear, mouth, and had cuts on his cheeks. His head had been resting in a growing puddle of blood from a large gash on the back of his head. Steve took out his handkerchief and dabbed at the wounds.

"Sarge, are you okay? Sergeant Hargrave can you hear me?"

No response.

As he was closer to the Green Parrot than he was the base, Steve decided he would get help from the pub. He stood and found those of the gang that could walk were making their way across the street. The fog swallowed them up once they were halfway across the road.

Steve passed the leader who was moaning and trying to rise and paused just long enough to kick him in the rib cage. The leader went down hard again with an explosion of air from his lungs and probably a broken rib or two.

Steve ran to the pub and once inside grabbed Arkee; he quickly told him of the problem, and then hurried back to Sergeant Hargrave.

Arkee, moments after telling the pub owner Glen to call an ambulance, hurried to help Steve. Several others from the Postal Squadron and pub were soon standing around Steve and Sergeant Hargrave. The Teddy Boys had evidently collected their leader and disappeared into the fog after Steve ran to the Green Parrot for help. Glen and Martin, the pub's head bartender, used the mass exodus from the bar to hastily close the Green Parrot. They turned off the lights, locked the doors, and hurried out to see if they could help Steve and the others.

A medic was attending to Sergeant Hargrave who was on a stretcher in the back of the ambulance. Steve was beside the driver in the front seat. With lights flashing and siren wailing, they were enroute to the USAF Hospital at South Ruislip. It was a thirty-minute drive from Denham and Sergeant Hargrave had lost a dangerously large amount of blood.

The dense fog made the trip much slower. It'd been a busy night at the USAF Hospital Emergency Room. An automobile accident at the round-about near Harrow had earlier filled that room with three survivors and put a fourth in the morgue. One of the survivors, with the rare blood type O-Negative, had nearly exhausted the hospital's supply of that blood group. It appeared doubtful that he would survive the night.

At the hospital Hargrave was examined and X-rayed. He had a severe concussion in addition to the gash on the back of his head and the many lesser cuts and lumps he'd received at the hands of the gang. A nurse began an I.V. and pressure bandages were applied to his wounds to stop the bleeding. He was still unconscious and badly in need of a blood trans-fusion. His dog tags revealed his blood type to be O-Negative.

An emergency call was made to the nearest hospital and several units were being rushed to aid Hargrave. The fog, distance, poor driving condi-tions, and the Sergeant's massive loss of blood concerned the medical staff. He was given the last of the O-Negative available, but it wasn't nearly enough. An announcement was made over the P.A. system asking for any O-Negative donors.

The medical team was also examining Steve. His nose was broken and the cut above his eye had been reopened. When he learned of Sergeant Hargrave's problem he checked his dog tags. He had been told his own blood type, but like most, had not paid much attention to it. He was surprised to learn that his was O-Negative also. Steve was immediately prepped and within minutes his blood was flowing into the veins of Sergeant Hargrave.

A corpsman cleaned the blood from Steve. His nose was taped. His eyebrow was stitched up again, and he was told he could ride back to Denham with the ambulance. Steve declined and asked if he could remain near Sergeant Hargrave. He was given a chair next to the Sergeant's bed.

It was nearing 0400 when Hargrave began to stir. He mumbled a few words, and Steve immediately summoned the doctor. Hargrave came to with a splitting headache and cursing. His hangover probably bothered him as much as the beating he'd taken. He didn't remember a thing relating to the incident. He was given a sedative and went immediately back into a deep sleep; then he was moved from the recovery ward to a two-man room. Steve remained constantly by his side.

Later, in his ward room, Phillip looked at Steve.

"The corpsmen told me what you've done for me. My thanks to you laddie, for coming to my rescue. That took courage, and you paid the piper for your efforts on my behalf. I'll not forget that. Maybe some day I can do you a favor."

"No thanks needed, Sergeant Hargrave. Anyone would have done the same."

"I'm not so certain of that, lad."

"No one's ever called me Lad or Laddie before. Sounds what? Scottish maybe?"

"Sorry. If it bothers you, I'll not repeat it."

"No, no. It's not that at all. In fact I kinda like it. I've just never had anyone other than you call me by that name before."

"Years ago," said Hargrave, "when my mother and father first returned with me to the States, we lived near Hattiesburg, Mississippi. There was a kind, old black gentleman there who used to take care of our lawn and garden. He was sort of like a handyman. He'd call me laddie. Guess that's where I picked that up.

"Anyway, by the by we became good friends. His children would come over and play with me. Sometimes they'd stay all day while their father worked. His children affectionately called him Pappy. After awhile I began to call him Pappy as well.

"Your calling me Sergeant Hargrave all the time sounds so damn formal, especially now that we've become friends, blood brothers of a sort, and the two Fighting Vigilante Yanks of Denham Studios—although rather one-sided—namely you. I propose, and certainly only with your concurrence, that my nickname for you be Lad and that yours for me might be Pappy?

Obviously, I'm not all that much older than you, but I've always been rather fond of that moniker, and only the good Lord knows when I'll have a family of my own. I don't want to embarrass you with this and will understand if you'd prefer otherwise."

"Well, now that the Doc says you're doing fine and will be out of here in a couple of days, guess I'll catch the bus back to the base. Doc also said you shouldn't talk too much, and we've probably already talked more than we should've. I'll see you tomorrow Pappy. Rest well."

He placed his hand on Hargrave's shoulder and Pappy quickly covered Steve's hand with his own. He patted Steve's hand lightly once, twice, smiled and quietly said, "Thank you, laddie."

At that moment a bond of friendship between the two men was forged. It was the beginning of a strong friendship and a lifetime relationship that would jointly share unlimited trust and devotion to one another—one that would know no constraints.

London's Monday morning newspaper, *The Daily Inquisitor*, headline read: *"Yanks in Guest Houses Shouldn't Throw Stones."* Beneath the caption was a photograph of the Teddy Boy Gang leader. The photograph had obviously been taken upon his arrival at the hospital. His head and clothing were bloody, and he was supported by the other members of the gang. They hardly looked better than their leader, some even worse. Beneath the photograph the story read:

Timothy Walden of Rickmansworth and three of his mates were set upon by a wild stone-throwing Yank near Denham Studios this past Saturday night. Walden and his friends were standing at the bus stop near Denham Station when suddenly they were bombarded by an unknown assailant. Within moments after being struck by the flying stones, Walden and his friends were beaten and kicked by a group of Yanks who had been summoned from the nearby Green Parrot Pub. Walden, shown here in the center, had two fractured ribs in addition to numerous head wounds from the savage beating. The attack was unprovoked, unwarranted and, unfortunately, once again serves to remind us that we do have a price to pay for allowing young, unruly Americans to remain as guests in our country. The identity of the stone tossing Yank is being investigated. The Commander of the USAF Forces at Denham Studios will have a statement with tomorrow's paper.

By Monday afternoon Steve had been identified as the "stone throwing Yank." The Base Commander had already issued his statement that the culprit of the incident: "Staff Sergeant Steve Scott was restricted to the base and that other punitive measures have already been initiated." When asked what those measures were, the Commander responded, "An Article 15 under our Uniform Code of Military Justice or perhaps a Court Martial." He assured the British press that the punishment would be correct and swift, and he apologized profusely for the incident. The press acknowledged that these kinds of incidents were rare and that, unfortunately again, there's always a bad apple mixed in with the rest of the good lot.

Tuesday afternoon, against his doctor's advice, Pappy along with Steve, First Sergeant Gage and Major David Ekridge, Steve's Squadron Commander, all met with an irate USAF Commander of Denham Studios, Colonel Chester L. Howard. All his guests saluted the Colonel and stood at attention upon entering. The Commander told all but Steve to have a seat.

He left him standing at attention.

Colonel Howard began: "I assume you have all seen or heard about the news coverage our hero here has earned for us?" Not waiting for a response he continued, "This rock throwing spree of yours has done irreparable damage to our otherwise good US/UK relations. You just can't seem to stay out of trouble can you, boy?"

"Sir, I'd like to explain—" Steve began, but was cut off abruptly by the Commander.

"Just stand there and shutup! I know your kind. I've had lots of thugs like you to deal with. You're given every break possible, and you have no appreciation. No respect. Assholes like you are a dime a dozen. I don't know why we even bother! All your kind wanna do is booze and fight. In your case though, I gotta admit that I was surprised to see that you've been through OCS and you've nearly completed your college degree. Shame you couldn't stay clean. You mighta made something of yourself. You pissed her away good, didn't you boy? Dumb. Dumb!" He continued his angry attack.

"Coincidence I guess, but a timely one, my receiving this letter yesterday from the Sheriff of Wadhigh County, Missouri. It was addressed on the outside to Commander, Denham Studios, but the inside letter was addressed to you, Major Ekridge. In any case Scott, it tells of yet another incident where you were fighting and put someone else in the hospital. You have a history of fighting, don't you boy? No discipline. No respect!"

Pappy interrupted and said, "Colonel, this is all a big misunderstanding. This young man came to my rescue. That gang of Teddy Boys may have killed me if it weren't for Sergeant Scott. I could, probably would have, been killed. He didn't attack them, they attacked him. I just got out of the hosp—"

"Don't bother trying to defend him, Sergeant. I know you two are roommates; it's obvious—"

"Commander, we haven't met but I am Sergeant Scott's First Sergeant and I've looked into this incident. May I speak sir?" Gage asked.

"Make it short, Sergeant. I'm on a tight schedule thanks to all the press and higher headquarters' concerns over this mess."

"Sergeant Hargrave is correct in what he's saying. I've talked to the proprietor and bartender at the Green Parrot Pub. I've also talked to several others who were there Saturday night. Hargrave was knocked unconscious and was being beaten by the gang when Scott came upon them. I've learned that two of the four gang members have admitted that they were the instigators and the press may shortly have a retraction. I'd like to suggest that you wait until we've gotten to the bottom of all this before you pursue UCMJ, a court-martial, or any other punitive action against Scott."

"Okay Sergeant. Nice speech. Are you through now?"

"Yessir."

"Then I suggest you and Sergeant Hargrave here get your asses up and outta my office. I'm sick and tired of Senior NCOs who think they're running the goddam military. If I need your advice on how to handle a situation under my command, I'll ask for it. I know all I need to know, and this Sergeant is gonna be busted!"

Gage, smoldering with anger, stared at Howard and said, "Commander, you, sir, are making a big mistake."

The Base Commander's face reddened. "That's enough out of you Sergeant! Who the fuck do you think you are to talk to me like that? One more word and I'm damned if I won't have your ass up on charges too. Get out of here, all three of you! Major Ekridge, you remain!"

Major Ekridge had silently taken all this in with a smug, satisfied grin. He was still chaffing over his initial conversation with MSgt Gage. He had reservations because of Gage's rumored relationship with Lieutenant General Berg, but he had some doubts about that as well. Both inwardly and outwardly he was pleased to see Sergeant Gage being raked over the coals by Colonel Howard. He had no concern regarding Sergeant Scott's predicament one way or another.

As soon as the three sergeants left, Colonel Howard turned to Major Ekridge.

"Dave, you're Scott's immediate commander, so it's up to you to determine the punishment. I'd like to see an Article 15 with a reduction in rank, and I'd like to tell that to the press if that's okay with you."

"If that's what you want sir, it's fine by me. I'll get started on the paperwork right away."

"And Dave," Colonel Howard concluded, "what about Sergeant Scott's pending commission and request for marriage?"

"That's shit-canned as of now. I'll start a letter on both as soon as I get back to my office."

"Good. Let me know if you need anything from me."

On their way back to the Orderly Room a subdued Steve said, "It didn't go well, but I want to thank you both for standing up for me. I'm grateful for your support and I'm sorry the Commander wouldn't listen to us. Seems like he's got a deaf ear and already made up his mind on all this."

"That's for certain lad. Also, the bugger seems to me to excel more than most at being a proper bastard," Pappy said.

"Yeah," said Gage, "'fraid you're both right." He patted Steve on the shoulder. "But don't give up on things just yet. And don't sign any disciplinary paperwork. In fact, don't sign anything unless you talk to Sergeant Hargrave or me first, okay?"

"Okay," responded a disheartened Steve.

Once in the privacy of his office, MSgt Gage placed a priority call to Lieutenant General R.P. Berg at the Pentagon in Washington, D.C.

"I'm sorry Sergeant Gage," the General's Executive Officer said, "General Berg is at Hickam Air Force Base in Honolulu. He was called by CINCPACAF for an emergency meeting. He'll be over there for three days. Can this wait or do you want me to patch you through to him?"

A sleepy Inspector General of the United States Air Force answered his bedside phone on the second ring.

"General Berg here."

"Rufus, this is Cal. We've got a problem . . . ." said Sergeant Gage.

The Wednesday morning's *Inquisitor* had an article on page 3a that read:
Banner Retraction: Upon further investigation of our Monday morning's lead article concerning the supposed stoning and beating of Timothy Walden of Rickmansworth, we add the following: It appears the American, Staff Sergeant Steve Scott, who was accused of throwing the stones in this incident, was, in fact, defending himself when he was attacked. This has been corroborated by two of the four involved in the fracas. Further,

*the four British youths were not set upon by other
Americans as previously reported in error. We are both
embarrassed and disturbed by the prior erroneous report
and apologize to all concerned. We point out with this
apology that this might indeed be a good time to pause and
reflect on the outstanding good relations the United States
and Great Britain have enjoyed for many thankful years,
both in peacetime and in war.*

The Air Police guard at the entrance to Denham Studios was
surprised to see the three star flag waving as he snapped to attention,
saluted smartly, and waved the sedan of the Commander of Third Air
Force on base. Normally, guards had prior notice when flag officers
were inbound.

The general's car pulled up in front of the Studios at the entrance to
the Base Commander's Office. The gate guard hurried inside and was
straightening his post. He quickly substituted his brilliantly shined
garrison hat for the run-of-the-mill one he had been wearing. He
donned his handsome USAFE neck scarf and arm cuff. He was giving
everything the once over, when, fifteen minutes later, the General's car,
flag still showing, indicating the general was yet a passenger, exited
the base.

"Damn, that was a short visit," the guard said putting his bright and
shiny articles back inside the wall locker.

By that afternoon word had spread like wildfire. Colonel Chester L.
Howard had been relieved on the spot from duty as USAF Commander
of Denham Studios. The Deputy Base Commander was now acting
commander. Also, Captain Earl Keene had been appointed as
Commander, Third Air Postal Squadron, replacing Major David
Ekridge who had likewise been fired and relieved. Both of these
actions were effective immediately.

Chapter 17
Mistaken Identity

Captain John Clemont flew into Milan, Italy, and as always breezed past all customs officials by flashing his ARFCOS credentials and handcuffed attaché case with the appropriate form declaration affixed. From prior visits he was well acquainted with the airport and the car rental locations. He leased a Porsche and headed directly for the USAF Annafiorno Air Base, which was north of Milan, near the Swiss border in breathtakingly beautiful country.

With this stop he had planned, requested, and received ARFCOS permission to vacation in the area for four days. Captain Clemont had already reserved his Swiss type chalet near Lake Como. He felt good about having made prior arrangements with Carla, a gorgeous and sexy Italian woman. This would be their third and longest interlude. A little over a month ago the couple had enjoyed a brief stay together when he was there accompanied by his boss, Captain Karl Miller, during an overnight courier drop.

On that prior occasion Clemont arrived in Milan first. He rented an automobile and delivered his courier material to the appropriate U.S. Navy office. He then reserved a hotel room for himself and another for his boss and returned to the airport later in the day to meet his boss' incoming flight.

Miller had joined Clemont in Milan after having made a hurried, diverted trip to the Salzdorf mine. He deplaned carrying two sealed ARFCOS bags—one contained some highly classified documents which Clemont would courier from Milan to Jidda, Saudi Arabia, the next day— the other bag contained a miniature sixteenth century painting, 'Portrait of Charlemagne,' which was destined for Miller's Milan art dealer. Clemont, of course, knew nothing of Miller's blackmarketing operation; nor had he mentioned to Carla that he was meeting with his boss, Miller on that trip.

A blossoming romance and nothing having to do with business or Miller was the only burning issue on Clemont's mind that previous stop. While

John Clemont and Carla renewed their acquaintance over dinner, drinks and later, a lively romp in the rack in her hotel room, Miller had met with his art dealer at a secluded park.

The dealer was waiting inside his car parked beneath a glowing park light. Miller blinked the headlights twice as he pulled Clemont's rental car to a halt in back of the other car and with the painting in hand he swung open the car door. The pre-arranged transaction took but minutes and as the art dealer turned, excited and happy with his purchase, he noted and memorized the sticker on the rental car's front windscreen. Back in his car he quickly jotted the name of the rental agency, the make, model and license number of Clemont's vehicle.

It was not at all difficult for the Mafia boss who purchased the Charlemagne portrait to learn later that an American USAF officer, Captain John Clemont was the person who had leased the car, and obviously transported and sold the stolen Nazi painting. The Mafia, through its underground connections, had learned of the selling of masterpiece paintings, fabulous pieces of sculpture and other rare objets d'art, known to have been stolen during the war by members of the Third Reich. They had alerted all their contacts to be vigilant for any foreigners who might be considered a conduit for that form of blackmarketing. Those contacts included the art dealer and, by chance, a beautiful Mafia prostitute named Carla who frequented popular tourist hotels. The same Carla who now, a month later, was on Clemont's mind from the moment his commercial flight had wheeled up and left London Heathrow's air traffic pattern headed for Milan.

The four o'clock afternoon sun re-emerged after a short but heavy rain shower. Captain John Clemont noted with pleasure that the tiled roof tops, the cobblestone roads, the walks, and all the wet surfaces were tinted a buttery yellow hue. The grandeur of a magnificent rainbow was heightened all the more by the dark blue, almost black sky, behind it. This contrasted beautifully with the golden haze of the setting sun. The freshness caused by the rain and the deep green of the trees, lawns, and fields were all exhilarating. It gave the area a feeling of undiminished cleanliness. He was excited thinking about being with Carla in the chalet, yet he was thoroughly relaxed in the lovely setting. But duty first, and he had some ARFCOS classified to deliver.

The Captain's drive to Annafiorno Air Base was pleasant. He had no reason to check, and thus did not notice, the black car following him at a considerable distance. The black car had immediately pulled off the side of the road and stopped when the Captain parked briefly, once out of Milan. Clemont unlocked the handcuff and the courier bag, removed the article he would need later, then resecured the locks. The black car resumed its tail when the Captain continued on toward the base.

At the USAF Post Office Registry Cage the transfer of classified materials went well. Clemont, as usual, retained the now empty courier bag in the event he might need it to again bypass customs with his return trip. He might still have something he didn't want the officials to view or possibly confiscate from his personal luggage.

It was early evening when he parked next to the chalet office, registered, and collected the key. He made certain his room telephone was activated, then removed and closeted his military uniform. Naked, he lay down on the bed to wait for the lovely Carla to call. He was dozing lightly when the phone rang.

In her beautiful, lilting accent Carla said, "I'm calling you from a telephone kiosk near Lecco."

"It's great to hear your voice again, Carla. I'm excited already thinking about your being here. Where is Lecco? How far is that from Lake Como?"

"It isn't far, perhaps thirty or forty klicks. I should be there shortly. How long can you stay this time?"

"We have four wonderful days and nights ahead of us. Much, much better than the last two overnighters huh?"

"Yes darling, I'm looking forward to it and I, too, am excited to be so near to you again."

"Hurry then. I've brought you a gift that I'm anxious for you to see. Oh, and if you aren't that far away, I may still be in the shower when you arrive, so just come on in. The back door will be unlocked. We're in Chalet number five. It's the last one near the edge of the woods. Just drive right past the office and follow the curve of the road. See you soon."

When he emerged nude from the bathroom a short while later he was surprised to find all the lights off in the chalet. He had left the desk lamp and the two bedside table lights on when he went for his shower. He was also surprised to find himself walking, very tentatively, on what appeared to be a thin sheathing of plastic that had been placed on the floor.

Envisioning her lying nude on the bed, he said delightedly, "Carla, you did get here fast. But why are all the lights off, and what's this plastic on the floor? Carla?"

A small light, as from a pen type flashlight, flicked on from the settee in the far corner of the room as the Captain's arms were roughly grabbed and pinned behind his back.

"What the fuck's happenin—" Captain Clemont tried to ask as he was savagely struck in the stomach doubling him over and then just as savagely hit on the side of his face, the blow gashing his left jaw and knocking out three of his teeth.

Someone lit the desk lamp. Its glow showed the Captain doubled over and being held from falling by two men holding each of his arms. Blood poured from his fractured jaw and jagged mouth wound. The blood splattered onto his feet and the plastic sheet he was standing on. He raised his head slightly and saw the clenched fist of the figure in front of him. The fist was encased in a cestus, a covering of leather straps with pieces of metal that looked like heads of bolts protruding from several pieces of the leather. These things were worn by life or death combatants in the gladiator days of ancient Rome.

The Captain was nearly unconscious and his head was swirling, dizzy. He felt nauseous. The space where his teeth had been knocked out felt as big as a cave when he ran his tongue over the area. It was through a heavy fog he heard people talking.

"Did you find anything in the luggage?"

"Yes, it looks like a piece of jewelry. A large piece. A necklace with huge stones, perhaps emeralds, rubies and with diamonds," said the cognoscenti, the Mafia connoisseur of art. "However, it doesn't feel authentic—maybe high grade costume—but it's impossible to say in this light."

"Is that all? Is there nothing more? No sculptures, paintings, or coins? What about the car?"

Another voice answered, "We've checked the car. There's nothing. And there's nothing more in this room. That piece of jewelry and the lira in his wallet and the dresser drawer. That's all."

The person that seemed to be in charge, the one asking the questions, stepped in front of the Captain and smacked him hard on the left side of his battered face.

With his head drooped downward blood flowed from the gaping wound in the American's mouth. He raised his head to look at the person who'd hit him; he then choked and coughed. The Italian cursed and jumped back.

Too late. Some blood from the Captain's mouth dotted his expensive suit cuffs and shoes.

"Hit him again!" the Italian shouted, and the leather and metal encased fist tore off the upper portion of the Captain's lip and knocked out two more of his teeth. Mercifully, he slumped into unconsciousness.

The Captain awoke when they poured cold water onto his face. He was lying on his back in his blood and void and he felt excruciating pain in his mouth, head, and testicles.

"Not what you expected, is it Captain? By now you had visions of being between the lovely Carla's thighs, buried snugly in her gorgeous bush of dark, pubic hair, with her moaning pleasantly in your ear, and her legs wrapped tightly around you. That's what you expected. However . . ." and the Italian nodded to one of his cohorts, "instead—"

The Captain screamed until his mouth was gagged as a tremendous tightening and squeezing was administered to his scrotum. The pressure remained for several moments and was then relaxed. Once again, waves of nausea swept over him and now a numbing pain paralyzed his right side. The Italian spoke softly, but the tone of his voice was chilling.

"All right Captain, I will ask you this only once. I expect to have your full and complete cooperation and truthfulness with your immediate response. These magnificent artworks that you are black marketing, where are they stored and to whom do they belong?"

"You crazy son-of-a-bitch, you've got the wrong—" and again the beginning of a scream was muffled by the gag being replaced as the Captain's testicles were slowly squashed together in a box-like vice.

It took longer this time, and several dousings of cold water to revive the Captain. In great pain and rolling waves of nausea, he awoke to the sharp point of a stiletto being pressed against his jugular vein. He was standing, though swaying, and being supported under his arms by two thugs who stood on either side.

"Not very smart Captain. The piece of jewelry you were bringing to Carla belies your denial that you are not the individual we seek. You gain nothing but pain by lying to us. Now, you and this room stink, and I have grown weary of being here. You have only one more chance to answer—"

Clemont attempting to get his naked footing beneath him slipped in the puddle of his own blood and waste. He fell forward bringing the two at his side with him. They collided with the assailant who was standing directly in front of them. Surprised, the Mafia leader jerked backwards, but his hand still holding the stiletto slit the Captain's throat from ear to ear. He had not intended to do this.

Captain Clemont died within moments, and the last words he heard were the shoutings and cursings of the Mafia members in the room. They were swearing at the person with the knife for killing their only known source to the German loot.

The Italians rolled the Captain's body in the plastic, secured it tightly with metal bands and a chain. They put his body in the car trunk and drove it to a deserted part of the lake's edge. There they put the body in a boat and rowed it out to the middle of the lake where the corpse, weighted with concrete blocks, was dropped over the side.

In the chalet office, the day's registration slip was removed and burned. Another without Clemont's name on it was substituted. The Captain's rented Porsche was driven to a back alley in Torino, the inside doused with gasoline and set afire.

At that moment nearly seven thousand miles away in Tacoma, Washington, Karl Miller, the USAF Captain the Mafia assassins had sought was resting comfortably. He was eagerly anticipating his momentary return to Europe, to see and walk again among the most fantastic wealth and art ever collected. This biggest and grandest prize had been personally obtained for and belonged to the Führer himself! And now it was his—the thought caused the blood coursing through his veins to tingle.

Miller thought too of his undeniable appetite for the special thrills he experienced on those occasions when he had tortured and murdered. He derived an intense sensual pleasure in killing—it was sort of like having an orgasm, a fantastically wonderful orgasm. That appetite was growing and seemed insatiable. *What the hell*, he thought while holding his father's military medal, the German Iron Cross that he now wore on a gold chain around his neck, *everyone has secret demons, mine just happen to be the best!*

Chapter 18

The Newcomer's Briefing

All base newcomers from full Colonel down to Airman Basic were required to attend the two-hour quarterly Newcomer's Orientation.

This mandatory meeting explained everything concerning the fact that all U.S. personnel in the United Kingdom were, basically, guests of that country and therefore should always obey all English laws, practices, customs, and courtesies. The briefing also covered the practice of driving on the opposite side of the road, different from what Americans were used to, and pointed out that while Americans, supposedly, spoke the English language, there were many noticeable American differences. Some of these, the newcomers were told, could offend their British hosts.

Briefed, too, were the dangers of the common Pea Souper fogs, British holidays, Black marketing, Scrip (military money), U.S. Greenback dollars, English currency, social diseases, and Off Limits areas.

Pappy told acting Commander Keene he would accompany First Sergeant Gage and Sergeant Danbury's new clerk, Heather MacVickar, to the quarterly meeting at the Headquarters' Third Air Force Conference Room at South Ruislip Air Base that Monday morning.

"Good idea Phil," responded the Captain, "and while you're over at Ruislip, how about you and Sergeant Gage stopping by and looking at the building they're offering us for use as our new ARFCOS Detachment?"

Pappy said he'd be happy to do that. He rounded up and loaded Gage and Heather into his new twelve hundred dollar Volkswagen and headed for Ruislip. Pappy fussed all the way during the drive trying to get the Blaupunkt radio in his dash to work. It had a loose connection and played only intermittently.

By the time Pappy found a parking space, and they reached the theater conference room, the doors had just closed. As Pappy reached for the door handle, a full Colonel appeared out of nowhere. He grasped the Sergeant's wrist and said quietly, "Please follow me." The three were led through a side door and into a dimly lit hallway. The Colonel said in a low voice, "We'll explain this in a moment or two."

Finally they rounded a corner and came to another door, this one guarded by an armed Air Policeman. He was standing at parade rest but snapped to attention, stepped aside, and opened the door in one quick movement.

The three found themselves in the plush conference room of the Commander of Third Air Force, Lieutenant General Leslie Putnam. General Putnam was standing beside his overstuffed chair at the head of a beautiful cherrywood conference table. A movie screen extended from the ceiling to the floor on the opposite wall. A 35mm projector was humming softly. The General offered his right hand to Airman MacVickar and said, "Nice to see you again Cathy. How are things going?"

"Just fine, thank you, Sir. I'm settling in nicely."

"That's good," said General Putnam. He added, "You may as well take the position nearest the projector as we need to get on with this briefing. We want to get you three back into the Newcomer's Orientation Meeting as soon as possible."

Turning to the First Sergeant and grasping his hand, the General said "Sergeant Gage, pleasure to see you again, too. Have you spoken with Moose lately?" Moose was also known as Lt. General R. Peter Berg, the USAF Inspector General.

Gage, returning the firm handshake said, "Yessir, weekly, and he sends his regards."

The General turned to Pappy. "Sergeant Hargrave, rather, Mr. Hargrave, I suspect some of this may be a bit of a surprise to you, but, hopefully, most of it will be explained shortly with the briefings we'll receive."

General Putnam hurriedly introduced Gage and Hargrave to several others in the room whose names the two sergeants would try to recall later. They did remember two offices associated with the strangers as being Interpol and Scotland Yard.

"On behalf of the U.S. Government," General Putnam announced to the gathering, "I would like to welcome you to Headquarters, Third Air Force. We have been asked to host this meeting due to our secure location, aircraft landing strip and global network of communications. We are pleased and honored by your presence and look forward to working with each of you and your activities on this sensitive matter. Please, everyone, help yourself to coffee or tea if you wish, and have a seat." General Putnam then introduced the Interpol spokesman who added his welcome and told the gathering that due to time constraints on the USAF briefers, they would be the first to present.

"Miss Moberly, will you begin then?" the gentleman from Interpol concluded.

Flicking a switch on the projector, Cathy, a.k.a. Airman Second Class Heather MacVickar picked up a briefing pointer, and nodded to the full Colonel in the back of the room as he dimmed the lights. In her crisp Scottish accent, Cathy began.

"Gentlemen, this briefing is classified Top Secret. My name is First Lieutenant Catherine Moberly, Special Agent with the USAF Office of Special Investigations. I am working as an undercover operative assigned, as some of you know, to the Third Air Postal Squadron with the USAF at Denham Studios, Buckinghamshire."

Pappy looked at Gage, raised his eyebrows and smiled as if to say, "I'll be damned. She sure had me fooled."

Gage smiled back. He raised his hand touching his thumb and index finger together forming an "O" indicating "Top Drawer—this young lady!"

Cathy continued. "I will be briefing you on the classified operation dealing with the recovery of precious gems, artifacts, paintings, rare manuscripts, coins, books, gold bullion, currency, and other valuables amounting to untold millions, perhaps billions, looted by members of Adolf Hitler's Third Reich during the period from 1938 to 1945. This operation has been assigned the Codename DROPHAMMER, which is, by itself, classified SECRET/NOFORN-DISSEM. The Unclassified Nickname is CABLE-TOW. CABLE-TOW will be used in all cases to inform of operation activities for meetings like this one. Also for notices of art and other DROPHAMMER black marketing transactions, pending or completed, as well as for individual contacts between ourselves and the following offices who have each been briefed on the operation.

"This slide shows you the listing of those U.S. and friendly foreign activities/agencies involved in Codename DROPHAMMER thus far." She slid a dark blue view-graph with black printing onto the projector. It read:

SECRET/NOFORN-DISSEM

Countries/Agencies Involved with DROPHAMMER

United States:	Foreign:
Department of Defense	INTERPOL
CIA	U.K.Scotland Yard
Secret Service	Germany Kriminal-Polizei
Customs	Customs
FBI	British Field Security Service (FSS)
U.S. Army Counter-Intelligence (CIC)	British MI5 Security Service

SECRET/NOFORN-DISSEM

GROUP 1
EXEMPT FROM DOWNGRADING

The slide was self-explanatory. Cathy continued. "All possible measures have been taken to restrict knowledge of the operation for obvious reasons. Only those with critical Need-To-Know criteria have been briefed."

"Excuse me please, Lieutenant," (he pronounced it Left-tenant) interrupted the English gentleman from Scotland Yard. He pointed to the slide with his large Meerschaum pipe, which emitted a very pleasant, sweet odor of tobacco. "Do I understand the British War Ministry has not been made privy to this?"

"It is my understanding the Ministry has been briefed, but a specific office or department to work with us on this has not, at the moment, been identified," Cathy responded and continued. "Hopefully by our next meeting we will be joined by their representative and our slide will then be updated. Thank you for the question, sir.

"We have reason to suspect that a member or members of the U.S. Air Force and/or our U.S. friendly military allies may possibly be engaged in efforts to disperse and sell portions of the Nazi loot alluded to above.

"For some time now Customs and Law Enforcement agencies have been tightening all border and port inspections in efforts to apprehend a new rash of black marketing dealings. Thus far these attempts have met with no success."

"Did those inspections include ocean going vessels and large item cargo loads from international flights as well?" questioned the man with the pipe again.

"Yessir, they did and I have some related comments on that. The majority of the items being smuggled are known to be a part of the Nazi contraband just mentioned," Cathy continued. "With the exception of items turning up in England and Scotland, the art, sculptures, porcelains, and such have all been small in size, dimensions, which would lend themselves to concealment in attaché cases and smaller luggage pieces. Currently, just why the larger pieces, mostly paintings by Old Masters, are turning up only here in the U.K. and not elsewhere on the continent, is a puzzle to us. However, we suspect one possible answer may be the items are brought into the country via military, postal, or courier channels, thus avoiding international custom searches. More on that in a moment."

"I'm curious as to what sort of confirmed Nazi loot might be turning up elsewhere on the continent," Pappy said.

"And that shall be addressed by this Operation's lead agency and our Interpol representative who will follow me shortly." Cathy said with a smile. "The works of Rembrandt, Monet, Van Gogh, and other pieces of art known to have been confiscated by the Nazis, have recently been seen, or mysteriously reported to have been seen in areas near USAF and other military bases. That is another reason for our heavy concentration on the military postal/courier and embassy activities.

"We suspect the larger items may possibly have been shipped into England either via postal channels or hidden aboard military equipment. Undercover operations with all European military postal and courier activities have been implemented simultaneously."

Another participant questioned, "I assume then all military equipment such as automobiles, trucks, heavy equipment and so forth, U.S. and Allied, are given a close search?"

"Yessir, to the fullest degree possible—everything is being looked at. However, with this, we do have some sensitive areas that mandate we tread lightly. Our country-to-country agreements have granted diplomatic courier status to our military couriers. They, as well as our respective Embassy and other diplomatic couriers enjoy, of course, unrestricted ease of international travel. Presently, it is impossible to monitor that courier activity. We're hopeful our various undercover initiatives will be productive. We shall, of course, keep you advised on all of this."

All attention in the room was immediately focused on the Scotland Yard official who accidentally banged his pipe in the ashtray trying to empty its burnt contents. "Sorry," he said. "It slipped out of my hand."

"Initial, small steps," Cathy continued, "have been taken to determine if, with the cooperation of all participating friendly foreign nations, and in the presence of an in-country embassy representative, a one-time stop and search without opening any sealed packages of diplomatic and military courier bags is possible. This is being explored via the appropriate diplomatic channels."

The English Customs official asked, "Is this operation, ring, or whatever, suspected to be of a considerable and widely-spread size then?"

"Quite frankly sir, at this point, we have absolutely no idea as to the composition or numbers of those involved," Cathy answered, then returned to speaking to the group at large.

"Through our web of international contacts we, again with Interpol acting as point in all matters, have alerted law enforcement and customs agencies throughout Europe to be on the lookout for contraband, with an emphasis on Old Master works of art, pictures, drawings, statues, figurines, also rare coins and books, the majority of which have not been seen since 1938. Some of these precious items have already surfaced, as indicated on this slide, in Athens, Paris, Madrid and Naples, and the western United

States. Most all of this, with the exception of the U.S. West Coast, has appeared within the past two years."

Cathy put her pointer down. She looked at each man present. "This operation has the highest U.S. Executive, Judicial and DoD levels of interest as well as that of our European Allied counterparts. We must maintain the utmost level of secrecy in all our actions regarding this operation. For the USAF, I shall be your point of contact for any emergency or follow-on meetings."

Cathy then reintroduced the Interpol and Scotland Yard officials who briefed on their offices' involvement and concerns. After the foreign officials, Cathy was again given the floor.

"In the space of time we've been allotted this morning, this concludes our initial briefing. Are there any further questions, gentlemen?"

There were several additional questions, which were promptly and efficiently answered by First Lieutenant Cathy/Heather MacVickar.

Finally, when it grew quiet, General Putnam stood. "Thank you Cathy."

While the European official guests were being served coffee and tea, General Putnam excused himself to visit and chat briefly with the two sergeants and Cathy.

"How's your cover working out Cathy, any difficulties?" he asked, his concern evident.

"Doing just fine, thank you, sir. I feel confident that I've been accepted." With a smile, Cathy/Heather MacVickar went on. "I'm beginning to receive cute little notes from my fellow airmen such as, 'If it's a problem for you, I can cure your virginity,' and 'Now that I've had optical intercourse with you over five hundred times, don't you think we oughta think about getting married?' and stuff like that."

"I don't suppose the young GIs will ever change, but don't let this become a problem," cautioned the General.

Turning to Gage, the General said, "Next time you speak to Moose Berg, please pass along my "Hello" and best wishes. By the way, what does the initial R stand for in his name—R. Peter Berg? Guess you know that's been an Air Force-wide question for some time now."

"Sir, with all due respect," Gage replied with a smile, "you don't have a clearance high enough for that level of data." Gage believed that only General Berg's mother and himself knew that the R was for Rufus. They were the only two that ever dared call the General by his first name, and that was strictly in private.

The General shook Pappy's hand. "We're especially grateful for your agency's assist with this. Please let me know if you need anything and thanks for stopping by."

Gage, Pappy and MacVickar were escorted back to the main conference room area in time to mingle with the Newcomer's Orientation crowd at break time and enter the conference room for the last hour of the briefing. The final portion was devoted to the U.S. and the United Kingdom's long friendly alliance and the need for U.S. servicemen to be respectful of all British customs and courtesies.

After the meeting when the three of them were walking back toward the VW, Pappy said, "Damn fine and very impressive briefing you gave us Cathy—ooops—Heather."

"Thank you, Mr. Hargrave, rather Sergeant Hargrave," she responded with her cute, dimpled, smile. "We both learned something new about the other today. This marks my first dealing with a GS-14 CIA Civil Service agent. It 'tis indeed my proud pleasure to do business with you sir."

As they approached Pappy's car, a GI a short distance in front of them yelled to the British driver of a passing lorry, "Hey bloke! How's your old lady and my three kids?"

Gage said, "Now, that oughta help cement good U.S.-U.K. relations."

The three of them laughed and enjoyed one another's company during their return trip to Denham Studios. The fact that their number would shortly be reduced by one would have been the farthest thought from their minds.

Chapter 19

London Calling

I t had been eight months since Steve left for England. Eight lonely months for LaRae. The time had been just as lonely for Steve. LaRae had her family, and they were very supportive of her. Dunc came to visit from time to time, but she missed Steve terribly.

They wrote to each other, sometimes daily, but never less than three times weekly. On special occasions, like LaRae's birthday, at Christmas, and another time or two when he felt he couldn't stand not hearing her voice a moment longer, Steve would book a transatlantic call to LaRae. Both were busy with their jobs, and each was also taking college courses. Active, demanding schedules helped to absorb their free time, but they still missed and longed for one another.

In early June Steve had enrolled in his last college course. It was an accelerated course, and was the last needed for his commission. The course would be completed in August. That meant LaRae could begin making arrangements to join and marry him in England, come early September. This was what the both of them had been most eagerly waiting and praying for.

When Steve called to tell LaRae that everything was being finalized, and just that morning he had purchased her wedding ring, she became so overcome with excitement she burst into tears and couldn't talk for several moments. She handed the phone to her mother.

"Hello Steve, what have you said to get our little girl so thrilled she's suddenly speechless?"

"Hi, Mrs. Prentiss. I was telling her that I'm finishing up my last college course and that I'll soon receive my commission. I also told her that I've purchased her wedding ring and was trying to explain some of the things she needs to get started on right away to prepare for her trip over here. That's when she got so excited. Is she okay?"

"Oh, yes son, she's fine. She's just overcome with happiness. She'll calm down in a minute or so. What does she need to do first? I'll jot all this down so we won't forget anything."

Steve explained LaRae would need to get started on her passport, immunizations, and a certified copy of her birth certificate. He told Mrs. Prentiss of several things that would have to be done. Finally, LaRae calmed down to the point where she could talk to Steve without crying, but said she was still covered in goosebumps from her head to her toes. The receiver shook in her hands as she held it tightly. It was an impassioned phone call for both of them. They found they were both laughing and excitedly trying to talk at the same time—overjoyed with the fact that they would soon be together, again—and forever.

Steve felt lightheaded and for the first time in his life, an overwhelming sense of happiness that he wouldn't have believed possible. Finally, at last, he would belong to someone. A caring, loving person who wanted him. And a someone who would, likewise, belong to him. He had never experienced such a feeling. Just before hanging up, LaRae said, as she always did at the end of their phone conversations and the closing of each letter, "Hey boy, somebody loves you." Steve discovered that he, too, was suddenly covered in chill bumps from head to toe.

"Somebody loves you back," Steve replied.

The Prentiss household was total chaos with excitement. Plans, notification of the wedding to all the relatives, shopping for a wedding dress and other clothes, the purchasing of travel bags and a hundred and one things were being worked. LaRae, overwhelmed with joy, was beside herself in happiness and emotion.

Dunc was excited and happy too, but admitted that he was going to miss his visits to their house for dinners or to watch special sports events with Mr. Prentiss. He also acknowledged that he might miss his pal, LaRae, as well. Dunc would be leaving shortly for a month's vacation in Canada with his father. He had decided to stop by to say his farewell to LaRae early and to give her the wedding present he had already purchased and wrapped.

LaRae promised that she wouldn't open it, but send it on to England in the box of things she had been collecting. After visiting for a while with the family, Dunc and LaRae went out for dinner.

Later, on their way back to the Prentiss home, they stopped at the Steamboat Ice Cream parlor for LaRae's favorite Pralines and Cream. They were just finishing and preparing to leave when Ernie Thompson walked in.

"I thought I recognized your Studebaker outside, Dunc. Okay if I join you all?" Ernie asked cheerfully.

136

They had seen Thompson only a time or two since they had visited him in the hospital and they, like everyone else who knew Ernie, were pleasantly surprised by his very obvious change of character. He actually turned out to be a nice guy. Although still an extrovert, he had stopped his bragging and all attempts to dominate conversations and friendships. He seemed to be more mindful of the feelings of others and some said, "Anymore, he's almost downright likeable."

"We were just getting ready to leave," Dunc said to Ernie, "but you can sit and join us for a minute or two if you want."

Pulling back a chair and sitting down Ernie said, "Aw c'mon you guys, you can stay for just a little bit longer and have a Coke with me. Probably be the last time I'll get to see you for a long while LaRae, and you too Dunc if you're going outta town."

"Okay Ernie, we'll have a Coke with you, but then we have to go 'cause I have tons of things to do, and we have to stop by Dunc's to pick up some photos he wants me to take to Steve," LaRae said.

"Great, I'll go get 'em." Ernie scooted back his chair and walked to the counter. When the drinks were set on the tray, he slid the tray to his right and paid for them. When he put his change in his pocket, he withdrew two small pills and without being seen, dropped one each in LaRae's and Dunc's Cokes. The pills were Picabo, commonly called the date-rape drug sold by prescription in Mexico, but increasingly popular in the United States for five dollars a pill.

Ernie reached for some napkins and straws, giving the tablets time to dissolve and stop fizzing before returning to the table. "So, when're you guys leaving?" Ernie asked, setting the drinks on the table.

They each told of their plans and chatted about things in general while they hurriedly drank their drinks.

"Well, Ernie, I know this hasn't been much of a visit, but we really gotta go. LaRae's folks're waiting for us, and like LaRae said, we still gotta stop by my house first. Thanks for the Cokes. Take care. Be seeing you."

Ernie stood, and offering his hand to LaRae said, "Tell Steve I said Hello, and I wish you both the best of everything. I hope you'll enjoy England; it sure does sound exciting."

"I'll be sure and tell him Ernie, and thank you."

Goddam, I hope they get to Dunc's house before the pills take effect—they usually hit in about twenty minutes—he might go to sleep just driving over there! Ernie worried. He quickly got in his car and followed Dunc and LaRae at a safe distance.

Dunc and LaRae entered Dunc's house and were seated at the dining room table. They were laughing at photographs they had taken while Steve was home on leave when the drug took effect. Dunc had a writing tablet before him and had started a note to Steve. By the time Ernie crept into the house, Dunc and LaRae had both slumped forward onto the table and were out cold. Ernie stepped around Dunc and walked quietly to where LaRae slept. He put his arm around her waist and coaxed her floppy arm around his shoulders. With barely more than a sharp grunt of exertion, Ernie lifted the unconscious woman and carried her into the nearest bedroom and placed her gently onto the bed. Then he took off her clothes.

Everything seemed dream like to LaRae. There was a man. . . . was it Steve? What is he doing to me? Pain. Hurt. Through a haze she wondered why *now?* We've waited so long. It wasn't gentle, slow, caring and loving. Wrong. This is wrong! So tired. Then, again, deep sleep.

When Ernie was finished, he lugged Dunc into the bedroom, stripped and laid him next to LaRae's nude body and covered them both with a sheet.

Hours later Mr. Prentiss entered the bedroom. Neither Dunc nor LaRae had heard her parents' loud knocking on the front door of Dunc's father's home, or their entering the house and calling their names.

Dunc was the first to awaken and saw Mrs. Prentiss standing in his bedroom door with her hand to her mouth. Her eyes were wide and she had a look of astonishment on her face.

It wasn't until LaRae's father bent over the bed and shook LaRae's shoulder that she opened her eyes and said, "Daddy, what's the matter?"

Dunc slowly became aware of being in his own bed, nude, and was shocked to see LaRae next to him, also nude.

Mr. Prentiss yanked the sheet off them and saw blood on the bottom sheet. "LaRae, in the name of God, how could you and Dunc have done such a stupid, foolish thing? Don't you realize what you have done?" He threw the sheet at LaRae and said in a voice choked with anger and disbelief, "Cover yourself and get dressed!"

LaRae was in shock and just lay there. She didn't understand any of what was going on. Finally her mother came around the bed and helped her up and into the bathroom.

"Mr. Prentiss, I swear to God, I don't know what happened. We went to dinner, stopped at the Steamboat for ice cream and then came by here so we could both write on the same letter to Steve. That's the last I remember. I swear it! I don't remember anything after our coming in the front door. I wouldn't hurt LaRae or Steve. I know I wouldn't. I couldn't. I love them both. I don't understand any of this. My God, what have we done?"

After returning home LaRae had experienced symptoms of drifting in and out of unconsciousness, hallucination followed by amnesia, delirium and hot flashes. Her body provided ample evidence that she had had sexual relations, and she felt as if she had been drugged.

"I just do not remember anything. I should remember, shouldn't I Mom?" LaRae asked. "Oh God, what am I going to do now? I feel so ashamed. What can I say to Steve? I know Dunc didn't rape me. He couldn't. I know he wouldn't do that. He just couldn't. But I don't remember agreeing to have sex with him, and I know I wouldn't do that either! I've never wanted anyone but Steve, and we both agreed we'd wait until we were married. Oh God, Mom! What am I going to do?"

Steve, as usual, was down at the AMT every day when the mail for the Orderly Room was put up. He was hoping and looking for a letter or package from LaRae. He'd written precise instructions telling her of the documents needed for their marriage and her continued stay in England after the wedding. It had been over a month since Steve had called.

He had written to her every day since. He sent her money to buy luggage and other things she would need for the trip. She also would want to buy those American items she might want that perhaps she wouldn't be able to find in England. Sometimes he wrote to her twice a day.

Strangely, he had received no word back from LaRae. No post card, letter, nothing. This was very unusual because he would always receive two, three or four letters from her weekly. And she was so excited and happy when they'd last talked. He couldn't understand it.

Concerned she might be ill, he made arrangements with his Adjutant, Captain Keene, to make another transatlantic call to LaRae's home and have it billed to Keene's residential phone. It was complicated and difficult to make those kinds of calls from the public phones near the barracks. It was also noisy and hard to hear well there. Steve booked the call during the day. There was a six-hour difference in time between Denham Studios, England and Ancell, Missouri. He would make the call using the phone on his office desk over a weekend, usually a Saturday, and then pay Captain Keene when he received the bill.

Steve's clothes were damp from his running to the office in the rain. The palms of his hands were moist, but not from the rain. He was nervous and flinched when the phone rang on his desk at 8:00 p.m., that stormy Saturday. The operator asked for Steve by name.

"I'm trying your call to America just now. One moment please."

Steve heard the rings echoing as if in a chamber, three, four, five rings. Finally he heard Mrs. Prentiss pick up the phone.

"Hello?"

"This is London calling for a Miss LaRae Prentiss, please," the operator, in his crisp British accent, said.

"Oh dear God, it's Steve, Father! (the name she always called Mr. Prentiss) It's Steve calling for LaRae!"

"Hello?" Mr. Prentiss said.

The operator said again, "This is London calling for a Miss LaRae Prentiss. Is she there?"

"May I take the call please? LaRae is my daughter," Mr. Prentiss said.

Steve broke in. "That's fine operator, I'll speak with Mr. Prentiss. Thank you."

Steve, his voice on edge and anxious said, "Mr. Prentiss, is anything wrong with LaRae? I haven't heard from her in weeks. Is she all right?"

It was silent for a long moment on the other end. Steve's anxiety built as he gripped the receiver tighter.

Steve could hear his next words as if in an echo, "Is LaRae there? May I speak to her, please?"

Finally Mr. Prentiss said, "Steve, yes LaRae is here, but she can't talk to you."

"What?" said Steve, his emotions rising even higher. "What do you mean she can't talk to me—why not?"

"Steve, LaRae and Duncan have written to you. We hoped you would have already received their letter. You should have it any day now. The letter will explain everything.

"LaRae is too upset to speak to you on the telephone and Mom and I, well, we're all heartbroken over this situation. I haven't cried in years, son. And right now it's all I can do to keep from breaking down this very minute, just hearing your voice."

"What's going on Mr. Prentiss? What situation? LaRae's gonna be over here in just a few weeks. None of this is making any sense to me. I don't understand. Why can't LaRae speak to me?"

The line was silent again for a long period with just muffled conversation occasionally heard by Steve from the other end. He suspected Mr. Prentiss had placed his hand over the receiver.

Momentarily he thought he heard the Prentiss' talking and LaRae's voice crying and in a sobbing tone of desperation say, "We can't keep him wondering. Oh God, Daddy, tell him."

Mr. Prentiss came back on the line. "Steve, it breaks my heart to have to say what I'm going to say to you, and please understand son, we couldn't love you more than if you were our own. And Steve, LaRae loves you. She worships and adores you, and Duncan loves you too. That's what makes all this so hard. I can't explain what has happened, that is, how or why it happened. I guess only God knows or ever will know. LaRae can't talk to you because she's too heartbroken. Steve, LaRae is pregnant with Duncan's baby. She won't be coming over there."

Steve's heart skipped several beats and his entire body went cold. He heard what Mr. Prentiss had said but thought, *This must just be a sick joke; this can't be happening. LaRae is mine. She's my world. We love each other; we're gonna be married. We're going to be together forever. This can't have happened! Please, dear God, please let this not be true!*

"Mr. Prentiss, please tell me this isn't so. This can't be happening—" Steve said, voice trembling.

"Steve, I . . . we are so sorry son," Mr. Prentiss tearfully said.

It seemed to Steve that the last word "sorry" must have echoed ten times before the telephone line faded into silence. He was still holding the instrument next to his ear long moments after the connection was broken.

Finally he heard the operator say, "This is London. Are you through?"

Steve placed the receiver back on its cradle, stood, turned off the lights and walked out into the rain.

Pappy was sitting at the bar having his usual "Cutty and water" with several of the regulars. As was his wont, he had instigated a heated discussion, arguing that England's rugby was a far tougher game than U.S. football. Pappy had this talent for using his British accent and super pissing off his American comrades anytime he claimed the United Kingdom or its colonies were better in sports, arts, products, anything over the U.S. and its territorial holdings. He did this only to be a rascal and to stir things up. And he always did a magnificent job of it.

"The Brits, as you bloody well know, wear no, that is no shoulder pads, helmets, cod pieces, shin guards or any of that rot when they do battle on the playing field. And you Axle, with your wretched Chicago Bears who are supposed to be rough and ready, come out onto the field looking like ruddy tanks what with all the armor they wear. In addition to their cup, they probably have a tube, a short, very short and well insulated metal tube they put their cock in so it won't be damaged should they stumble, be bumped, or tripped up with one of their pansy-assed plays."

Alexander, whom Pappy always referred to as Axle, all flustered and stuttering over Pappy's charges, was just building a response when Arkee, dripping wet, walked up to the bar and stood beside Pappy.

"Excuse me, Sergeant Hargrave, I think there's something wrong with Steve. I saw him walking toward the bridge down by the mansion. I yelled at him and he just kept walking. I ran down to him and asked if he was okay and he just stood there in the pouring rain, no raincoat or jacket, and looked at me like I wasn't even there. Didn't answer or nothin'. Then he motioned for me to go away. I couldn't get him to talk or to come back with me to the barracks."

Pappy stood, and leaving a considerable amount of bills, change, his new drink, and his friends at the bar, left immediately with Arkee.

"Where is he?" Pappy asked Arkee once they were outside.

"You can't see him in this rain and dark, but he's over there." Arkee pointed around the curved drive to the back of the club and the edge of the base where the old studio mansion stood separating the base by a shallow stream of water. It was raining hard and Pappy also had no raincoat and was already as soaked as Arkee.

"Thanks Arkee. I'll see if I can find out what's wrong. Go on back inside."

Pappy walked down the road to the bridge and then slowly up to Steve and placed his hand on Steve's shoulder. "Well, what do you think, laddie? Any possibility of rain today?"

He felt rather than saw Steve's shoulders shaking convulsively and realized his friend was crying.

"What is it, lad? What's the matter?"

Lightning flashed well off in the distance and the low rumble of thunder came rolling in seconds later. The rain continued to pelt them.

Steve spoke in just barely over a whisper. "She—she's not coming Pappy. I've lost my LaRae."

"What do you mean you've lost her? What happened?"

"She's pregnant, Pappy. She's pregnant with Dunc's baby."

Pappy stood with his hand still on Steve's shoulder. Shocked and puzzled, he said nothing for several moments, trying to take in the impact of what Steve had said. He knew Steve and LaRae worshipped one another.

Pappy sat down on the curb of the bridge, rested his arms on top of his knees and laced his hands together. He bowed his head and watched the rain drip from his nose and chin.

Steve stood silent beside him. They remained like this for a long time, neither saying anything. The lightning moved in closer and the thunder continued to rumble, engulfing them. The rain, now in sheets, was being driven by a strong wind from the north.

Finally, Pappy rose, put a hand on each of Steve's shoulders and turned Steve to face him.

"Laddie, words come hard for me just now. At a time like this they are all hopelessly inadequate. No one can truly know the depth of your pain, but I share some of it with you. It's like when someone very near and dear, someone extraordinarily special dies and takes your heart with them. There are no fitting words. All I can say to you, and as weak as this may sound, I mean it from the bottom of my heart, I am sorry. I am so very, very sorry. But you must go on, lad."

Steve looked into Hargrave's eyes and in a voice choked with emotion, again, barely more than a whisper said, "Pappy, this is the hardest day of my life. No matter what else may happen to me, where I go or what I do, no day will ever be this hard."

"Yes, laddie, I know," said Pappy. "I know."

He turned, and with his arm around Steve and the rain at their backs, the two men walked across the bridge and back up the road to their quarters.

Unfortunately for Steve the darkness and sorrow of the day's events were far from finished, even more sadness and heartbreak over LaRae was to come.

Chapter 20

A Fortuitous Stop

The day after his return from leave in Tacoma, Washington, Captain Karl Miller learned of a courier trip to Denmark. He had wanted to go there for sometime to revisit his art dealer. He promptly took the assignment. It would be a short one.

He had always been a "loner." Antisocial. Karl was very selective as to those with whom he would associate and drink. He recalled always the single occasion when he had drunk too much and talked more than he should have about the Salzdorf Mine. For these reasons he had been reluctant to go to the bar with the Diplomatic Courier and the two employees from the embassy. He had delivered his classified ARFCOS package to the Air Attaché Officer at the embassy in Copenhagen and, by chance, had met the other courier there. When pressed to join them he acquiesced and agreed to one quick drink. The one drink turned into several. This, primarily, because the bar hosted a topless-bottomless show and waitresses.

One of the waitresses, a cute Scandinavian blonde who had been very creative with the trimming of her pubic hair, had given Karl several flirtatious winks. He had the night free, and it turned out to be a fortuitous stop for him.

The two couriers stayed long after the other members of their party had left. As the night and drinks wore on, it developed that the diplomatic courier was sharing a bed with the female Chief of Staff at another embassy. From her, the courier had learned of a secret Allied multi-national inquiry and request for cooperation.

Certain law enforcement agencies, it seemed, suspected paintings by Old Masters, sculptures, jewels and other objets d'art were possibly being smuggled into several European countries. Emphasis concerning this smuggling was now being focused on diplomatic courier channels and other military or governmental conveyances. All other normal channels for that type of underworld activity had been closely monitored for some time now, and ruled out.

A letter had been received by several select embassies, querying the possibility of a one-time random check of couriers, utilizing embassy and Interpol officials. It was not known if the request would be honored or, if honored, when the stop and search might be implemented.

"I will have to keep this in mind. At least for the near term when I want to bring back those items that customs wouldn't ordinarily pass. And so now probably also you, neh?" questioned the diplomatic courier.

"Yes, I suppose so," responded Karl. "Do you know anything more about these items they're looking for?"

"Nothing more. Other than those being smuggled in are small in size and believed to have been stolen by the Nazis during World War II."

"Interesting," said Karl as he intimately caressed the buttocks and crotch of the blonde waitress when she placed another round of drinks on their table.

The waitress smiled in response to the caress. Later, the next day, she would tearfully and painfully regret that smile in the hospital where she tried to describe to the police the stranger who had so viciously sodomized and brutally beat her.

Back at Denham Studios, Acting Squadron Commander Captain Earl Keene had called a meeting of the local officers and senior NCOs. Captain Karl Miller, who just that morning returned from a hurried trip to Denmark, was present. So were three other Captains who were local Postal Squadron Detachment Commanders, Sergeants Gage, Hargrave, and Danbury.

Captain Miller was angry, and it showed in both his attitude and disposition. *I'll wait my turn to speak*, he told himself.

"Well," began Keene, "we've got ourselves a new Squadron Commander on the way. Should be here in about three weeks to a month at the longest. He has prior Postal command experience and should be a big asset. He's rated, so he'll be flying from time-to-time. Born and raised in Texas and from what little I've heard he's a damn good Commander. He has a promotion line number for Lt. Colonel."

"What the hell happened with Major Ekridge?" asked one of the Detachment Commanders. "He was here one day and gone the next, never saw anybody clear out and leave so fast. Same with the Base Commander, wasn't it? Did they screw up or something?"

"That's still a mystery to lots of people I guess," said Keene. "And I don't know anyone who knows the answer. I damn sure don't. I was talking to Ekridge when the Deputy Base Commander came in and asked to speak to him privately. Ten minutes later Ekridge was gone and an hour later some folks from commercial transportation were in here packing up his office stuff. Haven't seen or heard from him since."

First Sergeant Calvin Gage betrayed no expression, but smiled inwardly when he remembered the return call he'd received from Lieutenant General Moose Berg shortly after he had contacted the General in Honolulu.

"Cal," the General had begun, "did our problems over there get cleared up fast enough for you?"

"I think it took 'em about two minutes to pack up and leave Rufus, many thanks."

"Well, they won't be troubling anyone else. They've both decided to retire. Are things okay with our young troop there now?"

"Not really, but there's nothing we can do to help. He's having some personal problems, believe it's with his fiancée back home. He won't talk about it. His commission is back on track though and his records are sterling. Much obliged, again, for your help. He was being railroaded." Gage snapped back to the present as Keene continued.

"Anyhow, we've got some more changes coming," Captain Keene said. "Captain Miller and his ARFCOS operation are gonna be moving over to South Ruislip. And they're gonna be needing more augmentation on their courier trips. You all know that Captain Johnny Clemont is still missing?"

"Yeah, what is that all about?" one of the officers queried.

"Once again, this, too, is a big mystery for us. We know Johnny delivered the classified to the Registry Cage at Annafiorno Air Base in Italy, but don't know anything after that. He just vanished. No trace. He had some leave approved and listed an address at a resort near Lake Como. According to the investigation, he never showed up there. His rental car was torched in Torino, and that had no clues. He's just disappeared.

"Johnny's being carried as absent without leave, AWOL. If he hadn't already turned in the classified, we'd have an even bigger worry. That's all we know. Maybe Captain Miller can add some more on this later."

Captain Keene carried on with his update. "We're still having little to no luck on the rifling and stealing of personal mail, government checks, and the *Playboy* magazines. We continue to work with the OSI on this and, unfortunately, there's not a lot I can tell you about it. Whoever's doing it is doing it in cycles. Course *Playboy* is a monthly magazine and it comes over here via boat mail. The government checks are also sent at the end of the month. Son-of-a-bitch seems to be snatching the magazines every other month and alternates his routine. Hate to say this, but there are strong suspicions that the stealing is going on at one of our bases here in the local

London area. You probably know as much about this from your local OSI as I'm telling you. We're all asked to keep a sharp eye on this."

The discussions went around the room, and when it came to Captain Karl Miller, it was obvious he was disturbed. He didn't seem to like enlisted personnel and NCOs in particular. He wasn't pleased that Keene had invited the three non-coms to the meeting.

"I do not want any more decisions being made affecting my operation unless I personally approve of them," he said brusquely. "ARFCOS is affiliated with the Postal Squadron for logistical support—not for command or management!"

"What're you talking about?" asked Keene.

"The decision to move our location to South Ruislip, additional guards for courier runs, manpower requisitions, all sorts of actions have been taken without my approval. I want these kinds of things stopped. And stopped now! I am the Commander of my detachment and I, no one else, will decide what will be done!" His fist hit the top of the table for emphasis.

"If you're upset over the move to Ruislip, we had no choice with that Captain," Sergeant Gage said. "That was a packaged deal that went with our getting a new barracks. As you know, it was put forward while you were here, but approved by the Base Commander and HQ Third Air Force while you were home on emergency leave. It was coordinated through your ARFCOS Headquarters. We had no control over that or the other things you've mentioned," Gage added in a controlled fury.

The Captain, his eyes and words filled with menace, his tone and attitude combative, turned to face Gage. "Sergeant, if I want to know anything from you, I'll ask for it. I don't know who in the hell you *think* you are, but I want you to keep your nose out of my business! If you can understand anything, understand this. I want nothing to do with you, and you will have nothing to do with my operation. Is that clear enough for you to comprehend, Sergeant?"

Gage, in wordless silence, but with his eyelids narrowing, revealing his anger, looked at the Captain for long seconds. He would not, he decided, lower himself to Miller's level by responding. However, at that moment, both Gage and the Captain knew that other, far more serious confrontations between the two of them loomed directly ahead.

Gage stood. "Commander, I'll be in my office if you need me, Sir." In a single nod to all present in the room except Captain Miller, he said "Gentlemen" and left.

Alone after the meeting, driving to South Ruislip Air Base, the Captain thought, *I'll have to make some changes. I'll stop the sales altogether for the time being. Let things cool off. I can still bring anything I want back from Salzdorf and store it, no problem and continue to build up my supply here in England by logging my flying time. That'll be okay. Just have to wait until the possibility of any government, non-military customs stop and search efforts pass.*

Miller felt comfortable with nearly everything. The veterinarian's real estate nephew in Salzdorf had been managing the mine site property for him for a long time.

He paid what bills there were and drove out to the area from time-to-time, checking to make sure all was secure. He had no knowledge of the building's contents or of the mine shaft. He'd perceived the impression he shouldn't be curious about such things. At Miller's request the area was maintained in a very low profile. It was not discussed with anyone outside the veterinarian's family and rarely discussed within the family. Miller paid Horst handsomely for his attendant services.

Karl visited the site at least monthly, sometimes twice monthly. He would always fly the military plane into Fürstenfeldbruk just outside Munich. There he would rent a car and drive to the mine, parking out of sight in back. He slept in the building in his sleeping bag on the old family couch. Electricity was the only utility convenience available. He brought water with him. They had an old Aladdin type kerosene heater he used for warmth, and he kept the tinned food storage cabinet well stocked. His father's large upholstery table rolled easily to expose the entrance to the mine. With the building's only door bolted from the inside, Miller enjoyed many hours of just walking amongst row upon row of plundered art, jewels, gold, and medals. Over time he had collected and sectioned off the pieces he could easily carry within the ARFCOS courier bags he always brought with him.

He had, long ago, greased the skids with the military customs personnel he had to clear through. The majority of those dealings were with the RAF and USAF personnel at Northolt and Bovington. Those were the bases he always flew out of and returned to. He consistently, whether bringing contraband back or not, presented the Customs Inspectors with bottles of the best wine, brandy, and whiskey. He went out of his way to procure for them any requested purchases from the Continent. French magazines, special books, favorite musical recordings, anything the inspectors showed the slightest interest in, he procured for them, at his own expense.

On a few occasions, when he knew he would not be bringing anything back from the mine, he flew an inspector or two with him to Germany to attend the Oktoberfest or Fasching celebrations and maybe a visit to the

Hoffbrahaus or the Moulin Rouge in Munich. Captain Miller always looked them up. They never had to come to him. After a fashion this resulted in his never being inspected when he would bring items back from his flying assignments. The ARFCOS bags were exempt from inspection anyway. The bags, supposedly, contained only the highest classified military documents and items. The Captain was very well liked by all the customs personnel. However, they thought it strange that he would not allow them to help him offload all those mailbags. They knew he had to be tired from all the flying, but he always insisted on handling each mailbag and doing the work himself.

Hell of a dedicated officer, they thought. *Conscientious too.* Now and then he brought back presents for the customs guys to give to their girlfriends and wives. He owned the customs troops.

So, this will give me time to tighten my dealings here in England and Scotland. No problem with that, Miller thought. *In fact, this might all be for the better. I will make some expanded, normal ARFCOS trips and possibly enlarge my field of operations by adding some new cities. Everything is working out just fine. Everything is perfect—almost.*

The only discomfort he felt was *"with that swine Gage! I have bad feelings about him; something tells me I must be careful with that man. But other than that, it won't hurt to let things calm down a bit. Mustn't hurry or take needless, foolish chances. I have all the time in the world, and the Führer's mountain of treasure continues to wait, patiently, for me,"* he thought to himself as he drove toward South Ruislip.

Chapter 21

Olga, the Nordic Beauty

Sergeant Gage as the First Sergeant of the Squadron saw every piece of paper coming into the unit. Early on Friday morning he received and scanned the Key-Personnel Activity Schedule for the next seven days. Maybe it was because he was still smarting over his most recent run-in with Captain Karl Miller that he noted Miller, according to the schedule, would be logging flying time over the coming weekend. Miller would RON at the Fürstenfeldbruck German Luftwaffe base near Munich, and return to England Sunday evening. His estimated time of arrival back at RAF Northolt was 1600. The report showed Captain Miller would be flying a C-47, commonly referred to by its nickname—Gooney Bird. Gage stared at the listing for long moments as if daydreaming. Something was tugging . . . something was trying to get through to him.

Slowly a smile formed at the corners of his mouth. It was the kind of smile that comes on a person who has struggled with an elusive problem, a puzzle, or some kind of a nagging question, and then suddenly he sees the solution unveiled.

It's him! That son-of-a bitch! And that's the way he's doing it—he's using Gooney Bird flights! Why didn't I think of this earlier. That's gotta be it and it's gotta be him!

During his long and active career Gage had met and had trying experiences with many officers. He had worked closely with his officers in countless demanding situations, oftentimes during periods of intense stress when the actions of one or the other depended on the safety and lives of themselves and many others. Gage had respect, tremendous respect for the officer corps. But with Captain Karl Miller there was something different. Just something about him. Gage had this gut-feeling. He couldn't put his finger on it, or describe it and he couldn't shake it off. *It's gotta be him!* Gage said again to himself.

With the Activity Schedule still gripped tightly in his hand, Gage walked down the hall to Hargrave's office.

"Phil, are you going to be using your VW this weekend?"

"Nope, wasn't planning on it. Do you need some wheels, Cal?"

"Well, yeah, maybe. I've just come across something that perked my interest."

"Something good I hope." Pappy said with a smile. He had been wanting his friend to relax and unwind some. Seemed to Pappy that Gage was kinda wound tight and on edge for quite some time now. "Are you gonna get out of town?"

"Don't want to discuss it now, but can we meet and talk privately after work?"

"Sure, let's have a beer at the club around 5:30. You can pick up the car then, okay?"

"Yeah, thanks, Phil. See you at 5:30."

"Gawddam that's gross!" Alexander shouted.

Pappy, sitting next to him, startled by the exclamation, turned and asked, "What's gross?"

"Boyd here. He just took his front teeth outta his mouth. Stuck 'em in his shirt pocket and now he's gummin' the hell outta them boiled, pickled eggs and sausages. That's gross! Makes me gag."

Pappy, Alexander, Boyd, Steve and Arkee were all sitting at the bar in the NCO club. Pappy was waiting to see Gage before going into town to meet gorgeous Olga, the young lady from the Little Sweden Club in Soho. Today, he was convinced, was *the day!*

Pappy was lustful. The others were just killing time.

Steve had dropped his college course and began to go to the bar and pubs with the troops regularly. He was still, obviously, very depressed over his situation back home.

Pappy hoped time would help in the healing process. But he was becoming more and more concerned about his young friend.

"If a guy's got false teeth and gonna eat, he oughta leave his fuckin' teeth in his mouth. Damn near gag every time he does that. He knows it too. You know that Boyd! You just do that to piss me off, don't 'cha? You like to see me gag!"

"Please don't bother me when I'm dining, Axle," Boyd calmly lisped. Not helping the situation, he accidentally sprayed a few tiny particles of crackers from his mouth with his response. Boyd was not at all successful in trying to conceal the smile that had become apparent with the knowledge of the distress he was causing Alexander.

"How'd you lose them teeth anyways?" Alexander persisted.

"I don't wanna talk about it. That's personal. Besides, Axle, why don't you mind your own fuckin' business? Do I ask you what kinda underwear you're wearing?"

"What's my underwear got to do with you taking your teeth out to eat?"

"I don't know—let's drop it."

Alex pressed, "How'd you lose them front teeth? Some jealous boyfriend or maybe a pissed off husband evacuate your mouth, Boyd?"

"Axle, if I promise to miss you, will you please go away? I don't wanna talk about my teeth dammit. Geeesch!"

"Go on Warren, tell 'em about it," Arkee interjected. He resumed his barstool seat after playing Connie Francis' recording of *Who's Sorry Now* on the jukebox. "You're among friends," he said with a smile.

"It's embarrassin'. I don't wanna discuss it. Will you get off my ass, Axle? My snack here's gettin' cold."

"Hell, it's 'sposed to be cold. C'mon Boyd, tell us about it. You know you're gonna sooner or later anyways. Did some sweet young thing's feller bop you in your bicuspids?"

"Dammit, Axle, you just flat-assed won't leave a guy alone when he's eating, will you? Go ahead Arkee, *you* go ahead on and tell 'em. Maybe then he'll leave me alone."

"Happened at our last base," Arkee began. "Squadron picnic wasn't it, Warren?"

Boyd, munching on his snack, gave Arkee a sideways nod and frown and continued eating.

Arkee punched in the tab on his new can of beer, took a sip and settled back into his barstool to begin the tale of Boyd's lost teeth. Everyone at the bar, including the bartender, Waldo, gave Arkee their undivided attention, much to Boyd's chagrin.

"Back at Luke AFB, my pal here Warren Boyd, Steve, myself and most all the other single guys had been hitting the iced down beer pretty hard on that hot, Arizona desert Saturday afternoon.

"From the next table over, Edwards, probably the heaviest guy in the squadron, saw that Warren was easily three sheets in the wind, walked over to our table. He tapped Warren on the shoulder and issued a challenge.

"Boyd, betcha ten bucks I can beat you in a footrace from here to that concrete building and back," he said.

"Warren had a hard time even focusing his vision and looked at the building, easily a couple hundred yards away.

"You mean the latrine, that green building?" Warren asked, pointing to the same structure as Edwards.

"Yep, ten bucks says I can beat you running there and back."

"You're on Edwards. That's damn sure a bet. And I'll bet you another five on top of it, that you just made a bad bet."

"Gotcha covered," replied Edwards.

"Our hero, Warren rose, sorta wobbly like, to his feet. With a sly, and very self-assured grin to all of us at the table, he showed every confidence in the world that this was gonna be the easiest footrace and the fastest fifteen bucks he'd ever win. He put his money down on the picnic table. Edwards followed suit.

"Steve drew a line in the sand just beside the table that would be the start and finish line.

"Boyd and Edwards started loosening up, shaking their arms, and legs. Boyd, maybe, showed off just a little bit for us and did a jig, shuffle and derrière wriggle to boot. Boyd then gave all of us supporters another of his exaggerated winks that signaled his confident, assured win, and then joined Edwards at the line."

"Goddammit Arkee, you don't have to dramatize everything so fuckin' much!" Boyd interrupted in between gummin' bites of his snack. "You make it sound like I was purposely showin' off and stuff."

"Shut up and let him finish the story Boyd," Alexander refereed. "And you probably was showin' off. You're always showin' off cause that's your nature. Asshole! Go on Arkee, what happened next?"

"Well, Steve here got Boyd and Edwards all lined up and says, 'Okay guys, on the count of three then, One, two, three—go!'

"Both Boyd and Edwards sprinted, kicking up sand behind them. Warren stumbled and damn near fell when his right toe dug into the sand; he lurched, staggered a bit, but kept running and shortly straightened himself out. All us troops, a good number of supporters for both runners were yelling and shouting encouragement for our guy.

"It was kinda like the *Tortoise and Hare* tale. In no time flat Boyd was way the hell out in front of the much heavier and slower Edwards. Boyd later told us he had laughed to himself and poured on the steam thinking, *I'll show his smart ass. I'll get to the latrine, turn around and be back at the finish line before he even reaches the building to turn around. Fat fart. I'll teach him to challenge me to a foot race!*"

153

"Waldo, give me another beer will ya?" Boyd asked the bartender with a frown, interrupting Arkee's story once again.

"Get it yourself," Waldo responded, "I wanna hear the rest of this." Boyd, mumbling to himself got up and walked around the bar to the cooler and got his beer. While back there he opened the lid on the gallon jar and got himself another pickled egg.

"Decision made," Arkee continued, "Boyd doubled his effort and speed. His feet were flying! As he neared the concrete building he turned around and saw Edwards still struggling, but chugging along, way the hell back in the distance.

"At this point Boyd figured he had it made and told himself, *No sweat, GI. I'll be back at the finish line long before he even makes it halfway*.

"Warren put his hands up in front to brace himself when he reached the building. He'd then turn around and push himself away for the return run. *Like stealing candy from a kid*, he thought to himself. *Easiest race I ever won*!

"But instead of bracing himself, stopping, and turning around, guess all the beers he'd drunk affected his reflexes. The momentum of his speed kept him going as he slammed face first into that goddamned concrete block building. He just kinda stood there for a moment. Looked as if he was plastered to the side of the latrine, and then, almost as if in slow motion, he fell backwards, knocked out colder'n a cucumber. Also knocked out were his top four front teeth. His four front bottom teeth were all loose.

"We all ran to him and someone called an ambulance. They took him first to the hospital where they discovered he was a whole big bunch of drunk, but okay except for his bent nose, bruised chin, and broken teeth. Warren was then taken to the dentist office. That's where we caught up with him again. Damn he looked a sight! Drunker'n a loon.

His mouth and shirt was all bloody, teeth missing and he smelled like yesterday's busted beer keg. Kinda turned my stomach to look at him, mouth open and all settin' there spread out in that dentist chair."

"I can damn sure believe that!" Alex said with a grin. "Probably looked and smelled like Ca-Ca. He turns my stomach 'bout half the time him just lookin' his natural self."

"Kiss ass Axle!" Boyd tossed back in response.

"Anyway, eventually they gave him a partial bridge. Ever since then," Arkee concluded his story, "Boyd has never been without his four front false teeth—'cept when he eats. Years later, even till today, he still takes his teeth out to eat. Just can't get used to eating with that bridge huh Warren?"

Ignoring Arkee's question, Boyd said, "Okay Axle, I hope you're satisfied. Now will you please get off my ass about my fuckin teeth? Geesch! Gotta tell you everything for Crissake!"

"Ran face first into a fuckin' concrete building. Never did credit you with a whole lotta smarts Boyd," Alexander said, "but smacking into a cinder block wall for God's sake—that takes the prize."

Everyone at the bar laughed. Boyd rolled the napkins he had used with his snack into a ball and threw it at Alexander.

"See you guys later," Pappy said, excusing himself when he saw First Sergeant Gage enter the club. Gage and Pappy sat in a corner booth.

"You sure you won't be needing your Volkswagen this weekend?" Gage asked Pappy.

Giving Gage the car keys, he said with a smile, "No, not this weekend. I'm meeting beautiful Olga in town. She's coming in on the underground tube. We're gonna spend the night in Uxbridge, and am I ever looking forward to this. Wow, has that gal put a bounce in my britches! In fact I won't need the car back till next weekend when I'm going to meet with the lovely Brooke again. Brooke was my childhood sweetheart while we lived here in England. We sort of grew up together, always kept close and in touch over the years, and here of late we've become even closer. Damn, all of a sudden I'm sounding like a real Casanova, aren't I? With the lovelies, it's feast or famine in my case, Cal. What are you up to this weekend?"

"I'm just gonna do a little snoopin' around. I have a couple of things I'm wanting to check out. Nothing really concrete yet so don't want to jump the gun."

"Sounds intriguing. Are you onto something?"

"Just some unfounded suspicions at this point. More of a gut feeling than anything else. I'll keep you posted if anything turns up," Gage said.

"Yeah. Well, don't take any chances and please call me if I can do anything. If you don't mind, I might ride back with you to Uxbridge."

Pappy had been "cultivating" this rendezvous for several weeks. Around Olga, he had been on his best behavior and, under great strain, had been acting as the total and proper gentleman. Calm, cool, and collected—butter wouldn't melt in his mouth; he was extremely courteous, patient, and mannerly. Very proper indeed. And reserved. While all the time he was so damned horny he could honk!

All this in the attempt to seduce the ravishing Nordic beauty Olga that he had met at the "Little Sweden" in Soho. Finally, *finally*, all was now ready. Today was *the day*. He just knew it. He had given her bouquets and candy, wined and dined her. He'd made prior arrangements at the Wayside Inn.

The bottle of gin, Olga's favorite, and everything else he could think of was all set.

Opening the door to the hotel room and seeing the gin on the dresser top, he remembered he'd forgotten to get any sort of a mix or chaser. *Damn, not even a drop of vermouth!* he thought as he ushered Olga in and seated her comfortably on the bed. He then tore downstairs to learn the only thing available was a small bottle of warm Coke. Of course there was no ice for the rooms. He grabbed the Coke and in seconds poured Olga a stiff shot of gin, which she chased with a tiny sip from the warm Coke.

In a short while the gin was drunk, the bottle of Coke, a thimble full at a time, was drunk and also drunker'n David's sow were both Pappy and Olga.

In between heavy belts of gin, some wild petting had taken place and Olga, now standing nude before the full-length mirror, was the absolute picture of female sexuality and perfection.

With her hairbrush in hand, she was stroking her gorgeous blonde hair— its entire length—from the back of her head down to her beautiful buttocks.

Turning, she viewed a naked Pappy reclining on the bed with his penis standing at a rigid attention. She continued to brush her hair. The movement caused her magnificent, firm and youthful breasts to jiggle slightly as they pointed toward the ceiling. They were tipped with delicious raspberry-colored nipples. Pappy was excited beyond belief.

My testosterone level had to have maxed out long ago! he thought. Through the gin-drunken haze in his mind, he couldn't believe his good fortune. *This ravishing beauty, this magnificent, luscious, absolutely marvelous female body is mine for the weekend to do with whatever I desire. For reasons I'll never know, the gods have truly blessed me!*

Looking at the tawny blonde, almost white, triangle of hair between her legs, Pappy absentmindedly gripped his penis. Olga looked at him and said something in a slurred, rather drunken voice.

"Wha? Whassamatter?" Pappy asked.

Olga responded, "I said I theenk you have the verrry nice Schlonk."

"What?" Pappy said. "What I got?"

Olga smiled and put the brush down on the dresser.

With her head spinning from the gin and with a very pronounced stagger, she made her way over to the bed.

She removed Pappy's hand from his penis, replaced it with her own and began to stroke his throbbing phallus.

"Whoa baby!" Pappy tried to shout, but having some difficulty locating his voice, squeaked instead. "Careful darlin'. Please be careful with Ole Herman there. He's really not used to a lot of this foreplay business."

Lately, the extent of Pappy's involvement in foreplay had been to say to the lady of the evening, "Cor Blimey luv, don't 'alf got a bit of a rise-on. Let's just drop the undies and have a little bend over then." And as fast as that the romance session was underway.

"What were you just saying?" he asked Olga.

"Schlonk. I vars sayink Schlonk." Olga shook her head and blinked her eyes several times. She was having trouble focusing on Pappy's dick, which now seemed to be rotating, of its own accord, in small circles. Finally after several failed grabbing attempts she again seized his penis. "I say I theeenk you have the verrry nice Schlonk."

With her hand solidly gripping and stroking him, Pappy began to moan.

"Hmmmmmmm. Yeahhhhh, that's true. I got the verrry nice Schlonk."

Olga, now completely and totally in control of everything—except the gin prompted spinning of the room—said, "Ya? You like this ya? You maybe like this even more I theeenk?" Straddling Pappy she guided him inside her as she gingerly lowered herself upon him.

Everything on and about Pappy was throbbing! He'd never been so excited sexually. He was a milli-milli-micro-second away from the most fantastic orgasm ever achieved on this third planet from the sun. No one, absolutely no one in the history of recorded man had ever before, or would ever again have an orgasm like this one!

Wonder if I'll need some help pulling her back down out of the ceiling where the force of my climax will propel her within the very next instant, he thought to himself.

He tried to think of anything just to take his mind off the situation in an attempt to prolong the ecstasy.

This could be embarrassing if the 999 Emergency Response folks come rushing in and alls they can see is Olga's beautiful butt and legs protruding from the ceiling. Hell, she might even ricochet off the ceiling and walls, bouncing around the room four or five times!

His eyes rolled and he moaned again as Olga raised herself, ever so slowly, then, once more, lowered herself upon him. She did this twice, then the spinning room and physical exertion got to her.

Olga stopped abruptly, and, with a great force, jettisoned vomit that splattered all over an astounded and wide-eyed Pappy's face and chest.

Ole Herman, of course, immediately lost interest in all of this stuff and wilted like last week's rosebud.

Chapter 22

The Gooney Bird Round Robin

The C-47 USAF aircraft, the Gooney Bird, was the workhorse that augmented the C54 Skymaster Berlin Airlift Operation from June 1948 until September 1949. These aircraft carried the mountains of food, fuel, and supplies to West Berlin after the Soviets attempted to blockade and push the Western Allies out of Berlin to consolidate Stalin's grip on Eastern Europe. Sergeant Gage had flown in C-47s many times and knew the cargo capacity of the aircraft. *Plenty of room to bring a large quantity of contraband back into the country if a guy wanted,* Gage opined to himself.

The First Sergeant had a roster, as did each officer and senior NCO, of all key squadron personnel, showing their addresses and phone numbers. He familiarized himself with the location of Miller's apartment in Eastcote on Elm Avenue. He then zeroed in on a good place to park near the Northolt runway and observe Miller's return and deplaning from his trip to Germany. Pappy's borrowed Volkswagen had a military bumper sticker that would allow access to any US/UK base.

The Sergeant found a location near the flight line that would permit him to observe incoming flights without his vehicle being readily seen. He hoped when he returned Sunday evening the parking space would still be available. He decided he would come early enough to make sure he got it.

In a heavy drizzle of rain, Gage drove Pappy's Volkswagen through Uxbridge toward RAF Station Northolt at 2:00 p.m. the next day. On the outskirts of Uxbridge, just before crossing over the canal bridge, he saw the huge sign by the road identifying the entrance to the Wayside Inn. He smiled as he thought of Hargrave with Olga in their hotel room. *Wonder if Phil still has that bounce in his britches?* Gage found the parking space he wanted was vacant; he pulled the VW to a stop and turned off the engine. On the passenger's seat were some sandwiches, a thermos of coffee and night vision binoculars. He anticipated a long wait and settled himself comfortably. The sound of rain on the roof lulled him into short periods of sleep. With the infrequent arrival or departure of aircraft, Gage would immediately become alert, check the aircraft to determine whether or not it was a C-47 and then relax and catnap again.

At 1720 Gage opened his front window side vent to permit the condensation on the windshield from his opened thermos of coffee to clear. The rain had become a fine mist and was carried by the rolling fog that had come in off the channel. Unquestionably, the airfield's tower would be using Ground Control Approach to guide Miller's delayed flight through the rain and fog. Gage thought he heard the sound of an approaching plane and lowered the side window to hear better. Yeah, it was an incoming aircraft and he felt certain this would be Miller's. He rolled the window up and wiped the front windshield dry with his handkerchief. Visibility was going to be poor from inside the car. Shortly he saw the front of the C-47 emerge, ghost like, from out of the roiling fog bank. It came to a stop on the apron to the left of the Operations Building. The wheels were chocked as the two engines shut down.

Through the binoculars the Sergeant observed four uniformed people emerge from the aircraft. None was Miller. Twenty minutes later Gage saw Captain Miller step down out of the plane with two ARFCOS courier bags in each hand. He set the bags down near the rear of the plane, reentered the craft and momentarily came out again with four more bags. Within minutes Gage counted nine bags Miller had unloaded and placed in a pile. A military pickup truck with a large FOLLOW-ME sign across the back pulled up near the aircraft and the Captain gently loaded the bags into the truck bed. He got inside and they drove out from behind the Restricted Area chainlink fencing to the parking lot and the Captain's car.

Gage had to exit his car to keep the pickup truck in sight. He was certain it wouldn't leave the base. He didn't know the Captain's vehicle and didn't want to move his car to draw any attention to himself at this point. When Miller had loaded all but two of the bags inside his car, Gage reentered the Volkswagen, started it, and without lights for the moment, backed up and prepared to follow the Captain at a distance. As they neared Ruislip Manor and Eastcote, Gage was confident Miller was enroute to his apartment. He dropped well back behind the Captain's auto and parked several spaces away when Miller pulled into his driveway. The fog had remained, but there were patches of clearing. Gage could see the officer storing the mailbags inside the garage attached to his flat. He secured the door with two locks and then entered his apartment.

Gage waited several minutes before leaving.

From behind the front drapes in the darkened living room, Karl Miller watched as Gage's car pulled out from its parking space and drove away. He was certain the driver was that damned new First Sergeant.

"Did he follow me? That, most definitely is a certainty! Was I monitored at the airport? Had the son-of-a-bitch seen me with the courier bags?"

Having napped off and on during the afternoon, Gage was not sleepy. He was, instead, keyed up over his suspicions. He now strongly suspected that Miller was bypassing customs, using ARFCOS courier bags to bring items back into the country illegally. He couldn't be one hundred percent certain that the bags Miller had removed from the plane and stored in his garage contained only mail or classified materials, but he was at the ninety-nine point nine percent mark.

If the courier bags were being used in an official capacity, they should have been taken to the AMT and stored in the Registry Vault on base rather than the garage at a personal residence overnight. This was, at minimum, a king-sized security violation.

But, Gage's gut told him it was considerably more. He decided he should make a "CABLE-TOW" contact to report what he suspected. He called the number he had for Heather MacVickar, but she was out. The Charge of Quarters said she thought Heather had gone to Edinburgh for the weekend and wouldn't be back until possibly Monday afternoon. Could she take a message?

Gage then thought about calling Hargrave, but smiled when he remembered Pappy and his weekend mission—The Nordic Beauty. He, maybe, could reach Pappy at the hotel, but why bother at this point? Owing to the late hour, and feeling confident Miller wouldn't be doing anything with the courier bags until the next day, Gage decided he'd wait until morning to pass on his concerns.

Finally, half way through with the umpteenth reading of Sir Arthur Conan Doyle's, *The Sign of the Four*, Sergeant Gage, drowsily laid his book aside and turned off his bedside lamp.

A light sleeper for years, Gage awoke, fully alert, knowing he'd heard a noise from somewhere inside his apartment. Quickly and silently he got out of bed and stood beside his closed bedroom door.

He strained to hear anything, a quiet footstep, clothing rustling or brushing against a wall, a squeak in the floor, anything. He remained there for long moments listening, but heard nothing. He cautiously and very slowly grasped the knob on his bedroom door and gently turned it.

Thankfully, the door made no noise as he silently opened it and glanced to his left. Nothing. As he was turning to look to his right, he stepped barefooted out onto the hall carpet and was struck a crushing blow to the side of his head. He collapsed, unconscious.

Using the lead pipe he'd hit Gage with and a towel to muffle the noise, the Captain opened the kitchen's back door he had previously picked. He broke the glass above the doorknob. He dragged Gage into the kitchen and laid him near the opened door. He felt for a pulse and found it very weak and erratic. He noted that Gage was barely breathing, struggling for each breath.

The Captain hurriedly, but quietly, ransacked Gage's apartment. He looked for any kind of a journal or note pad that might be a record of either of their activities. He found nothing. He took Gage's wallet and watch and knelt again beside the unconscious Sergeant. Bending over Gage, he raised his arm to strike again. This time it would be a definite killing blow to the temple.

At that moment the entire rear of the building was illuminated by a resident's car entering the back lot. Miller darted immediately backwards and ran to the front of the building and out the front door. He rushed through an alley then went to the front street two blocks from Gage's apartment where he had parked. He jumped into his car and drove past the Sergeant's flat, noting the neighbor's headlights still lit up the rear of the building.

He also observed the Sergeant's inside apartment lights were now also on. The break-in and assault had already been discovered!

"Damn," fretted the Captain, "is he still alive? Should have hammered the son-of-a-bitch again. He was barely breathing and his skull was split wide open. Surely no one could survive such a blow. He must be dead by now."

Captain Miller drove a few blocks and pulled to the side of the road and stopped. Still wearing gloves to avoid leaving any fingerprints, he found it awkward to remove the bills from the Sergeant's wallet. Finally he pocketed the money and threw the billfold and watch out the window into a nearby hedge. Driving home, he thought, *if he isn't dead I'll have to finish the job and that'll probably have to be done in the hospital—damn, that will be tricky because everyone knows I don't like the schwein-hund. Why did that car have to show up at that instant? One more rap with the pipe would have done it! Oh well, if he's dead, fine. If he isn't, I'll just have to fix it, done it before, can do it again. But this time I'll enjoy it all the more with this stubborn, cocky arschloch. Tomorrow is another day . . . .*

Chapter 23

And Then They Were Gone

"So, how was the weekend with the lovely Olga?" Steve asked sleepily from his bunk as Pappy, the sexually frustrated Don Juan, entered their room. The first dull gray light was just breaking dawn on Monday morning. It was still foggy and drizzling light rain.

"Somehow, it was not quite what I'd expected. In fact, it was not a cracking good time at all. Seemed to be rather an ill-planned undertaking straight from the beginning." With a furrowed brow and pained expression, Pappy continued, "Just now, during my taxi ride back to base, it has prompted me to wonder if the game is worth the candle. I'm seriously pondering the advantages of celibacy." Pappy appeared momentarily lost in thought on the subject. "I heard once there are three stages to a man's life: stud, dud and thud. I calculate that I'm floating somewhere betwixt dud and thud presently. Oh, and by the by, Laddie, never, absolutely never drink gin and warm Coke in a hurry! Disastrous. I'm off to the shower. Feel as though I've been run over by a ruddy Sherman tank. Everything aches, even my nuts. In fact, especially my nuts. We'll talk more later. Sorry I woke you."

Just a few minutes later Steve pounded urgently on the bathroom door. Not waiting for a response, he rushed in and announced to Pappy in the shower, "Lieutenant Harris, the Officer of the Day, (OD) is here. He says Sergeant Gage was attacked in his home and is in the hospital at Ruislip. He says it looks like he's not gonna make it."

Pappy yanked the shower curtain aside. "You're bullshitting me!" He took a hard look at Steve. "No, I guess you're not. Ask the OD to wait just a moment."

Moments later Steve and Pappy bombarded the Lieutenant with questions.

"We're not sure at all what happened," the Lieutenant responded. "A neighbor of the Sergeant was returning home around midnight. When he pulled into the back of the apartments he saw Gage's back door was open and thought he saw a figure running from the kitchen. When the neighbor went to investigate, he saw Gage lying on the floor in a pool of blood. He immediately called an ambulance and they rushed him over to Ruislip. He's in a coma in the Intensive Care Unit. I've called Captain Keene, and he asked me to pass this on to you. Said he'd meet you at the hospital."

Steve and Pappy sat in a small waiting room just around the corner from the ICU. A plainclothes policeman and Bobby were speaking to them quietly.

"He was attacked in the hallway just outside his bedroom," said the plainclothed official. "He went down there, losing a great deal of blood. From that point he was dragged into the kitchen, and I surmise the arrival of the neighbor sent the intruder packing. What puzzles me is, if this were a simple burglary, why would the assailant drag the body to the kitchen? Why not just leave him where he fell initially?"

"You suspect it maybe was not a burglary then?" Pappy asked.

"It has all the markings of that, sir," responded the Bobby. "Entry was obtained by breaking the glass in the rear door. The flat has been hastily searched, ransacked actually, and the victim's wallet is missing. We, of course, can't know what else may have been taken. If he wears a watch, that's gone as well. Why would the body be dragged to the kitchen? Puzzling, that one. In any event, we have people at the flat dusting for fingerprints and the investigation there is still under way. Nasty business this. Poor chap. Doesn't look good for him from what we gather."

"We haven't spoken with the doctor yet," Hargrave said to the policemen. "If you'll excuse us, we were just going to try and do that. We're very grateful for your help. Thank you very much indeed."

"We shall be in touch. Good luck and good day gentlemen," the policeman said.

"Does he have any immediate family?" the doctor asked Pappy and Steve.

"No," responded Pappy. "There's no one else for you to notify, but we'll take charge of those matters."

Actually, the "Next of Kin" block in his 201 File said to contact Lt. General R. P. Berg at the Pentagon in the event of an emergency. They had booked a call to the General but wanted to speak with the doctor first.

"I'm amazed he's made it this long," said the doctor. "The entire right side of his head has been caved in. The life support equipment is the only thing keeping him going, and I've no idea how long that might continue. His life is hanging by a thread."

"May we see him please, doctor?" Pappy asked.

"Yes, but unfortunately only one person. If you want any time with him, you'd best go in now."

"You go on Pappy. I'll brief Captain Keene," Steve said as they saw their Commander, Captain Keene rounding a corner making his way toward them.

Pappy went in alone. The feeling of dread and the pungent hospital odor of phenol hung heavily about him. He pulled a chair over next to the bed and put his hand on top of Gage's. Just barely above a whisper and choked with emotion, he said, very slowly, "Jesus, Mary, and Joseph, what the hell happened Cal? What did you get into? Who did this to you? Would it have made a difference if I had gone with you this weekend? You said you had some things you wanted to check out. For Crissake, what could they have been?"

Pappy hadn't known Gage long, but they had become close. They shared common military backgrounds and WWII experiences. There was a kinship between them, a quiet, respected bonding that was rare and unique. Neither had a family—wife nor children. They were what many would call loners even in the military, but their ties were the same, their jobs and their comrades, the military and their country. That was their family; that's what they lived for. Shortly after their initial meeting, each, through some unknown sense, recognized the other as a professional. It was just one of those things, innate maybe, that happens when men of their caliber meet. Unspoken, but the flicker of recognition is unmistakable, loud and clear. They were both truly dedicated men, and they felt their obligations keenly. "Duty, Honor, Country," the famous hallowed words spoken by General of the Army Douglas MacArthur on the "Plain" at West Point was the code these men lived by. Duty, Honor, Country was the blood that ran through their veins.

Pappy sat immobile, as if thunderstruck, for a long time. His hand held Gage's with a gentle but firm grip. He was deeply saddened by the certain knowledge that he was losing this friend as he had so many others during the war. But with this man whom he had known for such a short period of time, it was different. He identified with him on a personal basis. And each, in his own way, had loved the other as only men and soldiers of their breed can love another—truly a once-in-a-lifetime, if fleeting, association. "I'll get him Gage," Pappy whispered. "By all that's holy, I promise you I'll get the bastard who did this."

Suddenly he felt Gage's hand tighten, it squeezed Hargrave's several times as if trying to communicate, and when it relaxed, Master Sergeant Calvin Gage was dead.

Pappy sat there for several moments and silently wept.

The doctor came in and examined Gage. He stood briefly beside the bed then, patting Pappy's shoulder he whispered, "I'm sorry Sarge. There was absolutely nothing more we or anyone else could do. I'm amazed he lasted as long as he did." The doctor left the room as quietly as he had entered.

Finally, Pappy stood and gently placed Gage's hand atop his now quiet, unmoving chest. He slowly pulled up the sheet and lowered it over Gage's head. He put both his hands on top of the sheet covering Gage's hands. Then sadly he turned to leave the room. Pappy knew, as do all men, the inborn fear of dying alone. At the foot of the dead Sergeant's bed, he stopped, turned around and said loudly, "Goddammit Gage, you didn't die alone!"

It was another typically British day, cloudy and drizzly. A low ceiling hung over RAF Station Northolt where a hastily erected bier with Sergeant Gage's coffin rested on top.

Four Scottish military men stood behind the U.S. flag-draped coffin, playing their bagpipes. A squadron each of U.S. Army troops, USAF airmen, British soldiers, British sailors and British airmen marched in tribute to a muffled drumbeat. Each contingent snapped their heads smartly at the command, Eyes Right! as they passed the coffin. Lieutenant General R.P. Berg, Inspector General of the United States Air Force, standing beside the bier of his fallen comrade and closest personal friend, viewed the salutes through tear rimmed eyes and returned them smartly.

Suddenly, a flight of British, then another of USAF fighters, flying in the missing man formation, filled the sky. Finally, a B-17 aircraft, the type Gage had flown in as a gunner during World War II, passed low overhead, dipping its giant wings in a final salute.

Within minutes of the closing ceremony, an honor guard in funereal lockstep placed Gage's coffin on board General Berg's military aircraft. Receiving a last salute from all those present, Master Sergeant Calvin Gage left England for the last time headed for Colorado, cremation, and the scattering of his ashes in a stream in the mountains close to the personal cabin of General Rufus Berg.

Over the years Gage and Berg, close as brothers, had enjoyed hunting and fishing trips in the splendor of the beautiful mountains. Each had expressed the desire to have his ashes scattered there and extracted a commitment from the other to ensure this would be done.

Three days later, on a sunny afternoon, General Berg fulfilled his obligation. Gage's ashes were gently scattered, falling slowly into the mountain stream swollen by the melting snow. He watched as most of them, drawn together in the rushing water, were caught momentarily in an eddy. They circled a large rock and Rufus couldn't help but think his friend, maybe, was waving farewell. And then they were gone.

Chapter 24

Mon Amie La Femme Ashley

P appy found himself in a hell of a quandary. He was still grieving the death of Calvin Gage, and yet discovered he was more concerned with his young friend Steve Scott. Steve had become like a younger brother to Hargrave, and he had taken a very personal interest in Scott's welfare. He hadn't wanted to become that close, but the relationship and circumstances caused the evolution and, like it or not, dammit, he loved the kid! He felt compelled to do everything possible to bring Steve out of his sorrow.

Steve, since calling the Prentiss' back in Missouri, had sort of gone into a shell. This state of affairs was compounded by the death of Sergeant Gage whom Steve highly admired and respected. His depression had grown even deeper—far deeper. Steve's sorrow was overwhelming. It had begun to affect every aspect of his life; it was destroying his spirit. He had developed a pessimistic, totally negative view of everything. Now Steve hardly spoke to anyone, including Pappy. He rarely ate and was well on the way to even more serious problems if he didn't snap out of it.

During the war, Pappy had seen more than one buddy crack-up from depression and for the exact same reasons his close friend Steve was now experiencing, receiving a "Dear John" letter or news of the death of someone very special. He had tried repeatedly to talk to Steve and to try and get Steve to talk to him about LaRae. As soon as her name was mentioned, Steve would withdraw immediately into his shell. Steve, Pappy was convinced, was showing the unmistakable signs of depression. Pappy was driven to find some way to help his friend. He put Steve on leave for a week and took several days off himself to try and straighten things out.

Pappy decided to make a special trip on the Metro down to the Picadilly Circus and Soho area. There he went to a particular house that he had frequented on several past occasions. Over time Pappy had established a pleasant and friendly relationship with the Madam, apart from the business end of things he conducted with her employees. On the rare occasion lately when he visited the establishment, he would always present Louise, the Madam, with a beautiful red rose and a bottle of Pouilly-Fuissé White Burgundy French Wine, Louise's favorite.

On this visit, and with the second glass of the wine he had delivered, Pappy was explaining his dilemma and concerns for his young friend Steve.

"He's no longer himself at all Louise. His sorrow is overwhelming. It is affecting every aspect of his life, destroying his spirit and he's developed this bitter, pessimistic view of everything. If he continues on I fear he'll have a total breakdown. It's that severe. He won't speak with a doctor or the clergy. Hell! He rarely speaks to me. I was at my wits end in trying to think of anything that might help him when I thought of you and your lovely lassies here."

"So," said Louise, "he was totally devoted to this young lady back home, and she gave him up for another? In this case absence did not make the heart grow fonder, is that it?"

"Well, no, I don't believe it was quite like that, but, I don't really know. He's since received a letter from the girl, but didn't open it. In fact, he threw it away, and when he wasn't looking, I retrieved it. I'm saving it for him in the event he might want to read it later on. But, yes, he truly worshipped the young lady. Louise, I don't believe he ever knew love from anyone before and only for and with her. And now, he feels as though his world has ended."

"Yes, I understand, Phillip. Devilish difficult to try and aid someone under such circumstances." The two were quiet for several moments then Louise continued, "And so you think one of my girls might be able to help him out of this fit of depression he's experiencing?"

"Hell's Bells, I don't know. For Crissake, I doubt seriously that I'll even be able to get him to come down here. But if I can, do you have a nice young lady who can be sensitive to his situation? To tell you the truth, I have my doubts that she or anyone will be able to get him to talk, much less perform sexually. But I think something like this with a beautiful lass his own age might help—if anything will—I just plain flat-assed don't know what else to do."

"Yes, Phillip, I see your point and I do believe I have just the young lady you've described. She claims she is twenty-three; however, I suspect her to be nineteen or there abouts. She is French, but speaks English quite well. She has a way about her. Sensitive and understanding. Yet she can be both quiet and a proper hellcat. She favors, quite remarkably in appearance, this new French starlet Brigitte Bardot. She is a very popular young lady here.

I wish I had a dozen like her. Her name is Ashley Simmone. Would you like to meet her and perhaps have a chat?"

From there Pappy went to Bayswater Road to the Marquette Hotel not far from the downtown London all ranks Military Douglas House, or D House as it was commonly referred to. Any enlisted military member with guest, could go to the D House for the finest American style meal—steaks, chops, ribs, whatever, with a fantastic salad bar, cocktail bar, slot machines, and top entertainers from the states as well as from all over Europe. And the prices were reasonable.

After talking with Louise and also at length with Ashley, Pappy made reservations for himself, Steve and Ashley at the D house for dinner the next day. And then, hoping and praying things would work out as planned, he also made reservations and paid for a nice suite at the Marquette Hotel for Steve and Ashley for the following two days.

On the way back to Denham, Hargrave stopped by Louise's bordello and delivered the hotel key to Ashley and also paid her for her services in advance. Now, all he had to do was get Steve to come downtown. And he feared that would not be easy.

"You've not been off this blasted base for ages, lad, and I believe we could both do with a good thick Porterhouse steak, French fries, mushrooms and onions, and a terrific salad. Sounds larapin (delicious) eh, what do you say?" Pappy was working hard on Steve.

"And, also, I have a friend I want you to meet who has a bit of a problem which I believe we might be able to help with. I know you're not feeling the greatest just now, but this outing, I'm certain, will help us all."

Steve surprised Pappy by asking, "Who's your friend? What's his problem?"

This caught Pappy off guard, as he thought Steve had not been listening to him at all. He fumbled some with his response.

"Well, actually, it's a friend of a friend who's recently over here from France and, I believe there was a death in the family, some homesickness. I'm not sure of all the particulars, but I thought we could have dinner and maybe visit and talk some. That just might help, and besides, I'd like a good steak."

"Well, you don't need me for that, and I'm sure I wouldn't be much company anyway. I really don't want to go Pappy, guess I'm just not up to it."

His frustration evident, Pappy shouted, "Dammit Steve, I want you to come with me! I haven't asked you for a favor before, but now I am. I

169

need you to come with me and if you won't, I won't go either, even though I've given my word to my friend that I would be there!"

Steve pondered this for several minutes then looked up and said, "All right Pappy. If it means that much to you, I'll go, but I won't stay long. I'm just not in a mood to be with people."

Ashley was in the guest parlor just off the foyer in the Douglas house when Pappy and Steve walked up to her. Steve had expected a male and looked quizzically at Pappy when Ashley stood and shook his hand with introductions. Ashley was beautiful and Louise was right, she looked amazingly like France's sex kitten, Brigitte Bardot.

During cocktails and conversation, Steve found he enjoyed listening to her speak. She had a captivating accent.

With table wine Pappy said, "I propose a toast: To the lovely lady who graces our table." Steve stood with Pappy, as they saluted Ashley with their drinks and the toast.

The steaks were cooked to perfection. It was a wonderful meal and afterwards the trio went upstairs to the ballroom and there enjoyed the performance of "The Browns" who sang their current hit, *The Three Bells*. Ashley was thrilled. "I love that song," she said. "It is very popular in France. We call it *Les Trois Cloches*. It's sad, but lovely."

Out on the verandah during coffee for Ashley and Steve and hot tea for Pappy, the latter asked Ashley about her difficulty with recently coming to England from France. This had been rehearsed the day before.

Ashley, with her enchanting accent, did a marvelous job of describing how her mother and father had recently been killed in an automobile accident in France and how she had come to England to live with her auntie (and supposed friend of Pappy's). She went on to tell of how she missed her homeland, her friends, and of course, her parents. It was here that Pappy excused himself, saying he would be back momentarily.

Steve had very obviously warmed to Ashley and was sympathetic to her tale of woe. From that conversation they went on smoothly to others and eventually transitioned to Steve's recent heartbreak over LaRae. As he talked of this, somewhat reservedly, Ashley reached over to him and took his hand in hers and caressed it tenderly.

Pappy returned, looking pained. "I'm afraid I'm feeling a bit under the weather all of a sudden. I'm terribly sorry. I'm sure it's nothing, but I am a tad uncomfortable. If you two will forgive me, I think I'll call it an early evening and return to Denham."

"I'll take you back Pappy," Steve offered immediately.

"By no means," responded Pappy. "I feel badly enough that I've invited Ashley to spend the evening with us, and now I have to bow out. You'll have to carry on and represent the two of us.

"Ashley, I beg your forgiveness and thank you for your delightful company," Pappy continued. "Will you please pass my regards to your lovely auntie and tell her that I send my best wishes and hope to see her again shortly? And Steve, take good care of Ashley. And Ashley, dear, please take good care of me lad here. I'll see you back at the base Steve."

Pappy left the D House sporting a wide smile and a hopeful feeling of successful accomplishment.

Later, as night began to fall, Steve and Ashley walked along the Thames River by the Tower of London near London Bridge. They could hear the toll of Big Ben striking seven p.m. as they sat on a bench in a park between two large cannons near the water's edge. Holding hands, they continued to talk quietly about Steve's feelings of disconsolation and grief over losing LaRae.

A tear rolled down his cheek and he looked at her, embarrassed, and said apologetically, "Sorry, I'm kinda having a hard time with this."

Ashley touched him tenderly and erased the tear, "No, no *mon cheri*, no need to be sorry. It is good to speak of these things. To get them out in the open, and to grieve, and to then go on. If it were possible for us to change things, we would. Sometimes, as with this, events, unfortunately, cannot be altered. And we hurt. I would help you change things if I could. I will help you with the hurt, if you will let me."

She took Steve into her arms and held him tight and ran her fingers through the hair on the back of his head. Steve leaned back and at arm's length looked deeply into her eyes. He held her face in his hands and then, hesitantly, kissed her tenderly, with trembling lips. Ashley pulled him closer, tightly, her tongue explored his mouth as she kissed him back, long and hard and passionately.

In the hotel room only the bedside table lamps were lighted. Steve had undressed first and was in bed with the sheet covering him when Ashley emerged nude from the bathroom. She stood momentarily in the doorway, her beautiful body highlighted by the strange crepuscular glow from the bathroom window. She walked to the bed and slid beneath the sheet Steve had raised. She took his rigid penis in her hand, squeezed it gently, looked at Steve, smiled and said, "Monsieur, won't you please introduce me to your friend here?"

With a fresh double Cutty and a splash of water, Pappy turned to his drinking buddy Alexander, whom, much to Alexander's chagrin, Pappy again called "Axle" instead of his preferred nickname of "Alex."

"Right you are then. I'll draw you a bloomin' picture to prove it." Hargrave motioned to the bartender.

"What'll it be Sarge?"

"Waldo, fetch us a piece of paper from that tablet back there, and let me borrow your pen a minute. There, that's a good chap. Ta, mate."

"Now then Axle," and drawing a darn good picture of a bathtub and a stick man sitting in the tub, Pappy said, "I'm going to bloody well prove to you that the shower is much cleaner, probably ninety-nine point eight percent more hygienic, than the bathtub you're so fond of."

"Name's Alex dammit! If I tole you that once, I've tole you that a hundred times! And it ain't done it Hargrave. Shower has only tiny little sprinkles. Guy can't get a good scrubbin' in a few drops of water."

"All right then mate, give us a look and see here. What goes into the bathtub first? Damn right, your stinking feet, that's what.

"And, then, what's next? You can bet your Nellie on that one. Ole Rose splashes down in the water. That's what! So now you've got your dirty feet and arse setting smack dab in the middle of things. And then you reach down between your legs, probably directly in front of your tallywhacker, and god only knows where that rascal of a thing has been, and you scoop up a handfull of that already dirty water to jolly well wash your face with. You scrub under your arms and the rest of your grungy body and then, then you rinse yourself with the same water you've just gone and washed all those soiled parts with. Cor blimey, and after all this you've got the balls to sit here and tell me you call yourself clean?"

"Jesus, Hargrave, I never looked at it that way. You convinced me. I ain't ever gonna take another tub bath as long as I live. Damn! Feel dirty settin' here just thinkin' 'bout it. For Crissake, might even stink right now. Do I stink Hargrave? I probably stink, don't I?"

Envisioning Alexander coming in from his dirty motorpool job daily, unbathed, greasy, odoriferous and sliding upon the barstool immediately next to him, Pappy, realizing the sizable error he may have made said, "Wait a minute, Axle. If you can't use a shower, you have to use a tub."

"No sir, not me, I ain't ever gonna use a tub again. I ain't gonna wash my face with water my butt's been in first. Yucko!"

"Well, Axle, as you damn well know, very few rentals here in England have baths with showers. When you can't have a shower, you may have to change your bathing habits. Wash first things first, but don't go about without a bath for Crissake!"

"Nosireebob, I ain't washin' my face with buttfeet dirty water ever again! You've made a believer outta me Hargrave."

Acknowledging and regretting his sizable error, Pappy said, "Better give me another Cutty, please Waldo and make it a double."

Steve walked into the NCO club and up to Pappy sitting at the bar. He tapped Pappy on the shoulder. Pappy turned and when he saw Steve, he hurriedly set his drink down and stood facing Steve with a concerned and questioning expression.

Before Pappy could say anything, Steve took him in his arms, gave him a giant bear hug, and whispered, "Thank you." Still holding him, he patted Pappy on the back several times, then turned and left.

Pappy wiped a tear from his eye and shouted to Steve's retreating back, "Bless you, Laddie. Bless you. Damn it's good to have you back!"

Chapter 25

The Pain of Love

The "Dog Days" of August had arrived in Southeast Missouri. The days were scorchers. Humidity was high, often matching the blazing, record setting temperatures of the daylight hours. And the nights too were stifling. Even with every window open, the rooms were insufferably hot with not a breath of wind to stir the night air.

For too many weeks now the days passed interminably without breezes or any sign of rain. The corn stalks in the cracked and caked fields were twisting due to lack of moisture. The Mississippi was so low it was now showing sandbars previously unseen for years. Riverboat navigation was endangered and traffic had been halted altogether in some areas of the river. Farmer's ponds were also dangerously low and many were turning over with hundreds of stocked fish dying due to lack of oxygen in the water. Fruit crops, soybeans, and grain fields were all in jeopardy of being lost.

The first big drops of rain that fell came as a surprise. Station KFVS had reported earlier that there was a slight chance of pop up showers later in the day, but cautioned its radio listeners the rain would be extremely scanty and to not get their hopes built up for any real relief from the heat. Still, a huge black thunderhead had developed just past the Diversion Channel, the Big Ditch bridge, as Ernie Thompson was driving south on Highway 61 to Ancell to pick up his date, Angela Ryder. Ernie quickly had to roll up the front windows when the rain changed from intermittent large drops to driving gusts of rain pelting down in sheets. He pulled off the road by the Saveway Gas Station and Restaurant and waited until the rain let up.

While sitting there, he checked again to make sure he had the pill, Picabo, the date rape drug rolled up in the tissue and tucked securely in his pants pocket. He had used the pill infrequently, but always with success and none of the girls he had been with after drugging them ever caused a ruckus. Ernie figured when they'd come back around, if they suspected what might've happened, they probably had wanted to have sex anyway.

"Sure. They all wanted a good screwing or they wouldn't have gone out with me," he reckoned. Still, he didn't take chances and never dated the same girls after giving them the drug, removing their panties and having sex. "Old Picabo works like a champ for me every time," he said. *It served me double duty with LaRae Prentiss, he remembered with a smile. Got her cherry and put the blame for it on that simple shit Duncan. Also heard a rumor she's pregnant—if she is it's probably mine—wouldn't that be a lick! Guess she told that bastard Steve Scott about things 'cause I heard she's not gonna go to England and marry him now. So, I got even with Scott for our fight and had his tight poon-tang to boot. That'll teach 'em to fuck around with me!"*

Ernie pulled up in front of the Ryder's house in Ancell and blew the horn. Momentarily Angela appeared at the screendoor and yelled, "Be right out." It was early and they'd planned to go to the drive-in movie up by the Big Ditch so they stopped at the Saveway and ordered hamburgers and Cokes. While Angela went to the ladies room, Ernie hurriedly dropped the Picabo tablet into her drink and stirred it with the straw. When Angela returned, Ernie went to the jukebox and played *Wake Up Little Susie* by the Everly Brothers, and then he used the restroom. While he was absent Angela's best friend Shirley came into the restaurant, purchased some chewing gum, saw Angela and sat down in Ernie's vacant chair.

Shirley was obviously very thrilled about her recent engagement. She showed Angela her new ring and was bouncing up and down. Overcome with her emotions, she picked up Ernie's Coke and took a large drink. Angela laughingly said, "Shirley, you just drank Ernie's drink!"

"Oh my gosh!" Shirley shouted. "I'm so excited! Guess I thought that was yours. I'm sorry, here, I'll go get him another."

"No, that's okay," said Angela switching the sodas, "I'll just give him mine and I'll drink his."

"Are you sure? I'll be happy to get him another one."

"No, that's all right, I'm not real thirsty anyway."

"Okay," said the excited Shirley, "well, I've gotta run. We'll see you later." Shirley smiled and waved at Ernie who was returning to the table as she was leaving.

Ernie ate his hamburger and drank the drugged soda. He played the jukebox some more, and he and Angela smoked a couple of cigarettes passing time and waiting for it to get a bit darker before going to the drive-in. Ernie noted that Angela had taken only a small sip of her drink. He had big plans for Angela and a hot time in the back seat of his car a little later. He hoped he wouldn't have a hard time getting her pants off. Sometimes in the past that had proven to be a chore. And just sliding their panties to the side made things really tough! Ernie lit his third cigarette and began to feel sleepy and to have hot flashes.

"I ain't feelin' so good alla sudden," he complained to Angela. "Wonder if there was something wrong with that hamburger? You feelin' okay?"

"Yeah, I feel fine," Angela responded, "but you really don't look too good."

"Yeah, I feel . . . sorta funny, kinda sick. I think maybe I better take you back to your house and go back home myself. Startin' to feel really weird."

"No, you go on home, I'll call my mom or get a ride with a friend," Angela countered. "Are you feeling well enough to drive? Shall I call someone?" She was genuinely concerned.

"Naw, I'll be okay, just feel kinda weird. I'll call you later maybe."

Driving back north on 61 toward Cape Girardeau, Ernie caught himself nodding his head in drowsiness. He jerked himself upright from another nod just as he drove past the turnoff for the drive-in theater.

"Damn, screwed up the chance for a good piece of pussy tonight! Don't know what's the matter with me."

He caught himself dozing again just as his right front fender scraped the lower railing of the Diversion Channel's bridge. Thinking he was going to crash through the bridge and plunge into the water, he whipped the steering wheel sharply to the left and the front of his car collided with the middle section of the huge eighteen wheeler traveling seventy miles per hour in the opposite direction.

Ernie's car was crushed, twisted, rolled and dragged, screeching in a giant shower of sparks to the south end of the bridge and beyond before the truck driver could come to a stop. He jumped out of the truck's cab with a fire extinguisher and was immediately blown backward twenty feet by the explosion of gasoline and fire from Ernie's car.

Steve rarely received mail from home, or anyone. Since his phone call to the Prentiss' quite awhile back, he no longer expected to receive any personal correspondence. That's why he was surprised when Arkee came into his office with a letter addressed to him from his grandmother back in Missouri. With some trepidation he took the letter and opened it. It read:

> *Dear Grandson:*
> *I apologize for not having written more often, but as you know,*
> *I'm not one much for writing to anyone. So much easier just to*
> *pick up the phone and call, but, in your case, 'course I can't do*
> *that. We're all well here and hope the same for you.*

*My reason for writing is a sad one to pass on some bad news.
One of your friends, Ernie Thompson, was in a car accident up
by the Big Ditch and was killed. Guess he went to sleep driving
and ran into one of those big trucks that's always whizzing down
the road. His funeral was a week ago Saturday. And, some
more bad news son, our little sweetheart LaRae has lost her
baby . . .*

Steve stopped reading at this point, refolded the letter, and put it back in
the envelope. He stood and walked over to Sergeant Hargrave's desk.
"I'm gonna take a little walk Pappy," he said, "I'll be back in a few
minutes."

Pappy had seen Arkee deliver the letter to Steve. Concerned, he asked,
"Are you okay? Want some company?"

"Naw, thanks, I'm fine. Be back in a little while." When he left the
Orderly Room, Steve walked around the back of the building in the
direction of the bridge leading to the old mansion.

At the bridge he leaned his back against the top rail, withdrew the letter
and, holding it tightly, stared off into space. He pictured LaRae, radiant, as
always, her beautiful, brilliant eyes flashing as she looked at him so
lovingly, tilting her head to one side and then reaching for him, her arms
extended and clasping his hands in hers and at arms length, smiling her
captivating smile and miming the words, "Hey boy, somebody loves you."
Then quickly she pulled him to her and kissed his lips.

Standing there he remembered and heard again one of their favorite
songs, the Platters' *My Prayer*. He could hear it just as clearly as if he and
LaRae were once more standing side by side in front of the jukebox back
home. He would have his right arm around her waist and her left arm was
around him, her thumb hooked into a belt loop of his Levis. He could smell
her, feel her presence, and became excited and thrilled by the memory of her
nearness. He could feel, once again, her complete and total love for him and
only him, and, he felt overwhelmed with his heartache and love for her.

Steve unfolded the letter, and began to read again.

*. . . our little sweetheart LaRae has lost her baby. Tiny
thing—only three months along. She miscarried and the doctors
could not stop the hemorrhaging so they had to operate. While
they were in surgery, they discovered that LaRae has another
very serious problem. Stevie, it's the kind of problem they can't
do much of anything about, and it tears my heart out to tell you*

177

that they don't expect her to live much beyond eight months to a
year. If that long. Poor little thing.

The whole town is heartsick and LaRae looks to me like she's
lost the will to live. Never see her beautiful smile anymore.
She's lost her color and looks pale and drawn. She's skinny as a
rail now and seems like she just looks through you when you
talk to her. It's like she don't hear you. Like she don't care—for
nothing.

Hard for me to look at her without crying. Your uncle and
family are all doing well. He has the Cottonbelt run to
Jonesboro now, and that's pretty regular so he can plan things
and not have to wonder when he might be called to take a
freight out. The kids are all back in school and it's a lot quieter
round here now. The local preacher got another church down
south sommers, maybe Georgia. Some might miss him, but I'll
not. Guess that's all the news I've got, son, and I'm sorry most
of it's bad. Please remember to say prayers for LaRae. I send
you my love.

> *Grandma Bertha*

Steve turned, held the letter out away from the bridge and released it.
He watched the paper float down and alight gently upon the stream where it
was promptly carried away by the swift current.

He was still standing there, bent over the rail, watching the water and
listening to its tumbling ripples when Pappy walked up and stood quietly at
his side.

"Thought you might be here," Pappy said gently. "Wanna talk?"

Steve looked at him for a long moment, then his trembling voice
reflecting his grief and sorrow, said "Goddam the hurt and pain in loving
someone anyhow!"

Two weeks later Steve received yet another mailing from his grandmother. It contained only a short note and a newspaper clipping which read:

Obituary Notice:

LaRae Prentiss died at her residence Thursday, October
10th following a brief illness. Miss Prentiss is survived by
her parents Oscar and Fern Prentiss. Miss Prentiss was a
member of the Missionary Baptist Church of Fornfelt where
services will be held at 4:00 p.m. tomorrow with interment
following at Lightner's Cemetery in Illmo.

Chapter 26

Alex, the Pugilist

K arl Miller slowed his Mercedes sports car as he passed first the Denham train station and then the Green Parrot Pub. He noted, again, that the pub always seemed to have several cars parked in front and never lacked for a steady stream of patrons. He promised himself to check it out sometime. Miller clicked on his right turn signal and entered the main gate at Denham Studios. He received from and returned a sharp salute to the gate guard and drove directly to the Orderly Room of the Third Air Postal Squadron for his meeting with the acting Commander Earl Keene. He smiled to himself as he walked past the now vacant office of the former First Sergeant, Calvin Gage.

"Karl," said Captain Keene, "I've received a letter from the owner of the apartment building where one of your couriers rents a flat. Guess they sent it to me because your guy indicated he was attached to the Postal Squadron when he filled out the apartment rental application."

"What's it about?" Karl asked. He was, as always, curt, short-fused and now obviously irritated by this situation.

"It's a complaint about loud music, parties, cars coming and going at all hours of the night, drunks and a steady stream of gals and guys in and out of the apartment. Owner says some neighbors have complained about seeing outside hand, wall and knob-jobs in process and nude women running around inside the apartment."

"Sounds to me like those are simply American goodwill initiatives to cement better U.S.-U.K. relations."

"Well, the apartment owner doesn't look at it that way and threatens to contact our Ambassador if things don't calm down. Here," Keene handed the envelope to Miller. "It's your guy and your problem, you answer it. I've written a letter to the apartment owner telling him this is a matter under your command, and that you'll look into it and respond to the complaint."

"Yeah," Karl said as he stood, snatched the letter, turned and left the building. He then walked down the street to the Motor Pool and checked out a small pickup truck his couriers needed to haul courier bags, attaché case handcuffs, rotary locks and other supplies out to their airport supply lockers. After signing for the truck he crumpled and tossed the letter of complaint into an office waste paper basket.

Driving back to his South Ruislip office he again passed the Green Parrot Pub. *Gotta stop in there and check it out sometime,* he reminded himself.

"I don't give a shit if he is littler'n me, if he bumps my chair again or smacks me in the back of the head with his elbow one more time, I'm gonna coalcock the little fucker!" Alexander exclaimed none too quietly in the crowded corner of the Green Parrot Pub. In fact, he'd nearly shouted it to be heard over Paul Anka's recording of *Diana,* which was blaring away on the jukebox.

A British fellow pub patron was sitting with his young lovely at the table directly in back of Alexander, Steve, Arkee, and Boyd's table. Each time the Brit, a rather effeminate looking chap, arose to get drinks or put a shilling in the record player, he'd either bump Alex's chair or boink him in the head upon leaving or returning. Alex had had just enough liquor to become easily antagonized.

"He could be more careful. There's room a plenty. Could even drive a friggin' deuce and a half through here. Pissed me off. Little fucker! Probably don't like Americans."

"Mind your manners Alex," Steve cautioned. "Try to remember that we're guests here. This is their country and we're supposed to be friendly allies."

"Yeah Axle," Boyd, who loved to yank Alexander's chain, chimed in. "These folks didn't invite you over here. If you ain't happy, go on back home! Say, I'll bet your teacher gave you bad marks for not getting along well with others in school, didn't she? And, too, don't forget HSORI. Didja forget HSORI Axle?"

"Goddammit, my name's not Axle! It's Alexander and you damn right well know that! If you don't start calling me by my right name, I ain't gonna associate with you anymore! I don't mess up your name, you gap-toothed fucker! 'Sides, it's not like—" Alexander was cut off in mid sentence as the Brit, returning to his table, accidentally (maybe) spilled some of his overfilled drink down the back of Alex's shirt collar.

Alexander, who'd been a bit on the testy side all afternoon, flew into a rage. He jumped up, overturning his chair and grabbed the arm of the offending Brit. This caused the entire drink contents from the tray being carried to spill.

"Okay, that's it. That did it. Now you've done it! You been ridin' my ass all night, and I ain't takin' no more of it!"

As busy and crowded as the pub was, it was amazing how fast Glen, the pub owner, was around the bar and at the table even before Steve or the others could intervene. Glen stood between Alex and the Brit. "All right, you blokes. We'll have no trouble in here. If you want to discuss differences, pack 'em on outside then."

Before Steve could attempt to reason with or to calm Alexander down, Alex had grabbed the much smaller offender and dragged him out the front door. Three quarters of the pub immediately emptied to watch the fracas.

Steve was trying to smooth things over and, as hard as he tried, Alex was just as intent on doing some bodily harm to his evening's antagonist.

"You been bopping me in the head, bumping my chair all evening, and now you just poured half a drink down my neck a purpose. Don't tell me you didn't 'cause you did, and you did it a purpose. Piss me off, you fuckin' jerk, and now I'm gonna kick your ass up to your shoulders. I'm gonna knock a fart outta you that'll whistle like a freight train. I'm gonna whomp you clear into the middle of next week and teach you not to pick on a good Reb from Duck Hill, Mississippi!"

Alex, wobbling from too much bubbly, assumed a John L. Sullivan stance with his left leg, arm and fist well out in front of him. His fists were raised head high and spaced widely apart. His boxing position and the puckered frown and expression he wore made it difficult for the gathering crowd not to laugh. His opponent, with hands on hips, stood directly in front of the drunk Sergeant and was just barely above Alex's waist in height. With his feet planted firmly, Alex began to move his fists in alternating circles, creating an even funnier spectacle.

"All right you little fucker, you're gonna pay for all this harassment. C'mon, put 'em up! Been askin' for it all night. C'mon stick them dukes up. You're gonna get it!"

Yet to utter a single word, the Brit stepped forward quickly and grabbed Alex by his testicles and squeezed. Alex, with a surprised and bewildered expression, looked down at his crotch, then back up again into the smiling face of his opponent. Alexander screamed the highest pitched scream any of the onlookers had ever heard.

As he doubled over, the Brit brought up a knee to impact with Alex's nose and mouth. Alexander's face bounced off the Brit's knee, almost like in slow motion, as the drunk Sergeant crumpled to the ground.

The British fighter stood above the unconscious Alex. Smacking hands together twice as if dusting them off and surprising all, spoke with a voice that was definitely female. "His pugilist skills are an even match for his poor manners when in the company of ladies," the lesbian said aloofly. She then collected her lover lady friend and coolly walked back inside the pub.

Steve and the others struggled with a rubber-legged, half-conscious Alexander who was mumbling, "What tha fuck happened . . ." and looking at Boyd he asked, "what does HSORI mean?" It was no small chore trying to walk him back to the base.

Several hours later, nearing 10:30, Captain Karl Miller returned to the Denham Studios Motor Pool the small pickup truck his courier officers had used for a couple of runs to London's Heathrow Airport. Although it was late Miller didn't mind taking the truck back because he needed to pick up his car he'd parked at Denham near the Third Air Postal Squadron Orderly Room. After returning the truck to the motor pool Miller walked over to the All-Ranks Club intending to have a cognac or two. Upon entering the club he saw several members from the Third APS. Not wanting to be in their company Miller immediately turned around and left the club.

Passing the Green Parrot Pub Miller noticed the night light still shining on the outside sign. Now, all the more yearning for a drink, he stopped in front of the tavern and entered. There was a couple at a small table and another patron at the far end of the bar. Miller took the last barstool at the opposite end of the bar.

"Evening G'uvnor," Glen, the owner, greeted Miller. "You're just in time for a short nip or two. I've just given 'last call' for the evening." Throughout England the mandatory closing time for all pubs was 11 p.m. That hour having been fixed back during World War I was inspired by the fears of munitions workers getting drunk. Most pub owners and drinkers preferred scrapping established closing times, but the licensing laws prevailed. Noticing Miller's officer rating as he removed his jacket, Glen asked, "Wot'll it be then, Captain?"

"Cognac, rocks, please." He paused for a moment and then, uncharacteristically, he spoke to the proprietor. "Usually when I pass by here your establishment always looks packed, even at a late hour. Slow night for you?"

Setting the drink before Miller, Glen continued with his nightly cleaning of the bar. "No sir, we've had our usual crowd tonight, earlier, and a tad more than our usual bits of excitement." Speaking very quietly he continued, "One of your American chaps got into a row with that little lady sitting at the table over there." Glen nodded his head at the transvestite lesbian whose back was towards them.

"You mean that little guy?"

"She may look like a little guy but she's no bloke, that one. She's a she and she's a proper little scrapper to boot. She took care of that Yank what challenged her in extremely short order. The other little lovely setting beside her is her lover."

"She sure looks like a guy to me."

"Aye, that she does. I had a chat with her awhile ago. She's a professional make-up artist over at the Pinewood Film Studios. Says she works on the weekly television series, *Ivanhoe*, starring that actor, what's his name—Roger Moore—that's so popular just now. Me missus and son never fail to watch that one. Big fans, they are. Anyway, I told her of me family's interest and she's invited the lot of us over to the film studios set one day to meet the actors. Mind you, I may not approve of her ways, but I reckon that's her own business and quite obviously she's good at her job. I'd wager a bloke that just by lookin' at her wouldn't know she's not a male less'n he'd pull down her undies or listened to her speak. She's just moved into that row of flats across the street."

Miller once again turned casually and stared at the lesbian couple as they arose from their table and made their way, noticeably more than a little tipsy, towards the door. Through icy blue eyes now narrowed to slits he saw the two wave goodnight to the pub owner. Suddenly a curdling, bitter-tasting hatred welled within Miller as his hand unconsciously rested on the outline of the switchblade knife in his uniform trousers. He quickly tossed down the remnant of his drink and asked for a refill. That one, he also drank promptly. Placing a ten shilling note on the bar by his empty glass he picked up his jacket and rendered a two finger salute to Glen in response to the owner's, "'G-nite Captain. Come again, sir."

Miller backed his car up facing it towards the street with the lights off. He watched to see the couple enter the door, which was the last flat in the complex. He waited until he saw the front room lights go off then drove across the street for a closer look at the apartment—he made a mental note of the location. "*Untermenschen!*" subhumans, he hissed. Imaginary newspaper headlines momentarily flashed through his mind: **"IS JACK BACK?"** they might read. The reference being to London's notorious

Jack the Ripper who killed and horribly mutilated at least five ladies of the night back in the autumn of 1888. "If I had my way these two would have the body parts they love so much removed and openly displayed for everyone to see and marvel at. Maybe Jack will be back," he said as he sped out of the driveway onto the main road.

"Ohmygawd, it looks as if you've been run over by a ruddy lorry!" Martha exclaimed when she first laid eyes on Alexander in the cafeteria the following Monday morning. With a hand each on either side of his face she asked, "Wot on earth has happened to you Alex, you poor dear?"

"He may not look it at the moment Luv," Warren Boyd said, "but he made us all proud the other night. A regular gladiator he was, wasn't you Axle?"

"Tell you the truth I don't remember much about it. But I do seem to recollect the bloke I fought was a big bruiser. Whaddaya reckon he weighed? Probably a couple hundred?"

"That and more, easily," Arkee said. "Hell, he was probably two hundred fifty pounds. Big, muscled, tall guy too! But Axle told him right off the bat: Ask no quarter—draw no quarter. Axle took care of him good, huh Boyd?"

"Axle's foot work dazzled him! You could tell that right off. And when Axle unloaded that upper cut, it damn near lifted the guy right up off the ground. Knocked him out coldern' a mackerel, huh Axle? The uppercut's what did it, wasn't it?"

"Yeah and the guy barely touched you, huh Axle?" Arkee asked.

"Well, I dunno for sure. I'm havin' a hard time rememberin'. And I got this hell of a sore nose—boy, does my nose hurt! And uh . . . Old Slim and the twins are kinda tender down below. Wonder how that happened?"

Alexander did indeed look pitiful. His badly bruised nose resembled a small, flattened pancake. He was sporting two giant black eyes reminiscent of the large rings around raccoon's eyes. When he walked, he kinda waddled due to his bruised and very sensitive scrotum. But Boyd and Arkee had convinced him that he had performed as a championship fighter and had fearlessly, ruthlessly, but gentlemanly and professionally, taught the local pub bully a well-deserved lesson.

Pulling up a chair to their table, Pappy, taking in the Denham Studios Floyd Patterson at a glance, said to Alex, "How's it going Champ?"

Pappy had been spending at least every other night and most of the weekends with Brooke, his English childhood sweetheart and now very serious ladyfriend from Harrow on the Hill. In fact, the subject of marriage was a frequent topic of conversation between the two of them.

Shortly after Gage's death and his young friend Steve Scott's apparent recovery from his heartbreak and depression, a quiet but distinct change had come over Pappy. He quit drinking all together, had only a soft drink with his friends at the club or a pub from time to time. His relationship with his two closest companions, Brooke and Steve, had definitely become more intense and caring although this was well-hidden from others.

Outwardly he appeared to be the same on the job, but his secret contacts with "DROPHAMMER," interested European and stateside agencies, and personnel had increased considerably in tempo. Pappy still joked about with his friends and co-workers, but he was now rigidly mind set and absolutely convinced that he would find the murderer of Calvin Gage and the ringleader of the Nazi plunder operation. And, somehow, he could not shake the impression that the two were in some way connected.

Pappy had began carrying his Beretta Model 81 in the custom-made holster that fit in the small of his back. The 380 semi-automatic pistol was tucked away in his ankle holster. At nights, and whenever in new or strange places, he would become extremely aware of those around him, including any odd or unusual circumstances. The feel of the weapons against his body provided him a feeling of comfort and security.

"Will it be your usual cuppa, Sergeant Hargrave, strong as sin, black as hate, and hot as love?" Martha asked with her usual cheery smile.

"Top of the morning to you, and no, thank you, Martha, me luv. I believe I'll have a spot of your lovely tea and a crumpet this morning. Also, I'm feeling a tad on the randy side so, maybe I'll have a bit of your delicious orange marmalade, thank you me dear."

"And how's the ever lovely Lady Brooke?" Steve asked Pappy after all at the table had passed around their "Hellos."

"She continues to border on super fantastic, thank you laddie, and she sends you her love and hugs and asks that you stop over this coming weekend for dinner on Sunday. I've talked her into preparing my favorite meal—rack of lamb and Yorkshire pudding. I fibbed a bit and told her it was yours as well. Hope you don't mind. And Axle, what in the world has happened to you, old sod? You look an absolute wreck!"

Alexander, seemingly still in a semi-befuddled state, mumbled, "He was a big sumbish Hargrave—stood six foot eight and weighed over three hundred pounds. Boyd said he hit me with a baseball bat when I wasn't lookin'. And he insulted us and our country, so I hadda take him down a notch or two. Tell him about it, Boyd. Tell you one thing Hargrave, he'll not do that again. Pissed me off good is what he did. Go on Boyd. Go on and tell him all about it."

"You all excuse me please," Warren Boyd said, sliding back his chair, "I gotta go get started on that damn Morning Report."

Chapter 27

The Engagement Party

First Lieutenant Cody Foltz was one of the few people Captain Karl Miller was even halfway friendly with. Foltz worked for Miller as a courier and they had traveled together on several classified ARFCOS trips. Foltz had been dating one of London's loveliest models and was hosting a Saturday night engagement party at their downtown London flat.

On Friday morning Foltz and Captain Miller were having a rare cup of coffee together at the snack bar. It was not Miller's practice to associate with anyone, particularly coworkers.

"Hey boss, Camille and I are having our engagement party tomorrow night. How about stopping by if you don't have anything else planned?"

"Naw. I'm not much of a partygoer and I don't like crowds."

"There won't be any crowd, boss. Camille is inviting a few of her female modeling friends, and boy are they some lookers. I've invited two of my British friends, and with you, that'll be it. Four of us guys and the rest will be some of England's most beautiful gals! Why don't you come on down? You might get lucky with one of Camille's beautiful coworkers. Guarantee you won't be disappointed—in the looks department anyway—the rest of it is up to you."

Karl Miller, concerned about being stopped and searched by civil customs officials, had all but stopped his black market operation. He rarely traveled outside England on official business, opting to send his subordinates instead. His military flights to Germany and his subsequent stops at the mine in Salzdorf had also slowed down considerably. With the law enforcement and customs heat being applied, he didn't want to take any chances. But he had become extremely bored with all the inactivity.

It might be good to get out and mix some, he thought, *and it has been quite some time since I've enjoyed a good, robust roust with a cute little Schatz. What the hell—why not?*

"Yeah, Foltz, that sounds interesting. Maybe you can write some instructions or draw me a map on how to find your place."

"Sure thing boss. It's easy to find, and there's plenty of parking. Things're gonna start about seven."

By eight-thirty the next evening, Cody Foltz was seriously regretting having invited Karl Miller to the party.

"He's an absolute cad!" Camille was all but shouting to Cody in their apartment kitchen where they were alone. "He's barely able to walk he's so drunk, and he has been pawing and ogling all of my friends from the moment he arrived. How could you invite such a beast to our party?"

"I'm sorry, Camille. I've never seen him drunk before. I didn't know he'd act like this."

"Well, get him out of here. He's even tried to pull Kathleen into the bedroom awhile ago after he put his hand on her crotch! Tell him to leave Cody. He's ruining everything. Tell him to go—now!"

"Damn, baby, he's my boss. I can't just tell him to get out."

"Then I shall. I won't have my friends humiliated and embarrassed like this—and that's not to mention how I feel about it this very instant!" Camille flung back over her shoulder as she turned and was hurrying out of the kitchen.

"Oh shit!" Foltz said to himself as he barely cracked open the kitchen door to spy Camille making a beeline toward a drunken Karl Miller. Foltz busied himself at the fridge in the kitchen, preparing another unneeded tray of hors d'oeuvres.

"I'm sorry, Captain Miller, but I must ask you to leave. You have offended all of our guests and embarrassed Cody and myself tremendously. I shall be happy to call you a taxi if you feel you are unable to drive safely."

"Leave? Offended? Go to hell!" Miller responded, looking at Camille through angry, wavering eyes. "I don't need help from you or anyone. I can buy and sell the whole damn lot of you three hundred times over and never even miss it."

Miller made a move to shove her aside, but Camille quickly stepped backward out of his reach. Captain Miller staggered to the apartment door and left, leaving the door open and mumbling curses on his way out.

Once outside Miller leaned back against the door of his new black Mercedes Benz 190SL and took several deep drafts of the cool night air.

"Not much of a party anyway, although the cognac was good. I suppose the girls were being stand-offish because they didn't want one another to know they were or could be an easy lay. *Drekische sows*—who needs them? Probably not a good screw in the entire bunch. However, I do hate

to go home again, unsatisfied. Might swing down past Piccadilly Circus
and check the action there. Yeah, why not?" Miller said to the night
air. "It's not far away. Might help to relieve some of the pressure."

On the way he sobered slightly and determined he should not solicit
a hooker in the heavy traffic areas, but maybe some side street where
his impressive sports car would not be so ostentatious and noticeable.
He rounded a corner and decided to take a less traveled and darkened
street. Eventually he passed a group of prostitutes and noticed a single
figure standing well beyond the others. He pulled near the curb and
stopped beside her. He rolled the window down and the whore leaned
down to speak to him.

"Hello Luv, are you interested in some company?" she questioned in
a young, but rather gruff voice.

"Do you have some place we can go that's quiet, maybe off the
beaten track?"

"Yes Luv, I've just the place and it 'tisn't far. Shall I get in then?"

Miller opened the door and the prostitute slid in beside him.

"Take this right just coming up and then the first left. I'll direct you
on from there," she said as she placed her hand on his crotch and traced
a long fingernail across his penis now beginning to stir inside his
trousers.

Traveling only a few blocks, they were soon beyond heavy
downtown traffic and the well-lighted streets. The passenger unzipped
Miller's pants, removed his erect penis and was stroking it. After
several more turns, she directed Miller to a row of flats on a darkened
street. "Stop here then. That's all right Luv."

Miller struggled in the close confines of the car, awkwardly putting
things back in place, and making himself presentable. He followed the
prostitute up the walk and into the apartment.

Once inside, instead of turning on the overhead light, the prostitute
switched on a very pale bedside lamp. She sat on the bed and
motioned Miller over. Again she unzipped his trousers and removed
his penis.

Miller, slightly more sobered now and in a high state of sexual
stimulation said, "That's okay for in the car, but now I want some of
you. Take your clothes off."

"All in good time, Luv. Just let me work on things a bit here first.
My, you are well-endowed though aren't you," she said as she took him
in her mouth and fondled his scrotum.

"All right, that's enough! If you continue you'll make me spend, and I want your body," Miller said as he put his hands on her head to move her back away from him. With that effort the prostitute's wig slid backward and revealed the male head of hair beneath the wig.

Astonished, Miller just stared at the transvestite sitting on the bed who, with downcast eyes, still gently cradled Miller's testicles in his hand. Miller recoiled in shock and disgust. He reached down, grabbed the transvestite by the shoulders and jerked him up off the bed and into the air. Slamming the prostitute down on the bed, Miller grabbed the blouse he was wearing at the bodice and ripped it open. He grasped the brassiere and tore that from him. With his switchblade knife he slashed first the waistband of the skirt then the underpants and ripped those away.

The prostitute lay naked and frightened before Miller.

"I am afraid that you have tried to fool the wrong person with your silly game," Miller said as he glared down at the young man. His eyes had turned demonic and he wore a vicious grin.

"Please don't hurt me." The mascara and make-up was now smeared, exposing and betraying the young male face which, with the wig, had looked convincingly like a female just a few short moments ago.

Miller slit with his knife then ripped a bed sheet in strips; he rolled the homosexual onto his stomach and tied his hands behind him. He also tied his feet and gagged the now terrified prostitute. Miller walked over to the small gas fireplace, lit it, and rested a pointed steel poker against the blue, sputtering flames. He stared transfixed at the fire until the point of the poker had become red hot.

His bound victim, watching Miller's every move, lay whimpering on the bed. His eyes were wide in horror and feared anticipation.

Time had flown for Miller in grisly obsession. He looked at his wristwatch and decided he should be leaving. With the towel he had used to remove his fingerprints, he placed the bloodied poker near the fireplace and turned off the gas jet. He was walking toward the front door when he heard a key being inserted into the lock and saw the knob turning. He quickly stood behind the opening door.

"Doyal, are you here?" questioned the effeminate looking and sounding young man as he tentatively opened the door, stepped inside, closed and locked the door. His back was toward Miller and his attention focused ahead for any sign of his friend.

"My god, what is this horrid odor Doyal? It smells—what's burning? Doyal—? Uuuunh!" he groaned as Miller put a forearm chokehold around his throat and dragged him into the bedroom.

Near the fireplace Miller, again, grasped the poker. He pushed the newcomer onto the bed and savagely struck him on the back of his head.

Miller gagged him and tied the young man's hands behind him as he had done with the other. He removed the man's trousers and underwear then positioned his body on the edge of the bed beside his friend Doyal's tortured, emasculated and burned body.

Later, after he had cleaned himself and, again, wiped the rooms clear of any fingerprints he might have left, Miller stood smiling, shaking his head and looking down at the two dead bodies grotesquely spread on the bed. "Old Jack back in his time wouldn't have known what to make of this number. Women making themselves to look and act as men. Men making themselves to look and act as women. Oh well, a one-night special—two for the price of one—and I didn't even have to pay for the one. More fun than I've had in a while, but I'd much rather be traveling and working the Continent once more. Maybe soon—in the meantime," he said, while patting the buttock of the transvestite Doyal, *"Leben ist güte,* (Life is good) even if a bit strange."

Chapter 28

Autumn Mornings

Steve, Boyd, Heather, and Alexander passed through the double doors at the end of Denham Studio's long corridor, and stepped outside, making their way toward their workplaces. Their breath formed steamy clouds as they walked, huddled in their coats and wraps against the cold November air.

Suddenly a large flock of birds caught Steve's attention as they flew up from a group of trees. A month ago the tree's branches and leaves had been brilliant in autumn's glorious colors. In his mind's eye Steve, recalled similar settings back home in Missouri. *So many autumn mornings*, he thought, *just like this one that I anxiously looked forward to in hopes I would see them. I'd stand in Grandma's back yard, looking up at the first few rays of the morning's sun. I remember looking to the skies daily and wondering when it would be. Mostly the fall colors would have peaked and the leaves, though many continued to fall, lay heavy and thick on the lawns, the hills and in the woods. Still, sometimes there were plenty of beautiful colors on the leaves. If I was out in a field or the woods collecting pecans, walnuts, or digging sassafras roots, it was so pretty to top a high bluff and see off in the distance the dazzling patchwork of colors on the rolling Missouri Ozark hills. The world seemed to be at its most beautiful then. I especially liked the mornings. Most showed a thick cover of frost on every-thing. I remember standing there in Ma's yard, my breath in a steamy cloud like it is today, and seeing the curlicues of smoke coming from the chimneys of the homes where early risers had built a fire in their stoves, fireplaces, or smokehouses. Loved to smell the hickory and oak wood burning! It was a good, sweet smelling odor. Then, one morning after having looked disap-pointedly to the empty skies day after day for a long time—there they were! Huge flocks of geese flying in their giant inverted V formations. Sometimes other groups would be just long scattered lines. They were flying south for the winter.* He smiled to himself when he recalled, *If I happened to be*

driving I'd stop, whenever possible, to see them circle and land so grace-
fully in the fields or on the lakes and estuaries or backwaters of the nearby
Mississippi River. God, how I loved to hear them calling and to see them
flying. So incredible.

Frankie Lane's recording of *Wild Goose* had long been a favorite of
Steve's. He was fascinated with the birds and had taken a college elective
course to study them.

His thoughts continued: *As each bird flaps its wings, it creates an uplift*
for the bird that follows. That's why they fly in V formations—lot easier
and they can fly farther and faster. When the lead goose gets tired, it falls
back and another takes point. They honk to encourage those up front to
keep going. They mate for life, and when one gets sick, wounded or shot
down, its mate and another go down with it and try to protect it. They stay
with it until it dies or can fly again. Then they either join another formation
or try to catch up with the flock. Their navigation skills are fantasti—.

"Steve, you gonna go to work with Axle today?" Warren asked the
daydreaming Steve, who was walking trance-like as if he would by-pass his
own office location. Steve was jolted back to the present when the group
neared the outside stairs leading up to the Third Air Postal Squadron
Orderly Room.

"See you guys later," Boyd said to Alexander and Heather as they were
parting. Alexander's motor pool was at the far end of the street and
Heather still worked in the AMT just beneath the orderly room.

"By the way, don't forget HSORI," Boyd said to Alexander.

"That's a big ten-four on HSORI," Alexander nonchalantly tossed back
in response.

When Heather stopped walking, the others also stopped short.

"What does HSORI mean?" she asked Alexander.

Alexander, eager to impress the young lady, leaped at the opportunity to
explain. "Well, you know how the military's always using accrominisms to
explain and short—"

"You mean acronyms," interjected Boyd.

"What?" said Alexander, irritated.

"Acronyms. Acronyms is the word you're meaning. You said 'accrominisms,' but you meant acronyms."

"Boyd, how the hell do you know what I meant? You got a fuc . . .
excuse me Miss Heather. He gets me so riled up sometimes! Boyd, you
got a dictionary in your pocket to prove what you're sayin? I mean if
you're gonna try and correct me then have somethin' to back it up. Don't
just tell someone that's usin' the right word that they're usin' the wrong

word lessn' you got some proof. Who the hell do you think you are, Dr. Eisenstein or some other kinda genius? I'm talkin, so shut up already!"

Turning again to Heather, Alex continued, "All the branches of the military use these accrominisms to shorten long words and things up. It's like you. See, you're a WAF right? WAF stands for Women's Air Force. USAF stands for United States Air Force, USN stands for U.S. Navy. SNAFU stands for Situation's normal-all fu . . . well, stuff and things like that."

"Oh. Okay. Thank you. I understand now. But what does HSORI stand for?"

"So you go on ahead and tell her Boyd, I've done all the other explaining."

"Sure, I'll be happy to tell you, but it'll have to wait till another time 'cause I'm late now already getting started on that damn Morning Report. You can go ahead and tell her if you want Axle. I'll see you guys later."

Heather turned expectantly to Alex, but he had suddenly left the others on his way to work.

Alex had surreptitiously exhausted nearly all efforts trying to learn what the acronym "HSORI" stood for. No one, not even some of the oldest veterans he could locate, had the foggiest notion or recollection of the term.

"I'll be kiss my happy ass if I'm gonna let that punk Boyd know I don't know what HSORI stands for," Alex promised himself.

Heather had been on the job for many months now. She had been accepted, without exception, as a coworker. There could be no question that her fellow workers didn't still follow her every move in her tight-fitting fatigue trousers or her Class A uniform skirts whenever she wore them. However, with those aside, she was considered and respected as "one of the guys."

She roamed freely throughout all sections and areas of the AMT. Her pleasing presence was never questioned and was always welcomed. Heather had varied her working hours so she could be present with all shifts to observe routines. She knew all her fellow airmen better than any of their other comrades. She knew the names of the wives and children of the married airmen. She also knew the names of the many girlfriends and fiancées her coworkers had met since arriving in England as well as those back home. Heather often asked questions about family members and girlfriends by their specific names, which endeared her all the more. She had a record of those who lived off base, those who worked at the airport and boat docks most frequently; she knew the drivers of the huge trucks that transported the bulk mail, and those that also operated the smaller vehicles. The beautiful Scottish lass had become a close friend to most all the airmen. She had definite opinions about many and had categorized them in her secret notes. They fell into many different areas: dedicated, loyal, semi-loyal, lazy and uncaring, trustworthy, and those with questionable trustworthiness qualities. On the personal side there were those that were loving husbands, fathers, boyfriends, and fiancés. There were many who had nothing but sex on their minds twenty-four hours a day. She suspected a few were most likely homosexuals, and the list went on and on. It included the names of several prostitutes at Picadilly Circus, many at Soho and even some of the guys' favorite stand-up "quickies" in Hyde Park.

The pretty undercover OSI agent had formed some suspicions and recently concentrated her major efforts on those. This week being mid-November when the larger boat mail shipments would begin to arrive, Heather decided to work through the noon and evening meal hours when the AMT was mostly deserted.

Johnson, one of those on her "Questionable List," just recently seemed always to go to early chow. He was then alone for the most part when the rest of the workers took their noon lunch break. Always there were a few people in the AMT at all hours, but due to the immensity of the building, they were often widely separated. Individual activity during those times could, guardedly, go completely unnoticed.

At the direction of the OSI, motor pool personnel quietly installed several large oval mirrors. These, supposedly, to assist with the inside building traffic—the many different vehicles—dropping off and picking up the AMT mail. The mirrors allowed Heather, completely unnoticed from her second balcony office location, to view any activity taking place within the entire AMT. Inside her purse she carried and used, most discretely, the small fold up high-powered 8X23 binoculars.

Today she followed, very closely, the clandestine activities of Staff Sergeant Johnson during the lunch hour. She noted his selective screening of letter mail to outlying APOs and his occasional visit to his field jacket hanging, with the zipper zipped to the neck, on the coat rack.

She also observed him placing a medium-sized package inside a large Armed Forces Exchange paper bag that had been tucked inside his coat pocket. He stapled a white PX sales slip sealing the bag. This he placed on the top of the coat rack beneath his fatigue cap.

During her late lunch break Heather visited the small library just opposite the cafeteria. There in a deserted corner she silently handed a note to an Airman who stopped briefly next to her to look at a book. The Airman was another undercover OSI agent.

At the 1700 shift change, the entire AMT emptied to see Arkee's brand new canary yellow Renault convertible his girlfriend had driven to pick him up. Everyone was standing around admiring the car and most all of the single GIs were also admiring Judy, Arkee's fiancée whose skirt had ridden above her knees. Finally, when it was time for them to leave, Arkee replaced Judy behind the steering wheel. As he started the engine several of the Airmen hurried behind the car, grabbed the bumper and lifted the rear tires off the ground.

The wheels spun in the air as Arkee cursed and swore at his fellow workers. Finally they lowered the car and Arkee, waving and laughing, drove away. Heather noted that Johnson had stood off to the side with his field jacket zipped up to his neck even though the day had warmed considerably and it was now not cold at all. Johnson hadn't involved himself in the horseplay. He was holding the package Heather had seen him seal earlier in the day.

As Arkee's car was nearing the south end of the street, two air police vehicles with lights flashing swung in from opposite directions to seal off the connecting roadway. Two more police cars sealed off the north end of the street at the same time. Arkee was wondering what in the hell he had done wrong and why were all the USAF cops in England after him.

Several Air Policemen and plainclothes OSI agents approached the confused crowd and milled about looking at names on uniforms until they sighted Johnson. Two agents grabbed his arms and guided Johnson to the side of the AMT building. There they had him spread his legs and arms and made a quick search. Inside the bag he was holding they found a package addressed to a Colonel John Patterson, CMR Box 118, APO 179, New York, N.Y. The bonafide gift certification on the outside of the package revealed the contents to be a gold, Elgin wristwatch valued at one hundred and seventy-five dollars, a brown leather wallet with family photographs, value: seventy-five dollars, and a set of briarwood pipes, a tobacco humidor and tobacco valued at one hundred and forty dollars. When Johnson's field jacket was unzipped, two bundles of government checks held together with large rubber bands fell at his feet.

The OSI agents asked that Master Sergeant Danbury remain, then told the other workers to please leave the area. There was, of course, no hint of recognition between Heather and the agents.

Heather and the rest of the troops that lived on base made their way to the Studio's main corridor.

"Damn, did'ja see the way the cops sealed off both ends of the street all of a sudden like that?" one of the troops asked.

"Yeah, and boy, those OSI guys and the Air Police were on Johnson like a sparrow on a June bug," replied another. "And poor ole Arkee hadda be thinkin' Judy musta broke every law on the base when they boxed his car in like that!"

"I didn't know Johnson all that well," Boyd said, "but I guess I'm surprised that he'd do such a thing as steal other people's mail. He's been in the postal business for a long time; you'd think he knew better. I'm glad they got him!"

"Well, I thought I knew him pretty good," Sergeant Collins said. "We were in the Transit Barracks together when we both first arrived. Been out drinking with him several times, and we worked beside one another in the Registry Cage. Surprising how little you can really know about someone you work with daily."

"Yes, isn't that the truth though," said Heather with a smile.

Chapter 29
A Puzzling Occurrence

A daily reading of the unit Squadron Bulletin Board is a mandatory task for everyone in the USAF. The Third Air Postal Squadron is no exception. The board is posted each morning, usually by the First Sergeant or Chief Clerk of the Orderly Room. It contains the latest information on assignments, promotions, details, all unit and base special meetings, immunization schedules, off-limits areas—any and everything of interest. By prior agreement with Master Sergeants Gage and Hargrave, Heather, if she needed to speak privately or to pass a message to either of the NCOs, would visit the bulletin board. There, with no one else around, she would add a third thumbtack to the two posting the base bus schedule. She would then leave an envelope containing her message behind the overhead flush tank in the orderly room latrine that she used on occasion.

Hargrave, again filling in as acting First Sergeant, was posting a notice for Commander's Call when he noted the third thumbtack on the bus schedule. It hadn't been there when he'd visited the board earlier.

He went immediately to the latrine, closed and locked the door. There, above the flush tank, was Heather's envelope. The note inside read simply: "CABLE-TOW meeting, same place, 1930 today."

Everyone stood when the USAF Commander of Third Air Force entered the room.

"Good evening everyone," Lieutenant General Putnam said.

A chorus of "Good evening sir" responses was returned to the Commander.

He noted that the majority of his visitors had already been served coffee or tea. With his welcome greeting he invited any so inclined to please help themselves to refreshments and be seated.

"I understand we have some new events involving OPERATION DROPHAMMER.

"I apologize for disturbing your evening, but as it has been awhile since we last met, we felt it best to provide you this update.

"First, it is my sad duty to announce the death of Master Sergeant Calvin Gage whom you each met when we were last together. Calvin was a true patriot. He fought bravely and valiantly for both our countries during WWII. He was a quiet but solid hero in every sense of the word. He fought for most all his life against our common foes on many foreign shores. He placed his life and his duty, as he saw it needing to be performed, on the line for us countless times. He, as some of you may know, was murdered in his home a short while back. His lifelong friend, Lieutenant General R.P. Berg, who, by the way, was just yesterday nominated for promotion to four-star grade, full General, by President Eisenhower, came here to collect Calvin's body. Sergeant Gage was given the fullest, highest possible military honors with his funeral. My heartiest thanks to those of you present who were instrumental in that ceremony and for your many kindnesses and support. Lady and gentlemen, may I propose a toast to our fallen comrade. To Master Sergeant Calvin Gage."

All arose immediately and there was a shouted mixture of "To Master Sergeant Calvin Gage" and "Here-Here."

General Putnam continued, "Calvin's murder is still under investigation, and I'm certain we are all hopeful for an early, successful bringing to justice of the perpetrator?

"We'll keep you posted on this. Now, you all, of course, remember Lieutenant Cathy Moberly a.k.a. Heather MacVickar, who will be briefing us again this evening. Cathy, whenever you're ready."

"Thank you General Putnam," Cathy said as the dimming of the conference room lights and the quiet hum of the projector became noticeable.

The introductory slide was classified Secret and showed only the name "DROPHAMMER" covering the bright red background and a German Nazi swastika.

The next slide listed the names of various cities. Cathy continued, "These are the locations involving DROPHAMMER since our last meeting:

• Edinburgh, Scotland	• Paris, France
• San Francisco, California	• Naples, Italy
• Madrid, Spain	• Copenhagen, Denmark

"I shall address them in order. A Mr. Kevin McCloud was brutally murdered and savagely mutilated in his remote Leith residence near the Firth of Forth and Edinburgh. There are no suspects in the case; however, on the day of the murder, Mr. McCloud was known to have met and negotiated with an individual for the purchase of a Rodin sculpture. McCloud told another Edinburgh dealer friend the sculpture was, most certainly, from a collection supposedly confiscated by the Nazis in Paris circa June 1940." The lieutenant paused to let the information sink in.

"McCloud choked to death after his tongue and genitals were excised and forced into his mouth and partially down his throat. The German words *'Lügner warmebruder'* which, roughly translated, mean 'Lying homosexual,' were carved into his chest."

"This sounds to me as more of a crime of passion and hatred, perhaps cultist, rather than black marketing involvement," one of the attendees volunteered.

"Yes, it would. That's correct," Cathy responded. "However, Mr. McCloud, in an earlier telephone conversation with his Edinburgh dealer friend, spoke of a planned evening meeting with the black marketeer. Still and all at the residence there were no fingerprints, no Rodin sculpture nor any clues other than a pair of rather unusual handcuffs which secured McCloud's hands behind him. Those are presently being analyzed by our friends here in Scotland Yard. The German words, of course, would lead one to suspect the murderer, at least, has a German background, or, perhaps, those words were chosen to make us think the killer is German."

Someone in the audience, probably the representative from Scotland Yard cleared his throat and mumbled, "Poor bugger, beastly way to go." Another responded "Rather!"

Cathy pressed on. "The death was so macabre and grisly, we now think the murderer is, perhaps, more interested, excited and motivated toward causing pain and suffering than he is in the sale of the German loot. We suspect, too, that he is probably insane."

A general hum pulsed through the room. Cathy let it wane, then continued.

"The Paris event involved the sodomizing and murder of a German prostitute. Again, unfortunately, there's no suspect, fingerprints, or other clues to point to a killer. However, in this instance a piece of jewelry was discovered and traced. A diamond and ruby studded stickpen was found under the prostitute's mattress and an engraving identified the jewelry as being from an Austrian collection, stolen by the Nazis in 1939."

Cathy continued with her briefing, detailing the various pieces of Nazi plunder which were turning up or being reported as seen throughout Europe and on the Western Coast of the United States. She spoke of the failed attempt to conduct a one-time search of official couriers and the suspicions that, perhaps, some of the contraband could be making its way across international borders concealed in other custom-exempt containers.

"We recently discovered a black market operation within our Postal unit located at Denham Studios. This, however, was a small-scale activity, which, as it turns out, dealt primarily with magazines and other mails stolen from APO/FPO channels. Those, along with Military Class VI spirits/liquors and cigarettes were being peddled to dealers primarily in downtown London. That affair had nothing whatsoever to do with the DROPHAMMER OPERATION."

At General Putnam's invitation representatives from Interpol and Scotland Yard then briefed on their activities and findings. Finally, in summation, Cathy announced that strangely and suddenly, all DROPHAMMER activities had ceased with the onset of autumn.

"We're puzzled," she said "by this occurrence. However, it has given us a bit of a leeway and we're now better prepared to monitor any future dealings via our underground art and jewelry dealership contacts. We believe the net is narrowing, and we're confident of success in the near future. Thank you gentlemen. Are there any questions?" There were several.

Afterwards General Putnam thanked all for attending and began the rounds of shaking hands. When he reached Pappy, still gripping his hand, they moved to a quiet corner of the conference room. "Mr. Hargrave," the General said, "I haven't had the occasion to speak with you privately since Sergeant Gage's death. I apologize for that. I've learned from General Berg that the two of you had become close during this assignment. I know how it is to lose a close friend. I share in your sorrow—Calvin's death."

Pappy, moved by the General's kind words, returned the hard grip.

"General, we've both seen our share of war, death, and sadness. But I believe there are few things sadder or lonelier than to be beaten and die as Gage did. I've had very few friends in life, really true friends, and Gage was one of them. I'll not rest until I know I've killed the bastard who murdered him. I promised that to Gage, and no matter how long, no matter what it takes, I'll keep my promise," Hargrave said, his eyes narrowing in anger.

They looked deeply into one another's eyes and the General, patting the top of Pappy's held hand said, "Yes, Phillip, I know you will. Please, let me know if there's anything I can do."

Chapter 30

A Special Cargo

The fog began rolling in during the late afternoon. By early evening it was a proper Pea Souper. The night air, particularly around the Denham train depot, was heavy both with the roiling fog and the mist. The unmistakable odor and taste of soot which was ever present with the coal burning train engines, running at idle, prompted some to wear a folded handkerchief, bandit style, over their noses and mouths as they awaited the call to board the train.

Captain Karl Miller, Pappy, and Steve were busily at work inventorying and loading the ARFCOS bags, footlockers, and wooden crates. The Captain was working just as hard as the two Sergeants with the loading and stacking process. He never left that portion of the manual labor to others. Most of the Squadron troops claimed that was really the only good quality the Captain had. The majority of the other officers always just supervised the loading of the vehicles, trains, and airplanes. Miller seemed to want to be actively involved in placing every article. He gave the impression he actually preferred to do all the loading and unloading himself.

In reality, that was the situation. Practically every shipment Captain Miller was involved in contained portions of the stolen booty from the Salzdorf mine. With all the normal shipments of classified ARFCOS documents and materials, he, as Commander of the Detachment, would delegate those assignments to the other officer couriers.

Since learning of the possibility of a one-time search of all couriers, and following the death of First Sergeant Gage, the Captain had halted all black market activity. He, by that time, had accumulated a large stash of contraband, mostly smaller pieces of sculptures, statues and figurines, bronzes, and pieces of porcelain. He also had stored numerous masterpiece paintings, more diminutive in size, far easier to transport later. He had collected quite a cache of precious stones, jewelry, and medals, several bags of gold coins, and a large amount of U.S. currency. It was his intention to ferry these holdings back to the States with his required logging of flying hours from time to time. He'd store the items either at his Eastern storage site location near McGuire AFB in New Jersey or on the West Coast near Tacoma, Washington.

The perfect flying assignment that would allow the Captain to transport the largest shipment of plunder yet had come along quite suddenly and unexpectedly. He had been chosen to pilot a special C-118 aircraft from RAF Station Burtonwood-Croft to McGuire AFB, New Jersey. The aircraft would contain three "Davy Crockett" tactical atomic weapon systems, designed to give heavy firepower to the smallest infantry units. The Eisenhower Department of Defense had sent the systems to England for the sharing of technological information with its US Allies. The Davy Crockett systems were on their way back home and were guarded by US Army infantrymen. The aircraft and its contents would, most certainly, be exempt from any custom searches. The Captain quickly seized the opportunity to fill his stateside coffers with enough of the stolen riches to last him a lifetime—in fact several lifetimes! And then the fog rolled in.

He had intended to load the shipment, disguised as ARFCOS classified materials, on board the C-47 Gooney Bird ferry run he routinely flew to Burtonwood-Croft. There he would transfer it to the larger C-118 Davy Crockett flight that he would later pilot on to McGuire AFB. But the intense fog had grounded all flights. This necessitated the shipment traveling from Denham to Burtonwood-Croft via rail with two mandatory armed guards to accompany Captain Miller and the cargo. He didn't like and most certainly didn't want the others traveling with him.

On his other trips when he was senior pilot, he always had a copilot and navigator with him, but these individuals were selected at random and had nothing to do with the ARFCOS shipment which the Captain always handled himself. Now however, the guards, always members of the Third Air Postal Squadron, would inventory, load, guard, monitor, and accompany the supposedly highly classified cargo every mile of its journey. The token three or four bags of actual classified material was mixed in with the Nazi plunder.

Steve and Warren Boyd's names were next on the ARFCOS standby list to act as guards. Steve was in his room studying for finals on his last required college course, a Psychology 400 level course, The Abnormal Personality. He'd had no other plans, so when the trip came up he didn't mind, but Warren Boyd was running a fever. He said his throat was on fire, and he also had chills. He was, in fact, waiting for the Air Police to come up with some transportation to take him to the hospital at South Ruislip. Most of the other troops had long ago left the base for London or other locations. Pappy was spending a now rare weekend on base as his fiancée, Brooke, had gone to Land's End with her parents to visit an ailing aunt. When Pappy learned of the semi-emergency trip requirement, he volunteered to accompany Steve and the Captain. As he was dressing he wondered if he should carry his pistols which were presently locked securely in his wall locker. *Probably no need on this occasion*, he thought to himself.

The Captain and two Sergeants quickly loaded their compartment of the partitioned off, secured railway car. Once the large door was slid shut and locked on the inside, the train immediately continued its journey toward Burtonwood-Croft.

With the cargo properly inventoried and positioned, Captain Miller, for want of anything else to do and not wanting to talk to the two Sergeants, busied himself stoking the fire. He added a few pieces of the stacked wood into the potbelly stove in the front part of the car. Soon the compartment was toasty warm and the miles clicked by. With their first stop the opposite side door had to be opened and some United Kingdom mail was removed from the steel meshed, smaller caged end section of the car. With each stop and door opening, a mandatory inventory of the ARFCOS contents was required. It was done hastily by the Captain and Steve while Pappy annotated the record on a clipboard.

By moving bags to visually cite and call off bag numbers, Steve noted that one of the bags had been torn by a jagged corner of the steel meshed wall.

"Captain Miller, this bag has been ripped pretty bad and is still hung up on a piece of this metal partition. Musta got snagged with the loading or jerking of the train. We're gonna have to rip the bag more to get it unhooked," Steve said.

"Goddammit, leave it alone. Get away from that bag! Did you look inside—did you see any classified contents?"

"No sir, I just checked the bag number for the inventory and noticed it's torn and still caught on this piece of metal cage. I didn't see any of the bag's contents," Steve lied.

Captain Miller had grabbed another courier bag, a larger one than the one snagged. He pushed Steve away. "I'll take care of this," he said, ripping the bag loose and hurriedly placing it inside the larger one. He sealed the top with the leather strap and locked it. Miller was the only person to hold the keys to the locks. "This new bag number is ARFCOS

AG-404. Substitute that for ARFCOS AG-396, the other torn bag," Karl Miller shouted to Pappy who noted the change on the log.

Captain Miller knew Steve was not responsible for the torn bag, but he was nonetheless agitated by the incident. He wondered if Steve had seen the gilt-edged corner or any portion of the framed masterpiece painting inside the torn bag. No way to tell. Steve gave no impression or the slightest indication he'd seen the bag's contents. The Captain stewed. He was disturbed and uneasy over the situation. Another hour passed.

"I'm going to the dining car," Miller announced, not offering to get or bring anything back for the two Sergeants. Pappy slid the lock bar in place after the Captain departed. He had no more than returned to his chair when Steve hurriedly stood and walked to the door the Captain just exited. He looked through the small window in the door to confirm Captain Miller had left, the next car's corridor where he had gone was empty.

"Pappy, come here a minute!" Steve said excitedly.

Steve guided Pappy to the ARFCOS bag AG-404, the one containing the torn bag. "The bag inside here, the one that was ripped—"

"Yeah, what about it?"

"The ripped bag doesn't have any classified material in it. I got a good look inside before I called the Captain. I wouldn't have told him at all, but he was already close and was coming over there anyway. Figured I might as well mention it. Pretty sure he didn't see me looking inside."

"So, what did you see?"

"It looked like an old time painting. A gilt framed painting of a deer or an elk standing at the edge of a forest. C'mere you can feel the frame on the inside—feel it?"

Pappy complied. "Yeah, sure do. Let's check some of the other bags."

Pappy and Steve hurriedly felt several other bags and decided there were many that evidently contained frames and small statues or sculptures.

Captain Miller, who had been standing to the side of the outside door when Steve checked to see if he had gone to the diner, was cautiously peering through the small door window watching the Sergeants conduct their search. Their backs were toward him. A vicious grin slowly formed on the Captain's face. *Not a concern,* he thought, *I'll just kill them. No problem, in fact, I'm rather looking forward to the task. Don't have all night, but there's time enough to take care of them before the train stops again and the doors open. For the moment, I'll go get that cup of tea, relax, and plan my strategy.* Suddenly he was pleased, thrilled, and excited.

"Steve, laddie, listen to me—we may not have much time before the Captain returns. There are some things I need to tell you. First off, with the very next stop I'm going to get off the train and make a telephone call to try and arrange for some people to meet us up ahead. I don't want you to be left alone with Miller, and I don't want him to suspect we know anything. Just as the train stops, I'll make some excuse to leave, and you say you'll join me. Tea, coffee, sandwich, whatever, just follow my lead, but do not stay in this car with Captain Miller alone! Understand?"

"Okay, Pappy, understood."

Pappy had immediately decided he would attempt a CABLE-TOW contact at the next stop. *This blasted train carries no communication system other than the simple intercom connected to only a few of the cars. With the call I'll try to make arrangements to have the train met enroute at some advance station stop or at the end of the line, Burtonwood-Croft. If I'm not successful with the CABLE-TOW contact, then I'll just have to seize the Captain. We'll tie the bastard up, search the contents of a bag or two and notify the authorities once the train reaches its destination,* he thought. *I'd like to make certain of our suspicions. After all Steve just got a fleeting glance at the torn bag's contents, and we're not 100 percent positive about the other bags. But we can't take any chances. If Miller is responsible for what I suspect, this is a very dangerous situation.*

"Okay lad," Pappy instructed, as he motioned for them to return to their chairs, "carry on acting as normal as possible, but be alert."

When Captain Miller returned a few minutes later, he had to bang loudly on the metal door to be heard over the noise of the speeding train. Pappy unlocked the door to admit the officer. Captain Miller walked over close to the stove where Steve was sitting, trying his best to look interested in his psychology book. Pappy bolted the door and walked back to take his seat. As he turned to sit down, the Captain, holding the barrel of his pistol as a hammer, clubbed Pappy in the back of the head. Pappy fell near Steve's feet. As Steve attempted to rise, the Captain's pistol butt swung again, striking the surprised Steve a glancing blow to his temple area. Stunned, Steve stumbled backwards and fell on top of some of the ARFCOS bags. The Captain laid his .38 on the chair seat Steve had been occupying.

Fearing Steve's fall and weight might break some of the framed masterpiece paintings, porcelains or other priceless articles, the Captain, cursing, hoisted Steve up and off the bags, dropping his limp body heavily to the floor. Steve stirred and made groaning noises. The Captain savagely kicked Steve in the face several times, and then checking on Pappy, noted that he, too, was beginning to waken and was trying to get up.

Quickly grabbing a large piece of firewood, he swung it, striking the sergeant in the side of his head. Pappy's left temple and jaw area gushed blood and he slumped back heavily to the floor. Miller dropped the wood and hastily searched the NCO for any kind of a weapon. At first finding none, he rolled him over then discovered the holstered Beretta in the small of Pappy's back.

Pappy had decided, at the last minute to carry his weapons after all. Captain Miller placed the pistol in the right pocket of his field jacket and continued to frisk the NCO. Finding nothing more, Miller stood and kicked the unconscious sergeant in his ribs.

"All right you *schweinisch hund*, I'll get back to you in a minute!" the Captain hissed.

Returning to search Steve for any weapon, he was surprised to see the young man was again beginning to stir. He removed and flicked open his large switchblade knife. He was smiling an evil grin, and raising his arm as Steve opened his eyes. The Captain plunged the knife downwards, driving it to the hilt into Steve's chest.

"You sergeant bastards seem to have this rather annoying habit of being hard to kill. Your friend, the newer one—Gage, I believe was his name— he didn't want to die easily either. Took him the longest, even after I caved in his fucking head."

Steve moaning tried feebly to grasp and remove the Captain's hand still wrapped around the handle of the embedded switchblade. With his left hand the Captain slapped, then backhanded Steve's face. Steve was struggling to remain conscious.

"That's right Sergeant, hang in there," Captain Miller said, obviously enjoying himself. He withdrew the knife and passed the long blade, dripping with blood, in front of Steve's dimming eyes. "Stay with me Sergeant, hang in there you bastard, the party's not over yet."

Steve coughed up a mouthful of blood and began to wheeze, obviously gasping for air. Still grinning and delighting in the pain he was causing, the Captain said, "Looks as though we may have punctured a lung. Aw well, not to worry, you still have another, at least for the moment." Then, very slowly, he slid the knife into Steve's chest again. When the blade glanced off Steve's ribs he thankfully, passed out once more.

"I hate to have to end all this, but I've things to do before the next stop." The Captain removed the knife and still kneeling aimed the point of the blade for dead center on Steve's heart. He began the final downward thrust of the switchblade.

The 380 caliber bullet shattered the bone in the Captain's right shoulder and the knife fell from his hand as he spun around to see Pappy, blood streaming down the side of his head, but aiming the pistol with a rock steady hand directly at Captain Miller.

Struggling, Pappy propped himself up against a courier bag as the Captain slowly stood and stepped in front of the chair containing his .38 pistol. He knew it would be impossible to reach the Sergeant's Beretta he had earlier placed in his right jacket pocket. His right shoulder and arm were now useless.

Concealing the terrible pain he was feeling, the Captain said in as close to a normal conversational tone as possible, "Well, well Sergeant. You clever bastard, you've gone and pulled a sneaky on me, haven't you? Now, where did that gun come from? I checked you thoroughly earlier."

"What a shame then you overlooked my right ankle holster, Captain. I'm afraid that's an oversight you shall shortly regret, probably even more so than now."

"Perhaps, but it'll have to go some as my shoulder is throbbing like mad this very moment. Would you mind, Sergeant, if I have a seat?" the Captain asked, even as he was lowering himself, reaching with his left hand for the hidden .38 directly beneath him.

The inside of the car echoed again as Pappy's weapon fired once more. This time the cartridge disintegrated the Captain's left kneecap as he fell, screaming, to the floor.

"By all means sir, please have a seat," Pappy said.

"You bastard son of a bitch!" the Captain, writhing in pain screamed. "If you're going to kill me, do it! Stop this goddamned target practice!"

Pappy, taking the most casual attempt of an aim, then shot the officer in his left shoulder.

"Please do not defame my mother. I, as it happened, was not a mistake by birth. However, with you, sir, I'm not quite certain we can say the same. And even if you were not a mistake at conception, I rather strongly suspect your brain bucket was somehow messed up in the birthing process. Wonder if the doctor may have smacked you in the head instead of on the ass with your exit from the womb? If you're responsible for the things I'm thinking you're responsible for, you most certainly are the vilest, sickest piece of shit on God's green earth."

The Captain writhing and contorting in pain made an involuntary spastic move. Pappy, reacting automatically, pulled the trigger once more. This time the cartridge entered Miller's mid section and exiting carried an eight-inch section of intestines out of his side.

"Ooops," Pappy said with a smile. "You know you really shouldn't jump like that—things have been somewhat tense around here."

The Captain moaned and begged painfully, "Finish it, for God's sake! You son of a bitch, finish it!"

"Now, now, Captain. Now you've gone and taken all the fun out of it. You see with my oath of enlistment I swore that it would be my duty to follow the orders of all the officers and others appointed over me. Now you've gone and reminded me of that, so I guess I'll just have to stop all this fun and games lot and follow your order. *Auf Wiedersehen* from Calvin Gage. May you rot in hell you slimy bastard." And with that, Pappy raised his pistol for the last time and, without aiming, shot the Captain squarely between his eyes.

His broken ribs making any movement excruciatingly painful and with his head still streaming blood, Pappy crawled his way over to Steve's side. He felt for and found a strong pulse on Steve's wrist. He noted Steve's wheezing but steady breathing and then Steve began to stir. Pappy lightly put his hand on the side of Steve's head and patted him gently.

"It's all right now laddie," he said. "Not to worry. It's all right now."

Chapter 31

A Double Whammy

"Shhhhhhhhh, hold it down for Crissake Axle! You're talking so loud everyone sitting inside the Chapel can hear you."

"No they can't, the door's closed. And I ain't talkin' that loud in the first place. You're just always wantin' to ride my ass, Boyd! Why you always ridin' my ass? You always ride my ass!"

Warren Boyd and Alexander were having a last minute cigarette prior to entering the small Chapel at the USAF Hospital at South Ruislip.

"Besides," continued Alexander, "like I just told you, it is Friday the thirteenth for God's sake and there's also gonna be a full moon tonight. Heard it on the radio while I was shavin' this morning. That's a double whammy you know!"

"What do you mean that's a double whammy?"

"Dammit Boyd, you got a case of the permanent dumass? Ain't you ever heard that Friday the thirteenth is a bad luck day? And, not only that, there's gonna be a full moon out tonight. Everyone knows that the weird and crazies come out and all sorts of strange things happen on those nights. And this one's a double whammy! Friday the thirteenth and a full moon both! And Hargrave has to pick today to get married! Why in hell can't they wait 'till tomorrow? Saturday the fourteenth'd be a good day. They're lookin' for trouble, I'm here to tell you. They oughta wait one more day, just one more friggin' day!"

"Axle, today is just like any other day and the full moon don't matter a diddley squat. Where do you come up with all these crazy-assed ideas?"

"Boyd, I'm tellin' you this is bad medicine. Friday the thirteenth has been a bad luck day for years. And the full moon does make certain kinds of people do weird things. Read that in a book once. Remember? When you was a kid, didn't you see any of those Wolfman pictures? Fuzzy faced fucker, big teeth and claws. Ran around biting people on the neck and the only way they could kill him was to drive a stake through his heart, or pull him out into the daylight, or put a bunch of garlic in the coffin he slept in. And, then there was this big, tall assed guy, musta stood more'n eight feet. Had little miniature lookin' fire hydrant like things stickin' outta his neck. Both sides. They'd hook electricity up to those things on his neck and shock the piss out of him. Made him mad; then he'd go around yankin' people's heads off and stuff. And all this always happened on full moon nights. Probably on a Friday the thirteenth too."

"Axle, you got the Wolfman, Dracula and Frankenstein all mixed up. And those were just horror movies. You know damn well none of that stuff actually ever happened. You know that!"

"Well, today is Friday the thirteenth, and there's gonna be a full moon tonight and those are bad luck signs. Just look at Hargrave and Scott! Wow, if anybody ever had bad luck it's them two. Shit! They're both settin' in there in wheelchairs right now this minute. Got tubes and needles stickin' everywhere. All wrapped up in bandages from head to toe for Crissake. Probably even got their dicks in a sling. Don't ya know old Hargrave's gonna have one helluva time in the honeymoon rack? Kinda funny when you mental image it—him, still all wrapped up in bandages and slings and things—him and his Missus going at it like crazy. Old Hargrave's knee'd slip and he'd miss a stroke. Probably tilt, fall off the bed and maybe even crack another rib or somethin'. Boyd, reckon maybe we oughta tell him to leave that thing alone for a day or two?"

"What I reckon Axle is you'd best keep your nose out of other people's business and your sexual advice to yourself."

Pappy and Steve were still showing the battle scars from their recent run-in with Captain Miller during the ill-fated train ride to Burtonwood-Croft. Hargrave's head and ribs were bandaged, but of the two he was in better shape. He'd had several stitches to close the wound in the side of his head and with three fractured ribs, his chest area was tightly taped. He was scheduled to be released from the hospital the following Monday.

Steve looked as though he'd been mangled by a grizzly bear. His nose had been broken and his left cheek, eyebrow, and forehead had been badly cut and torn by the kicks from Captain Miller's brogan boot. He had suffered a collapsed lung—the doctor called it a spontaneous pneumothorax—and other punctures in his chest from the knife-wielding Captain. The punctured areas between the lungs and collapsed lung was what was keeping Steve in an unwelcome hospital regimen. He was assigned to strict bed rest for three weeks. The top half portion of his bed was elevated to ease his breathing. He had to sleep, when he could manage it, sitting up. No trips to the latrine, dining room, or anywhere. Couldn't get up even when they changed his bed linen. God, how he hated the bedpans and urinal! His only salvation was that Sergeant Hargrave was in the bed immediately next to him, at least for the moment.

All the troops from the Squadron had been by to see Pappy and Steve in the hospital, but Warren Boyd and Alexander were the first and most frequent visitors. Their initial visit had been refused by Pappy and Steve's doctors due to the serious condition of the two men. This was within hours after the two wounded NCOs had been admitted. With their second visit, Boyd and Alex had snuck in past the doctors and nurses.

"So, how's it going?" Alex had quietly asked Hargrave. At least he thought it was Hargrave. The patient's head was swathed in bandages, he had an oxygen tube in his nose, IVs in his arms, a catheter inserted, and was tightly wrapped from just above his belly button up to his Adam's apple. A small humidifier, which looked like one of the large-mouthed, short stemmed oil cans in Alex's motor pool, was quietly emitting a steady stream of medicated air directed straight at Pappy's head.

Their double room was illuminated only by a half-moon light located near the floor at the head of the bed of each of the injured NCOs. Both patients remained totally silent. The only sound was the hissing, steaming, humidifier.

Alex looked at Boyd, hunched his shoulders, with arms and palms extended out in front of him as if asking, "What now?"

Boyd, who was standing quietly by Steve's bedside whispered, "Steve, you all right? Can you talk pal?"

Feebly, Steve, who's head was also swathed in bandages, an oxygen tent enclosing his chest and head, IVs in both arms, and the catheter in place, pointed to Hargrave's bed.

Pappy weakly raised his right arm and wriggled his forefinger in a lean-down, come hither motion to Alex.

Alexander, patting Hargrave gently on his left shoulder said, "What is it Hargrave? I'm right here. You okay?"

Pappy whispered, just barely loud enough for Alex to think he heard, "HSORI Alex."

"What? What'd he say?" Boyd asked in his loudest whisper.

"I think he said HSORI. Ain't that what you said, Hargrave? Yeah, I'm certain that's what he said—he said HSORI!" Alex was quiet for a long time, a studious frown and expression on his face.

"So, what the hell does HSORI mean? I been trying to figger out what HSORI means for months! I've checked out every fuggin accrominism from Julius Caesar's army's time till now, and I'm yet to learn what HSORI stands for." Alex's voice had risen incrementally in volume and emphasis.

Alexander continued, "All right Hargrave, quit fuckin' 'round with me! I know you're hurtin', but you ain't that bad off. You don't tell me what HSORI stands for I'm gonna piss in your IV. I'm gonna tell the nurse your Doc said to give you a five gallon enema. I'm gonna bring you some big, glossy, 8x10 porno pictures, and you'll get a hard-on so stiff a damn cat couldn't scratch it. Then here'll come the ugliest nurse in forty-eleven wards; she'll smack you on the head of your pecker and you'll be out of commission for three months. You're jackin' round with me Hargrave. Been doing that for the longest. What the fuck does HSORI mean?" Alex was almost shouting.

"Help Stamp Out Rectal Itch," whispered Boyd.

"What?" screamed Alex. "What'd you say Boyd?"

"That's what it means, Axle. Help Stamp Out Rectal Itch. That's what HSORI stands for. Been pullin' your chain with that just to get your goat."

There was a complete and total silence for a long moment, then the entire room erupted with the laughter of the four NCOs. Seconds later the head nurse came flying into the room and ushered Boyd and Alex out with threats of jail time if they ever came back.

Now, several days later with encouraging but slow recuperation, Steve's doctor had agreed, most reluctantly and only at the urging of Lt. General Leslie Putnam, Commander of Third Air Force, to allow Steve to be wheeled to the hospital chapel to act as Pappy's best man at today's wedding ceremony. However, on the strictest of orders, Steve couldn't be out of his bed for more than a half-hour and had to remain seated the entire time. He could not stand, even for a moment, during the wedding service. The savage thrusts of Captain Miller's switchblade had done considerable damage, and the doctor was concerned over the potential for internal bleeding.

MSgt Hargrave had been informed that his sabbatical from the Central Intelligence Agency was drawing to a rapid close. Now that the DROPHAMMER mission was completed, his presence back in the headquarters had been subtly, yet firmly requested. Another problem—a hotspot was heating up in Southeast Asia—a place called Vietnam. Previously, this had largely been France's problem, but some U.S. counterinsurgency and CIA personnel were now involved. Along with his fluency in the German language, Hargrave was expert also in French. That and his knowledge of underground and guerilla warfare expertise were needed back in the headquarters. He was surprised to learn he would be going back to a one grade higher, promoted position.

Apart from all of this, his old boss and friend, the Director of CIA, Allen Dulles, had told him jokingly, but also straight from the cuff, "You've had enough vacation and goof-off time in London. Besides, it's been too long a time since I last saw your lovely Lady Brooke. Time to come on back home Pappy. We need you more back here."

Hargrave and his new bride Brooke would be leaving for the U.S. within the week. That was the impetus for the hurried wedding today. When agencies like the CIA and people of Dulles' stature wanted things to happen, they routinely happened fast. Hargrave wasn't ready to leave England and Steve just yet, but he, years ago, had learned when to speak up and when to zip lip, salute smartly, and move out. This was a zip, salute, and move out smartly time.

Pappy and Steve had been side-by-side since the train rolled to a stop following Pappy's putting a bullet between Captain Karl Miller's eyes. Steve, coughing and spitting up blood was unable to move. Pappy with his broken ribs amazingly performed the Herculean task of forcing himself to crawl to the door, and lift up and remove the heavy bar locking the secured rail car at the intermediate train stop. He then struggled the door open and signaled for help. The train was halted while police, medical, and ambulance crews were summoned and arrived. The train's car was disconnected and placed on a side rail, under heavy guard, until MI-5 and USAF personnel could arrive. Pappy and Steve were taken to a local hospital, then later transferred by ambulance to their current location, the USAF Hospital at South Ruislip.

"Excuse me gentlemen. The ceremony is about to begin," an usher announced to Alexander and Boyd. The two sergeants snuffed out their cigarettes in the Butt can by the door and entered the Chapel, taking their seats in the last pew on the right. It was a small crowd. Lt. General Putnam, Commander of Third Air Force, was in the audience seated next to some of Sergeant Hargrave's relatives from his mother's side. Steve, acting as best man, was the only other member in Pappy's party. Just a few of Brooke's closest relatives were present, seated on the left hand side.

Pappy and Steve's wheelchairs were slowly turned about by two attending corpsmen. As the rest of the congregation stood, the organ began the first strains of "Here Comes the Bride" and a beaming, radiant Brooke was escorted down the aisle by her father and her hand placed in that of a smiling Phillip Hargrave.

A loudly weeping Alexander could not control his emotions and was embarrassing Warren Boyd something fierce!

Chapter 32

The Anonymous Client

I t seemed to Steve like this suddenly was the time for unexpected goodbyes—and surprises. Just a couple of hours before Pappy was released, he and Steve were visited in their hospital room by Heather MacVickar, a.k.a. Cathy Moberly. Steve did a double-take as Heather entered their room wearing the uniform of a first lieutenant which sported a name tag showing her last name to be Moberly rather than MacVickar.

Cathy's beautiful dimpled smile tried but could not quite conceal her sadness as she stared at the two with teary eyes.

"I'm afraid I'm not very good at this sort of thing, you know, saying goodbye," Cathy said awkwardly in a voice that cracked. "Yesterday was my last day at the AMT. They, the OSI, told me I couldn't go back. Tomorrow morning Sergeant Dan and all the guys will be told I've left on an Emergency Leave and will be transferred immediately from that leave status on to a Humanitarian Reassignment. I think I'd liked to have said goodbye to the guys, but I guess it's best this way. I would have gotten emotional. However," she continued, "I just could not leave without stopping by to see you two. Damn it all, I hate these things! Anyway, I guess this is farewell then Mr. Hargrave, Pappy. It was indeed a pleasure knowing and working with you sir. I've learned a great deal from you, and it has been a valuable experience. Thanks for all your help and all you've done."

"You're entirely welcome, Luv, and I return the compliment. It has been a pure delight working with you Cathy. And, where are you off to now, if you are at liberty to say?" Pappy asked.

"Actually, I'm not at liberty," she said, but with her index finger next to her lips in a 'Shhhhhhh' fashion Cathy whispered, "I shall shortly be a nurse at an Air Force hospital on the Continent. I'm afraid one of our illustrious physicians is not being very illustrious." She leaned over and gave Pappy a kiss on the cheek.

"I hate to rush," Cathy said, but there's a car waiting for me, and I really shouldn't be seen publicly in this uniform now that the assignment is completed. She walked to the side of Steve's bed and gave him a kiss and an affectionate hand squeeze. "Bye Steve. Good luck, dear. I shall miss you."

"Thank you for coming by," Pappy said with genuine emotion. He had grown fond of the young agent. "And Hells Bells, who knows," he added, "the three of us may meet up again somewhere sometime. In our line of business it's sometimes a small world."

Steve simply said, "Bye Heather."

At the door, Cathy paused, turned, kissed the fingertips of her right hand and blew the kiss to the two NCOs. She was wiping tears from her eyes as she disappeared into the hallway and was gone.

Steve was still hospitalized a week after Pappy and Brooke had come to say their "Goodbyes." It had been an emotional farewell. The three of them had become very close.

"Pappy—Brooke, what can I say to you?" Steve said haltingly during their last visit. "You both mean so much to me. I've never had anyone . . ." his voice broke as he said, "except LaRae, that I've really been close to, and you guys."

"We understand, lad," Pappy said with feeling. "You don't have to say anything. This is hard on us all."

"You've done so much for me. I can never thank you enough." Steve was having a hard time with his goodbye.

"Well old boy, that feeling is mutual," countered Pappy. "By my latest count we have both saved one another's life at least once. As for any of my part with the rest of it, whatever that might be, don't mention it. It's all in the past. And for the future, who knows? With that, all I've done is, perhaps, point you, I hope, to a good road. The rest of the journey is now yours. You know how to reach me any time day or night, just mention the code I gave you and you'll be put through immediately, no matter where I am." Pappy hugged Steve. Choking up he turned and said, "God bless and keep you, me laddie."

Brooke, realizing the extraordinary bond that existed between her man and Steve had soon found that she, too, after their first few meetings, quickly developed a caring, loving place in her heart for this quiet and sensitive young man. Initially, after learning from Pappy about Steve's problems, she was guided by the sympathy she felt for Steve, his heartbreak over LaRae, the unrequited love and emotional scars he silently but constantly carried with him. But those feelings were quickly replaced by friendship and genuine

affection once the two were acquainted. The three had become an insepa-
rable trio. Steve would miss them both. The Hargraves would miss him.

Later Warren Boyd and Alexander paid Steve another visit. They had
said their goodbyes to Pappy and Brooke at Denham Studios earlier.

"You ain't gonna believe this," Alex said to Steve. "Hell, I can't hardly
believe it myself and I know its true cause I've talked to her about it."

"Talked to who about it? What am I not gonna believe?" Steve asked
Alex.

"Old Gap-Tooth here's engaged. He's gonna marry that sweet young
thing he's been dating off and on all this time. Hey, Boyd, that reminds me,
does she know you don't have any front teeth? Bet'cha she don't, does
she? She probably wouldn't marry you if she saw you with your teeth out,"
Alex said giggling. He continued, "She probably wouldn't even look twice
at you. Bet she flat-assed don't know. Huh, ain't it so, Boyd?"

"Kiss ass, Axle!" Boyd directed caustically with a frown to Alex. "My
romancin' ain't none of your business. Besides you're just pissed off
'cause I ain't gonna let you be my best man."

"Congratulations Warren," Steve said sincerely to Boyd. "I'm happy for
you. Have you set a date? Why don't you want Alex to be your best man?"

"Axle's getting his rotation orders pretty soon now. He's going to
Barksdale Air Force Base near Shreveport, Louisiana. I'm gonna wait till
he's gone before we get married. I don't want him around and for sure I
don't want him to be my best man! He gets too damn emotional at
weddings."

"Don't either!" Alex said indignantly.

"You do too, Axle. You embarrass the cowboy shit out of me! 'Member
how you boo-hooed at the Hargrave's weddin? Couldn't even hear the
preacher for Crissake cause of your cryin' and carrying-ons!"

"Well, I couldn't help that," Alex said in defense. "My emotions snuck
up on me—they got away from me a little bit there. I wouldn't cry at your
wedding though—'cept maybe in hysterics from laughing so hard picturing
your new wife's expression the first time she rolls over in the mornin' and
sees you without your teeth. Face it Boyd, you're an ugly fucker."

Before they left his hospital room, Boyd and Alexander agreed with
Steve that they would all stay in touch and meet at a central location once
they returned stateside.

Steve was still stuck with his strict bed rest routine. Once Pappy had
been released and Steve was on his own, he found he had lots of time to
think. He'd completed his last course and received an official diploma

from the University of Maryland, which serviced the European military's educational needs.

After discussing the matter at length with Pappy prior to his release, Steve decided to turn down his commission and leave the Air Force. Pappy had made several suggestions for job opportunities to him. Steve, at that time, had been uncertain and also seemingly unconcerned about his future. He was, however, leaning toward a Special Agent position Pappy said he could help him with.

Steve had had several conversations with Sergeant Gage about Colorado. The First Sergeant had talked nostalgically about returning to Colorado and eventually retiring there. He'd described some of its marvelous country—mountains, streams and rivers to Steve. Steve had been highly impressed. He thought he wanted to go to Colorado, but his head was a muddle. He had no reason now to go back to Missouri. He had been frugal and saved as much as possible for him and LaRae to get started on, but he would, of course, have to get a job shortly. He missed Pappy and Brooke, and, damn, did he ever hate that hospital bed!

In the short span of a little more than a fortnight, following the death of Captain Miller, Scotland Yard, working in concert with its U.S. and European counterparts, was instrumental in several discoveries associated with the Nazi loot. Thanks to the meticulous records Karl Miller had maintained, the authorities were able to immediately locate the captain's storage sites in the U.S. the U.K., and all the other European cities. All had been opened and inventoried and their contents were being analyzed and researched as a first-step in returning each and every item possible to its rightful owners.

Also, and this was a worldwide headline grabber, the vast holdings of Adolf Hitler's personal cache had been zeroed in on at the Salzdorf mine location. Untold billions of gold, silver, currency, diamonds and other jewels, hundreds of paintings by Old Masters and sculptures, porcelains, unbelievable wealth and art was being sorted. It was impossible to project when all of the discovery could be returned to its rightful owners or heirs. However, with those items possible—all the works of art, pottery, porcelains, jewelry and others that carried identifying marks, features or known histories—those returns were made immediately.

One such return was to the tremendously wealthy Austrian family of Baron Richard Von Bucknell. Shortly after the Germans had occupied Vienna, the entire art collection of Von Bucknell had wound up in the hands of Hitler and much of this had been stored at Salzdorf. Other families whose artworks and wealth had been stolen would have to endure a much longer delay in its return. While the world anxiously watched and waited, the sorting and identification process, although hurried, would yet be cautious. The time involved to sort all of this would seem interminable to many waiting people, including, unfortunately, families of the Holocaust victims, and some victims themselves, who had lost everything.

The news of the discovery was a media blitz. Pappy and Steve were the reluctant heroes and their roles, their backgrounds, wounds and recovery were daily press fodder. Hargrave's World War II and Korean heroics were detailed; his strong British background and love of England were mentioned frequently. Steve's prior press record, the battle with the Teddy Boys and, unfortunately, his personal tragedy, the death of his fiancée (thankfully no mention was made of LaRae's pregnancy) while planning to come to England to marry him were made known.

There were countless articles of praise and congratulations and talk of reward for both Pappy and Steve. The USAF had issued a statement that its NCOs had acted in a military and duty bound capacity. Although their actions were indeed honorable and truly heroic, rewards were discouraged.

During this the third, and hopefully final, week of his hospitalization, Steve, going nuts with not being able to get out of bed, had a strange visitor. Two corpsmen had come in early one morning and wheeled Steve, in his bed, into a large private room down the hall from the open ward he had been moved to once Pappy was discharged.

"Don't ask us what it's all about," the corpsmen said in response to Steve's question. "We were just told you're gonna have a private hush-hush meeting and to move you in here." The corpsmen positioned Steve's bed and left him to his thoughts. *I wonder what this is all about,* he mused to himself.

Shortly after the noon meal, an Air Force Colonel who identified himself as the Staff Judge Advocate for Third Air Force and a formally dressed and distinguished gray haired English gentleman entered his room. The Colonel introduced himself and then introduced the Englishman as Mr. Stewart Halbington, Barrister. Later, Steve learned the impressive civilian was the most respected and highest priced attorney in all of England.

"Mr. Scott," the Englishman began, "I have been directed by my client whom shall remain anonymous, to deliver this envelope to you. In the presence of Colonel Anderson here, representing the U.S. Air Force and your country I declare to you, and to him, that the contents of this envelope are not a reward for your recent heroics, the results of which have placed you here in hospital."

In true British demeanor he staunchly went on. "The envelope and its contents thusly are simply of a personal and private nature between my client and yourself. This has absolutely no legal, military, or other connection involving additional people, property, activity or any other state of affairs. If you will, sir, please sign this receipt acknowledging I have given you this sealed envelope, coded LGV10-228, this date."

Steve, with a somewhat bewildered expression, signed the receipt.

Turning to the Staff Judge Advocate, the English attorney said, "Colonel Anderson, I have here a short statement acknowledging that you, representing the United States, were present and understand these proceedings are correct and proper. Further, it is understood that this is not, in any form, representative of a reward, but, rather, simply a personal and private correspondence between my client and Mr. Scott.

The Colonel signed the statement.

"Thank you both, gentlemen."

Turning to Steve the Englishman said, "Sergeant Scott, good luck to you, sir. It has been my distinct pleasure meeting you, young man. I sincerely hope that the remainder of your stay in our country shall be more pleasant. We are indeed proud to have had you here." He handed Steve his card. "Please call me if I may be of any service to you whatsoever. Speedy recovery. Cheerio."

For a long moment after Steve had been left alone, he studied the red wax sealed envelope. It looked to him like the Coat of Arms on the reverse contained the initials RVB, but he couldn't tell for sure. Other than the lettered, numbered code, nothing else showed.

He opened the envelope.

Inside was a small, folded, half sheet of obviously, very expensive stationery which bore no identifying heading, imprint, or markings. In beautiful script a message read:

"Sergeant Steve Scott:
Please accept the grateful thanks of our entire family,
both past and present.
We shall remain, forever, beholden to you."

There was no signature.

Attached to the slip of paper was a cashier's check for two hundred thousand pounds sterling, the approximate equivalent of five hundred and sixty thousand dollars.

Steve felt weak—who? Why? He thought hard for awhile—then the answers came.

Epilogue

Never wonder where I am
because although we are apart,
know always that I am at your side,
you are always with me
and that I love you so.
                                        —Thoreau

Steve took the new section of Interstate I-55 out of St. Louis. He headed
south toward Memphis, returning to his old hometown of Ancell, Missouri.
He noted a lot of changes from the old Highway 61 that used to carry all
the north/south bound traffic. Many of the old towns and cities were now
bypassed completely.

His new XK-150 Jaguar carried him along like a breeze through the
steady, but light rain. Although dreading this part of the trip, his spirits had
been buoyed with the recent completion of all his training. First the FBI
Agent's course at Quantico, Virginia, and then the Investigator/Agent's
Course at the DoD Security Institute, a little further south of Quantico, near
Richmond, Virginia. He had spent weekends, when the training permitted,
with Pappy and Brooke at their townhouse in Midlothian, Virginia.

Hargrave, still instrumental as his mentor, had secured a position for
Steve as a Special Agent with the DoD's Defense Investigative Service
(DIS), a Federal Law Enforcement and Investigative Agency. While he
could have selected a position at nearly any stateside location, and despite
Pappy and Brooke's wanting him close to them, he had, instead, chosen
Colorado Springs, Colorado. He was on his way there now, after this next
short stop.

Just beyond Cape Girardeau and crossing over the new four lane bridge
that spanned the Diversion Channel, called "The Big Ditch," where he had
camped and fished as a youngster, he looked east. A short distance from
the new span stood the old, rusted, two-lane bridge. That is where Ernie
Thompson collided with the eighteen wheeler and was killed.

The Saveway Gas station, the tavern, roller rink, and grade school were all gone. In their place was a new cloverleaf exit for the towns of Ancell, Fornfelt and Illmo—all consolidated now with the new name of Scott City. The old granary still stood.

Steve felt a strange sensation in the pit of his stomach as he drove slowly past the town's many reminders, the mostly sad memories of his having grown up there, and the memory of LaRae.

He stopped at the funeral home and received a map of the graveyard. It showed the location of LaRae's resting place.

Thunder rumbled and the rain continued as he opened the car door and turned off the ignition. He gently closed the door and walked to the grave. On her marker, attached in the center just over her name, was an oval photograph. Her reflection showed a trace of a smile and, he thought, a trace of sadness in those hauntingly beautiful, deep, brown eyes.

"Wonder what you were thinking when the picture was taken?" Steve asked. "Maybe at that time you were lonely and thinking of me? Maybe your thoughts were about coming to England and our being together—were you thinking about us Rae?"

He noticed she wore the necklace he'd sent for her birthday. *God, she was so beautiful!* he thought.

The sky turned darker and the rain became heavy. Steve was oblivious to this and also the lightning and thunder that had intensified and was moving in closer.

With his pocketknife he removed a small patch of sod and set it aside. He dug down and removed several handsful of the dirt and placed the tiny box containing the wedding ring he'd bought for her in the space. He repacked the earth and replaced the grass covering.

Still kneeling at the foot of her grave, he looked again at her picture. He sat like that for a long time, just looking at her picture. Then he closed his eyes and bowed his head. His thoughts swirled with a thousand memories of LaRae. He remembered their first meeting, and later, her asking him, "What'll it be, hug, mug or slug?" He saw her again, looking deep into his eyes with her own beautiful brown eyes brimming with tears, saying goodbye when he'd left for England. He could hear, so clearly, her last words to him when he'd called from London . . . "Hey boy, somebody loves you."

Finally, he slowly stood. He wiped his eyes and looked at her smiling, yet sad face on the photograph one last time.

"Somebody loves you too," he whispered. "Goodbye Rae."

He turned, walked back to his car, and headed West.

Acknowledgments

I owe an enormous debt of gratitude to the following for their contributions and help, for without them this book, most likely, would not have been written: D.J. Stevenson, J.M. Dauphine, R.P. Berg, Pappy and Hilda, D. Semmel, P. McElroy and H. Eynouf. Special thanks for their encouragement and support goes to Kathy Wong, Barb Schmidt, Doris Rohret, Ellie Ross, Vikki Petraitis and to my publisher, Craig Nelsen. Finally, to the wonderful library staffs at Marble Hill, Missouri (all dear friends), and Loveland, Colorado, my heartfelt thanks for their kind, professional and ever willing help.

About the Author

Wade Stevenson is a retired Special Agent from the U.S. Department of Defense Investigative Service, a Federal Law Enforcement and Investigative Agency. His thirty-five year career with the U.S. Government ranged from performing duty as an armed guard and courier with the Armed Forces Courier Service in Europe, to serving as a U.S. Intelligence Officer. He has worked on espionage cases involving offenders such as Boyce and Lee (the infamous *Falcon and Snowman* team), James Durward Harper, William H. Bell, the Navy Walker family and others.

He held an executive position with Presidential and other Departmental level clearances in the most secret of all Pentagon operations—the Black World Special Access Programs Office—Office of the Secretary of Defense. His assignments have involved working closely with the CIA, NSA, FBI, the Secret Service, NASA and numerous other agencies on classified projects. Mr. Stevenson is bound by lifetime security restrictions on many past assignments that he can never reveal. While there is no intent to represent the characters or the events in *The Salzdorf Wellspring* as anything other than fictitious, portions of the book are based in truth and involves one of his assignments he could write about.

Author Notes

When my idle curiosity turned to compelling interest in the legacy of Adolf Hitler and his Third Reich's rape of the European continent's tremendous art works and much of its wealth from the late '30s through WWII, I started thinking—What if?

History did indeed reveal that the Führer had dotted the German landscape with numerous secret hiding places—vaults, castles and abandoned mines, which were filled with the most magnificent paintings by Old Masters, priceless sculpture, porcelains, rare coins, book and jewels. Large numbers of those storage places were discovered after the war. However, hundreds, perhaps thousands of fantastic works of art and great wealth plundered by the Nazis still, to this very moment, remain missing—waiting to be discovered. The search continues.

With my "What if" scenario I wondered: What if Hitler had an ultra-secret hiding place where the had stored, for his personal use and enjoyment, the most coveted paintings of Rembrandt, da Vinci, Raphael, and other valuable paintings, jewels and riches. And what if a trusted guard of the mine who was thought to have been killed in an SS assassination attempt, had escaped to return after the war, years later to find Hitler's mine with its treasure still intact? Thus, some five years ago, in the beautiful Ozarks near Marble Hill, Missouri, I began my first notes on *The Salzdorf Wellspring*. I soon discovered that more than a half century later there remains worldwide both a stigma and fascination with Hitler and the Nazis. My research and contacts from Germany, Austria, Switzerland, England, Scotland, Australia and elsewhere show that Hitler's looting and subsequent storage of fabulous art and wealth affected, sometimes dramatically, sometimes horribly and sometimes deadly, the lives of many, long after his ignoble end in 1945.

So, using the above for the the catalyst of my story, I introduced subplots in a fictionalized vein, which among other things, deal with young love, the coming of age, and rascally military characters and events. *The Salzdorf Wellspring* is wide ranging in locale. It is brutal and sensitive, it has love and hate, it is sad and humorous, and it is my most sincere wish that you will enjoy the reading.

Highly instrumental in my research and strongly recommended for further reading is *The Rape of Art* by David Roxan and Ken Wanstall. I owe them a debt of gratitude for their outstanding contribution to the history of WWII, which details Hitler's plunder of Europe's great art and wealth.

Wade Stevenson may be reached by email at: WASteve@Concentric.net

Glossary of Terms

AC: Aircraft Commander
AFB: Air Force Base
Airman: Term used to identify USAF military personnel
Amt: Office (German)
AMT: Aerial Mail Terminal.
APO: Army Post Office
ARFCOS: Armed Forces Courier Service
ASAP: As Soon As Possible
AWOL: Absent Without Leave
CABLE-TOW: Unclassified nickname for operation dealing with Nazi plunder
CO: Commanding Officer
CIA: Central Intelligence Agency
CINCPACAF: Commander-In-Chief Pacific Air Forces
DoD: Department of Defense
DROPHAMMER: Classified codeword for blackmarketing of Nazi stolen loot
Flight: Formation of aircraft and term used for group of marching airmen
First Shirt: Unit First Sergeant (also Top Shirt)
Gestapo: Secret political police force of Nazi Germany
G.I: Government Issue
Guidon: Drill instructor and point of reference for marching troops
I.D: Identification
Interpol: International police organization.
K.P: Kitchen Police (work detail, mess hall duty)
MSgt: Master Sergeant
NCO: Non-Commissioned Officer
NCOIC: Non-Commissioned Officer In Charge
OCS: Officer Candidate School
OSI: Office of Special Investigations (USAF)
RAF: Royal Air Force
RON: Rest Over Night-term used for pilots in travel status
SchutzStaffel (SS): Hitler's elite bodyguard and security corps
Sgt: Sergeant
SSgt: Staff Sergeant
TDY: Temporary Duty-identifies travel and duty away from primary station.
Third APS (3rd APS): Third Air Postal Squadron, UK, Hqs-Denham Studios
Troop: USAF Airman or Army enlisted person
Twelfth APS (12th APS): Twelfth Air Postal Squadron, France, Hqs-Paris
Soldier: Army enlisted person, but also referred to USAF Airman in early '50s
U.K: United Kingdom, England
U.S: United States
USAF: United States Air Force
USAFE: U.S. Air Forces, Europe
WAF: Womens Air Force